CARNIVAL
BLUES

ALSO BY DAMIEN BOYD

CARNIVAL BLUES

DAMIEN BOYD

THOMAS & MERCER

Text copyright © 2022 by Damien Boyd
All rights reserved.

Published by Thomas & Mercer, Seattle

www.apub.com

Amazon, the Amazon logo, and Thomas & Mercer are trademarks of Amazon.com, Inc., or its affiliates.

ISBN-13: 9781542023610
ISBN-10: 1542023610

Cover design by @blacksheep-uk.com

Printed in the United States of America

For Winnie

Prologue

Succinylcholine.

It had been the obvious choice, until he'd found his target in intensive care. What use is a drug that paralyses the respiratory system if the intended victim is already on a ventilator?

He leaned on his trolley while he waited for the lift outside the operating theatre and examined the clinical waste crate in front of him; the novelty of taking a peek and trying to guess what the surgeons had cut off or out had long since worn off. He'd got quite good at it, mind you; amputated body parts and internal organs were easy, tumours a bit more of a struggle.

Three months working as a porter; Andreas Kalda from Estonia. The agency hadn't asked too many questions, or looked at his papers too closely, and neither had the hospital. Nobody had recognised his accent wasn't exactly Estonian either.

It was the perfect cover.

He was earning his money this time, that was for sure. Still, it was being made worth his while, and he'd be back in the old country before the post mortem took place; only a three hour flight.

Would a hospital porter look out of place in the intensive care unit? Hardly, although he'd need to pick his time carefully. And the drug.

'No one must suspect a thing,' Zavan had said. 'It must look like natural causes.'

Easier said than done.

It had never mattered before. A bullet in the back of the head and over the side of the boat in the middle of the Bristol Channel, suitably weighted down. Sometimes he didn't even bother with the bullet. All he'd had to worry about was not getting stopped with his victim in the boot of his car. This time was different though, which explained the bigger pay cheque – enough to retire on.

Somewhere by the sea, on a clifftop overlooking the Adriatic.

He stood at the back of the lift, hoping the doors would close before anyone else appeared.

It really was a shame; sux would have been perfect. Readily available in the hospital, the only real risk was getting caught in the act. Even the victim being in the ICU had its advantages; the cannula in the back of his hand was one, the feeding tube another. It gave him options, and there'd be no injection site for a pathologist to find.

'Going down,' he said, jabbing the button and glaring at the porter pushing an empty bed along the corridor towards the open doors. 'I send it back up.'

'Thanks, mate.'

Sux would have been hard to detect too. That's if the police had suspected foul play. An ordinary toxicology screen would never pick it up – a pathologist would have to be looking for it – and then all they'd find was traces of succinic acid. Hardly surprising, that.

It had been a problem, finding a poison that would kill quickly and then disappear, but now he had the answer.

Potassium chloride.

Cause of death would be cardiac arrest – not unusual for a man on life support for eleven months – and, once it had done its job, all that would be left would be potassium and chloride, both substances a pathologist would expect to find.

He might even go as far as injecting a lower dose a few days before the fatal one, just so raised potassium levels were noted in routine blood tests. He was known for being thorough.

Zavan had given him a name but not much else, and he knew not to ask too many questions. That was the way of things. Eleven months on a life support machine though.

It had come as an unpleasant surprise that his victim was a fellow Albanian.

Still, ours is not to reason why, as the English are so fond of saying.

Chapter One

Fish and chips. Candyfloss. Beer. Coffee. Tobacco. There was even the sweet smell of cannabis in there somewhere. Bubblegum too, although that could have been one of those electronic cigarettes belching out God knows what.

'Follow the lights,' Jane had said. 'You can't miss it.'

She hadn't mentioned the smells.

Apple and cinnamon now; clouds of sickly vapour enveloping him as he approached the back of the crowd lined up along the pavement.

Detective Chief Inspector Nick Dixon had seen the lights from the window of the train as it crept into Bridgwater railway station two hours late. The blare of the music had reached him as soon as he opened the train window, the smells as he strolled along St John Street, his overnight bag slung over his shoulder.

Walking in time to the music now, whether he liked it or not; the last time he'd heard the song he had been on a first aid course, practising cardiopulmonary resuscitation, to give it its proper name.

Stayin' Alive.

'Chest compressions in time to the beat,' the instructor had said. 'Everyone knows that one, surely?'

He wondered whether the Bee Gees would have approved.

The carnival cart was something to behold. Dancers in white suits on rotating platforms, giving it their best John Travolta; *Disco Fever* the theme, the huge neon sign over the bar giving it away. Avalon Carnival Club had managed to squeeze a whole nightclub on to their cart, and more light bulbs than you'd find on the Clifton Suspension Bridge, some of them flashing and all of them reflecting off more glitter balls than you could shake a stick at. An old red Ford Mustang was the centrepiece, although what that was doing in a nightclub was beyond him.

The giant articulated flatbed lorry crawled along Broadway, following the cart in front; even the driver of the towing vehicle was wearing a white suit and dark sunglasses, several rotating platforms above his head to hide its true purpose. At the back, the power unit had been disguised as a balcony with more dancers, all of them standing in cradles if you looked closely. God bless health and safety.

Stayin' Alive faded out, then started again, soon drowning out the noise of the engine and the diesel generator once more.

'Want a programme, mate? Two quid.'

'It's almost over,' shouted Dixon in reply, glancing down at the man's Bridgwater Rotary Club fluorescent tabard as he rummaged in his pocket for the change.

'It's all in a good cause,' said the man, rattling his bucket. 'And you'll soon catch up with the stragglers if you walk round to Cornhill.'

Dixon dropped a two pound coin into the bucket being held up in front of him. 'Can I cut across?'

'No, mate, sorry. You'll have to walk around.'

Bollocks to that, thought Dixon, fishing his warrant card out of his jacket pocket.

Disco Fever gave way to *Those Magnificent Men in Their Flying Machines*, the Ham Hill Carnival Club opting for a diorama of old biplanes, hot air balloons and airships, the clouds illuminated by yet more light bulbs. No dancers this time, and if the pilot of the triplane hadn't scratched his nose, Dixon might have mistaken the people for mannequins.

He squeezed through the crowd on the pavement and stepped out into the road in front of *Curse of the Kraken*. Middlezoy Carnival Club had gone for green lighting that cast an eerie glow across a cart featuring a Spanish galleon flying the Jolly Roger and rocking from side to side on rolling waves. Blackbeard was standing on the poop deck, waving a cutlass at giant tentacles threatening to drag his pirate ship down to Davey Jones' Locker.

'*Yo-ho-ho, and a bottle of rum.*'

The stewards moved faster than Dixon had expected, but a wave of his warrant card stopped them in their tracks when they tried to intercept him, and he quickly disappeared into the crowd on the opposite side of the road.

Eastover was closed, the road blocked by several mobile food kiosks, the sizzle of hot dogs and burgers adding to the sounds and smells of carnival night in Bridgwater. Tempting, but Jane was waiting for him and he'd already eaten on the train anyway.

'We'll be outside the Carnival Inn,' she had said.

Dixon looked along the River Parrett from the middle of the bridge and watched *Disco Fever* crossing on the main road further down. The lead carts must be on their way out of town already; best get a move on, he thought, choosing to ignore the drug deal taking place by the telephone box on the far side of the Eastover bridge. Something was definitely changing hands.

'Sod it,' he grumbled, turning back with his warrant card at the ready. 'Oi.'

'Shit.'

'Smile, you're on *Candid Camera*,' he muttered when buyer and seller sprinted off in different directions.

Detective Sergeant Jane Winter was waving at him with both arms from the other side of the road as he weaved his way through the crowd. Crossing would be a matter of waiting until the stewards had their backs turned and then making a run for it.

The Storm Carnival Club cart was smaller than the rest, and must have made the sharp turn into St Mary Street far quicker; the gap behind it was his chance. He glanced up at the self-conscious teenagers in sleeveless T-shirts and stick-on moustaches dancing to *I Want to Break Free* and wondered what Freddie Mercury would make of it all.

'You took your time,' said Jane. 'We waited for you. We're starving, and Roger's had far too much beer on an empty stomach.'

'Nice to see you too.' Dixon kissed her on the lips. 'I did send you a text. The train was late.'

Dr Roger Poland was standing behind her with a pint of beer in each hand. 'I got you one in,' he said. 'They're plastic glasses, so be careful.'

'Thanks,' replied Dixon, frowning at the glass in Jane's hand. 'Is that—?'

'Tonic water,' she hissed. 'Drink up. They're holding a table for us in the English Raj.'

'What about the carnival?'

'You can watch the rest at Burnham on Monday. We're only here for the squibbing anyway.'

'Where's the car?'

'Express Park. And, yes, I'm driving.'

Poland grinned. 'I remember when my ex-wife was pregnant,' he said, raising his glass, a conspiratorial glint in his eye.

'We got a lift in with the Rural Crimes Unit,' said Jane.

'Nigel's here?'

'Said he'd give us a lift back after the squibbing.'

'I'm staying with you tonight,' said Poland, taking a swig of beer.

'Lucy's on the sofa.' Jane was standing on tiptoe, trying to pick out her half-sister in the crowd further along the pavement. 'She's here somewhere with Billy.'

Purple steam trains with comedy skulls on them, lurching from side to side and backwards and forwards, the lights on rotating wheels illuminating fluorescent skeletons on the suits of the dancers lined up either side. *Spirit in the Sky* this time, mercifully not too loud.

'You have to admire the ingenuity,' said Poland. 'Takes them all year to make these things. Must cost a pretty packet too.'

'How was the assessment centre?' asked Jane, shouting in Dixon's ear as another cart passed by, *Right Here, Right Now* belting out from speakers at head height.

'Fine.' Dixon turned his back on the cart. 'Why they had to hold it at bloody Hendon I don't know.'

'How many were there?'

'Twenty.'

'I didn't know there were that many going for the super's job.'

'Only three for the Avon and Somerset vacancy. The rest were from other forces.'

'What did you have to do?' asked Poland.

'Just the usual crap, Roger. Presentations, mock briefings and interviews, that sort of stuff.'

'When d'you find out?'

'No idea.'

Poland drained his glass and left it on the windowsill of the pub. 'Why do I suddenly feel the urge to perform CPR on someone?' he asked, tipping his head.

'Let's go,' said Dixon, turning to Jane. 'Before he tries it on one of us.'

'*Disco Fever*, Avalon Carnival Club, sponsored by Eastman and Webb Estate Agents.' Poland was reading the sign on the front of the cart. 'May vote for them just because of the song,' he said, his shoulders swaying from side to side in time to the music. 'I had all the moves, y'know.'

'And the white suit?'

'Don't take the piss.'

'You can't vote for the song, Roger,' protested Jane. 'What about the work that's gone into the cart?'

A big cheer went up from the crowd outside the pub, an Avalon CC banner waving. 'Must be family and friends, I suppose,' said Dixon. 'Sponsors, maybe.'

'I thought there were two "o"s in "tandoori"?' asked Poland, looking up at the sign.

'I'm sure they know how to spell their own cuisine.'

'We won't hold it against them. I'll see if they've kept our table.'

Dixon watched Poland duck inside the English Raj, the noise and lights of the carnival fifty or so yards away on High Street. He was hoping the restaurant hadn't kept a table for them after all – he was still feeling sick after the microwaved bacon roll from the buffet car on the train that had accompanied his evening insulin injection. Being diabetic was a pain in the arse at the best of times.

Then Poland was tapping on the inside of the window, grinning from ear to ear and waving.

'Just don't tell Lucy, for God's sake.' Jane was following Poland to a vacant table at the back of the restaurant. 'She'll do her nut if she finds out she's missed a curry.'

'I won't.' Poland dropped down on to the bench seat and slid along. 'I've ordered two pints of Kingfisher, a tonic water and some poppadoms.'

'We could go on *Mr and Mrs*,' said Dixon, kicking his overnight bag under the seat.

'Have you done your jab?' asked Jane, sitting down opposite Dixon.

'I'll give myself a few extra units, don't panic.' A discreet glance around, then it was six units of insulin through his shirt.

'I've told you before about that, injecting through your clothes,' grumbled Poland.

'Yes, Mother.'

'Thought any more about your honeymoon?'

'It's a bit difficult when you're getting married on Christmas Eve. There's a posh hotel on the banks of Lake Windermere that takes dogs – we go there on Boxing Day for a couple of nights, then we've got a cottage in Borrowdale over New Year.'

'Sounds cold.'

'Hopefully. I thought about getting her an ice axe for a wedding present, but she'd probably hit me with it.'

Jane was examining the menu and spoke without looking up. 'I wouldn't hesitate.' No hint of a smile either.

'I wouldn't blame you.' Poland let the waiter leave the beer and poppadoms, taking a swig before he continued his questioning. 'How was the scan?'

'It's not till next week.'

'I was hoping you'd tip me the wink, seeing as I'm your best man. Dave Harding's got a sweep going and I could make a few quid.'

'A sweep? The cheeky sod.'

'Lucy seems to have settled down,' said Poland, watching Jane sniffing her tonic water.

In and out of foster care for much of her life, Jane's half-sister had been a bit of a handful to begin with. Jane had just about got over the guilt of being adopted at birth by parents who had spoilt her rotten. She had been spared their mother's drug taking and alcoholism, unlike Lucy, who bore no grudge against anyone, oddly enough. It must have been a bit of a shock finding she had a sister at all though, let alone one who was a police officer.

Jane was old enough to be Lucy's mother, legally. Just. Sometimes she behaved like a mother rather than a sister; so much so that Dixon wasn't entirely sure whether he was going to be Lucy's brother-in-law or her stepfather. But there was order in the girl's life now, and that was what mattered.

'She's doing all right. Passed all her GCSEs, gone to college; she's even joined the police cadets. Steady boyfriend. She stays with her foster parents during the week and comes home at weekends.'

That had slipped off Jane's tongue easily – *home* at weekends.

'Still with that lad Billy?' asked Poland.

'Yes.'

'And she's all right after seeing Peter Lewis shot at point blank . . .' Poland hesitated, not wanting to bring back the memory, probably.

'I arranged some counselling for her,' replied Jane. 'But she's a level-headed kid, in spite of everything.'

'Pleased to hear it. That was a hell of a case, wasn't it? A bloody scythe as a murder weapon. A first for me.'

'And me,' said Dixon, raising his glass. 'Here's to Peter.'

'A good lad.'

They ordered without looking at the menu, Dixon opting for a sheek kebab.

'You had something on the train?'

'A revolting bacon roll, if you must know.' Dixon ignored Jane's scowl. 'I had to, so I could do my evening jab.'

'Why don't you get Lucy an onion bhaji?' asked Poland, a smile creeping across his lips. 'You could wrap it in a napkin for her.'

'I'd end up wearing it,' muttered Jane.

'I'm looking forward to the squibbing. I haven't seen it for years. And it's been ages since anyone died, so we should be fine.'

Dixon sat up, surprised by the sudden change of subject. He flashed Poland a concerned look. 'Died?'

'I'm just pulling your leg. It was before my time.' There was mischief in Poland's voice. 'In the old days, when the squibs were homemade, they used to blow up when you least expected it. There were garden sheds and barns going up all over the Levels. We'll stand at the back, just to be on the safe side. It'll be fine, but then that's probably the eternal optimist in me.'

'Too much beer in you, more like,' said Dixon. 'I'd much rather things stayed nice and quiet, thank you. I'm quite enjoying my paid holiday.'

'Holiday?'

'Feels a bit like it. Janice took over as managing DCI at Express Park, so I'm based at Portishead and Charlesworth's got me going for this superintendent's job. Until then, I'm "in between jobs", as actors like to say. Last week I was chasing kids in Bristol – the little buggers have been burning homeless people's stuff in shop doorways. I've got a couple of trials coming up as well.'

'Enjoy it while it lasts. Word is you're a shoo-in for the promotion.'

'I suppose there's a sweep on that as well?'

'Sadly not.'

'Anyway, I'm not holding my breath. The advisory board have to meet to review the report from the assessment centre.'

'You'll still be around though, I imagine?'

'You don't get rid of me that easily, Roger.'

Chapter Two

I've found her! Jx

Dixon tapped out a reply, phone in one hand, beer in the other. The sheek kebab had seen off the feeling he was going to be sick at any moment. Either that or it was the beer.

Outside Carnival Inn. They're getting ready. Hurry!

He was standing on tiptoe, looking along the pavement, when the crowd in front of him parted to allow Cole through – Jane, Lucy and Billy following right behind him. A police uniform, hi-vis jacket and a shout of 'coming through' had done the trick.

'They're just getting in position now,' said Lucy, catching her breath. 'How many of those have you had?'

'Only a couple,' replied Dixon.

'Have you eaten?'

'They had a table in the English Raj,' said Poland. He was still swaying from side to side, although the last of the carnival carts had long since passed by, taking the music with them. 'I wanted a kebab, but he insisted.'

'You weren't supposed to say anything,' grumbled Dixon.

'Oh, that's great, that is. Thanks very much.' Lucy was lifted on to the windowsill of the pub by Billy, placing her hands on his shoulders when he turned around. 'We had to make do with a slice of pizza.'

'We'll get you something when the squibbing's over,' offered Dixon, watching a large red tractor crawling along High Street. Following behind were two lines of people dressed in orange overalls and hard hats; some were wearing hi-vis jackets. Each carried a long pole with a giant firework on the end.

'You not seen it before, Sir?' asked Cole.

'No.'

'It's quite something. Imagine hundreds of giant fountains held up on the end of poles – "coshes", they call them – all going off at the same time.' Cole was the only one tall enough to get a proper view over the heads in front of them. 'They're putting the rags down now; it won't be long.'

'Who are they?'

'Carnival club people mainly. Sponsors, that sort of thing. How they still get permission for it, I'll never know,' said Cole, with a shrug. 'Health and safety will see it off one day, I expect. Either that or they won't be able to get insurance for it. It used to be bloody dangerous when the squibs were homemade, but it's not so bad these days – been years since there was a fatality. A bit like the tar barrels at Ottery St Mary.'

The tractor had disappeared, leaving behind it two lines of squibbers standing either side of the road, some waiting more patiently than others, some looking nervous behind their goggles, balaclavas protecting long hair.

'Five minutes and counting,' said the voice over the tannoy.

Squibbers the whole length of High Street, on both sides of the road; Dixon had counted fifty on one side before he gave up halfway along. He glanced at Jane, her blonde hair tied back safely in a ponytail. He was tempted to pull the hood of her coat up over her head, but maybe that was being a bit too protective.

Maybe not.

'Don't do that,' she snapped, with a swish of her hand. 'We'll be fine back here.'

It was a good wide pavement, the crowd ten deep, and they'd have a fire extinguisher in the pub, if push came to shove.

'Did you miss me?' whispered Dixon in Jane's ear.

'You were only away for one night, you soppy—'

Jane was cut off mid-sentence by a loud horn blasting. 'Light the rags!' came the instruction over the tannoy.

A figure started running down the white line in the middle of the road, stopping at intervals to light small piles of rags on the ground in between the lines of squibbers.

'Let the countdown begin!'

The crowd joined in with gusto, none more so than Roger Poland. 'Ten, nine, eight . . .'

It started slowly, the squibs taking a moment to get going, then the first of them was held aloft, others joining in quick succession, sparks on both sides of the road rising twenty feet in the air, the hiss and crackle almost drowned out by the cheers of the crowd.

'Told you it was quite something.' Cole was leaning over and shouting in Dixon's ear. 'You won't see this anywhere else in the world!'

It was a blaze of light, reflecting off the shop windows, sparks cascading into the road and on to the crowd at the edge of the pavement; the cheering louder if anything, drowning out the few screams coming from children who had been dragged too near the front by enthusiastic parents.

'He's a bold lad,' said Poland, gesturing to a small boy sitting on a pair of broad shoulders at the front, sparks bouncing off the hood of his coat.

The smell of cordite masked even the e-cigarette a few paces upwind of them, thick smoke from the squibs drifting along High Street at rooftop height.

A soft 'pop' seemed out of place, the flash that went with it visible even in the dazzling display from the two hundred or so squibs lining High Street. Then a gap appeared in the line on the far side of the road. Whoever it was had dropped their squib, the sparkle of the firework replaced by flames.

A figure engulfed in flames – orange and yellow – arms flailing.

Cole had spotted it too and was already pushing his way through the crowd in front of them. 'Police, coming through!'

Dixon dropped his overnight bag on the pavement and fol-lowed, turning to see Jane dragging Lucy off the windowsill.

'There'll be a fire extinguisher in the pub, Roger,' said Dixon, when he heard Poland right behind him.

'I'll get it.'

The crowd was starting to twig to what was going on, cheers and laughter turning to screams at the front. Some turned to run, others reached for their phones. Some stepped forward to help.

Cole ducked under the rope. He grabbed the nearest steward, who was rooted to the spot, staring in disbelief. 'Fire extinguisher!'

'Yes, yes, there's one on the tractor.'

'Get it. Now.'

The burning man had dropped to his knees and was tearing at his orange overalls with hands of fire as Dixon and Cole crossed the road, jumping over the smouldering piles of rags, the screaming in the immediate vicinity now drowning out the cheers from further along the road. Some squibbers had dropped their squibs, sending sparks flying along the tarmac towards the man on fire.

Dixon tore off his coat and threw it around the man's shoulders, glancing up at the gap in the line. 'His name's Richard,' mumbled the next squibber in the line, a woman with goggles and a balaclava covering her hair. 'Richard Webb.' She had dropped her squib in a puddle, the fountain of sparks all but fizzled out. 'He's my business partner.'

Webb's hard hat had come off and his greying hair was on fire.

'His goggles have melted,' said Cole.

The flames reignited as fast as Dixon could dampen them down with his coat, Cole trying the same thing with his hi-vis jacket, wrapping it around Webb's head.

Squibs were still being held aloft further along High Street, the cheer of the crowd gradually fading, replaced by gasps and screams as the realisation of what was going on spread along the pavement.

Sirens in the distance, fire officers sprinting towards them down the middle of the road carrying extinguishers.

Then Poland arrived. 'Stand clear.'

'We can't, Roger. He's covered in accelerant,' replied Dixon. 'Just do it!'

Poland pulled the lever, directing the nozzle at Webb, covering him with white foam.

'We need to get his goggles off,' said Cole.

'Leave them. Let them do it at the hospital,' said Poland.

Dixon was holding Webb up now. 'He's passed out.'

'Get him in the recovery position.' Poland dropped the fire extinguisher and helped Dixon lower Webb to the ground. 'We need to clear his airway.'

Dixon stepped back and watched Poland kneeling over Webb, two fingers in Webb's mouth, clearing out foam. Then he pressed his fingers to the side of his neck. 'There's a weak pulse and he's breathing. Get this off him.' Poland rolled up Dixon's sodden coat and threw it into the gutter. Then he covered Webb with his own.

Firefighters were directing their extinguishers at squibs still alight in the road.

'What d'you want me to do?' asked Jane.

'Get uniform taking names and addresses from anyone and everyone who saw what happened, before the crowd disperses too much.' Dixon had sat down on the kerb and was watching Poland briefing the paramedics who had arrived, running ahead of the ambulance that was creeping along High Street, its siren blaring, the crowd parting to let it through. 'Phone footage too.'

'Leave it to me.'

'And you'd better look after this lady,' said Dixon, gesturing to the woman who had been standing next to Webb, still rooted to the spot. 'She knows who he is.'

Poland slumped down next to him. 'He's going to need to go to Frenchay for this. Maybe even the Queen Elizabeth in Birmingham. I've told them to put the air ambulance on standby. It can get down on St Matthew's Field, I think.'

'Life threatening?'

Poland puffed out his cheeks. 'Shouldn't be.'

'There was definitely an accelerant, Roger,' said Dixon, staring at his hands. 'Every time you put him out, he just burst into flames again.'

'How are your hands?'

'They were protected by my coat this time.' Dixon winced at the memory of turning up at Poland's house in the middle of the night nearly eight months ago, his hands wrapped in wet towels. 'I've been stabbed and shot with a crossbow bolt, but the burns were the worst.'

'They always are,' Poland said, the slight slur that had been creeping into his voice now well and truly gone. 'Grievous bodily harm at the very least.'

'Attempted murder, assuming he makes it.'

'He should do, but sepsis is always the risk in these cases.' Poland shook his head solemnly.

A second ambulance had arrived and was pushing through the crowd from the opposite direction.

'Maggie's on her way from Express Park,' said Jane, sitting down on the kerb next to Dixon. 'She's picked a good night to be duty SIO.'

'Where's that lady gone?'

'Hilary Eastman,' replied Jane. 'Her husband was there to film her squibbing, so he's taking her home. At least she won't be on her own. The victim is Richard Webb. He was the one who persuaded her to have a go, would you believe it? They're both estate agents, Eastman and Webb, in College Street. D'you know them?'

'Their lettings department rented me our cottage.'

Webb was screened from them now by a circle of paramedics and doctors kneeling around him, working furiously. Dixon tried to listen to what was being said, but the tannoy drowned out any conversation.

'*Thank you very much, everyone. That's the Bridgwater carnival over for another year, but we'll see you in Burnham-on-Sea on Monday night. Please travel safely and don't drink and drive. Good night!*'

Dixon picked up his coat, watching the fire extinguisher foam dripping into the gutter, and fished a wad of sodden dog poo bags from the pocket. 'They've had it,' he said, stuffing them back in, before dropping the coat back into the gutter. He sniffed his hand. 'That's the foam. I thought it might be accelerant for a minute.'

'That will have burnt away,' said Poland.

Steam was still rising from Cole's hi-vis jacket, wrapped around Webb's head.

'Where's Nigel?'

'At the ambulance over there,' replied Jane, pointing. 'Getting his hands looked at, I think.'

Webb's feet were twitching; Dixon hoped it was the paramedics moving him. 'God help him if he regains consciousness,' he whispered.

'They won't let him. The doctors have got morphine on them and that's one of the A&E consultants from Musgrove.' Poland stood up. 'I'll just go and have a word.'

Jane waited until Poland had gone before taking Dixon's hand. 'You all right?'

'Cordite and burning flesh,' he said, watching the last of the crowd being ushered along the pavement by uniformed officers, leaving behind them lines of rubbish, like the tide going out: takeaway boxes, bottles, plastic pint glasses, fish and chip paper, napkins, cigarette ends; all of it masked by the cordite and burning flesh.

'It's a horrible smell,' Jane said, under her breath.

'Lucy really didn't need to see that.'

'She didn't see it, don't worry. I got her off the windowsill, and after that she couldn't see over the crowd.'

'Does she know what happened?'

'I just told her there'd been an accident. Billy's taking her home.'

'Back to Westonzoyland?'

'His father's there, and you know what, she's sixteen now and there comes a point when I just have to trust her.'

'Did she want to get something to eat?' asked Dixon, turning to Jane.

'Said she's lost her appetite now.'

'It's as I thought.' Poland was standing over them. 'He's going straight to the Queen Elizabeth. The helicopter's going to land at St Matthew's and they'll run him over there in an ambulance.'

Chapter Three

The crowd had all but gone by the time Detective Inspector Margaret Baldwin arrived, flanked by Detective Constables Dave Harding and Mark Pearce, just in time to watch Webb's stretcher being loaded into an ambulance for the short drive around to St Matthew's Field, the helicopter already on the ground.

Dixon had ordered High Street sealed off and Cole had bagged up Webb's cosh and the remains of his squib; a group of uniformed officers gathering for a fingertip search of the immediate vicinity when Scientific Services arrived.

'Donald Watson is on his way,' Maggie said. 'Did you see what happened?'

Dixon nodded. 'Webb's squib had been tampered with. There was definitely an accelerant, and it must have been rigged to blow back on him. You'll need to get on to the Forensic Explosives Lab at Porton Down. They'll send someone down to have a look at it.' It was odd, seeing Dave and Mark working with another inspector. Dave had even ironed his suit.

'You can explain that to Donald Watson.'

'Scientific are your problem, Maggie,' said Dixon. 'I'm just a witness this time.'

'Will he live?' she asked, turning to Poland.

'I'd have thought so, although he might wish he hadn't.'

'The poor bugger.' Maggie leaned back against the side of Cole's patrol car, now parked on the pavement outside the Carnival Inn. 'Can you stay and help me, Jane? I'm guessing you've not been drinking.'

'No, I'll stay.'

'Looks like it's just you and me again then, Roger,' said Dixon. 'Any chance of a lift home, Nige? We'll never get a taxi now.'

Cole dropped them in the car park of the Red Cow, opposite Dixon's cottage in Brent Knoll, just after midnight. The pub was shut and the streetlights had gone off. Dixon and Poland watched the tail lights of the patrol car fade into the distance.

'First time I've seen something like that,' said Poland. 'I'm usually involved after the event. Never during.' He followed Dixon across the road. 'You've seen more than your fair share – how do you deal with it?'

'I have help.'

'He never made a sound.' Poland steadied himself, a hand on Dixon's shoulder. 'You'd have thought he'd have screamed, or something. Shock, I suppose.'

'You're the doctor,' replied Dixon, fishing his door keys out of his pocket. 'And let's hope we never have to find out.'

Poland frowned. 'What help?'

'You've met him before.' Dixon smiled as he slid his key into the lock; a loud thud against the inside of the front door before he had a chance to turn it. Then the barking started.

He squatted down as he pushed open the door, throwing his arms around the large white Staffordshire terrier that came charging out, jumping up at him and licking his face.

'Your very own therapy dog.'

'Something like that.'

'I've often thought about getting one, but I work long hours in the lab and live alone. Maybe when I retire.'

'Jane knew you were coming,' said Dixon, gesturing to the bottle of Scotch on the side in the kitchen.

'Are you taking Monty for a walk?'

'We'll go up the hill, I think. Hardly feel like sleeping.'

'You bring the dog, I'll bring the whisky.'

Cold and clear, the first frost of winter already; a gossamer-thin layer of ice forming on the shallower puddles in the lane was just about visible in the moonlight. It had taken Dixon a few minutes to find a pullover and an old waterproof jacket; green, with a hood rolled up in the collar.

'You're going to need a new coat,' Poland had said.

Scientific Services had taken his old one to test for residues of whatever accelerant had been used, but even if they hadn't, Dixon wasn't wearing it again. That had been an easy decision.

Over the stile and into the field at the top of the lane; they walked in silence, the only sounds the frozen grass crunching under their feet, the barking of a fox in the distance, an owl hooting somewhere in the copse below them; Poland taking the occasional swig from the bottle.

'What degree were his burns?' asked Dixon, watching the flashing lights on an aeroplane high overhead.

'Third on the exposed areas. Full thickness. Not good.' Another swig.

'And what were mine?'

'First mainly. You had some blistering, so that's second degree technically, but you got off lightly. I know it didn't feel like it at the time.' Poland handed him the bottle. 'Here, you have some.'

'Ta.'

'He's looking at multiple operations, skin grafts.'

Dixon hooked Monty's extending lead over a fence post, leaned back and took a swig of Scotch. The towns and villages below had been plunged into darkness when the streetlights had gone off, but the lights of Hinkley Point were visible several miles away across the estuary, the steelworks at Port Talbot even further away to the north-west, the lights twinkling on the horizon.

'He'll probably survive, so you're looking at one charge of grievous bodily harm,' said Poland, the slur creeping back into his voice.

'Attempted murder. And there'll be explosives offences too, under the Explosive Substances Act 1883.' Dixon was deep in thought, talking to himself as much as Poland. 'There aren't going to be many people capable of rigging a squib to blow back like that, are there? They'd need access to the squib and the technical knowledge. Should narrow it down a bit.'

Poland reached over and slid the bottle from Dixon's hand, murmuring his agreement at the same time.

'Then there's the public nature of it – if that isn't making a statement, I don't know what is. Sending one hell of a message.'

'Who to?'

'If we knew that, Roger . . .'

'D'you think they'll cancel the rest of the carnivals?'

'I doubt it. There's no more squibbing now, so why should they?'

'Burnham next then, on Monday night.'

'Do you ever get used to the smell of burning flesh?'

Poland took a large swig of Scotch, then handed the bottle back to Dixon. 'No, you don't,' he said.

◆ ◆ ◆

'What time is it?' asked Dixon, rubbing his eyes.

Jane was sitting on the edge of the bed holding a mug of coffee, a toothbrush sticking out of the corner of her mouth. 'Half past seven.'

'Where's Monty?'

'I've fed him and he's sitting on the windowsill downstairs, waiting for the postman.'

'What time did you get in?'

'Three,' she mumbled in reply. 'I grabbed a few hours on the sofa. Maggie wants me back at Express Park by nine and I've got to pick Lucy up from Westonzoyland and get her on the eight-fifty train. It's her foster mother's birthday party tonight and there's no way she's missing that. What would Judy think?'

'Have you seen Roger?'

'I couldn't wake him up. I did knock. You must have hit it pretty hard when you got back last night. That bottle of whisky's half empty.'

'That was him. We took Monty for a walk and Roger took it with him.'

'How much did you have?'

'Not a lot.' Dixon took a sip of coffee. 'You know I can't drink a huge amount since I've been diabetic.'

'I'll try him again before I go.'

'Any news?'

'Webb's still with us, if that's what you mean,' replied Jane, talking and brushing her teeth at the same time. 'And Scientific have got the middle of Bridgwater closed off.'

'How's Maggie doing?' Dixon was out of bed, pulling on a pair of jeans.

'Fine.' Jane was out on the landing now, still brushing her teeth, the tap running in the bathroom behind her. 'It's going to be a big one to keep on top of. No shortage of witnesses and CCTV.'

'Bet you wish you were still safely tucked up in the Safeguarding Unit.'

'No fear.'

The door of the spare bedroom opened slowly. Poland was still fully clothed, yawning and blinking furiously as his eyes adjusted to the light.

'How's the head?' asked Jane.

'Don't ask.'

'I'll see to him,' said Dixon. 'It's nothing a couple of headache pills, black coffee and a good fry-up won't sort out.'

Jane arrived at Express Park just before 8 a.m. She drove up the ramp on to the top floor of the staff car park to find Maggie standing on the far side, inhaling cigarette smoke deep and blowing it out through her nose. Her arms were folded tightly across her chest. Not a good sign.

'I didn't know you smoked.'

'Only on special occasions.'

'What's up?'

'I've got the assistant chief constable on his way down to see me.'

'Charlesworth?'

'Deborah Potter's coming too.' Maggie was screwing her cigarette end into a brick on the top of the wall. 'The ACC and a detective chief superintendent – means only one thing, doesn't it?'

'A major investigation team.'

'He wittered on about media interest, it being a high-profile case and all that. You can just imagine it, can't you? They want to make sure the force has it under control, he said.'

'He has a point.' Jane gave what she hoped was a reassuring shrug. 'It'll need a big team too, just to take all the witness statements.'

'At the moment there's just the five of us, which is no bloody good, is it?'

Jane knew a rhetorical question when she heard one. 'What about the CCTV?' she asked, changing the subject.

'Dave and Mark have been at it all night. There's going to be hours, from multiple cameras. And we've already had several clips emailed in by members of the public.'

'Are Dave and Mark here?'

'Downstairs.'

Jane swiped her card in front of the sensor and opened the back door. 'C'mon, you don't want Charlesworth to find you skulking about up here.'

Dave Harding was grinning at Jane as she walked along the landing towards the CID Area on the first floor. His suit was a bit more crumpled than usual this morning, but then he had spent the night in it. 'Nice to have you back doing some proper police work,' he said.

'You two need to go home and get some sleep.' Maggie flicked on the kettle and reached for a jar of coffee. 'I've rustled up a couple of uniformed officers who can take over the CCTV. Brief them and then bugger off.'

'What time d'you want us back?' asked Dave.

'Four will do. I'm guessing somebody else will be in charge by then anyway.'

'I think we should speak to Hilary Eastman,' Jane said. 'Somebody has almost killed her business partner. I'll ring her, see if she's up to giving a statement.'

'Did you say you had some headache pills?' asked Poland, rinsing his mug under the tap while he watched Dixon frying eggs.

'That cupboard. There's a selection, some with codeine, some without. I might have some Tramadol left if you're desperate.'

'It's not that bad. Paracetamol will do.' Poland was snapping two tablets from the foil sleeve. 'Can you drop me back to my car?'

'Where is it?'

'The visitors' car park at Express Park.'

'Are you sure you'll be all right to drive?'

'Probably.'

'Not good enough. I'll drop you down to Musgrove Park. You can get a taxi back this evening, when you've sobered up a bit. A couple of post mortems and you'll be as right as rain.'

Monty was sitting at Dixon's feet, waiting for a piece of bacon, when he started growling.

'Bit early for the post,' said Dixon. The knock at the front door was loud and slow. He glanced over Poland's shoulder at the car parked in the road outside, the flashing blue light on the dashboard visible through the front window of the cottage, the uniformed driver still sitting behind the wheel. It could mean only one thing. 'There goes my paid holiday.'

'Who is it?' Poland was standing in the kitchen doorway, leaning on the frame while he waited for the painkillers to kick in.

'You two had quite a night of it, I gather.' Charlesworth stepped into the cottage when Dixon opened the door.

'You could say that,' replied Poland.

'Come in, Sir,' said Dixon, trying not to sound unduly sarcastic.

'Thank you.' Charlesworth balanced his hat on the back of the sofa. 'Flying colours at the assessment centre. Well done.'

'Thank you, Sir.'

'I'll come straight to the point. The word from the QE in Birmingham is that Webb's stable and likely to make it, so it'll probably end up being an attempted murder. Either way, the media attention is going to be huge. The official line at the moment is that it was an accident, but we're putting a major investigation team on it straight away because we know otherwise, don't we? You're to be the SIO.' Charlesworth paused, not long enough for Dixon to put up even token resistance. 'You were there, so it makes sense. And you're twiddling your thumbs at the moment anyway.'

'Yes, Sir.'

'Deborah's at Express Park now, breaking the news to DI Baldwin. She'll stay on the MIT, though, and I suggest you team her up with DS Winter.'

'For obvious reasons.'

'Quite.' Charlesworth raised his eyebrows. 'Take as many people as you need from uniform for the rest of today, CID too, and we'll send two teams down from Portishead in the morning. There'll need to be a press conference at some point tomorrow as well. I'll get Vicky Thomas to sort that out and she'll let you know the where and when.'

'Thank you, Sir,' replied Dixon, doing his best to sound sincere.

'You can have the open plan area on the top floor. You usually seem to take it over anyway.'

'What about Monday night at Burnham?'

'You think this is just the start?'

'I don't know that it isn't.'

'You'll need more if you want me to get it cancelled.' Charlesworth snatched his hat off the sofa and turned on his heels for the door, which was still standing open. 'Nice to see you, Roger,' he said, with a wave of his hand. 'We must have lunch.'

Jane's text arrived ten minutes later, just as Dixon was putting on his seatbelt, a bacon sandwich held between his teeth.

Potter here. MIT. No news on SIO. Jx

His reply didn't take him long.

I know Nx

Chapter Four

'Is this it?'

'For the time being,' replied Deborah Potter.

Dixon had taken the stairs two at a time, arriving on the top floor of the police centre just as Potter was leaving. Six of the workstations were occupied, Jane and Maggie Baldwin perched on the edge of the table in front of blank whiteboards, DC Louise Willmott filling the kettle from the water cooler.

'Uniform were flat out last night for the carnival.' Potter had stopped at the top of the stairs, her hand on the banister, ready for a quick getaway. 'They've got the fireworks in Burnham tonight, then the carnival tomorrow. And it is a Sunday, don't forget.'

Dixon glanced at the two uniformed officers sitting idly at workstations, the computers in front of them switched off. 'Where are Dave and Mark?' he asked, turning to Maggie.

'I sent them home,' she replied. 'They'd been at the CCTV Hub all night; I told them to be back by four.'

'Did they find anything?'

'No.'

Dixon's short stint as managing DCI at Express Park had included umpteen team meetings, so he just about recognised the four detectives sitting at workstations on the far side of the room. He'd certainly never worked with them before and putting names to the faces was a non-starter. God help him if he'd done their performance reviews.

'DS Hobson, Sir.' She was dressed casually – jeans and a pullover. 'We were there last night, so came in to see if we could help. We thought it might be all hands to the pumps.'

'Thank you.'

'I'm Jenny, this is Lisa, Ness and Kim.' She smiled in a feeble attempt to hide her embarrassment, painfully aware that most police officers don't go to the carnival unless they're being paid; overtime rates, preferably. 'It was a girls' night out.'

'Right, well, I'll leave it in your capable hands, Nick.' Potter was already halfway down the stairs. 'There's somewhere I need to be, I'm afraid.'

Dixon was staring at the blank whiteboards. 'How many witnesses have we got?' he asked, spinning around.

'Contact details for eighty-two,' replied Jane. 'Not including the staff at Eastman and Webb. Some of them were there to watch the squibbing. It was their staff night out.'

'Jenny, can you and your team start ringing them? Separate out any who saw anything remotely suspicious, and we can take statements from them first. All right?'

'Yes, Sir.'

'Maggie, I'm going to have to ask you to focus on the CCTV for the time being. Charlesworth's fixing a press conference for tomorrow afternoon, and he'll want images of persons of interest. People we need to speak to.'

'Fine.' Maggie was clearly less than impressed, but did her best to hide it.

'Whoever rigged that squib to explode may not even have been there, but my guess is he or she wouldn't have missed it for the world. Jenny, if you come up with anything on the phones, let DI Baldwin know so her team can find it on the CCTV.'

'Will do.'

'You two.' Dixon turned to the two uniformed officers. 'Can you help with the CCTV?'

'Yes, Sir.' In unison.

'You know what to look for?'

'We do.'

'What about me?' asked Jane. 'I rang Hilary Eastman, but her husband said she's taken a sleeping pill and gone to bed.'

'Populate those whiteboards. Victim first, you know the drill. Lou, you're with me.'

A Scientific Services van had beaten them to it and was parked outside a large, green painted corrugated barn set back from the road, the huge steel doors standing open. It reminded Dixon of an aircraft hangar, only this time it was a carnival cart taking refuge from the sleet.

Disco Fever really did look like a nightclub the morning after the night before, only this time there were no beer bottles on the floor, no broken glass. The strip lights revealed exactly what had been hidden by the darkness, disguised by the bright lighting and glitter balls. The reality behind the sparkle.

The cart had been backed into the barn, the towing vehicle and power unit reversed in alongside it, health and safety cradles standing empty on the wooden platforms.

'I've never understood the attraction,' said Louise, as Dixon turned into the lane leading out to the barn, the gateway wide and newly concreted. 'Must cost a bomb too.'

'Some people get involved in football clubs, others carnival clubs. I should imagine it's a social thing as much as anything.'

'And what d'you do?'

'I walk my dog.'

Louise turned away, hiding her amusement no doubt.

'Can I help?' shouted a man with a clipboard, striding over to greet them as Dixon and Louise climbed out of the Land Rover, parked next to the Scientific Services van.

'We're looking for the club secretary, Ray Smith,' replied Dixon, with a cursory wave of his warrant card.

'That's me. We've already got your forensic lot in there.'

'Shouldn't the cart be lined up on Queen's Drive, ready for Burnham tomorrow night?' asked Louise.

'We would be, usually, but we've pulled out as a mark of respect. Truth is, no one's got the stomach for it. It's a shame because we got Best Feature Cart last night and thought we might do a clean sweep this year.'

Dixon was looking up at the barn. 'There's no Avalon Carnival Club signage.'

'We don't want to advertise what's in here, do we? There's thousands of pounds' worth of stuff. The generator's worth thirty grand on its own. Then there's the tools, the cart, everything. It'd be a burglar's dream come true. As it is, it's just a barn on a farm in the middle of nowhere.'

'Apart from the concrete turning circle.'

'There's no way round that, really.'

'Any CCTV?'

'No, sorry. The farmer's a club member and he only lives over there. He keeps an eye on it and there's always people about. It's a working farm.'

'We'll need a word with him.'

'Of course.' Smith waved his clipboard at a teenager standing in the doorway, gawping as if he'd never seen a police officer before. 'Don't just stand there, go and find Amos.' Smith was clearly used to barking orders.

Even the bright strip lights inside the barn weren't powerful enough to mask the arc lamp that had been set up, pointing at the steel cabinet against the rear wall.

'They're dusting for fingerprints,' continued Smith. 'They won't find anything, I'm afraid. God knows how many people have been in and out of that cupboard in the last couple of weeks. It was supposed to be an accident, anyway, wasn't it?'

'What's in it?' asked Dixon, ignoring Smith's question.

'It's where we keep the squibbing stuff.'

'And the squibs?'

'Aye.'

'Richard Webb was a club member as well as a sponsor?' asked Dixon, squeezing down the side of the towing vehicle to get out of the sleet.

'He's our club president. Been a member for as long as I can remember. His kids used to come along too, but they're away at school these days. Is there any word on his condition?'

'Stable but still unconscious, mercifully,' replied Dixon. 'He's at the Queen Elizabeth in Birmingham, the specialist burns unit.'

'Always been a strong supporter of the club. Never misses the squibbing either, the poor sod. Of all the things to bloody well happen.'

'Were you there?'

'A bit further along. I saw the flash and then all hell broke loose. I gave my details at the time.'

'Where do you get the squibs?'

'We buy them in from Semper Fireworks down Willand way. They have to make them specially, mind. They're not regular fireworks by any stretch.'

'When?'

'We had the delivery last Wednesday, just after lunch, so about two, I suppose. I signed for them and put them in the cupboard as usual. Same every year.'

'When were they attached to the coshes?'

'That evening. We did it after the committee meeting. Tape and cable ties it is these days, but some of them have got metal straps. It used to be rope, but it stretches, and we had one burn through.'

'And who has access to the cabinet?' Dixon had edged his way along to the back wall of the barn, turning sideways to get past the power unit, and ducking under several ladders sticking out from the shelving opposite. Giant shelves, right to the ceiling, covered with pots of paint, rolls of cable, tools, paintbrushes. It looked more like an aisle at B&Q.

'Everybody,' replied Smith, holding his stomach in as he followed Dixon.

'Surely it's locked?'

'Padlocked, but we keep the key on top.'

Dixon thought better of replying, opting for a silent count to ten instead.

'It's bolted to the wall, Sir.'

'Which makes all the difference.'

The Scientific Services officer had been trying to help, but was left wishing he hadn't bothered. 'I'm getting loads of prints,' he said, trying a change of tack. 'Most of them overlaid or smudged, though. I might get a few clear ones, but I wouldn't hold your breath.'

Both doors of the large cabinet were standing open, several ornate carved poles hanging on hooks from leather straps, the remaining hooks empty. 'They're the coshes,' said Smith hesitantly. 'Some people brought theirs back last night, when we brought the cart in. Others will have taken them home.'

'They're usually stored here?'

'Aye.'

'And that would've been Richard Webb's?' asked Dixon, pointing to an empty hook with a little brass plaque above it: 'President'.

'And that's mine,' said Smith, a cosh hanging from a hook marked 'Secretary'. Third in the pecking order, after President and Chairman. 'May I?' he asked, making to reach into the cabinet.

'Best not, Sir,' said the Scientific Services officer, intercepting him before he touched anything.

'Oh, right. Well, the squib we attach to the bottom end, then we hold it up like this.' Both hands above his head now.

'I was there,' said Dixon. 'Last night.'

Smith shook his head. 'I'm afraid I just froze. We all did.'

'How many carnival club members were there?'

'We had twenty squibs and we used them all. Hilary Eastman had one as our main sponsor with Richard, and the rest went to club members. Oh, and a local councillor had one. Not sure why, really, but we occasionally accommodate local dignitaries.'

'Who was it?'

'It was a bloke from Curry Rivel way. Richard set it up. Crony of his, I think.'

Dixon glanced at Louise, who was resting her notebook on a large bucket of paint, taking notes.

'The coshes, then. If they're labelled like this, then they're specific to each person.'

'Touch another fellow's cosh on pain of . . .'

'Amos is here!' A shout from outside the barn.

'You go, Lou,' said Dixon. 'Anything unusual – Wednesday afternoon onwards.'

'Yes, Sir.'

'Have you got any squibs left?' he asked, turning back to Smith.

'No, never do. We only get however many we need – they're not cheap. Back in the old days we used to make them ourselves, but health and safety put a stop to that in the end, back in 2001 it was. There was the occasional incident, shall we say.'

'Of a squib exploding?'

'That happened a couple of times.'

'And there were fatalities?' Dixon was watching Louise standing outside with the farmer, trying to keep her notebook dry.

'A couple, both from the resulting barn fire. Nobody died on a carnival night, although we did have some nasty burns.'

'What about access to the barn itself – who has keys?'

'Are you suggesting someone tampered with Richard's squi—?'

'I'm not suggesting anything, Sir,' interrupted Dixon, with his best disarming smile. 'I'm just looking at all the possibilities, until we know one way or the other. It's my job.'

'All club members have keys.' Smith's hands were on his hips now, a sure sign he was getting defensive.

'Do you have a list of members?'

'You want it, I suppose?'

Smith disappeared into an office at the front of the barn, the slamming of filing cabinet drawers letting Dixon know what he thought of it. 'It must have been an accident,' he said, emerging from the office, a pair of glasses now sitting precariously on the end of his nose. 'It must've been.'

'We'll be getting an explosives expert to look at the remains of Mr Webb's squib, and forensic tests will confirm whether or not an accelerant was used.'

'It was you, wasn't it?' said Smith, squinting at Dixon. 'I'm sorry I didn't recognise you. You were the bloke with the coat, trying to put him out. And you think an accelerant was used?'

'We'll see, Sir. We'll see.'

Chapter Five

'Were you there last night, Lou?' asked Dixon, making polite conversation when the third set of traffic lights stopped him on the run back into Bridgwater. It was either that or thumping the steering wheel.

'No, we're taking Katie to the fireworks in Burnham tonight and then I've got – *had* – tomorrow night off to take her to Burnham carnival.'

'You'll be going to both, don't worry.'

'Yeah, that's not quite what we . . .' Louise thought better of it.

'What did the farmer have to say?'

'Not a lot, really. He thinks people were there the whole time until the cart pulled out on Saturday afternoon. It's always a bit of a last-minute rush to get it ready – painting, usually. And something electrical always goes wrong, he said.'

'People were there working right through the night?'

'He thinks so – they usually do – but he goes to bed about ten and wouldn't have seen anything after that anyway.'

'Was he at the carnival?'

'No. He used to be heavily involved in it, but not so much these days. He's an honorary member of the club now, mainly because he charges them a reduced rent for the barn.'

'So, he was no use at all?'

'Pretty much.' Louise was flicking through the list of members of the Avalon Carnival Club. 'Don't know any of them,' she said. 'You think something's going to happen at the fireworks tonight?'

'A squib is a firework, isn't it?'

Dixon parked on the pavement outside the Vodafone shop. A small gaggle of onlookers were standing along the blue tape that blocked off High Street, uniformed officers on hand to stop the more inquisitive among them. A couple of photographers were there too, one with an ID card hanging on a lanyard around his neck; both took photographs when the tape was raised for Dixon and Louise to duck under.

'Is he dead, Inspector?'

'Is it a murder investigation?'

Gits.

'When can I open my coffee shop?' A third voice, anxious rather than inquisitive. 'I've missed the morning trade already, and it'll be lunchtime soon.'

'I'll find out for you,' replied Louise.

A line of officers in hazmat suits were crawling on their hands and knees, some on the pavement, others in the road, sifting through the litter of carnival night.

Dixon stopped at a second line of blue tape, scorch marks visible on the tarmac twenty yards ahead of them, his plastic pint glass still sitting on the kerb.

'We'd better wait for the crime scene manager,' said Louise.

'Is there one?'

'There always is now. An email went round. It's the new rules.'

A third line of tape crossed High Street fifty yards further along, and beyond that two flatbed lorries were waiting to get through, black bin liners piled high on the back of both. The council street cleaners were taking a tea break, by the looks of things.

'What are you waiting for?' asked Donald Watson, waving his clipboard at Dixon.

'The crime scene manager. There was an email, apparently.'

'That's me this time.' Watson lifted the tape. 'No need to suit up, we're almost finished – just doing a final sweep for anything we might have missed. You wait till you meet the new bloke. He'll have your guts for garters.'

'I'll soon have him wrapped around my little finger,' replied Dixon, ducking under the tape. 'Just like you.'

'Piss off.'

'What about the shops?' asked Louise.

'They'll be able to open in half an hour or so.'

'Found anything interesting?'

'The remains of his squib, obviously,' replied Watson. 'There's someone on the way from Explosives to look at it this afternoon. It blew out, which is unusual in itself. If you look at the others, you're left with an intact cardboard sleeve on the end of the cosh, just like an old Roman candle or something, but this one blew just above where it was attached. We found this in the gutter.' Watson reached into a plastic crate on the pavement and pulled out an evidence bag. 'It looks like a funnel, and it's partially melted. Definitely tampered with.'

A curved metal sleeve, small enough to fit inside a squib, it was charred on one side, the edges buckled.

'It would be enough to direct the blast back towards the squibber,' continued Watson.

'What about the accelerant?' asked Dixon.

'Acetone, probably, if the flames were orange and yellow. They're already looking at Webb's clothes back at the lab, so I'll get back to you on that. We've got various tests to run. I take it you don't want your coat back.' Watson lifted another evidence bag from a different crate.

'No.'

'Thought not.'

'Better let everybody know, Lou.'

She turned away, dialling a number on her phone.

'We're just going down to the corner,' Dixon said, walking off.

'We'll still be here,' replied Watson.

The streets beyond the furthest section of blue tape had been cleaned, the cleaners enjoying a well-earned rest and fag break. 'How much longer, mate, d'you know?' one shouted.

'About half an hour,' Louise replied, interrupting her telephone call.

'Typical, innit. We could've gone back to bed.'

Dixon stopped in his tracks. 'Were you here last night?'

'No fear, mate. The carnival loses its appeal when you have to clean up after it every year.'

'Find anything?' asked Watson.

'I'm not sure what we were looking for,' whispered Louise.

The Scientific Services officers were clambering out of their hazmat suits and carrying plastic crates to their vans by the time Dixon and Louise arrived back outside the Carnival Inn. The street cleaners had started work too, litter picking along both sides of High Street.

Dixon was standing over the scorch marks on the road surface, where Webb had fallen, burning; the smell bringing the images roaring back, of burning flesh, hair, melting goggles, the flames reigniting as fast as he and Cole could put them out.

He spun round. 'Get on to the social media team at Portishead, will you, Lou. Ask them to monitor the usual channels and I want to know about anyone uploading images.'

'Yes, Sir.'

'Right, we're off,' said Watson, his hand on the open driver's door of his van.

'You're not leaving this here?'

'No choice, sorry.' Watson cleared his throat. 'We haven't got a jet washer.'

'I'll go and see if the street cleaners have got one,' said Louise.

'Shall we take the tape down on our way out?' asked Watson.

'No.'

'But there are people waiting to get through.'

'They'll have to bloody well wait.'

'They've got a pressure washer,' said Louise, trotting back from speaking to the street cleaners. 'They use it for the chewing gum. He said he'd be over in a minute. Is that it then?'

'We'll wait.' Dixon was still standing over Webb's outline on the tarmac. 'I'm not having this lot popping up all over bloody Instagram.'

◆ ◆ ◆

Jane had done well, the whiteboard a mine of information.

The images had come from Facebook by the looks of things, the people smiling, holding glasses with floating lemon slices, some on a beach somewhere. It was amazing the information people gave away these days.

Richard Webb, age fifty-six. Jane had written 'ex-wife Anita, son Rupert and daughter Rachel' underneath images of a woman and two teenage children. Even his parents must have been on Facebook – the photograph taken on a cruise, possibly.

'So, that's it then,' she said. 'Attempted murder.'

'Till we know otherwise. His profile says "in a relationship", but there's no photo. Who's he in a relationship with?'

'He's married to a bloke called Ian Szopinski,' replied Jane. 'No mention of him at all on Facebook.'

'Where can we find him?'

'A friend drove him up to Birmingham in the early hours. He's likely to be up there for several days, so I've arranged for local family liaison to look after him.'

The images of the staff members at Eastman and Webb looked more formal, with the E&W logo in the background, so had probably come from the firm's website. Dixon remembered it well from his days in the legal profession; the mugshot for the website and a paragraph of outside interests to make the lawyers seem like human beings. 'Outside work, Nick enjoys . . .'

There were eleven staff, including Webb himself; even the admin assistants and the receptionist must have had their photos on the website. Richard Webb was listed as 'director', with one assistant residential property agent, Andrew Platt.

'We'll need to speak to Platt, Jane. At the office, preferably. Did you get anywhere with Hilary Eastman?'

'I did ring again, but her husband said she was still in no fit state—'

'Try her again.'

'Yes, Sir.'

Dixon had expected one, but there was no barb in Jane's voice, no sarcastic edge. She understood.

'We'll need to get Szopinski interviewed. They can do it at the hospital. We need his whereabouts since Wednesday afternoon, phone records, the usual stuff.'

'I'll see if someone local can do it.'

'Someone senior.' Dixon pointed at the photos on the whiteboard. 'Tell me about Anita, Rupert and Rachel.'

'I've spoken to Anita,' replied Jane. 'They get on for the children's sake, apparently, even though he walked out on her – "acrimonious" was the word she used to describe the divorce. She's gone over to the school to tell the kids.'

'Where are they?'

'They're both in the sixth form at Millfield.'

A summons to the headmaster's office, mother waiting, it could mean only one thing. Dixon had seen it all before.

Poor kids.

The phones were busy on the far side of the incident room, a fifth casually dressed officer having joined the girls' night out ringing around the witnesses.

'We've had three come in so far,' said Jane. 'Maggie's got the other two on the CCTV, so they're getting through that a bit quicker. There are a couple of off duty PCSOs on the way in too.'

'Have we come up with anything on the CCTV?'

Maggie stood up from her workstation, picking up several bits of paper from the desk in front of her. 'Four, so far. They look out of place or are behaving oddly. We've isolated the footage, but these are some stills.'

Dixon flicked through the grainy images, time stamps in the bottom left corner.

Several people were hanging out of an upstairs window of the Carnival Inn, a shadowy figure in the background, a mobile phone in his hand. Two more were filming the lighting of the squibs on their phones, hoodies obscuring their faces, but then it had been a cold night and hoodies were ten a penny.

The fourth was a steward, possibly, lighting a pile of rags that had gone out; a hi-vis jacket and bobble hat, collecting bucket in one hand, lighter in the other.

'These look like they were taken when the squibbing was just getting going. Were they still there when Webb's squib blew?'

'We're just looking for that now, but it's difficult,' replied Maggie. 'The cameras white out with the brightness of the squibs when they get going properly and you can't see a bloody thing. We'll see if High Tech can do anything with the footage, but it's a long shot.'

'What about afterwards?'

'We're checking that too.'

'Can we identify the steward, at least?' asked Dixon.

'I've emailed the image over to the carnival press officer,' replied Jane. 'He's going to make some enquiries and get back to me as soon as he can.'

'Let's get High Tech over to Eastman and Webb today – we need to be having a look at their computers.'

'Already done,' said Jane.

'And let's have an increased presence at the Burnham fireworks display tonight. An ambulance on standby too.'

'Really?' Jane frowned. 'You think something else is going to happen?'

'Better safe than sorry,' Dixon replied, trying to hide his uncertainty. 'I'll see you there. Lou?'

'Yes, Sir,' spilling her coffee.

'We'll start with the ex-wife and then wake up Hilary Eastman. She's right in the middle of this whether she likes it or not.'

Chapter Six

'The car's here,' said Dixon, trying the doorbell again. 'Maybe she's round the back.'

They followed the footpath around the side of the house, past manicured lawns, not a dead leaf in sight despite the line of oak trees along the fence. The rose bushes were all pruned too, the flower beds covered in bark.

'She must have a gardener,' whispered Louise. 'She'd never do all this herself.'

Voices were coming from beyond a timber stable block at the end of the garden. 'Now, change the rein, "M" to "K", and don't forget to sit for two at "X".'

'Oh, Lord, you didn't leave the gate open, did you?' shouted the woman, when Dixon and Louise appeared around the corner of the stables. 'I don't want the dogs in here.'

'Didn't see any dogs, sorry. And we closed the gate.'

'They've probably gone back to bed.' She was still leaning on the top rail of the fence, watching a teenage girl taking a grey around the sand school. 'Are you the police?'

Dixon took out his warrant card.

'Oh, don't bother with all that, either you are or you aren't.'

'We are, Mrs Webb.'

'Anita, please.' Shaking hands. 'I thought someone would be along sooner or later. Poor Richard. I shot over to Millfield this morning and picked up Rachel. Rupert wanted to stay. He's got a play rehearsal this afternoon.'

'How are your children?'

'They took it rather better than I thought they would, actually.' She closed her eyes fleetingly. 'They haven't seen much of him lately anyway.'

'Is now a good time?'

'Yes, fine. Now "A" to "C", halt at "G" and salute.' Anita was watching her daughter's rising trot on the far side of the arena. 'Dressage is the current fad. It was jumping last month, until she fell off.'

'Can you think of anyone who might have wished to harm Richard?'

'It was an exploding firework, squib-thing – an accident, surely?'

'It was an unusually large firework that had been rigged to explode and shower him with accelerant. We're waiting for confirmation at the moment, but we're proceeding on the basis that it was a deliberate act.'

'Someone tried to kill him?' Anita quickly checked her daughter was out of earshot. 'Ten minutes on this rein, Rachel, then cool him down before you take him in. I'm going up to the house.'

'Tea?'

'No, thank you.'

'I'll have something stronger, I think,' said Anita, reaching for a bottle of gin on the side. 'I can take her back to school in the morning. Richard's unconscious and he's not allowed visitors yet anyway, apart from his husband. I did ring, in case you were wondering.'

Louise sat down on the end of the bench and dropped her notebook on the kitchen table.

'You were going to tell me about his enemies,' said Dixon, watching Anita pour at least a triple.

'He had plenty, I'd say, but I'd be astonished if any of them felt strongly enough to have a go at killing him. And like that?' She took a deep breath as she added a small amount of flat tonic to her glass. Then she took a swig. 'I suppose I hated him the most, when he left me for that man, but that was yonks ago and we got over it.'

'What about business deals?'

'He always used to say there are disappointed people in every property deal. Some getting a better deal than others, some missing out altogether. An occupational hazard, he called it.'

'Was he involved in property development?'

'Not when he was with me. He is now.'

'No specific instances of complaints, threats to sue?'

'Not that I remember.'

'What did you think of Hilary Eastman and her husband, Bob? I'm guessing they're the Eastmans behind Eastman Homes?'

'That's Bob. It was when Richard got involved with Hilary that he started getting big ideas – dealing in plots of land, and he went more upmarket in the properties he dealt with as well. It worked, because we bought this place. He must still be doing well, because I got to keep it and the kids are still at Millfield, although that's more about his guilt than anything else, I expect.'

'Anything else you can think of?'

She sighed. 'There was a rumour doing the rounds a while ago. This agent's been doing that, that agent's been doing this. Estate agents are a soft target for the gossip mongers. After all, everybody thinks their house is worth more than it is, don't they?'

Dixon waited.

'There was a suggestion he was deliberately undervaluing properties and then a related company was buying them. Eastman Homes, surprise, surprise.'

'A suggestion from whom?'

'I really don't know, specifically.'

'What about former staff? Are there any ex-employees who may have a grudge against him?'

'Trevor Bishop is the only one I can think of,' she said testily. 'I remember the trouble he caused. Richard had to sack him, and he set up on his own practically next door. Money had been changing hands to get probate sales. It caused a lot of bad feeling with the other agents in the area. Richard put a stop to it when he found out, but the damage had been done. It took ages for him to repair his working relationships after that. They're still cordial, at best.'

'When did your marriage break down?'

'Two years ago. It was all very bitter at first. Acrimonious, shall we say.'

'How did he meet Ian?'

'Online, I think. I'd always thought he might be gay, deep down, but never in a million years was I expecting that.' Another swig of gin. 'He's a nice lad, actually, when you get to know him. Polish, works over at Hinkley, something to do with the new pylons, I think.'

Dixon stopped on the gravel drive, turned and looked back at the house when the front door slammed behind them. 'D'you think there's that much money in estate agency, Lou?'

'I don't know. Maybe. Ordinary residential stuff, probably not.'

'Or d'you think it's in the property development?'

'Are you asking me or telling me?'

'You and I have been working together for too long.'

'Really?'

'No, not really.' Dixon smiled. 'I'll drive. You've got some calls to make. Let's check her movements against her phone records and find this ex-employee, Trevor Bishop.'

'Where are we going?'

'Semper Fireworks. They'll be on the jetty at Burnham, setting up tonight's display. It'll give Hilary Eastman another hour's sleep.'

Dixon's phone pinged just as his diesel engine rattled into life, the text from Jane not coming as much of a surprise.

Richard Webb woke up. Now in induced coma. Likely to be days. Ian S staying up there for now.

'The jetty's closed, I'm afraid.' A hi-vis jacket with the Sedgemoor District Council logo on it barred his way. 'They're setting up for the fireworks display tonight.'

Dixon and Louise had parked on the double yellow lines opposite the amusement arcade, and were looking down the jetty towards a scaffolding platform that had been built halfway along, just beyond the vehicle access slip to the beach.

'Police.'

'Oh, sorry.'

The tide was out, the murky grey water of the River Parrett racing past the end of the jetty, the sand and mud shelving away steeply to the water. The marker buoy was sitting on the mud on the far bank, waiting to be lifted off by the incoming tide, the

56

outline of Hinkley Point visible through the gloom on the other side of the estuary.

'What time's high tide?' asked Dixon.

'Eight-twelve,' replied the man. 'Nine point two metres, with a light offshore breeze. Should be perfect.'

Dixon squeezed past a van that had been reversed down the jetty, the only sounds the cry of seagulls and the scream of a cordless wrench tightening scaffolding bolts. The platform was ten or twelve feet high, enough to keep the fireworks clear of the water.

'That's me done,' said the man sitting on top of the platform. 'I'll be back tomorrow to take it down.' Then he started climbing down an aluminium ladder.

'Thanks, mate.' The reply came from inside the Semper Fireworks van, the back doors standing open.

Dixon looked in the back of the van to find two men sorting through large plastic crates on shelving units. 'Police.'

'We had your lot come to the depot earlier. We really haven't got time now, I'm afraid. I've got to get this lot wired up for tonight.'

'Make the time.' Dixon waited while the man clambered out of the back of the van. 'Name?'

'James Yule.'

'You make the squibs?'

'We do.' He sighed. 'We went through this earlier with someone from your Scientific Services. They even took away a couple we had left over. For testing, they said. Look, we're really pressed for—'

'We can talk while you work,' said Dixon.

'Thanks.' Yule climbed the ladder up on to the platform. 'Pass them up, Mike,' he shouted.

'How easy would it be to rig one of your squibs to blow in a particular direction?' asked Dixon.

'Easy. We do it anyway, don't we? We rig them to blow upwards.'

'What would you have to do?'

Yule frowned. 'Are you saying it wasn't an accident? That our squib didn't—'

'It had been tampered with.'

'Did you hear that, Mike?' Yule took a deep breath. 'Fuck me. We thought we'd . . . that it was our . . .' He was rubbing the back of his neck with his hand. 'Whatever we can do to help, I mean . . . fuck me.' Dixon felt sure Yule wiped away a tear. 'The bloke from Scientific never said.'

'He may not have known, and he certainly wouldn't have been authorised to reveal that information anyway.'

'Yeah, well, you'd need to cap it so it didn't blow upwards, then weaken the side you wanted it to blow out on. It's thick cardboard, just like a normal firework, so you'd cut it out on one side. It'd be hidden by the label, I suppose. Maybe put a funnel in as well, to direct the blast.'

'Would there be room for an accelerant?'

'Plenty.' Yule sat down on the edge of the platform, his legs dangling over the side, and reached down for a plastic crate that Mike was handing up to him. 'I'd put that in something like a balloon or a condom. The heat would soon burst it, and whoosh. I mean, it's not got to blow far, has it, just down on to the operative. It's not as if it's pushing sparks up into the air for a display, like.'

'What tools would you need?'

'A Stanley knife, some glue maybe.'

'Gunpowder?'

'You wouldn't need any explosive. You'd use the stuff that's already in the squib. How's the bloke who got . . . ?' Yule let his voice peter out; sorry he asked before he'd even finished the question.

'In an induced coma,' replied Louise.

'Bit of a random way to try and kill someone, isn't it?' Yule shook his head. 'I can think of better ways.'

Dixon was staring into the back of the van, watching Mike lifting the plastic crates off the shelves. 'Does one of you stay on the platform, to light the fuses?' he asked.

'Not these days. It's all done remotely. We'll be up there,' Mike said, gesturing to the top of the sea wall, 'controlling it all from an iPad.'

'Squibs are very old fashioned,' said Yule. 'Pretty much the only firework we make with the old style fuses nowadays.'

Chapter Seven

'You drive,' Dixon said, lobbing his keys to Louise. 'I need to read the statement she gave last night. Such as it is.'

The sound of gravel under the wheels of his Land Rover coincided with him finishing the short handwritten statement.

'Is this it?'

'Sexey's Orchard,' said Louise. 'Posh, isn't it?'

Faded red brick with a black painted timber frame you could play noughts and crosses on, and leaded windows; the gable end painted white.

'If Nigel was here, he'd be telling me how much it was worth,' said Dixon.

'Was he an estate agent in a past life?'

'Watches too much daytime telly.'

'I'll go for a million plus,' said Louise, looking up at what was left of a wisteria. Someone had given it a vicious pruning. 'You'll be able to afford it on a super's salary.'

'Hardly.'

A matching red brick car port was a more recent addition, a Jaguar and a Volvo sheltering from the November frosts. They liked their SUVs and their private plates: RTE 1969 and HRE 1971. Beyond the car port was a walled garden, raised beds visible through an open gate.

The barking started as they approached the front door.

'Labradors,' said Louise.

'Spaniels.'

'How can you tell?'

'I can see them through here.'

A scowling face appeared at the small leaded window in the front door.

'Is this really necessary? I mean now?' Two liver and white springer spaniels tore out when the door was ajar and began chasing each other around the front garden.

Dixon took a deep breath, but resisted the temptation. A dutiful husband, trying to protect his wife. He would give him the benefit of the doubt.

'You'd better come in. She'll be awake now anyway.'

'Mr Eastman, is it?'

'Bob.' He whistled, the dogs responding immediately.

'They're well trained,' said Louise, stepping to one side as the dogs raced past her towards the kitchen.

'Gun dogs.' Eastman gestured along the passage. 'There's some coffee on the side – help yourselves. I'll just go and see if she feels up to it.'

'Before you do that, Sir,' said Dixon, 'I gather you were there last night?'

'Yes, I was there to film Hilary squibbing. They sponsor the Avalon Carnival Club and they'd finally badgered her into having a go. She was terrified, to be honest.'

'Have you squibbed before?'

'A few years ago. Richard organised it.'

'We'll need to see the film you took last night.'

'Yes, of course. I can AirDrop it to you, if that's any good. It's on my phone, but it won't be much use, I'm afraid. I stopped when . . .' Eastman took a deep breath.

'I'll switch my phone to receiving from everyone, if you could send it to me, please, Sir?' said Louise.

'There. Done.' Eastman dropped his phone on the worktop. 'Let me go and get Hilary.'

Double doors opened out on to a patio, a large garden and an orchard, rotting apples and dead leaves lying in the grass underneath the bare trees; open fields beyond.

'Coffee?' asked Louise, walking towards the percolator on the side, her heels clicking on the stone floor, the dogs watching her every move.

'Not for me.' Dixon was looking at the photographs along the mantelpiece and on the wall above the sideboard: family stuff, holidays, school photos, the odd certificate framed too.

If Hilary Eastman had been in bed, she'd taken the trouble to pull on a pair of jeans and a jumper. She'd had a go at taking off the previous night's make-up too, although traces of mascara remained on her cheeks.

'I took a sleeping pill,' she said, holding on to the door handle with one hand, the back of her other across her forehead. 'That was at about four in the end. Sorry.'

'Quite understandable, Mrs Eastman,' said Dixon.

'You'd better have a coffee,' said Bob, pulling out a chair at the kitchen table.

'Just a glass of water.' She slumped down on to the chair, holding the table to steady herself. 'How is Richard this morning?'

'They've put him into an induced coma and it's likely to be a while before there's any news,' replied Dixon, sitting down opposite her. 'His husband, Ian, drove up to Birmingham in the early hours and we've got a family liaison officer there as well.'

'It looked bad.'

'I'd be lying if I said it wasn't.'

'Will he live?' asked Bob.

'I really don't know.' Dixon was watching Hilary Eastman sipping from the glass of water handed to her by her husband. Time to start asking the difficult questions. 'How long had you worked at Eastman and Webb?'

'Richard and I set up on our own, what, maybe fifteen years ago. He'd come down from Bristol and I'd just left where I was. I was going to go it alone, then I met him and we set up in partnership.'

'How did you know him?'

'Professional colleague, that's all. We all know each other because we've got deals on all the time. Chains, you know how it is. We got on, and setting up with someone else reduced the risk for me.'

'What about you, Sir?' asked Dixon, turning to her husband. 'What d'you do for a living?' Asking a question he already knew the answer to, just to make it look as though he didn't.

'Property developer. Eastman Homes. We've got several sites on the go at the moment, you may have heard of us?'

'Sorry, no, Sir.' A little lie goes a long way. 'Why did Mr Webb leave Bristol?'

'No idea,' replied Hilary. 'I don't think I ever asked, and he never said. He was working for one of the big nationals and I suppose he just got fed up; everyone does. And like he always says, you never make any real money working for somebody else.'

'He had a young family at the time?'

'Just Rupert, from memory. Rachel was on the way.'

'And you?'

'I was pregnant with twins. It was the flexibility I was after, working for myself.'

'Tell me about the break-up of Richard's marriage.' Dixon glanced at Louise, who was leaning on the kitchen worktop, taking notes.

'Lead balloon,' said Bob, still hovering.

'It was difficult for Anita.' Hilary took another sip of water. 'Being left for a younger model is one thing, but for a younger man . . .' She curled her lip. 'She struggled with that.'

'I'm told they get on well now?'

'It took a while, but they worked at it, for the sake of the children more than anything else.'

'Has the business done well?'

'Yes, very. We've had our challenges, like everyone else – the property market goes up and down, competitors come and go, but we're still here after fifteen years.'

'And what about last night. Who was there?'

'Everyone, almost. It's our annual staff "do". We have a table in the Italian restaurant and afterwards we all watch the carnival. Same every year. Then Richard and I did the squibbing. He does it every year, but it was my first go. And my last.'

'Did he have a guest?'

'He'd invited a councillor along, trying to butter him up, if you must know.' She hesitated. 'He sits on the planning committee.' Blushing now.

'Which of your staff weren't there?'

'Andrew Platt was the only one, I think. He does our residential lettings and property management.'

'Can you think of anyone who might have wanted to kill Richard?'

'Look, we have problem clients, we've had deals that have turned sour, we've been sued for negligence and had to sue people when they've tried to dodge our fees. Nothing out of the ordinary for an estate agency, I can assure you.'

'Anyone in particular?'

'Not really. Not that I can think of.'

'Let's talk about Trevor Bishop, then.' Dixon let that hang in mid-air for a moment, watching for a reaction.

Hilary's features stayed blank, although that may have been the sleeping pill. 'That was ages ago.'

'Staff come and go all the time,' said Bob. 'There's a high turn-over in estate agency. Everybody's worked everywhere else at some point.'

'Have you had any dealings with him lately?'

'That turned sour, you mean?'

'Let's start with those.'

'We had a chain collapse a couple of weeks ago. His clients were buying from mine, but their buyer pulled out. Trouble getting a mortgage.'

'It happens all the time,' said Bob. 'You're not going to kill someone for that.'

'Richard had nothing to do with that deal anyway.' Hilary was leaning back in her chair, her arms hanging down by her sides. 'It doesn't make sense. He's more commercial and land than residential anyway.' She glanced at Bob, who nodded, not quite imperceptibly.

Dixon waited.

'We had to let Trevor go, if you must know.' Hilary sighed. 'Five years ago, maybe. We never had any proof, but there were rumours. Complaints.'

'Who from?'

'Other agents in the area.' She folded her arms. 'There were rumours money was changing hands with local solicitors, small brown envelopes if they placed a probate property for sale with him. He was on a bonus, so it would have been worth his while, a couple of hundred quid here or there – if he got the property and a sale went through, his bonus was twenty per cent of our fee. Plus it got the property on our books. He was good at getting the properties in, I'll give him that. I never looked too closely, to be honest, until the other agents started grumbling, threatening formal complaints and what have you.'

'And you confronted him with it?'

'Richard did. He denied it, but we sort of gently suggested it might be time for him to move on. So, he did.'

'The little shit set up four doors along the road,' grumbled Bob. 'Bishop Property Services.'

'The premises were vacant, and if it hadn't been him, it would have been someone else. It was an estate agent before, remember.'

'Did he carry on buying probate work from solicitors?'

'We still got our fair share of it, so if he did, he was careful not to make it too obvious.'

'Which solicitors, do you know?'

'This is just rumours, but there was a clerk at Holman and White. He's long gone now anyway.'

'Where?'

'Prison. He was caught with his fingers in the till, helping himself to money from estates. He's doing six years, I think.'

Chapter Eight

Dixon counted seven more photographs stuck to the glass partitioning at the far end of the incident room, printed off in colour, the paper curling at the edges.

'These are the people using their phones at the time Webb's squib blew,' said Maggie. 'They're the best we can get with all the lights. The ones from the security cameras on the pub are better, but we're just seeing the backs of people's heads.'

'These two are both employees of Eastman and Webb and there's the steward on his phone as well, so we should be able to identify him,' offered Dave. 'That leaves the four on the end unaccounted for.'

Holding their phones aloft, apparently filming the squibbing, it was difficult to see exactly where the cameras were directed. Grainy, at best – light trousers and a dark top; dark trousers and a dark top; a hoodie – little chance of getting an ID. The public might recognise someone, but it was unlikely.

'Which ones do we use at the press conference?' asked Jane.

'All four,' replied Dixon.

'If we get an ID from any of these photos, I'll eat my hat.' Maggie turned away. 'I need another coffee.'

'She still hasn't been home,' whispered Jane.

'After the fireworks, Maggie,' said Dixon, 'go home and get some sleep. And the same goes for anyone else who's been on duty all night.'

'A few more have come in to work the phones.' Jane gestured towards the workstations where the girls' night out were still hard at it, their ranks swelled by five more plain clothes detectives. 'Jenny's team have come up with a handful to interview first. And we've had a load more footage emailed in.'

Louise handed Dixon a mug of coffee and a bundle of paper off the printer. 'This is that company search you wanted.'

'Thanks.'

'Richard Webb's condition is stable and Ian Szopinski is coming home tomorrow.' Louise shrugged. 'He's got a dog, apparently, and can't leave it for too long. The elderly neighbour's got it at the moment.'

'Did we get a statement from him?'

'Someone went to the hospital and there's a statement on the system. It doesn't say much, though. He works for Energen Land over at Hinkley and was there all day Wednesday, Thursday and Friday; evenings he was at home with Richard. He wasn't at the carnival – hates it apparently – and was with Richard all day Saturday until he left at about five. We're checking his phone records match that.'

'We'll need to see him when he gets back. Ring him and get him to come straight here.'

'You found out anything?' asked Jane.

'Only that Webb had plenty of enemies, but none likely to want to kill him. Or try to, anyway.' Dixon flicked straight to the Register of Members. 'Did you look at this, Lou?'

'No, Sir.'

'They're all shareholders in Bob Eastman's company – Hilary, Richard and Anita Webb.'

'A nice little racket.'

Dixon noticed Jane's frown. 'Hilary Eastman and Richard Webb undervalue property, Bob Eastman steams in and snaps it up for development.' Another swig of coffee. 'Then there's a former employee he sacked, Trevor Bishop, paying backhanders to get probate sale instructions from local solicitors. We need to dig a bit more into that, see if it's still been going on. The clerk involved is in prison for an unrelated fraud so that may have put an end to it. Where have we got to with Trevor Bishop, Lou?'

'No sign of him,' replied Louise. 'We've checked his office, just in case, but it's closed. He's divorcing and back living with his parents, but they've not seen him since yesterday. They weren't expecting to though, they said. Oh, and he does the electrics on the Markmoor Carnival Club cart, but he's not at their depot and no one's seen him at the cart either. I've left messages for him and sent him an email.'

'You need to see this,' said Jane. 'Donald Watson's just emailed it over. The explosives expert has got a squib to explode in exactly the same way.' She flinched. 'I wouldn't want to be on the receiving end of that.'

'I saw it last night.'

'Yeah.'

'What about the accelerant?'

'An odourless kerosene.' Jane was reading aloud, paraphrasing. 'You get it in barbecue lighter gel. Traces of acetone too. We need to start thinking about tonight's fireworks,' she said, changing the subject before Dixon was tempted to watch the footage.

'We've got a good crowd,' he said, peering over her shoulder.

'I think some of them are hoping to stay on the major investigation team,' replied Jane. 'I told them there were no guarantees. Several of them were keen to work with you, apparently – jumped at the chance, they did.'

'They must be mad.'

'That's what I told them.'

'Thank you all for coming in on a Sunday, and as a reward you get to go to the Burnham-on-Sea fireworks tonight.'

Dixon ignored the mock cheer from the back of the incident room, his audience scattered among the workstations.

'What you've achieved today will give the MIT a flying start in what is going to be a huge investigation. We'll need a big team too, so any of you who wish to do so can stay on the MIT and we'll worry about the kicking and screaming from your line managers later. The ACC can sort them out.'

There was definitely a high five from the girls' night out.

'Take a minute to have a look at these boards and familiarise yourselves with our victim, if you haven't done so already. He's an estate agent in Burnham. At the moment, the public thinks that it was an accident, and let's keep it that way until the press conference tomorrow.'

'Four o'clock, Sir,' said Louise. 'Vicky Thomas just rang.'

'We need to find Trevor Bishop. He's a former employee of Eastman and Webb and there was a good deal of bad feeling when they went their separate ways. He's just going to be helping with our enquiries, but he's the closest we get to a suspect at the moment.'

'What do you think's going to happen at the fireworks?' asked Mark.

'Nothing. Hopefully.'

Chapter Nine

Waves were lapping gently against the base of the sea wall, the water either side of the jetty flat calm, the offshore breeze hardly sufficient to force even the slightest ripple. A perfect evening for ducks and drakes; he might even have allowed Monty in for a paddle. Perfect for the fireworks display too; the reflections on the water would magnify the spectacle, what wind there was taking the sparks away from the crowds on the promenade.

Fireworks were going up from the holiday camp behind the yacht club at the southern end of the seafront, but the loudest noise was coming from the drinkers piling out of the Reeds Arms. They drowned out even the cries from excited children sitting on the rail on the top of the sea wall, the hands of parents clamped around their waists, hopefully. It was a long way down.

The tannoy on the beach lifeguard hut near the top of the jetty was used to shout at bathers occasionally, especially those venturing towards the end of the jetty. In the winter months, its only job was the countdown to the start of the fireworks display.

'Ten, nine, eight . . .' The crowd joining in, of course.

Dixon and Louise were standing outside Castle Amusements, the cheers of the crowd drowning out the bells and whistles of the fruit machines; not that he was tempted.

'Let's hope you're wrong, Sir,' she muttered.

He had updated the Policy Log earlier, DCS Potter clearly holding the same view. Her text had arrived just as he was leaving Express Park.

A brave call. Let's hope you're wrong!

Dixon hated the Policy Log. A record of the SIO's decision-making process; only he didn't have a process. It just happened. And all the log really did was provide evidence against the SIO when it all went horribly wrong.

'Shouldn't you be asleep or something?' asked Dixon, when Nigel Cole appeared next to him, leaning on the Winnie the Pooh crane machine.

'Wouldn't miss this.'

'He's probably wrong,' said Louise.

'Has he ever been before?'

'I'll get back to you on that one.'

Dixon slid his phone out of his pocket and sent a text to Jane's father, Rod.

How is he?

Rod's reply arrived just as the fireworks were really getting going, the flashes and bangs merging into a wall of sound and fury, all of it reflecting off the water.

Monty asleep on sofa. Got the footie on nice and loud :-)
Some fireworks in the next street but not too bad so far

73

He spotted Jane and Maggie down at the front, by the lifeguard hut; Dave and Mark at the top of the jetty. There were plenty of excited gasps and cries from the crowd, but that was the extent of it, as far as Dixon could tell. He was listening for the sort of screaming and crying he had heard the night before in Bridgwater, but none came.

'How long does it go on for?'

'About half an hour,' shouted Cole, the bangs still getting louder, the flashes brighter and higher in the sky.

Then Jane was pushing her way through the crowd at the front, an urgency to her movements, her eyes fixed on someone or something further along the sea wall. She stopped, jumped up, before carrying on elbowing her way through the throng of people, their eyes fixed on the fireworks lighting up the sky above their heads.

'This looks like it, Nige,' said Dixon.

He sprinted across the road, Cole and Louise following close behind him.

Cole was shouting into his radio. 'Sea wall; fifty yards north of the jetty.'

Uniformed officers came running along the road from all directions, converging on the spot.

'What is it?' asked Louise.

Dixon was standing on tiptoe, looking over the heads towards the front. 'Jane's seen something.'

'Excuse us. Can we get through, please?' The crowd parted to reveal Jane, dragging her half-sister Lucy by the coat, the girl wriggling and trying to free herself from Jane's vice-like grip.

Lucy looked at Dixon and gave a guilty smile.

'You little shit,' huffed Jane. 'You're supposed to be spending the day with your foster parents. It's Judy's birthday party tonight. I even put you on a bloody train this morning, for heaven's sake.'

◆ ◆ ◆

'Well, that's a relief,' said Louise, watching the two lads from Semper Fireworks wading out to the scaffolding platform. They had parked their van at the top of the jetty, the scene lit by their headlights. 'Nice to be wrong sometimes, isn't it, Sir?'

'We'll try that letting agent from Eastman and Webb who just happened to be off sick yesterday. He lives around here, doesn't he?'

'Andrew Platt. He's got a flat above a shop in Regent Street.'

'There's something to be said for sitting on a riverbank all day,' said Dixon a few minutes later, looking in the window of the fishing tackle shop at the rods lined up along the side wall. They had walked in silence along the promenade, only the seagulls to keep them company now the crowd from the fireworks had gone. Even the pavilion was closed, the fruit machines silenced.

A seaside town out of season.

The entrance to the flats was to the side of the shop, a tiled floor leading to the front door and an Entryphone with three buttons mounted on the wall.

'Flat 3,' said Louise, her finger on the top button.

'Yes.'

Dixon leaned in to the microphone. 'Police, Mr Platt.'

'What d'you want?'

'To speak to you.'

'I'm not really . . .' A loud sigh. 'I'm in the middle of something . . .'

'We are too, Sir.'

'All right.'

Louise grabbed the door when the lock buzzed and followed Dixon up the stairs, the sound of a door opening above them echoing down the stairwell.

Platt was leaning on the frame, arms folded, when they arrived on the landing.

'Not a fan of the carnival, I take it,' said Dixon.

'I had food poisoning.'

'Of course you did.'

'I bloody hate it, if you must know. You don't *have* to go, but Richard makes it clear you do, if you know what I mean?'

Dixon was following Platt along the corridor, Louise glancing into the kitchen as they went past. Not a fan of washing up either, by the looks of things.

'He had us doing a line dancing display one year. I mean, what the fuck was that about?'

The living room was cluttered, old vinyl records lying on the dining table in the window, piles of CDs on the mantelpiece, smoke rising from an ashtray on the end.

'You live alone?' asked Dixon.

'I do.'

You hardly needed to be Hercule Poirot to work that out.

'In a relationship?'

'Sort of. She's got kids, so it's a bit on and off at the moment. Look, I heard what happened and I wouldn't wish that on my worst enemy, but me and Richard never got on. Anyone will tell you that, so there's no point me trying to hide it, is there?'

'None at all, Sir.'

Empty foil trays were piled up on the side, a plastic fork balanced on the edge. 'The source of your food poisoning?' asked Dixon.

'That was today's.' Platt's face reddened. 'I wasn't ill. I just wasn't going to that bloody carnival. Again. It's the same every year, and every year we have to go and pretend we're loving it. Flying the flag for Eastman and Webb, networking and crap like that. If you really don't want to go you have to take a day's holiday, so I threw a sickie.'

It sounded a bit like the office Christmas party when Dixon had been training to be a solicitor. And he could sympathise with Platt's hatred of networking; nobody liked that. It was always a job dumped on the trainee – representing the firm at this breakfast or that lunch, when nobody else could be bothered to go.

'How long have you worked for Eastman and Webb?'

'Three long, gruelling, miserable years.'

'There have been various suggestions Richard was undervaluing properties.'

'I don't know anything about that.' Platt was standing by the mantelpiece, lighting a cigarette. 'I just deal with the property management and lettings.'

'You rented me my cottage opposite the Red Cow.'

'Really?' Platt frowned. 'When was that?'

'Last year.'

'Yeah, I remember. You're the one who had the break-in and it needed replastering after the shotgun went off. We had complaints from your neighbours after that.'

'I'm sure you did.' Dixon was resisting the temptation to run his finger along the top of the television. Louise had given up trying to clear a space on the coffee table too, and was resting her notebook on her knee. 'Everybody else seems to have heard these rumours,' said Dixon, getting the conversation back to where he wanted it. 'Hilary and Richard are both shareholders in Bob Eastman's property development company. They undervalue the land, Bob buys it at the reduced price, and—'

'Like I say, I just deal with the lettings. But, yeah, I heard that's what they're doing.'

'Are you comfortable with it?'

'Nobody has to accept their valuations, they could get another, *should* get another. And they don't have to sell either.'

'It sounds like fraud to me,' said Dixon. 'And I wonder what the National Association would make of it?'

'Not my problem.'

'Have you ever considered blowing the whistle on them?'

'What, and slit my own throat? I'd be out the door faster than you can say "knife" and I'd never work again in the local area, that's for sure. Not as a letting agent anyway.'

'You could always set up on your own, like Trevor Bishop did.'

'He was gone before I started working for Eastman and Webb. And he was getting all the probate work in the town as well – gave him a solid platform to start off with. I wouldn't stand a chance.'

'Do you know Trevor?'

'I've seen him around.' Platt stubbed what was left of his cigarette out in the ashtray. 'He's a pain in the arse, if you must know, always contacting my landlords and trying to get them to transfer their business to him. Every time a "To Let" board goes up, a leaflet of his goes through the letterbox. Then he gets the landlord's details off the Land Registry website and contacts them direct.'

'What have you done about it?'

'I've tried warning him off.'

'Do you do the same to him – contact his clients?'

'No.'

Platt sat down on the edge of the sofa and lit another cigarette, the flicker of the flame glinting in his narrowed eyes. 'Ask them about Markmoor Farm,' he said, picking up an open can of lager off the floor and taking a swig.

'Ask *who* about Markmoor Farm?'

'Hilary and Richard.' Platt smirked as he scrunched up empty can and threw it in the fireplace.

'What about it?'

'I'm not saying any more.' His smug look evaporated, replaced by a nervousness. 'And you didn't hear that from me. All right?'

'You were here yesterday, all day, on your own, I suppose?' asked Dixon, changing the subject before Platt clammed up completely.

'I was.'

'Doing what?'

'*Call of Duty: Black Ops*. I'm not far off turning pro. I was playing online with other people, so they could vouch for me, I suppose.'

'Professional computer gaming?' asked Louise.

'Some of the online tournaments have a prize fund of three million dollars.'

Chapter Ten

Queen's Drive had been fun when he was young and irresponsible. Off the roundabout, hammer down, it was possible to get up to well over a hundred on the long straight before the railway bridge. He winced at the memory; of driving a friend's Porsche, the accelerator floored a touch too early off the roundabout, the car snaking wildly. Thank God for traction control; if it hadn't been for that, they'd have ended up in the field.

Doesn't bear thinking about, thought Dixon, glancing down at the speedometer in front of him, his Land Rover creeping up to thirty miles an hour.

Carnival carts lined the other side of the road, parked nose to tail facing Burnham, their nearside wheels on the grass verge. A sorry sight with their lights off.

'They'll have been here since the early hours,' said Louise, dropping her phone back into her handbag. 'Ready for tomorrow night.'

'Which one is the Markmoor cart?'

'*Highway to Hell*,' replied Louise.

Dixon drove slowly along the line, past cars and vans parked on the nearside grass verge, people milling about, some carrying torches, others tools and pots of paint. Bright lights were coming from the backs of several of the carts, the back doors of *Curse of the Kraken* standing open, feet sticking out of the crawl space underneath the main platform.

Dixon pulled on to the grass verge behind a van. 'Problems?' he shouted across the road.

'Just the electrics to the galleon,' came the reply, the man reaching in with a screwdriver in his hand.

'Did you win?'

'Avalon did, with their *Disco Fever*. We got second.'

'Bad luck.'

The towing vehicle looked like it had once been a tractor – or a lorry perhaps, it was difficult to tell – that had been stripped back to the chassis and engine, new controls put in underneath a platform and hidden by one large turntable with four smaller ones mounted on it. Someone had gone to a lot of trouble, painting rolling waves all around the cart.

Two doors were standing open at the back of the power unit behind the main cart, a large generator on a trailer boxed in and hidden under more platforms and a rowing boat. The cables were visible now, a bunch of them as thick as Dixon's forearm, held together with plastic ties, disappearing through a hole in the base of the main section of the cart.

'We've still not found Trevor Bishop, I suppose?'

'No,' replied Louise.

'Where's the Markmoor cart?' he shouted, leaning out of the driver's window of his Land Rover. '*Highway to Hell.*'

'Round in Edithmead Lane,' came the reply. 'You can cut through just up there.'

Dixon left his Land Rover on the grass verge opposite *Curse of the Kraken*, and he and Louise walked along the main road, past *Those Magnificent Men in Their Flying Machines*, and through the bollards where the rat run that was Edithmead Lane had long since been blocked off, leaving a turning circle large enough for a carnival cart. A similar sight greeted them: cars and vans, people milling about with torches.

Highway to Hell was parked at the far end of the lane, a van parked opposite it, against the hedge.

Dixon tapped on the window.

'What?' The man sat up sharply. 'What's going on?'

'You from the Markmoor club?'

'Yes,' winding down the window.

'How long have you been here?'

'All afternoon. Why, is there a problem?'

'Have you got a set of keys?'

'No, I'm just here to keep an eye on it. Someone's got to, the police are bloody useless.'

Louise waved her warrant card at the man.

'Oh, sorry,' he mumbled.

Dixon walked over to the back of the cart, glancing up at the Harley-Davidson motorbikes on the platform. He stopped at the back, standing by two small doors apparent only from the 'Authorised Personnel Only' stickers and the keyhole.

'Who's got the key to these?' asked Dixon, turning to the man who had followed them, albeit tentatively.

'The committee members, probably. That's the electrics, so Trevor Bishop will have one as well, I expect.'

Dixon banged on the door with his fist. 'Trevor, it's the police. Open up.'

'You are shitting me,' groaned Louise under her breath, noticing a muddy footprint on the tow hitch.

'There's the Rural Crimes Unit,' said Dixon. 'Flag them down, Lou. They'll have a battering ram in their van.'

'You can't do that!'

Then a voice from inside. 'All right, all right. I'm coming out.'

Chapter Eleven

A key was inserted in the lock from the inside, then the door opened, an unshaven face blinking furiously in the light from Dixon's phone.

He snatched open the door, light streaming into the crawl space underneath the cart, illuminating the large electric motors that powered the turntables above. Dixon stepped forward, shining the light on his phone through the open doors into the back. Mounted on a wooden board just inside on the left was the electrical control panel, a big red switch at one end of the junction box, just like the one in the cupboard at his cottage. There were a few more fuses, mind you, and more cables. And a sleeping bag stretched out on the floor.

'Bloody hell, Trevor. I've been sitting in my sodding car all afternoon in the freezing cold and you were in there all the time?'

'Sorry, mate.' Bishop was sitting cross-legged on the sleeping bag, his eyes adjusting to the light. 'Where's the battering ram?' he asked.

'There isn't one. But there would have been, pretty damned quick, if you hadn't opened the door,' replied Dixon. 'You'd better come with us.'

'Am I under arrest?'

'If you come with us voluntarily, then no. If you refuse, then I'll have to arrest you.'

'For what?'

'On suspicion of the attempted murder of Richard Webb,' replied Dixon, watching for a reaction. None came; not a flicker of surprise. Nothing. Bishop knew what he was talking about, all right.

Louise stepped out on to the main road and flagged down a patrol car that had slowed on the approach to the carnival carts.

'Get him back to Express Park, Lou,' said Dixon, setting off towards his Land Rover. 'Book him in and stick him in an interview room. Better let everyone know we've found him, as well, so they can get back to what they should be doing.'

'These are for you,' said Jane. She was holding a packet of sandwiches in her outstretched hand when Dixon reached the top of the stairs at Express Park, the incident room all but deserted. 'I got them in the canteen before it shut. I bet you haven't eaten.'

Egg and cress. Nice.

'No KitKat?'

'You're diabetic.'

'D'you want the good news or the bad news?' asked Mark, his head popping up from behind a computer screen.

'The good.'

'There isn't any.'

Dixon ripped open the packet, knowing that the bad news was on its way whether he liked it or not.

'Bishop's got himself a solicitor,' continued Mark. 'They're down in interview room one now.'

'Anything else?' mumbled Dixon, through a mouthful of sandwich.

'Forensics have finished over at the Avalon Carnival Club depot. There's no CCTV, as you know, and the cabinet the squibs were kept in is clean – no viable fingerprints, I should say.'

'What about the witnesses?'

'We're working through them, but not really getting anywhere,' said Jane.

'We've got a few more photos over there.' Mark gestured to the back wall of the incident room; the glass partition papered with more grainy images. 'There's some additional video footage too. One with the sound of Webb's squib blowing.'

'We need a team focusing on the carnival club members – anyone with access to that cabinet.'

'We'll have more people in the morning, won't we,' said Jane.

'Have we got Eastman and Webb's file on Markmoor Farm, Lou?'

'Yes, it's here,' she replied, holding up a red box file.

'All right, let's go and see what Bishop has got to say for himself.' Dixon dropped the empty sandwich carton into the bin. 'The rest of you go home. Eight a.m. sharp.'

'You've got no grounds to hold my client, Insp—'

Dixon raised his hand, silencing Bishop's solicitor mid-sentence. 'I'm not holding your client. He is here of his own free will and has very kindly agreed to help us with our enquiries.'

Trevor Bishop was wearing grubby jeans and the same suit jacket he had been to work in the previous day, and spent the night in. His tie was hanging out of the hip pocket, dragging on the floor as he slumped in the plastic chair in interview room one. He hadn't brushed his dark hair, but it was short enough to get away with it.

He was sitting next to Dixon, rather than opposite him with a table between them. Dixon hated the new layout; designed by someone who had never conducted a police interview.

'You're not under arrest, Trevor. You've not been cautioned either. You're here purely as a witness. All right?'

Bishop shifted in his seat, sitting up with his hands on the metal frame either side of him.

'I'm assuming you know what happened to Richard Webb?'

'I was there.'

Dixon handed Bishop a bundle of CCTV stills from the Bridgwater carnival. 'Can you identify yourself in any of these photographs, Trevor?'

'I was in the pub, the Carnival Inn. I do the electrics on the cart and once it's underway my job is done. So, then I go to the pub.'

'You don't squib?'

'Used to. Not any more.'

'How long have you been involved in the carnival?'

'Since I was a kid. My stepfather got me into it. We used to make the squibs as well as do the electrics.'

'How did you make the squibs?'

Bishop turned to his solicitor. 'Do I have to answer these questions?'

'No, you don't. I've told you that.'

'How well did you know Richard Webb?' Changing tack.

Bishop sighed. Loudly. 'You know the answer to that, otherwise I wouldn't be here, would I?'

'I'd like to hear your side of the story,' said Dixon, turning in his seat to face Bishop.

'I worked my arse off for those people. I suppose they've told you about small brown envelopes changing hands, but they bloody well knew what I was doing and turned a blind eye, until it suited them to get rid of me.'

'And you set up on your own a few doors up the road?'

'It's a free country.'

'How would you describe your relationship with Richard Webb?'

Bishop folded his arms tightly across his chest. 'Last time I saw him I knocked him down, the—'

'I think you've said enough,' interrupted his solicitor.

'They'll hear about it soon enough, so there's no point trying to hide it.'

'When was this?' asked Dixon.

'The first Friday in October, the fourth or fifth, something like that. It was after the annual dinner.'

'And what was the fight about?'

'It wasn't a fight.' Bishop hesitated.

'Markmoor Farm and the amazing moving electricity pylons?' continued Dixon. 'I've looked at the Eastman and Webb file. There's correspondence from you on there.'

'It belonged to my mother and stepfather. Webb was trying to get them to sell it at an undervalue and I was trying to see to it they got a fair price. That's all.'

'And did they?'

'No.' Bishop stood up. 'Can I go?'

'Why did you punch Richard Webb?'

'I'd like to leave now, please.'

'I would strongly advise you to stay and answer our questions, Trevor,' said Dixon, without looking up. 'You saw what happened to Richard Webb and, at this point, I see you more as the next victim than anything else.'

'I'll take my chances.'

'Will you be at the Burnham carnival tomorrow night?'

'I've got to check the electrics on the cart before the procession starts. I need to do that by six in case there's anything that needs fixing.'

'Where will you be for the rest of the day?'

'The show home at Brent Knoll.'

'Where were you on Wednesday, Thursday and Friday?'

'In the office all day, working on the cart in the evenings, then at my girlfriend's flat. Liv will confirm that.'

'And Saturday?'

'The show home in the morning, then we took the cart over to Bridgwater in the afternoon.'

'You've no evidence my client has done anything wrong, Inspector, except for his admission of a historic assault for which you have no complainant and which we would argue was self defence in any event,' said the solicitor. 'Can someone please show us out? Now.'

Dixon stifled a sigh, looked at Louise and nodded.

Chapter Twelve

Dixon arrived home just before midnight, a diversion via Worle to pick up Monty from Jane's parents thrown in for good measure. It turned out it was later than he had thought, and he'd got them all out of bed, but Monty didn't mind, at least.

'I got you a curry out,' said Jane, when he pushed open the back door.

'Thanks.'

Jane slammed the microwave shut and jabbed the button.

'Where's Lucy?'

'In bed. She wanted to stay down for the carnival tomorrow night, but I told her no way. I'm dropping her at the railway station in the morning – *again* – and she's bloody well going back to Manchester this time. I told her they'll probably call it off anyway.'

'They won't. There's no reason to, on the face of it.'

'For God's sake don't tell her that. Who'll make the decision?'

'Charlesworth. There's a press conference at four, so he'll have to have made up his mind one way or the other by then.'

'How did you get on with Trevor Bishop?'

'He seemed a bit reluctant to answer questions, and his solicitor was there, which didn't help. In the end we had to let him go.'

'Let him go?'

'There was no reason to keep him. There's no evidence he had anything to do with Webb's exploding squib, although he did used to make them for the Markmoor club when he was younger, so he'd have the knowledge needed, I suppose.' Dixon was filling Monty's water bowl with fresh water. 'Motive and opportunity too.'

'But you still don't think it was him?'

'Where the bloody hell did this come from?' growled Dixon, staring at a jar of no-added-sugar mango chutney.

'You're diabetic and you're going to be a father. You have to look after yourself.'

'Yeah, but mango chutney.' Dixon's protest was punctuated by the ping of the microwave. 'Is nothing sacred?'

'How many are we getting from Portishead?' asked Jane, trying a change of subject.

'Another sixteen.'

'That's—'

'Not enough, I know.'

'Is the Burnham carnival really going be cancelled?' Lucy was standing in the doorway, yawning.

'Probably.'

'Yes, it is,' said Jane. 'And you're going back to Manchester.'

Lucy's eyes narrowed as she glanced at the jar of mango chutney in Dixon's hand. 'Your fiancée hid the proper stuff at the back of the cupboard,' she said with a mischievous grin, before running back upstairs.

'You little . . .'

◆ ◆ ◆

Dixon woke early to the sound of his phone buzzing on his bedside table, the alarm rather than a phone call, mercifully. Jane was leaning on her elbow, watching him.

'I don't know how you do it, I really don't,' she said. 'How you keep all this information coming at you in any sort of order in your head.'

'I remember what's important and forget the rest,' said Dixon, yawning as he tapped at the snooze button on his phone. 'The knack is knowing the difference. Trouble is, the important bit usually turns out to be something I've chosen not to remember.'

'Don't tell anyone else that, for God's sake.'

'I won't.'

'Which bits are you remembering this time?'

'Markmoor Farm. The whole thing stinks. We need to be having a word with Trevor Bishop's mother and stepfather. I'll ring Maggie and get her to put some people on it. The other thing that keeps going round and round is an off the cuff remark from one of the blokes doing the fireworks.'

'What did he say?'

'He said it seemed "a bit of a random way to try and kill someone"; and it is. There's no guarantee your victim is actually going to die. And Webb hasn't.'

'So far,' muttered Jane, sliding out from under the duvet and wrapping herself in a towel.

'It makes me wonder whether it was an attempted murder at all; whether the intent was to kill or just maim.'

'And that's significant because?'

'No idea.' Dixon sat up. 'We'd better get going.'

'I'm having a quick shower,' said Jane, allowing her towel to drop to the floor. 'If you'd like to join me?'

'Turn left just up there,' said Louise, as they drove out along Mark Causeway, open fields either side of them. 'The pylons cross this road about here and go off across that field there.' She was point-ing out of the passenger window when Dixon made the turn. 'Markmoor Farm Holidays are just up here – *were* just up here.'

Dixon stopped by a new concrete bridge that crossed the rhyne on the nearside of the lane, a wide gravel track leading off across the field to a T-junction nearer the middle. Large concrete plinths were surrounded by wire fence panels on the far side of the field, one in each corner, men milling about in white hard hats and hi-vis jackets.

'Looks like the foundations are going in,' said Louise. 'Massive, aren't they?'

'About four hundred yards from those houses.' Dixon pointed over his shoulder at the first bungalow along the Causeway, just behind them.

'My mum had a friend who lived under a pylon near Market Harborough. Lymphoma, aged fifty-two.'

Dixon knew better than to challenge the science behind Louise's anecdote, not that there was any.

'And her husband died of leukaemia eighteen months later,' she continued. 'Go figure.'

'Get on to Energen Land, find out when it was decided to move these pylons further west and who made the decision.'

The line of the pylons angled away across the next field, judging by the positioning of the metal fence panels surrounding the next set of foundations. Further along the lane, a line of red, white and blue banners on the grass verge was fluttering in the wind.

Eastman Homes.

One of the old holiday lodges had survived the bulldozers and was being used by the workmen, judging by the line of them sitting outside with their feet up on the railings, coffee and a smoke being taken by all. A mobile office unit had been dumped on the grass beyond it, the area outside the front door a muddy mess, despite the plastic mats.

More metal fence panels surrounded the entire site, even the field beyond, the hedge between having been ripped out and burnt.

Dixon turned into the field, stopping in front of a man who had come striding towards his Land Rover, his right hand raised.

'I'm sorry, we're not open yet. The show home should be ready by the spring, maybe the end of March next year.'

'Too close to the pylons for me, thanks,' replied Dixon, showing the man his warrant card.

'What d'you want?'

'A look around,' replied Dixon, accelerating away from the man and parking behind Bob Eastman's Jaguar, the tyres caked in mud. 'It said there was a fishing lake on the internet?' he asked, pretending not to notice the man gesticulating wildly at the workmen with their feet up and pointing at the cabin.

'It's in the next field. It's just a small pond, really. We're leaving that for amenity value. There'll be a play area too. It'll make a nice feature when it's landscaped.'

One of the workmen had trudged through the mud and was banging on the door of the cabin, his cigarette still hanging out of the corner of his mouth.

'Incoming,' whispered Louise, watching Bob Eastman being told of their arrival on site.

Several sets of foundations had been laid out along the edge of the base layer of a road, only the kerbstones marking the line of it. Two small cement silos at the far end gave a sense of scale. Otherwise, the site had been marked out with poles, stuck in the ground, and string.

The hedge was still intact beyond the metal fence on the far side of the field, cows grazing around a set of pylon foundations in the next field over.

'Shall we rattle his cage?' asked Dixon, watching Eastman sliding on a pair of wellington boots.

'What is it now?' he demanded, marching through the mud towards them.

'Where was the farmhouse, Mr Eastman?' asked Dixon. 'I was given to understand the owners lived on site.'

'It was on the other side of the lane. We demolished it. We can get eight houses over there, twenty-nine this side. Look, what's this all about?'

'Someone has tried to kill a shareholder of yours, Sir.'

'That's got nothing to do with this, surely?'

'Then there's the matter of obtaining a pecuniary advantage by deception. I wanted to see the site for myself.'

'What deception?'

'The matter is under investigation, Sir, that's all I can say at this time; the circumstances in which the purchase price of this site was arrived at. I'll be speaking to the previous owners about it later on today, amongst other things.'

The blood drained from Eastman's face. 'It was all perfectly above board. The plans were real and showed the line of the pylons as first envisaged.'

'Then you've nothing to fear from the investigation, Sir.'

Eastman was dialling a number on his phone, his eyes darting from Dixon to his screen and then back again. Then he turned away. 'I need to speak to Peter Walmsley. Now, please.'

'His solicitor,' mouthed Dixon to Louise.

'Well, get him out of the bloody meeting!' Eastman rang off.

'You can never get hold of your solicitor when you need to,' said Dixon. He walked along the base of the road, dodging the puddles, and into the adjacent field, where the foundations of the holiday lodges were still visible, surrounding the pond in the middle. Several fishing platforms were still there in amongst the reeds, which were busily dying back.

'We netted the fish and sold them to a carp syndicate. Got a good price for them,' said Eastman, who had followed them.

'Did you ever have any dealings with the previous owners personally?' asked Dixon.

'No, Richard dealt with them. I never met them.'

'And when was the line of the pylons changed?'

'Much later. After we bought the site, actually. The locals got together and formed a pressure group, the local MP pitched in, and it did the trick. We gave them some money anonymously to help with printing costs: "No moor pylons" – moor as in moorland – that sort of thing. Then the Planning Inspectorate moved everything four hundred yards that way.' Eastman was waving his hand at the hedge. 'It was a godsend for us. We'd still have made money developing the plot on the other side of the lane, just not as much. That made it an easy decision for us; guaranteed a small site, with the possibility of a much bigger one. Much of property developing is really gambling, Inspector.'

'And the previous owners knew that?'

'I think so, yes. I really don't think Richard misled them in any way. "This is the line of the pylons, there's a chance it might move, a chance it might not, now I've got a client who will give you eight hundred thousand pounds for the site." What would you do?'

Chapter Thirteen

'His name's Lionel Harper,' said Louise. 'He's been living here since he and his ex-wife sold Markmoor Farm.'

'Where's his ex-wife?'

'Divorced him and remarried.'

Someone had gone to a lot of effort with the tree planting, the drive lined with conifers, freshly turned earth at the base of each. Leylandii had been planted all along the boundary of the park for additional privacy and were just getting going as well. Trinity Rise, according to the sign – a Brendon Park Homes development.

'What number is it?' asked Dixon, holding the Land Rover on the clutch.

'Plot 36b,' replied Louise. 'Just look for the Scientific Services van.'

Lines of park homes either side of the drive, all a different design, the smell of newly laid tarmac wafting in through the air vents.

'Nice the way they don't have two the same next to each other, isn't it?' She was staring out of the passenger window at the immaculately maintained gardens, freshly laid turf on the lawns. 'You can see the join above the bay windows,' she said, pointing. 'They must arrive in two halves and then get bolted together, I suppose.'

Some of the park homes had 'For Sale' signs in the windows; others small cars parked in the drive. Three steps up to the front door, a decking terrace with white painted balustrade. Every window was a bay to offer more space, except the small one with the frosted glass.

'It'll look nice when the trees have grown up a bit,' said Louise. 'There's the Scientific van, up ahead, just round to the right.'

Grey roof tiles, bay windows – the join visible on the gable end – and a black front door. An old Ford Mondeo, more rust than car, was parked in the drive, all of the doors open, a Scientific Services officer in a white hazmat suit leaning in the passenger side.

'The Sandringham. Looks lovely, but I suppose it should at a hundred and eighty-six thousand.' Louise dropped her phone into her handbag.

'You've been on Rightmove again, haven't you?'

'I'd cheerfully retire to one of these.'

'I bet they don't allow dogs,' said Dixon, parking behind the Scientific van.

'Yeah, they do. I saw a Yorkie sitting in the window of one back there.' Louise gave a nervous laugh. 'Anyway, Monty will be long gone by the time your turn comes.'

'Thank you, Constable.'

'I'll shut up.'

Grey crushed slate crunched under their feet as they walked up the path to the front steps. The decking turned out to be plastic, as did the balustrade; the plants in the borders were real though.

'Go in,' said the Scientific Services officer, through the open driver's door of the Mondeo. 'No need to suit up.'

The front door opened into a corridor; left to the living space, right to the bedrooms, kitchen and bathroom opposite.

'Two bedrooms, triple aspect living room . . .' Louise stopped mid-sentence when Dixon sighed. 'I'm just reading the . . .' She thought better of it, replacing the brochure on the hall table.

Several pairs of boots were piled up on the floor inside the front door, each pair in an evidence bag; clothes strewn all over the floor in the bedroom next to be bagged up, the door standing open at the far end of the corridor. A grubby looking duvet was half on the floor, revealing an even grubbier looking sheet underneath.

Dixon opted for the living space.

'Rents it furnished,' said the Scientific Services officer in the living room. 'The site manager came over when we arrived. Five hundred a month. It's only until they sell it, then he'll move to another vacant one, until they sell that one. He's moved three times already. He knows the owner, apparently, and he's doing him a favour.'

A sofa and armchair, dining table and chairs in the far corner.

'There's not a lot here. Not much personal stuff. There was an empty petrol can in the back of the Mondeo, but that's about it.'

'Petrol or kerosene?'

'Smells like petrol.' The officer sniffed, pinching the bridge of his nose through his face mask. 'Sticks in the nostrils, but it could be worse, I suppose. We haven't checked the loft yet, or the crawl space underneath. There's an access hatch round the back.'

That explained the steps up and the hollow sound when you walked.

The pile of papers on the dining table was not terribly enlightening: bank statements, letters from Vodafone and TV Licensing. The photograph on the Bridgwater Carnival Club steward's pass looked familiar though.

'They nicked him for assault PC. He took a swing at Nigel Cole when they went to pick him up. I've booked you the interview room with the table,' said Jane, when Dixon appeared at the top of the stairs. 'I thought you'd like it in between you. He's a big lad. Angry too.'

'Solicitor?'

'Doesn't want one. Says he hasn't done anything wrong, so why the bloody hell should he? And he was wearing a hoodie on the night, so he's not the steward on the CCTV.'

'C'mon then, Lou, let's get it over with.'

A quick check on the monitor in the adjacent room, Harper picking at the skin at the base of his fingernails, the camera looking down on his bald head from the top corner of the interview room. The hoodie had hidden that on the CCTV footage.

'About bloody time,' he said, when Dixon opened the interview room door.

'Lionel Harper, you've been arrested on suspicion of assaulting a police constable in the execution of his duty.' Dixon dropped his papers on the table in front of him and waited while Louise sat down. 'It is my duty now to arrest you on suspicion of the attempted murder of Richard Webb. You do not have to say anything, but it may—'

'Attempted murder? I haven't tried to kill anyone!' Harper stood up sharply.

'Sit down!'

Dixon waited.

Harper sighed, then did as he was told.

'. . . harm your defence if you do not mention when questioned something you later rely on in court. Anything you do say may be given in evidence. Do you understand?'

'Yes.'

'Taking that into account, do you now wish to consult a solicitor?'

'No.'

Dixon sat down opposite Harper. 'This interview is being audio and visually recorded on to a secure digital hard drive. Identify yourself for the recording, please.'

'Lionel St John Harper.'

Tall and heavy, but he carried it well; early seventies, probably. Dixon would have put him in the second row in a scrum back in the day; probably not fast enough for the back row. A missing front tooth, food down the front of a sweatshirt that had absorbed too much sweat; pockmarks and a touch of rosacea too, although that might have been the drink. Two laundry baskets full of empty bottles in the bath at his rented park home had spoken volumes.

Hardly the genial host of a holiday park, thought Dixon. Maybe Eastman had done everyone a favour knocking it down and putting houses on it?

Harper was looking up at the camera, breathing heavily through his nose, while Dixon and Louise identified themselves for the recording.

'Tell us about Markmoor Farm Holidays,' said Dixon, after a suitable pause.

'It was my life. A campsite, eighteen lodges, carp fishing; I'd built it up from nothing. There was a clubhouse with a bar and karaoke. We did all right. Till the pylons came along.'

'What about your divorce?'

'The bitch was playing away; met someone else over Wells way, tried to make out it was my fault.' Harper was sucking his teeth. 'Wanted half of everything, she did. And she'd done bugger all to help build it up.'

Dixon waited.

'We agreed a split. She kept the farmhouse and the land east of the lane. I got the bulk of the site, the clubhouse, lodges and fishing lake. I had to give her half the profits as well, until she remarried, even though she never showed her face.'

'Then what happened?'

'You know what happened. The fucking pylons *happened*. They'd been on the cards for a while, ever since Hinkley Point C got approval and the tight bastards said it was too expensive to run the cables under the sea up to Avonmouth. We all thought they'd follow the line of existing power lines. I mean, why shit on someone else's doorstep? Why not just use the existing line, even if you have to switch out the pylons themselves? It didn't make any sense.'

'Aren't they going to be smaller than the traditional steel lattice things?'

'Yes, but that just means the cables are going to be lower. Nearer us on the ground. Then the next thing I know I've got Richard Webb on my doorstep with a set of plans telling me they're going to be in the next bloody field, right behind my campsite. You'd have heard the buzzing in your tent. What d'you think that would've done to my business?'

'This was before the proposed line of the pylons was put out for consultation?'

'Yes. I still don't know where he got the plans from, but it was a couple of months before the official announcement was due. No one in the village knew about it.'

'And what did Webb say?'

'That he had a client who'd buy the site and take the risk.'

'What risk?'

'That the pylons wouldn't be moved. The locals were already gearing up for a campaign, but these things don't always succeed, do they? At least, that's what Webb said.'

'What was his client offering?'

'Eight hundred thousand. He said they might break even developing the site on the other side of the lane – *her bit* – where the house was, but it would only be really worth their while if the pylons were moved and they could develop the other side as well. They were prepared to take the risk, though, so I got the same bloke who valued it for the divorce out again to tell me what he thought of their offer. He said if the pylons went in according to that plan then I could forget any hope value for the land to the west of the lane, and that was the bulk of it.'

'Who was that?'

'Gerard Pollock. He's a chartered surveyor at Harrison Samuels in Burnham.'

'Are you sure the plan was genuine?'

'Yes. And the line was the same when the official announcement was made a couple of months later, although I'd already sold out by then.'

'What did your ex-wife say about it?'

'She was OK with it. The problem was her bloody son, Trevor. I never got on with him. I'm pleased to say he stopped being my stepson when I divorced his mother. Every cloud, and all that.'

'And he wasn't OK with the sale?'

'He said it wasn't enough money – said we'd get more if we hung on, that the plot would have real value to it if the pylons were moved. Pollock had said one point six million when we divorced, but that included hope value based on the *hope* we'd get planning permission to develop the site. And it was before there was any mention of pylons at all, let alone in the next field.' Harper was sucking his left middle finger, blood oozing from the torn skin around the base of the nail. 'Made a right bloody nuisance of himself, Trevor did, but anyway, we sold it. Then I find out Webb's stitched me up like a kipper. He even took his bloody one point five per cent commission on the deal as well. Trevor went for me, said I'd ripped off his mother and what have you. Accused me of being in on it with Webb. I mean, why the hell would I do that? It was my money as well. Bang out of order, he was.'

'Go on.'

'Anyway, Webb must've known those pylons were going to be moved. Must've done. Turns out he was batting for the other team, as they say, with one of the blokes at Energen Land.' Harper sneered. 'Yes, I found out about that, but only much later. And he's a shareholder in Eastman Homes. His bloody business partner is Hilary Eastman, for God's sake. The penny never dropped at the time.'

'And what did you do about it?'

'What could I do?'

'Kill him, for example.'

'Fuck no!' Harper gave an exaggerated shake of the head. 'I was there, saw it happen, and I'd never wish that on my worst enemy.'

'Was he your worst enemy?'

'What d'you think?'

'What about the valuer, Gerard Pollock?' asked Dixon, watching for any reaction. 'Did you ever suspect he was in on it?'

'I doubt it. Why would he be?' Quizzical.

'Money.'

'He's got more than enough of his own, from what I can gather. Turned up in a Porsche.'

'Let's move on. Look at these images of Bridgwater Carnival, if you will, and identify yourself?'

'That's me there,' he said. 'I was stewarding once the procession was underway.'

'How long have you been involved in the carnival?'

'All my life, pretty much. I started out in Markmoor Carnival Club as a lad, got involved in the committee, then got elected to the main committee. I was chairman for a while, now I'm the pro-cession marshal. It's my job to see to it that the carts get away on time and in the right order; manage the traffic. I organise the road closure applications each year, that sort of thing.'

'Were you involved in the squibbing?'

'Not any more. I used to make the squibs for the Markmoor club, back when it was a DIY job. Then they stopped that for health and safety reasons and I lost interest. You have to buy the bloody things now.' Harper chuckled at a memory, his eyes glazing over fleetingly. 'Burnt down an old shed on my farm once, yonks ago, before we had the campsite. Bloody thing went off in my face,' he said, pointing to a scar on his chin. 'It was fun back then.'

'Where were you on Friday night, the night before the Bridgwater carnival?'

'We had a main carnival committee meeting. We always have one the night before the season kicks off, just to run over any last things.'

'And the night before that?'

Harper shrugged. 'At home on my own.'

'Do you have keys to the carnival club premises?'

'Which one?'

'All of them.'

'Some we do, some we don't. Some are on a keypad anyway.'

'How long were you Trevor's stepfather?'

'I married his mother when he was seven. His real father's dead. He's got a new stepfather now, mind you.' Harper chuckled. 'She's on her third husband.'

'And you didn't get on with Trevor?'

'Not really. It was all right to begin with, but he always took her side and then he went through a difficult patch in his late teens: stealing, drugs. Wrote off my car once, the little shit. Left it upside down in a rhyne on the bend by the White Horse. His bloody mother even made me say I was driving, would you believe it?'

'Was there ever any violence?'

'No.' Indignant, softening with a sigh. 'Once. He took a swing at me. One punch and he was flat on his back. That was it.'

'What was that about?'

'Drugs. He had some pot plants in an outbuilding.'

'When you were a member of the Markmoor Carnival Club, what was your job on the cart?'

'Trevor and me did the electrics. He was doing an apprentice-ship before he switched to estate agency. Said he'd never make any money as a sparky. And he's doing all right, by all accounts. Got a swanky new Tesla, one of those electric things.'

Dixon stared at Harper across the table, putting on his best pained expression. 'That's pretty much a full house, Mr Harper,' he said. 'Are you sure you don't want a solicitor?'

'What d'you mean?'

'You've got motive, means and opportunity for the attempted murder of Richard Webb.'

'No I haven't.'

'And now you're going to tell me you didn't do it, I suppose?'

'Yes, I bloody well am.'

'Not to mention an admission to one count of perverting the course of justice.'

'Eh?'

'You lied about who was driving your car when Trevor left it in the rhyne.' Dixon's eyes narrowed, trying to hide his disappoint-ment. 'Then there's the assault PC. That was our Rural Crimes Unit you took a swing at.'

'I'm sorry about that. I was just about at the end of my string, what with everything that's been going on this season.'

'He's a barrel of laughs, isn't he?' said Louise, as they trudged up the stairs. 'Next time I need cheering up I'll check the old TripAdvisor reviews for Markmoor Farm Holidays.'

'Release him under investigation.'

'What about the perverting the course of justice charge?' she asked, still chuckling at her own joke.

'I'm more concerned about who tried to kill Richard Webb. That's assuming someone did try to kill him.' Dixon punched the code into the keypad and then wrenched open the security door at the top of the stairs. 'We've got nothing to hold him on anyway. We do need to have a word with his ex-wife. And we need to be clear about the main carnival committee and their access to the club premises.'

'I can deal with that easily enough.'

'Thanks.'

'You don't think he did it?'

'Nothing this complicated is ever this easy to unravel.' Dixon dropped his papers on the corner of Jane's workstation in the incident room. 'Anything from forensics?'

'Nothing at his park home so far,' she replied. 'His car's gone to the lab. Clothes too.'

'What about the CCTV?'

'He's outside the Town Hotel when Webb's squib explodes, maybe four hundred yards away; no phone in his hand, not that he could have filmed it from there anyway.'

'Where have we got to with bank statements?'

'Later on today, they said,' replied Jane.

'What was the name of the bloke who organised the campaign against the pylons?'

'Knott,' replied Louise.

'Simon Knott-in-my-backyard.'

'Shut up, Mark.'

'Yes, Sir.'

'Would you want it in your backyard?'

'Not really.' Mark kept his head down, hiding behind his computer screen.

'Let's pay Mr Knott a visit, Lou,' said Dixon.

Chapter Fourteen

Dixon could see what had happened – the bungalow on the corner, with the overly large garden, vehicular access off the lane at the side presenting no highway issues. Planning permission would've been waved through on the nod, probably.

Three years old, possibly more; red brick with sandstone cornicing on the bay window at the front, the double garage sideways on to the house. Even the fence looked new. Someone had made an effort with the front garden too, all of the plants arranged in neat rows.

Dixon parked across the gravel drive.

'What's that on the corner of the garage?'

'A charging point,' replied Louise. 'He must have an electric car. Never seen so many solar panels too.'

'What are you supposed to do if you've only got on-street parking?'

'You'll still be able to get diesel for a while, so you'll be fine in this old heap. And think of the carbon footprint involved in buying a new car.'

The front door opened before Dixon got out of his Land Rover, footsteps on the gravel alerting him to the approaching house-holder, no doubt about to complain about him blocking his drive.

'You can't park there.' From the hand gesture, Dixon was clearly expected to go elsewhere; forth and multiply, possibly.

'Simon Knott?' he asked, sliding out of the driver's seat.

'Yes.' Tall, looked like he'd been wearing ski goggles recently, from the tan lines around his eyes. Either that or he'd been on a sun bed. The cable sweater wasn't a surprise. Dixon checked for sandals: Crocs. Close, but no cigar.

Knott was blocking the five bar gate. 'How can I help?' he asked, not taking his eyes off their warrant cards.

'We're investigating the attempted murder of a local estate agent—'

'Not that poor bloke at the carnival? It said on the news he was an agent.'

'Yes, Sir.'

'But that was an accident, surely?'

'Sadly not, and we wanted to talk to you about the pylons.'

'God, it's not to do with that, is it? Bloody hell. You'd better come in,' Knott said, gesturing to the front door. 'I was standing for the county council at the time, so it was a good opportunity to get myself known, being relatively new to the area.'

'How long have you been here?'

'Four years. We moved down from Surrey.'

A framed photograph on the wall next to a mirror in the hall; Knott and a woman waving a wedding ring at the camera and beaming, on a beach somewhere.

'That's my wife. She works for EDF, which was a bit embar-rassing when it came to the pylons, but heigh-ho.' Knott gave a sheepish laugh at the memory.

'Did you get elected?'

'I did.'

Conservative then, although the blue rosette in amongst the car keys on the sideboard had already given the game away.

'Kitchen or living room?' asked Knott.

'You choose,' replied Dixon.

'Kitchen then, and I'll make us all a cup of tea.'

Open fields at the back of the house, the view not yet blocked by the conifers at the end of the garden.

'I suppose you know, but Mark's a linear village,' said Knott, filling the kettle. 'We're all spread out along the causeway, over a mile, only now we've got this large development at one end. Rather throws it out of kilter.'

'Did the pylons come as a surprise?'

'Not really. To some, maybe, but I'd been tipped the wink by council colleagues in the know. I think the locals were hoping they'd run the cables under the sea, but it all came down to money in the end. These things always do. Sugar?'

'No, thanks.'

'Me neither,' said Louise.

'The proposed line of them was a shock, mind you. We'd all expected them to follow the existing line, well to the west of us, but when the plans were published these bloody great "T" pylons suddenly appeared right on the edge of the village. That's when our campaign started, to get them moved; public meetings in the village hall, posters, letter writing. Every time we got wind of a visit from surveyors or planners, we organised a welcoming committee. I hate to say it, but it was good fun, actually, or at least it would've been if the stakes hadn't been so high.'

'Who for?'

Knott dropped a tea bag into each mug. 'Everyone. Look, I know the science has never been proven, or if it has it's been suppressed, but these things are a bloody health hazard. There's so much anecdotal evidence there comes a point, surely, when you have to say it must be right?'

'I wouldn't want to live near one,' said Louise firmly.

'Me neither.' Knott handed them each a mug. 'Milk's in the jug,' he said, placing it in between them. 'We'd not long moved in here – it'll be three years next Easter – and God alone knows what would've happened if we'd had to sell.'

'Was there a lot of bad feeling?' asked Dixon, stirring his tea.

'From some quarters, certainly,' replied Knott. 'It got a bit heated a couple of times, but most people understood that Energen were only doing their job. They sent a Polish chap to a couple of our meetings and he had a pretty rough time of it. Shouting, y'know. Nobody could understand why the pylons had to come so close to the village in the first place.'

'What about Markmoor Farm Holidays?'

'They'd already sold up and gone. I think someone must have told them what was coming, so they sold to the developer and got out. Eastman Homes. That was the start of another campaign, that was, when their planning application went in.'

Dixon spotted Knott's embarrassment and waited, letting it hang.

'I know how it looks,' said Knott, blushing. 'I'm sitting here in a newish house and I'm objecting to a new development in my backyard. *Knott-in-my-backyard*, some trolls called me on Twitter. Don't you just hate social bloody media? Pardon my language.'

Dixon had never really got the hang of social media, not that he'd tried. It was a useful source of evidence sometimes, though. 'What were your grounds of objection?'

'Altering the nature and balance of an established linear village, traffic obviously, the local school's too small. Loss of amenity, out of keeping with the rural character, too dense a development. I tried to keep people focused on planning reasons for their objections and we had hundreds of letters in the end. Didn't do any bloody good, though, did it, as you can see.' Knott took a swig of tea. 'I still say there was something funny going on. Money changing hands.'

'What makes you say that?'

'We were told we stood no chance whatsoever of getting the pylons moved, and we did it. Then we were told that with enough local objections we'd get the housing development reduced in size, and we failed dismally. It went through without any changes – thirty-seven houses.' Knott looked at Dixon for reassurance, but got none. 'There was definitely something fishy going on.'

'And you've got no evidence of this, I suppose.'

'None whatsoever. Look, it's not an allegation I'd make publicly, and I certainly don't want it going any further.' Knott realised he had overstepped the mark. 'Let's call it "off the record", shall we?'

'There's no such thing as "off the record" in an attempted murder investigation, I'm afraid, Sir.'

'I suppose not.'

'So, let me make sure I understand this correctly.' Dixon was watching Louise scribbling in her notebook. 'You take money from Eastman Homes to help with the campaign against the pylons, and then, when that's successful, you object to their application to build houses on the site.'

'It wasn't quite as simple as that.' Knott was starting to get defensive. 'Richard Webb offered us the money to help with the pylon campaign. I can't remember the exact amount, but it wasn't huge. Just enough for printing costs and suchlike. None of us had any idea he was anything to do with Eastman Homes. We only found that out later.'

'When?'

'During the campaign against the housing development. There was a lot of anger about it. We felt cheated, to be honest.'

'Cheated by Richard Webb?'

'You're going to tell me it was him at the squibbing, aren't you?'

'Yes, Sir.'

Knott took a deep breath, exhaling slowly.

'So, where d'you think the money was changing hands?' asked Dixon.

'I accept entirely people have got to have places to live and the council has government targets for the number of houses they have to build, so I can accept the decision on the housing development. Thirty-seven is a bit tight, and we might have got it reduced, but I was at the planning meeting – not on the committee, you understand – and I don't think there was anything untoward going on there. What unlocked the site, though, was the pylons moving in the first place. If that hadn't happened, it would have been eight at most on the other side of the lane. The campsite and lodges would never have been redeveloped.'

'What role did Trevor Bishop play in all of this?'

'Who's he?'

'The son of the former owners of Markmoor Farm Holidays and a local estate agent. Bishop Property.'

'None as far as I remember, in that case. A couple of the locals put their houses on the market around that time, hoping to get out before it was too late, and a few Bishop Property 'For Sale' boards went up, but I don't think he was involved in the planning side of things.'

◆ ◆ ◆

'We've got a bit of digging to do,' said Dixon, doing a three-point turn in the lane.

'What d'you think went on?' asked Louise.

'If I had to guess, I'd say Richard Webb and Ian Szopinski conspired to place the pylons so close to Markmoor Farm Holidays that the Harpers had no choice but to sell for whatever they were offered. Then, when Eastman Homes had got their grubby hands on the site, Ian saw to it that the pylons were moved, and hey presto, the rest is easy. They even funded the local pressure group, so it gave them a smokescreen for moving the bloody things.'

'Gives any number of people a motive for trying to kill Webb, I'd have thought.'

'We need to speak to Ian Szopinski sharpish.'

'He's driving down tonight, leaving Birmingham at nine, he said.'

'And we need another chat with Trevor Bishop too.'

Chapter Fifteen

Dixon sat down at a workstation and spun round on the chair to face the whiteboards.

'No sign of Trevor Bishop, I suppose?'

'His office is open,' replied Jane. 'But they've not seen him yet today. He's not at the Brent Knoll show home, either. They tried ringing him for us and got no reply. I've left messages for him everywhere I can think of. Charlesworth was looking for you as well. The press conference is in half an hour and he wanted to know what CCTV stills we'd got.'

'None that are any good,' said Maggie, 'but I didn't tell him that.'

'We'll go with those four you picked out,' said Dixon. He tipped his head. None were much good, Maggie was right. No logos were visible, or any other distinguishing marks for that matter, but there was a remote chance someone might recognise the build of the individuals highlighted. Still, it was something, and would keep Charlesworth happy; whether it kept the press happy was his problem.

'Anything from the social media team?'

'A couple of videos have popped up, but none of the squib actually exploding,' replied Dave. 'Or, if they have, the companies took them down pretty quick. We've got a request in, just in case. Apart from that, it's just the usual selfies and stuff.'

'The computers have all gone to High Tech as well,' said Jane. She was standing beside him, nudging his shoulder. 'We need to have a word. Outside,' gesturing with her thumb now.

Dixon followed her along the landing and out of the back door on to the top floor of the staff car park; all but deserted, given that almost the entire major investigation team were out taking statements.

Jane took Dixon by the arm and dragged him into the gap between his Land Rover and the wall. 'Charlesworth had two blokes with him,' she said, her eyes darting from side to side. 'No one's seen them before, so they must be down from Portishead.'

'Is that it?'

'Two blokes from HQ, arguing with the ACC on the landing – animated it was too. That's enough, surely?' She placed her hands on her hips. 'Charlesworth was waving his arms, then he stomped off. All we heard was "after the press conference", then the two blokes disappeared into the Professional Standards Department down the far end. They didn't look too happy about it.'

Dixon frowned. 'And you think it's got something to do with me?'

'Your name was mentioned. Dave was on the stairs and heard it.'

'It'll be something and nothing.' Dixon tried a reassuring smile. 'Maybe someone's got friends in high places and has lodged a complaint. Bob Eastman, possibly. Forget it. Really. I may have ruffled a few feathers, but apart from that I haven't done anything for Professional Standards to be interested in.'

'Yeah, but—'

Dixon waved away her protest. 'It'll be something and nothing.'

Once back on his swivel chair in the open plan incident room, Dixon spun round and looked along the landing to the far end of the atrium and the Professional Standards Department. Glass partitioned, soundproofed; he had been in once before for an interview. Failure to disclose a personal interest, the end result the capture of a prolific serial killer and a slap on the wrist; a price well worth paying.

A press conference, followed by a visit from PSD.

Things are looking up.

Standing room only at the back of the press suite, although Dixon knew most of the journalists were there just to find out if the Burnham carnival was going ahead. And it was.

Jane had taken up position against the back wall, next to two men in dark suits, each carrying a black leather briefcase. She had nodded and fidgeted in their direction through much of Charlesworth's prepared statement, written for him by Vicky Thomas, the press officer. She was also standing at the back, glaring at Dixon, her parting shot ringing in his ears.

'For God's sake, don't put your foot in it this time.'

The press officer was not a fan of his tendency to tell the truth. 'Yes, there is a serial killer on the loose' had done it last time. His defence had been that he hadn't been on the 'handling the press' training course, but that had done little to placate her.

This time, Charlesworth had suggested that he and Deborah Potter do the talking, unless a question was specifically directed to the SIO, of course.

'Can you guarantee the safety of those attending the Burnham carnival tonight?' The question shouted from the middle of the room.

Er, no, thought Dixon, grateful that Charlesworth dived in.

'There will be a significant presence of uniformed officers all along the route of the procession. The carts are being checked and double checked, every precaution that can be taken will be taken, and we see no reason to cancel it at this time.'

'Will there be plain clothes officers in the crowd?'

'That's an operational matter, which I will not be commenting on.'

The CCTV stills had given the journalists something to report on, but they hadn't been received with much enthusiasm.

'Detective Chief Inspector, is there a serial killer on the loose?'

Dixon recognised the crime reporter from the local rag. He had been there for the press conference last time and had asked the question that got Dixon in trouble – the same question.

Git.

'We have various lines of enquiry, but are yet to make an arrest,' he said, ducking the question.

Charlesworth dived in again, talking over the murmuring as he wrapped up the press conference with a final appeal to the public for information.

Dixon had been watching the two men at the back out of the corner of his eye. Distracted for a moment by the direct question, he looked back to find they had gone. Something was coming, he knew that. What, though, was another matter. Dixon had done his best to calm Jane's nerves, but now his own were rising in the pit of his stomach.

Maybe that was why Charlesworth had insisted on doing the talking at the press conference?

The scraping of chairs and dismantling of camera tripods rose above the chatter as the throng of journalists stood up and made for the door, eager to file their reports, the noise dragging him back to the present.

'This way, Nick,' said Charlesworth, gesturing to the door at the back of the press suite. 'Just stay calm and remember that we're on *your* side. All right?'

It hardly came as a surprise that the two suits were waiting for him in the corridor.

'Detective Chief Insp—'

'Let's take this in an interview room,' interrupted Charlesworth.

Dixon glanced at Deborah Potter, who mouthed 'good luck'.

The suits dumped their briefcases on the chairs, a brown envelope in the hand of the older man. He at least had the decency to wait until Charlesworth had closed the door behind them.

'Detective Chief Inspector Dixon, my name is Detective Superintendent Carlisle. I am obliged to serve on you a notice pursuant to Regulation 15 of the Police (Conduct) Regulations 2020. I am also the officer appointed to investigate the complaint.' He handed the envelope to Dixon. 'In the first instance, I would like to discuss the matter with you informally. You will not be interviewed under caution at this stage, but you are entitled to have your Police Federation representative present if you wish.'

Dixon had ripped open the envelope, his eyes scanning the notice for the two words that made all the difference.

And there they were.

Gross misconduct.

'Does the name Besim Raslan mean anything to you?'

'It does.'

'I regret to inform you that Mr Raslan died at Bristol Royal Infirmary on the first of November. He never regained consciousness following the incident at your home on the sixteenth of November last year. Cause of death was cardiac arrest.'

Chapter Sixteen

'Really, Nick, it's just a formality.' Charlesworth had done his best. The concerned looks from Jane and the others in the incident room hadn't helped, none of them taking their eyes off him as he rode up in the glass lift to the Professional Standards Department.

Still, at least he knew what was coming now.

Carlisle was a tall man with dark hair and piercing eyes hidden behind a pair of reading glasses balanced on his sharp nose. He could have been an accountant, maybe. 'This is Detective Inspector Larkin,' he said, gesturing to the man sitting next to him. 'You are not under caution, of course. This is purely an initial interview in disciplinary proceedings; you are not entitled to have a solicitor present, and you have indicated that you do not wish to have your Federation rep here. Is that correct?'

'It is.'

'Tell us what happened on the night of sixteenth November last year.'

Dixon folded his arms. It had been a long time since he had sat in on a police interview from the other side of the table; a couple of occasions when he was a trainee solicitor, perhaps. And those had been motoring offences. 'You know what happened. I gave a detailed witness statement at the time.'

'Tell us again.'

Maybe his legal training hadn't been a complete waste of time after all? 'My witness statement dated sixteenth November last year was written later that same day, when the events were fresh in my memory. The best I can do is refer you to that statement.'

Carlisle tried again. 'What first alerted you to the break-in at your home?'

Dixon sighed. 'My witness statement dated sixteenth November last year was written later that same day, when the events were fresh in my memory.' Matter of fact and spelling it out. 'The best I can do is refer you to that statement.'

Larkin shifted in his seat, his eyes fixed on Dixon. 'Failure to cooperate in disciplinary proceedings is itself a disciplinary matter.'

'Is itself a disciplinary matter, *Sir*.'

'Yes, Sir.'

'And I am perfectly happy to cooperate. I have nothing to hide. You have asked me a question and I have given a reasonable and entirely helpful answer. If you want to know what happened that night, read the witness statement I gave at the time. It was and remains the most accurate record of events.'

Carlisle was glaring at Larkin. 'Do you think you used reasonable force?'

Dixon had known that one was coming. 'The Independent Office for Police Conduct looked at it at the time and agreed that I had. But let's be clear: two men break into my home in the early hours of the morning, one armed with a shotgun and the other a machete. Yes, I used reasonable force. If I'd had a gun and shot them, it would *still* have been reasonable force.'

'You were armed with an ice axe and a trench cosh from the Great War.' Carlisle was flicking through his notes. He looked up, his brow furrowed a little too much. Clearly forced. 'Where did you get those weapons from?'

'They are not weapons. They are items of sentimental value kept by me for the reasons set out in the witness statement I gave at the time. It deals with all of those matters.'

'Have the items been returned to you?'

'They have.'

'Do you still have them?'

'I do. As I said, they have sentimental value.'

'We may need them again.' Carlisle reached across and tapped the blank page of Larkin's open notebook. 'I'm concerned by your reluctance to talk about the events of that night,' he continued, a pained expression on his face as he turned back to Dixon.

'You haven't asked me anything that's not already dealt with in my statement of sixteenth November last year, Sir.' Few things irritated Dixon more than being taken for a fool. Time to go on the offensive. 'I know the way this works. You get me to go over it all again now – the best part of a year later – and look for discrepancies between what I said then and what I say now.' He folded his arms. 'It's a fishing expedition, Sir, and I'm not playing that game. You haven't even given me the opportunity of reading my original statement to refresh my memory.'

'You'd recently been stabbed in the shoulder and were on painkilling medication at the time of the incident. Is that right?'

'That is in my statement as well.' Dixon had tried the deep breath and count to ten anger management routine several times already in what was looking increasingly likely to be a short interview. 'Look, if you've got anything new to put to me, Sir, then by all means do so and I'll comment on it, but I see nothing to be gained by trying to remember what happened that night when there is a detailed witness statement on the record.'

'You sound like a solicitor,' said Larkin, with more than enough sarcasm to ensure it wasn't mistaken for a compliment. At least he hastily tagged 'Sir' on the end.

'If you'd looked at my personnel file, Inspector, you'd see that I am a solicitor,' replied Dixon.

'Yes, Sir.'

'Have you got anything to say to the complainants?' asked Carlisle. 'Mr Raslan's parents.'

'Like what?'

'An apology, perhaps.'

'Their son breaks into my house, at night, carrying an offensive weapon, and I'm supposed to apologise?' Dixon stood up sharply, sending his chair slamming into the glass partition behind him. 'I've had enough. I've got work to do,' he said, wrenching open the door. 'You'd better add failing to cooperate to your list and see how far it gets you. Sir.'

Jane looked as if she was about to burst when Charlesworth appeared at the top of the stairs and intercepted Dixon on his way back along the landing towards the incident room.

'Let's nip in here, Nick.' Charlesworth pushed open the door of an empty training suite and stepped back to allow Dixon into the room. 'How was it?' he asked, closing the door behind them.

Dixon was still seething and knew he would have to choose his words carefully. The realisation that he had killed a man was also starting to sink in, taking the edge off his anger, for now. The rest would come later, on the beach with Monty. He perched on the edge of the long desk, his back to the line of computers.

'It's not your fault,' continued Charlesworth. 'It's routine whenever there's a death involving police, you know that.'

Dixon took a deep breath. 'I killed a man.'

'You killed an armed man who had broken into your house. And you didn't intend to. I read the file.' Charlesworth sat down next to him. 'If you'd intended to kill him, you'd have shot him when you picked up the gun, not hit him with it.'

'Seems I hit him too hard.'

'As hard as you needed to. For all you knew, he might have had another gun in his pocket, or a knife. I can arrange some counselling, if you think that might help?'

'No, thank you, Sir.'

'Did you cooperate with Superintendent Carlisle?'

'He didn't have anything new to put to me, so I just referred him to my original statement.'

'Then you stormed out. I heard your chair hit the glass.' Charlesworth gave a conciliatory smile. 'It does mean we're going to need to put your promotion on hold for the time being, I'm sure you understand that.'

Dixon had known that one was coming too, not that he minded. He'd only applied for the detective superintendent role at Charlesworth's insistence. Shame about the pay rise that went with it though.

'When the IOPC have finished their investigation, we'll look at it again. I'm sure there'll be other vacancies coming up. You could even apply for a transfer to another force, although I'd much rather you didn't.'

'Yes, Sir.'

'Look, I've discussed it with Deborah Potter and we're not going to suspend you pending the investigation. All right?' Charlesworth stood up. 'Technically we should, but there are clear mitigating factors at play here and, besides, we need you on this carnival thing.

So, get back to that and let this other business take care of itself. Are you ready for the Burnham carnival tonight?'

'There's a briefing at five-thirty.'

'Well, you'd best go and get on with that. But remember, Nick, we're all on your side. I know it may not seem like it when you're being quizzed by the PSD, but we are. What you did that night was quite something.'

'Thank you, Sir.'

◆ ◆ ◆

News travels fast, judging by the looks on their faces, thought Dixon, glancing around the now packed incident room. All of the workstations were occupied by plain clothes detectives; standing room only for the uniformed officers all around. Chief Inspector Bateman, bronze commander for the carnival, was briefing the uniformed contingent on their duties for the evening, but Dixon was miles away.

He remembered waking up – pitch dark, the streetlights off outside – Monty standing on him, licking his face. Then the dog ran to the end of the bed and started growling softly at the gap in the curtains.

His great-grandfather's trench cosh had been in his sock drawer under the divan bed, and he must have made a conscious decision not to hit either intruder over the head with it, instead using it to smash the wrist of the man holding the gun. A lump of lead on the end of a bamboo cane, wrapped tightly in brown leather; it was designed to kill a man through a steel helmet, for heaven's sake.

Yes, that was why he had picked up the gun and hit them with the wooden butt. He remembered the crack, wondering at the time whether it was the wooden stock or skull.

Skull, as it turned out.

He hadn't hit them with the ice axe either, using it to deflect the blow from the machete. Had he really kept it for sentimental reasons though? The photo on the wall of him waving it at the camera on the summit of Mont Blanc suggested he had – and, after all, it was the only piece of his climbing equipment he had hung on to – but if that was right, why had he kept it hidden down behind his bedside table?

He hadn't mentioned that in his original statement, of course. Nor would he now.

Charlesworth had been wrong about the gun. Dixon's television and DVD collection had been hit by both barrels when he smashed the wrist of the man holding it, so he couldn't have shot them even if he had wanted to. Maybe that explained why he had picked it up and swung it like a baseball bat instead?

Would he have shot them, if he could? Mercifully, that was a question he didn't have to answer.

Charlesworth was right about one thing though. Forget it. It was advice Dixon had received before: 'Box it up, put it to the back of your mind.' And he would, for the time being at least. Better move the ice axe, all the same, though.

Jane had summed it up best on the night. 'Fuck 'em.'

'Do you have anything to add to that, Nick?' asked Bateman, wrapping up his part of the briefing and turning to Dixon.

'Er, no, thanks.'

He kept his part of the briefing short. Most of those present knew what was going on anyway, as did anyone who had watched the news channels; the outside broadcast vans had gone from the police centre car park, taking up position in Burnham ready for the carnival procession. And the reality was there was no evidence to suggest anything was going to happen at the Burnham carnival anyway, as Charlesworth had been at pains to point out.

Everybody had already been given copies of the still images from the CCTV and knew what to look for. There wasn't a lot else to say.

'At least there's no bloody squibbing tonight,' said Mark.

'Quite.'

Jane was first out of the blocks when the briefing broke up. 'Is it true? Has one of those fuckers died?'

'I killed him.'

'He killed himself when he broke into our house. It was us or them, don't forget.'

'Are you all right, Sir?' asked Louise.

'I'll be fine.'

'It's just routine, Sir,' said Dave.

Routine, maybe, but they all knew what it meant: Professional Standards and investigators from the IOPC crawling in and out of every orifice for months. 'Yes, thanks, Dave. And I'm still leading this major investigation team, so let's get on with it. Lou, you're with me tonight, but go with Maggie in her car. I need to have some time with Jane.'

'The promotion's gone,' said Dixon, his hand resting on the gearstick while he waited for the electric gates at the bottom of the ramp to open. 'Put on hold until this is sorted out, according to Charlesworth.'

'I don't care about that.' Jane placed her hand on his, interlocking their fingers. 'I care about you.'

He glanced in his rear view mirror at Louise and Maggie behind them on the ramp, waiting to turn out of the staff car park. He'd never been very good at lip reading, and the mirror made it even more difficult, but he could imagine – Maggie wanting to know what it was all about, Louise telling her as little as she could get away with.

'What did he die of?' asked Jane.

'Cardiac arrest. He'd been on a life support machine ever since the . . .' Dixon wasn't sure what to call it; 'incident' hardly did it justice.

'Why don't you take some time off? Take Monty to the Lakes for a few days.'

'I can't. Maybe when this carnival business is over.'

'Did Charlesworth offer you any counselling?'

'He did, but it's not me.'

'I know it's easy to say, and you'll hear it a lot, but you did what you had to do.'

'I did, but it doesn't help.' Dixon accelerated on to the dual carriageway. 'When the anger subsides, all that's left is guilt. Could I have done something differently? Did I have to hit him so hard?'

'I'd have hit him as hard as I bloody well could.'

'I think I lost my rag with the suits from the PSD as well.'

'Did you take a deep breath and count to ten?' asked Jane, still holding his hand as he changed up through the gears.

'Several times.' Dixon was gripping the steering wheel tight with his right hand, his knuckles whitening. 'The bloke was on a fishing expedition, looking for inconsistencies between what I say now and what I said then, but I wasn't having any of it. I just kept referring him back to my original statement.'

'I bet he didn't like that.' Jane shook her head. 'He looked a right jobsworth.'

'It takes a certain type to work in Professional Standards and he's definitely *it.*'

The traffic was slow on the A38 as they approached the motorway roundabout, the turning to Queen's Drive, where the carnival carts were lined up along the verge, blocked by two patrol cars. A couple of cars in front showed passes and were allowed through; the remainder directed further along the A38 towards Brent Knoll.

A wave of his warrant card and Dixon was allowed through as well, Maggie and Louise following.

'I don't know what's going to happen,' said Jane. 'But the one thing I can say for sure is that we'll get through it together.'

'I never doubted it for a minute. And besides, I can always—'

'Don't give me any of that "I can always go back to the legal profession" crap.' Jane lifted his hand off the gearstick and rested it on her thigh. 'You know you don't mean it.'

Chapter Seventeen

Lines of cars were parked on the grass verge opposite the carnival carts, the rumble of diesel generators and engines on both sides of his Land Rover as Dixon crept along Queen's Drive. Some of the carts were lit up, others still dark; people milling about in the middle of the road, some in costume, others in hi-vis jackets.

The engine of *Right Here, Right Now* roared into life when Dixon was alongside, waiting for the crowd blocking the road to part, then a blast of the music rattled the windows of his Land Rover. A short blast, mercifully.

Dancers were climbing on to the carts and taking up their positions on the platforms, crouching down and then standing up inside their metal cradles, the steel loops around their waists.

'How long until the procession starts?' asked Dixon.

'About half an hour. They're off at six-fifty.'

Highway to Hell had pulled round from Edithmead Lane and taken its place in the procession, but the cart was still dark, the back doors of the power unit open, as was the hatch at the base of the main platform. Apart from torches, the only light came from the carts in front and behind, casting an eerie glow across the Harley-Davidsons that should have been rotating on turntables, their engines revving. Even the Hells Angels looked unimpressed, wandering up and down in the road, some of them glancing in the back of the cart at the electricians working frantically under the platform.

Spirit in the Sky had started up further along, and was soon joined by *Those Magnificent Men in Their Flying Machines* towards the back of the procession, the music drowning out the shouting coming from under *Highway to Hell*.

Dixon stopped in the middle of the road, Maggie and Louise still right behind him, and got out, leaving his engine running.

'Who are you?' asked one of the dancers, shining the light on her phone at Dixon.

'Police.'

She'd made an effort with her costume; they all had. Studded black leather jackets and waistcoats aplenty. 'There's something wrong with the electrics,' she said. 'Bloody thing won't start.'

'It was fine on Saturday night at Bridgey,' grumbled another, hands on hips. 'Where the bloody hell's Trevor?'

A van screeched to a halt in front of Dixon's Land Rover, Lionel Harper jumping out carrying a clipboard, his pass dangling around his neck on a lanyard. 'What's going on?' he shouted, not bothering to remove the whistle between his teeth.

Most just managed a shrug in response, but one of the dancers blurted out a rueful 'electrics won't come on'.

Harper glared at Dixon. 'Are you looking for me again?'

'No, Sir.'

'Bloody good job,' he said, disappearing into the gaggle of Hells Angels waiting by the base of a stepladder that would take them up on to the platform, a Marlon Brando lookalike at the front of the queue.

Then he reappeared at the back of the cart, leaning into the open doors in the base. 'What is it?'

'I dunno,' came the shout.

'Another five minutes and you'll lose your place.'

'Shall we get into town for the procession?' asked Jane, standing next to Dixon at the front of his Land Rover. 'We'll never find anywhere to park now as it is.'

Dixon glanced at Maggie's car behind his own, both Maggie and Louise watching the dancers climbing up the stepladder one by one and spreading out across the cart, some of them climbing on to platforms, others on to motorbikes. 'You'd better change places with Lou.'

Marlon Brando was already sitting astride his Harley, pretending to rev the engine; all of it lit by phone or torchlight.

The people at the back of *Those Magnificent Men in Their Flying Machines* were watching on, waiting, some less patiently than others, although Dixon felt more sorry for the dancers in skimpy costumes on *Spirit in the Sky*. A cold November night was not a good time to be kept standing around. At least their cart was lit, so they had hundreds of light bulbs to keep them warm.

'Right, that's it. We'll have to go without you,' Harper had shouted, the whistle still between his teeth. 'Just make sure you get it fixed for Friday at North Petherton.'

Getting all the cars off the road had proved a bit of a challenge, but the procession eventually got underway half an hour later than scheduled, the remaining carts pulling around *Highway to Hell*, still shrouded in darkness, one set of the wheels on the nearside verge.

All of the spectators along the grass verge had gone, but Harper and his clipboard had stayed behind, occasionally jabbing his radio aerial in Dixon's direction.

'I get the impression they think it's our fault,' Louise said. 'We nicked their electrician, apparently.'

Most of the Hells Angels had drifted off, some home, others to the pub. Those that had stayed behind were standing at the back of the cart, shining lights into the crawl space and glaring at Dixon.

'And nobody knows where Mr Bishop is?'

'No, Sir. He rang the club secretary when he got out of Express Park last night and said he'd be here in plenty of time, but no one's seen him.' Louise was backing away towards Dixon's Land Rover. 'Shall we get into town before we get lynched?'

'What about his parents?'

'They've still not heard from him.'

'Where are Jane and Maggie going to be?' Dixon asked, walking around to the driver's side.

'By the Baptist Church.'

Dixon overtook the carnival carts crawling along Queen's Drive, the blue light on top of his Land Rover. Some of the dancers on the carts were warming up, even though the procession didn't start officially until they were on the other side of the roundabout.

'You're not going to—' Louise stopped mid-sentence when Dixon made for the third exit. 'I thought for a minute you were going down the outside of the line.'

'Long way round,' he replied, smiling. 'We can get along the seafront and park at the top of College Street.'

'On the double yellows?'

Chapter Eighteen

A large police presence didn't include traffic wardens, so Dixon felt safe leaving his Land Rover on the double yellow lines outside the Pavilion, with the blue light on top just in case.

The smell of fried food wafted towards the seafront on the gentle offshore breeze, the tide rolling over the jetty at the far end of the promenade, moonlight reflecting on the flat calm water; the sounds of the carnival procession creeping along Burnham High Street, drowning out the bells and whistles of the amusement arcade.

Jane and Maggie were standing on the corner by the Baptist Church, the car park full of trailers, smoke rising from grills: hot dogs, kebabs, pizza, burgers; fish and chips too. Roger Poland was there, tucking into a pasty.

The first of the walking groups at the head of the procession had appeared opposite the end of College Street, the obligatory one-man band with his drums, followed by an assortment of dragons and dinosaurs.

'I got you a beer in,' said Poland, picking a plastic glass up off the wall and handing it to Dixon. 'Thought you might need a drink, after your run-in with—'

The bush telegraph had clearly been at work again. 'I'm on duty, Roger.'

'Of course you are, sorry. I'm driving too, so I'd better tip it away. Shame to waste it.'

'The little shit!' Jane was standing on the wall, staring at the queues for the fast food trailers on the far side of College Street. 'I put the little bugger on a train again this morning and there she is, getting a bloody hot dog.'

'She'll have got off at Weston and caught the bus back,' said Louise.

Jane was tapping out a text message, then she looked up, watching the crowd on the far side again. 'Yeah, she got that.' Both arms waving now.

'What did you say?' asked Dixon.

'I told her to be home by eleven, or else.' Jane jumped down off the wall. 'Sisters. Who'd have 'em?'

'You would.'

'Yeah.'

Dixon had missed most of the Bridgwater carnival thanks to a late train, arriving just in time to catch the last few carts and then the squibbing. Now he was seeing the ones at the front of the procession for the first time, and it turned his stomach.

The usual platforms and turntables, cells with bars at the windows, dancers in prison uniforms; *Jailhouse Rock*.

'I'm not bloody well voting for them,' he mumbled under his breath.

Jane reached across and put her arm around his waist. 'You're not going to prison. It won't come to that,' she said. 'Really, it won't.'

'I hope you're right.'

'Why are we here?' asked Poland, clearly thinking a change of subject might help.

'No specific reason,' replied Dixon. 'Just in case something happens.'

Poland took Dixon by the elbow and led him back up towards the seafront; not far, just enough so he could speak without shouting. Or being overheard.

'Jane rang me earlier, told me what happened. Is there anything I can do?'

'I was hoping you'd say that, Roger. If they pursue it, I'm going to need you to look at the post mortem. He died in Bristol, so someone up there will have done the first.'

'Yes, I can do that. Gladly. I still do the odd bit of private work. If it comes to giving evidence in court, I'm hardly going to be seen as impartial, though, am I? "How well do you know the defendant, Dr Poland?" I was the best man at his wedding.'

'I just need to know what I'm dealing with,' Dixon replied. 'If it gets as far as court, I'll have to get a second PM done. I'm sure you know someone.'

'I do. Just try not to dwell—'

Dixon raised his hand, silencing Poland mid-sentence.

'Sorry,' he said. 'I expect you've heard that umpteen times today.'

'Funny you should say that.'

'How about "You did what you had to" and "It was his fault for breaking in"?'

'Them too.'

'I'll shut up then.'

'It's enough that you're here, Roger.'

Poland took a swig of beer. 'So, what's the story with this case?'

'One estate agent fighting for his life in hospital, another missing. Both involved in the same dodgy deal.'

'Suspects?'

'The bloke who was ripped off, mainly.' Dixon was watching the estate agency opposite; lights on inside, an empty champagne bottle on one of the desks, the 'Closed' sign in the door.

'It's about time you bought somewhere,' said Poland. 'When this . . . er . . . business is . . . er . . . over.'

Saved by the bell, thought Dixon, watching Jane jogging towards them along the pavement.

'There are lights on in Bishop Property,' she said.

'Haven't we got people over there?'

'Dave and Mark were there, but they've walked up to the churchyard, I think.'

'Get them back.'

Jane ran back to the Baptist Church, shouting into her phone.

They pushed through the back of the crowd at the bottom of College Street, ducked under the rope and crossed High Street between *Grease* – black leather jackets and summer dresses – and *Voodoo Hack* – zombies in top hats and tails – the music a strange mix of *Summer Nights* and Jimi Hendrix belting out *Voodoo Child*.

The crowd parted to let them through on the other side of High Street. Lucy thought about making a run for it when she saw Dixon, but soon realised she was too late.

'You're in deep trouble,' he said as he ran past her, ducking through the queue for the fast food trailer on the pavement outside the bank.

Then he stopped to take in the scene two doors along from the Zalshah.

'There's no one in there,' said Poland, still holding his beer, although not much of it had survived the crossing from the Baptist Church.

Bishop Property was a small office, single fronted, with the usual property listings hanging in the window, a rack of the free property paper just inside the door. Several empty wine bottles were on a desk at the back of the office, a stack of plastic cups lying on its side on the floor.

'Looks like the staff "do" went ahead without him,' said Nigel Cole, appearing beside Dixon.

'Where were they?'

'They had a table in the Zalshah. Now they're on the pavement over there.' Cole was gesturing to a small group at the back of the crowd on the corner by the Railway Tavern. 'I counted seven of them,' continued Cole. 'They came out of the restaurant, went in their office, then came out again a few minutes later with a glass of wine each.'

'And there's no sign of Trevor Bishop?'

'Definitely not, Sir. I've been keeping an eye out for him.'

Dixon had been a police officer long enough to spot a back deliberately turned; the hood hastily pulled over a head when it wasn't raining confirmed it. It hadn't been there when he pushed through the queue either. He walked over to the line and placed his hand on the man's shoulder. 'Excuse me, Sir,' he said.

The man turned.

'Mr Platt,' said Dixon, trying to hide his disappointment. 'You hate the carnival and yet here you are?'

'I just came out for something to eat.'

'And drink?' The smell was unmistakable.

'I've had a couple. There's no law against it, is there?'

'None whatsoever, Sir. You enjoy your evening.'

A man in a flat cap and waxed coat walked back along the pavement and into the Bishop Property office, so Dixon followed, arriving in the window in time to see him refilling his wine glass.

'We're closed,' shouted the man, spinning round and spilling his wine when Dixon pushed open the door.

'Police.' Warrant card at the ready.

'He's not here, if you're looking for Trevor.'

'Do you know where he is?'

'No, I'm afraid not. He was supposed to be here for the dinner, but never showed up, so I ended up paying for it.'

'And you are?'

'Tony Johnstone. I work part time, doing viewings. Sometimes I help out at the show home over at the Brent Knoll development. It's our office party. Look, something must be going on. The Markmoor cart has been pulled out of the procession, apparently. Is he all right?'

'I hope so, Sir,' replied Dixon. 'The cart had an electrical fault, I'm afraid.'

'Is that all? We were thinking all sorts of things, especially after what happened to Richard Webb.'

'Do you know Mr Webb?'

'Not really. I know *of* him. Burnham is a small place.' Another top-up to make up for the wine he had spilt on the carpet; red to match the wine, mercifully.

'I'm guessing he's got an office at the back?' Dixon was looking over the man's shoulder. 'Do you mind if I have a look? See if he's . . .'

'Not at all.'

'What's upstairs?' asked Dixon, squeezing past between the desks.

'Residential flats.'

A small office, next to the kitchen area. He glanced along the corridor; toilet next, then the back door, bolted from the inside. He wasn't sure what he had expected to find in the time allowed, and the absence of a search warrant. Photographs of Bishop's children, tick, certificates on the wall, tick. Keys were in the filing cabinet locks, but he was just supposed to be checking for Bishop himself, not rummaging through his files, however tempting it might be.

'Thank you, Sir,' Dixon said, shutting the door behind him.

'D'you mind? I'd better get back out . . .'

Dixon followed the man back out on to the pavement, watching him drop the latch and then slam the office door before lurching from side to side along the pavement to where the Bishop Property staff were standing.

He arrived just as the screaming started.

Dixon began pushing through the crowd towards the screams coming from the edge of the pavement. Two young women were crying, several others holding their phones out in front of them, open mouthed and staring at the screen.

'Don't accept it,' said a girl leaning over the shoulder of another.

'Don't accept what?' asked Dixon, still with his warrant card in hand. 'Police.'

The girl passed him her phone.

AirDrop; Trevor Bishop would like to share a video.

The option to decline or accept was beneath the thumbnail image.

'Take a screenshot of that,' said Dixon, handing the phone back to the girl. 'Then accept it.' He turned to Jane, who had followed him. 'We need to get these people off the street. Let's get them in the Bishop Property office and get some help here *now*.'

Jane turned away, reaching for her phone.

Johnstone was ashen faced, still staring at his phone screen.

'Accept it,' said Dixon. 'Then let us back in your office.'

Those Magnificent Men in Their Flying Machines had gone past and was being followed by several walking groups out on High Street, so Dixon took advantage of the gap in the music. 'Police,' he shouted. 'Anyone who has received an AirDropped video on their phone, in the Bishop Property office now, please.'

He counted eight, filing through the open door as two uniformed officers came sprinting along the pavement, behind the crowds still largely oblivious to what was going on; hot air balloons and biplanes had seen to that.

'Hardly a rural crime, is it, Nige,' said Dixon.

'I'd just got down to the church when I got the shout.' Police Constable Nigel Cole was grinning and catching his breath at the same time. 'Getting paid to watch the carnival, my wife called it.'

'We've got someone AirDropping videos to people's phones. I want to know if anyone else in this section of the crowd has received it. We'll need the CCTV of this area too.' Dixon ducked inside the office, the door slamming behind him shutting out the music and flashing lights. All four desks were occupied, with two more people sitting on a sofa just inside the front door, the remainder standing.

'Cole's bringing another in,' said Louise. 'What's going on?'

'Someone's AirDropped a video of a dead body to their phones. A grim one.'

Johnstone frowned. 'What's AirDrop when it's at home?'

'It's a thing for transferring files and videos from one phone to another. It was just used to send you that video.'

A blast of cold air behind Dixon signalled the door opening again.

'One more, Sir,' said Cole, ushering in a woman wearing a long wool coat and a fur-lined hat.

'It's a bloody hoax. It must be,' Johnstone said, rolling up his cap and stuffing it into his pocket. 'A practical joke, surely? I'm having a drink.' He reached for the bottle of red wine on the desk in front of him.

'All in good time, Sir,' said Dixon. He picked up the plastic cups from the floor and dropped them in the bin.

Nine in total; all of them squeezed into Bishop Property's tiny office. Some were still staring at their phones, two of the younger ones sobbing quietly.

'Keep the door shut, will you, Nige,' said Dixon. 'My ears are ringing as it is. Right then.' He knocked on the nearest desk. 'Did everyone take a screenshot of the AirDrop thumbnail and then accept the video?'

All nine nodded. In silence.

'I accepted it, then deleted it when I saw it was from Trevor, I'm afraid,' offered the woman in the wool coat. 'It'll be in my Deleted Items though. I'll recover it.'

'Have you watched it yet?' asked Dixon.

'No, I haven't. There, I've recovered it. I always delete whatever he sends me.' Watching the screen now, a tear slowly rolling down her cheek, taking her mascara with it. 'Oh God, Trevor,' she mumbled.

'Does he send you a lot?'

'He used to. Not so much these days.' The tears were flowing freely now. 'I'm his ex-wife, Faye. Has anybody actually watched the whole thing?' she asked, handing her phone to Dixon. 'I can't bear it.'

'I did,' said Johnstone. 'It must be a wind up.'

'Liv watched it too,' said a girl sitting on the sofa. She had her arm around the shoulders of another girl, who was sobbing uncontrollably. 'She's his girlfriend. We were filming the cart when—'

'I've got it as well,' said another. 'When Liv screamed, I checked my phone to see if I'd got it. We all did. I've taken a screenshot and accepted it, like you asked,' she said, holding her phone out towards Louise. 'I can't bring myself to watch it.'

Jane was standing in the doorway. 'What d'you want me to do?'

'Detective Sergeant Winter here will take your contact details, please. And your phone passcodes,' said Dixon, raising his voice.

'You're not going to keep our phones?' Johnstone again, swaying backwards and forwards in his chair. 'I need it for work. It's got all my appointments on it.'

'We'll have to, I'm afraid, Sir. You'll get it back as soon as we can arrange it.'

'A lot of fuss for a practical joke.'

Dixon sat down in Trevor Bishop's office, opening the Recents photo album on Faye's phone, the video starting automatically when he clicked on it. Two minutes and fifty-nine seconds, shot that afternoon at 15.09; he had seen a thumbnail of the still image and knew what was coming.

It started innocuously enough – a woodland clearing, the camera panning around slowly; birdsong, the sun bursting through what was left of the canopy, the turning leaves of autumn hanging on for grim death, the ground carpeted in long wet grass battered by the rain and first frosts, now being smothered by leaf litter. A forensic ecologist might be able to tell where it was, if no one else could.

A white car, the boot popping open to reveal a shirtless man, his hands tied behind his back; throat cut.

The camera stopped panning; zoomed in. He clicked 'pause' on the still image, but there was over ninety seconds of video left.

Jane was working her way around the office, taking contact details from each of them in turn, the hushed voices the only sound apart from the distant thump of *Spirit in the Sky* as another cart passed the end of College Street, the bass beat rattling the sash windows in their frames.

Dixon turned back to the phone in his hand and clicked 'play' on the video. A black leather gloved hand – a man's – pouring liquid from a red plastic fuel can over the body and the back of the car. Then the sound of matches being struck, the film ending with them being dropped into the boot.

'Ask Dr Poland to come in, will you, Lou,' said Dixon, standing up. 'Do you all work at Bishop Property?' he asked.

'Yes, this is all of us, apart from Trevor, of course,' replied Johnstone. 'Oh, and Faye.'

'I work at Harrison Samuels now,' she said. 'The other side of College Street, opposite the Baptist Church. I just popped over to say hello.'

'Do you know everyone here?'

'Most of them.' Faye glanced around the office, seeking reassurance. 'We worked together for quite a while, didn't we?'

'We did,' confirmed an older woman, sitting at her own desk judging by the photographs on the wall next to it.

'Watch this, Roger,' said Dixon, handing Faye's phone to Poland, who had appeared in the doorway, the glass of beer gone, mercifully.

'Must I?'

'I need to know if it's real.'

Poland sighed as he clicked 'play' with his thumb. 'It looks genuine enough.' A grimace corresponding with the camera zooming in. 'I can't really tell from a video. I'd need to see the . . .' He caught himself, suddenly conscious of the people sitting opposite. 'Body,' he mouthed.

'Of course it's not real,' grumbled Johnstone. 'You can get fake slit throats in any joke shop; a bit of ketchup and Bob's your uncle.'

Liv started sobbing again.

'Did you watch the film to the end before you deleted it, Mr Johnstone?'

'No.'

'Anyone know where this is?' asked Dixon, looking at each person in turn, all of them staring blankly back at him.

'A woodland somewhere?' Johnstone again, sarcastic rather than helpful.

'Dave and Mark are outside, Sir,' said Louise, changing the subject before Dixon could draw breath. 'And I've brought some evidence bags for the phones.'

'Get them to check and see if a burnt out car's been found in woodland in the vicinity, will you. Yesterday or today.'

'Nothing's been reported, Sir,' replied Cole. 'Shall we get the helicopter up?'

'Waste of time,' said Dixon. 'It's November and the video was filmed hours ago. It'll be stone cold by now, so the thermal imaging camera won't work, and it's pitch dark. Let's find out where Trevor Bishop lives and get someone over there.'

'With his parents at North Petherton,' gasped Liv, between the sobs. 'Ken and Elaine.'

'Get family liaison over there. And we'd better have a trace on his phone as well. Whoever AirDropped the video must have been using it.'

'Yes, Sir.'

'He's back at his parents while he gets a divorce.' Liv spoke without so much as a glance in Faye's direction. 'We were together.' She closed her eyes, still sobbing quietly on the end of the sofa.

'You and Trevor?' Johnstone frowned. 'I never knew that.'

'I was going to ring him, but you've taken my phone,' said Liv.

'I'll try it in a minute,' replied Dixon, with his best reassuring smile. 'Maggie, a word outside, please.'

Dixon was careful to close the office door behind him, and spoke in a hushed voice, despite the carnival procession filing past not thirty yards away. 'I want you to focus on this AirDropping business. Find who sent the video and we find Trevor Bishop, his killer, and whoever tried to kill Richard Webb as well, probably. All right?'

'Yes, Sir.'

'Take Dave and Mark. You need to watch this.' He started the video, Maggie watching the footage, Dave and Mark peering over her shoulders.

'Is it real?' she asked, before the film had ended.

'Looks real enough, but then it could be make-up and you don't actually see the car go up in flames,' replied Poland.

'You know Home Office pathologist Dr Roger Poland, Maggie?' asked Dixon.

'Yes, of course.'

'Some dog walker somewhere is in for an unpleasant surprise in the morning,' mumbled Mark.

'I bought my house through Bishop Property.' Maggie dropped the phone into an open evidence bag being held in front of her by Cole. 'I thought the name sounded familiar.'

'Do you know how AirDrop works?' asked Dixon.

'Not really.'

'You can send photos and videos from one iPhone to another via Bluetooth. Don't worry too much about the technology, it's just short range wireless. The key is the short range bit. Whoever sent this video was within thirty feet of them when he or she sent it.'

'CCTV it is then,' said Maggie, turning to Dave and Mark.

'We're on our way.'

'It was targeted. Whoever did it must have been using Trevor's phone, so we've already got a trace on it. The video went to "contacts only", otherwise anyone on the pavement with "everyone" selected in AirDrop would have received it as well, and no one else has come forward – only Bishop Property employees and his ex-wife.'

'I've got their contact details, Maggie,' said Jane.

'We'd better get the bins and drains checked too. And the beach when the tide's gone out, in case it was thrown over the sea wall.'

'You never know, there might be a bit of carnival left for us to see,' said Poland, when Maggie disappeared back inside the Bishop Property office.

'I've got to get back to Express Park,' Dixon said, with as much enthusiasm as he could muster. 'And to be honest, Roger, I wouldn't mind if I never saw it again.'

'They've put him in interview room one, Sir,' said Louise, when they arrived back at Express Park. 'He was wondering how long it might take, apparently. Says he's tired after the drive down.' She handed Dixon a copy of Szopinski's handwritten statement. 'You'd have thought he'd be falling over himself to help, given that somebody's tried to kill his husband.'

Dixon had long since given up trying to read anything into people's reactions to bad news, having encountered tears and laughter and everything in between. 'Has he got a solicitor?' That was the question that often told him more than anything else, but even that could be misleading.

'No.'

Szopinski stood up when Dixon and Louise walked into the interview room. 'Inspector Dixon. They tell me you are the officer who got to Richard first.' Szopinski's eyes softened. 'Thank you, for what you did,' he said, his hand outstretched.

'I wasn't able to do much, I'm afraid.'

'You tried. So, thank you.'

'How is he?'

'Stable. They keep him in a coma for a while; weeks rather than days, they said. His face, neck, hands and arms are . . .' Szopinski wiped away a tear with the back of his hand. 'It's early days, and there are many operations ahead of us.'

'How did you meet?' asked Dixon, gesturing to Szopinski to sit back down.

'On the internet. He was very nervous about it at first. Unsure. I don't think he had accepted he was gay and was fighting against it. Almost embarrassed by it. By us. In the end he tell his wife and moved out that same day; came to live with me, then we got a place of our own. It was difficult at first, because of his children mainly.'

'Was there any hostility towards you, or threats?'

'Who from?'

'Anyone.'

'No. Richard went out of his way to keep our relationship quiet anyway. We were firmly "in the closet" as they say. That's the way he want it, and I was fine with it, so . . .'

'What about his ex-wife, Anita. How did she take it?'

'Not good. That was just to begin with, though. When his children accept the relationship, I think she decided she should do as well.'

'Can you think of anyone who might want to kill Richard?'

'They ask me this in Birmingham and there is no one. He has made enemies, of course he has, but there is no one who would do that, I'm sure of it.'

'What about Anita?'

'No way.'

'Where do you work?'

'Energen Land. We do the surveys for the new pylons that will connect Hinkley Point C to the grid. I am land surveyor.'

'Does Markmoor Farm Holidays mean anything to you in that case?'

'There are many farms along the route. It is thirty-nine miles across farmland.'

'What about the name Lionel Harper?'

'Some farmers were more difficult than others.' Szopinski shook his head.

'Richard arranged for the purchase of the farm by Eastman Homes. It was on the edge of Mark.'

'Yes, I remember it, in that case,' Szopinski said, his hand across his forehead. 'A campsite with holiday lodges. The pylons were in the next field but then the villagers started a campaign to get them moved and the planning people decided they should go two hundred metres west. I was already working elsewhere by then, on the route north of the Mendips.'

'Lionel Harper says he lost a lot of money.'

'I know nothing about that.'

'Did he ever make threats to you or Richard?'

'To sue, yes, but it never came to anything. I think Richard even threatened to sue him for libel or slander, or whatever it is.'

Chapter Nineteen

Where are you? Jx

Jane's text arrived just as Dixon switched off his headlights, plunging the beach back into darkness. The tide was on the way out, leaving lines of seaweed in its wake, the wet sand shimmering in the moonlight.

His was the only car, but then it was nearly one in the morning.

He slid his phone back into his coat pocket and opened the back of the Land Rover, Monty sitting patiently, waiting for permission to jump out, his tail thumping into the sides of his bed.

It had been a long night, and Dixon hadn't left Express Park until well after midnight, the image of a burning Tesla etched firmly on his mind. The search for Trevor Bishop was underway as far as it could be in the middle of the night. Carnival night – when most of the duty shift was policing the event. Coastguard search teams were out, police dogs, patrol cars. Even the helicopter was lined up for first light.

'Go on then,' said Dixon, picking up the dog's lead.

Not a breath of wind, the waves rolling gently up the flats a couple of hundred yards away, the only sound the thundering of Monty's feet as he pelted after his tennis ball.

Try as he might, the memories of that night a year ago had been flooding back all evening; the gap in the curtains – seeing the blade of a machete glinting. And the shotgun.

Standing in the dark, the blast of cold air when the back door of his cottage had been broken open, the gun barrels appearing in the doorway, a black gloved hand, finger on the trigger.

Yes, he'd told Carlisle his witness statement was the most accurate record, but he remembered every detail of that night, even those not mentioned in the statement: the crunching of the wrist bone, the crack of the skull. Sounds that had stayed with him ever since. Like the soft crack of a climber's spine all those years ago; Dixon could still see him falling, landing flat on his back next to him.

Nobody had died, though, and it had been easy to move on. The plaudits had come easy too: 'Great work, mate', 'You did what you had to, well done', 'They got what they deserved' or '. . . more than they bargained for'. But it had been easy precisely because no one had died.

He had known one of the intruders was still in hospital, the other having pleaded guilty to aggravated burglary; twelve years had been the price. Dixon hadn't seen him since the bail application, refused mercifully – if ever there had been a flight risk.

Then there'd been the visit from the big cheese. A gun in the ribs, a distinctly eastern European 'Get in the car', and Zavan had been sitting there, dressed in black with his white beard.

Twat.

It had been the one with the machete who'd died. Dixon remembered the blade glinting as the man had swung it at his head; there was still a deep gouge in the rubber handle of his ice axe where he'd parried the blow. Then Dixon had hit him with the shotgun butt, swinging it by the barrels.

How hard? As hard as he bloody well could was the honest answer to that question. Too hard, as it turned out.

Besim Raslan.

Dixon hadn't known his name at the time, but it was not a name he'd forgotten in the days since. A permanent vegetative state, or so they said.

Not so permanent.

Headlights on the beach ramp, then Jane's car bounced off the end where the tide had washed the sand away from the base. Her lights caught Monty's coat as she turned and parked next to Dixon's Land Rover.

'Thought I'd find you here,' she said, jogging along the sand. 'Is it going out or coming in?'

'Going out.'

She threw her arms around him and kissed him. 'You're not stewing on that Albanian tosser, are you?' she said, kicking Monty's ball along the beach.

'I—'

'Would you rather he'd shot us and thrown us over the side of a boat, out there?' waving her arm out to sea. 'That's their usual method, isn't it?' Monty was standing up at Jane, his paws scrabbling at her coat as high as he could reach. 'This one would've died too, trying to protect us. With the machete, probably,' she said, scratching the dog behind the ears.

'I get it.'

'It was them or us.'

'A man is dead.'

'He is, and that was his choice, his risk. He took the gamble when he jemmied open our back door. And he lost. The IOPC agreed at the time, and they will again. Besides, no jury in the

155

land would convict you of anything, even if the CPS did decide to prosecute. You've got to let this go, you really have.' Jane clearly decided that a change of subject was in order. 'Complicated, isn't it, this carnival thing? It just keeps coming at you.'

'Not really,' replied Dixon. He was tipping his head, watching a flashing light moving slowly across the sky above them. 'The carnival stuff's smoke and mirrors. When you cut that out, you're left with a murder and an attempted murder. Both local estate agents.'

'What about the AirDropping?'

'It is what it is: sending a message.' Dixon opened the back of the Land Rover and whistled, Monty jumping in and curling up in his bed. 'Where's Lucy?'

'Back at the cottage. I'll be sticking her on the train again in the morning, and she'd better bloody well stay on it this time.'

'Remind me to move the ice axe when I get home.'

'The carnival stuff is just a distraction,' said Dixon, facing a packed incident room the following morning. He had decided to ignore Deborah Potter standing at the back, snooping. His Policy Log was up to date, so he wasn't entirely sure why she had bothered to drive down from Portishead for the routine briefing. Still, it was her travel expenses claim. 'Let's stay focused on what's at the centre of this: an attempted murder and what looks like a murder, but we still haven't found a body. Very public, and with a killer determined to make sure everyone knows about it. Have we had anything in from the public in response to the appeal?'

'Not really,' replied Dave. 'A couple more sightings of the mysterious steward at Bridgwater Carnival, but no images with a face or an ID.'

'What about Bishop's phone?'

'Still dead, Sir,' said Mark. 'It didn't go live last night either. Scientific are searching the centre of Burnham in case it was dropped, but there's no sign of it yet. It could have been done without the SIM card in it, though. AirDrop works via Bluetooth so it doesn't need a SIM card in the phone.'

'And Trevor himself?'

'Still no sign.'

'Bishop Property is going to be closed today, so let's search the office. Computers to High Tech, and I want his file on Markmoor Farm Holidays. What about Eastman and Webb?'

'Their computers are still at High Tech,' replied Jane. 'Their office will be opening today, but with a reduced staff.'

Dixon took a deep breath. 'I'm going to take a team off the witnesses. I know it means we'll get through them a bit slower, but I reckon this killer's too clever; no one will have seen anything anyway. The key to unlocking this is in the business dealings of these estate agents, so Jenny, you and your team look at the files, please. Go with the search team into Bishop Property and look for any transactions involving both agents. Check the files at Eastman and Webb too. Go back three years.'

'Yes, Sir.'

Jenny and the girls' night out looked pleased to have been taken off the chore of working through witness after witness who hadn't seen anything interesting anyway, but a day or two of going through estate agents' files would soon wipe the smiles off their faces. 'Right then, Lou, we're off to see Trevor Bishop's mother.'

Chapter Twenty

'A Christmas tree?'

'The hotels on the prom at Weston have all got theirs up,' said Louise. 'We drove along there the other day.'

'It's only the start of November, for heaven's sake.' Dixon parked across the drive of the small dormer bungalow on the edge of North Petherton, set back from the main road in a lane running parallel to it. 'There ought to be a law against it.'

The metal gate swung back on a spring, the clang the signal for the yapping to start. Dixon glanced at the sign in the front window: 'Beware of the Dachshunds!'

'I've got ankle boots on,' whispered Louise.

'Lucky you.'

The door was answered by Karen Marsden – jeans and a fleece the uniform of the family liaison officer these days; or jeans and a T-shirt in summer.

'How are they?'

'His mother's not doing too well,' she replied. 'I rang 111 and they're sending the duty doctor. Ken's holding it together, though.'

'Have they seen the video?' asked Dixon, his voice hushed as he stepped into the porch.

'No. Liv's here – Trevor's girlfriend – and she's told them about it.'

'We've met.'

'They're in here.'

Karen made the introductions, although only Ken looked up; early sixties possibly, bloodshot eyes. Elaine and Liv were sitting together on the sofa, holding hands and sobbing into paper tissues, a photo of a young Trevor resting on Elaine's knee. He was beaming at the camera, sitting astride a large motorbike, his helmet on the fuel tank in front of him.

'Here's another,' said Ken, taking a photo off the mantelpiece and handing it to Dixon. 'He used to do a bit of racing when he was a lad. Speedway too. Amateur stuff, that's all.' Red and black leathers, helmet tucked under his arm this time. 'He had sponsors though, local ones.'

'I'm very sorry—'

'Have you found him yet?'

'Not yet.'

'Save it then.' Ken sat down on the arm of the sofa and began rubbing his wife's back. 'Just find who did it, that's all we ask.'

'Switch the tree lights off, Ken,' said Elaine through her tears. 'Trevor was supposed to be having the children this weekend. We don't get to see our grandchildren that much, so we were making a bit of a fuss.'

'We were going to take them to Wookey Hole before we dropped them back to their mother.'

'Tea, anyone?' asked Karen, leaning around the door. Making strong sweet tea was the most important skill of the family liaison officer. That, and gathering information without the family knowing it was happening.

'Yes, please,' replied Ken.

Dixon was admiring the collection of trophies in the glass fronted corner unit: motorcycling and darts, by the looks of things.

'The darts ones are mine. Not that I was ever very good at it.'

'Can we see the video?' demanded Elaine.

'No, I'm very sorry, that's not going to be possible,' replied Dixon. 'I don't have a copy on my phone, and we haven't yet confirmed it's genuine either.'

'I did try to explain, Sir,' said Karen, handing a mug of tea to Ken.

'Have you seen it?' he asked, looking at Dixon.

'I have.'

'Just please tell me her boy was dead before the fire started.'

'Oh, God. I can't bear it.' Elaine buried her face in a bundle of tissues and started sobbing again.

'We can certainly ask the pathologist to confirm that one way or the other, if it comes to that. At the moment, we still haven't found—'

'He was no saint was our Trevor, but he really didn't deserve that.'

'He used to say he was the Del Boy of the property world,' replied Ken, quickly clarifying Elaine's remark. 'A wheeler dealer. He made friends and he made enemies, but it was purely business and, before you ask, he never mentioned being threatened or anything like that.'

'He should never have married so young either,' said Elaine, her tears drying up. She was rubbing the back of Liv's hand. 'He never managed to stay faithful for very long; still sowing his . . .' Her voice tailed off. 'Sorry, Liv,' she mouthed.

'I'm told he left Eastman and Webb under a cloud.'

'Who said that?' demanded Ken. 'That bloody Richard Webb, I suppose?'

'Mr Webb isn't capable of saying very much, I'm afraid, Sir. It was his squib that exploded at Bridgwater Carnival. He's in an induced coma.'

'That was Richard?' Ken looked embarrassed, and rightly so. 'God, sorry, it just said on the news it was a local estate agent. It was an accident, though, wasn't it?'

'No, it wasn't, although we only released that information to the media yesterday.'

'He was a two-faced bastard, but even he didn't deserve that.'

Dixon waited for Ken to explain himself.

'It was that business about the probates,' said Elaine. 'It was all lies. They cooked that up to get rid of Trevor.' Ken was pacing up and down on the rug in front of the fire, Elaine trying to take his hand each time he came within reach. 'They used him to run their residential property sales for years, targets that would make your eyes water – paid him a pittance too, while they ran around buying up land and developing it. They made millions while he was left scratching around for a couple of hundred quid here and there in bonuses. I gave him the money to set up on his own in the end. This was before Ken and I met.'

'There was more to it than that though.' Ken sat down in the armchair, looking up at Dixon. 'They were undervaluing land and then buying it themselves. Trevor was going to blow the whistle on it, which is why they cooked up that probate thing so they'd have something on him. "Tell on us and we'll take you down too", was the message. It rumbled on for years.'

'They had a fight,' whispered Liv. 'Trevor and Richard. After the local association annual dinner at the County Ground. It was in the car park as we were leaving.'

'You saw what happened?' asked Dixon.

'Yes.' Liv was trembling, on the verge of breaking down again, her sentences punctuated by sharp intakes of breath. 'Richard came off worse. Brian Townsend stepped in and separated them.'

'Who's Brian Townsend?'

'Another agent and the president of the local association. He's at Harrison Samuels.'

'And what was this fight about?'

'Everybody knows what it was about,' said Ken, with an abrasive edge. 'It's what Trevor was going to blow the whistle on originally, only this time they did it to his mother. The same old story: Hilary Eastman and Richard Webb undervalue a property, and then her husband steams in and buys it at the knock down price. That's exactly what they did with Markmoor Farm, Elaine and Lionel's place over at Mark. It's how Eastman got started in the first place. Bungalows to begin with; a good sized plot, knock it down and put four houses on it. He was doing it all over Somerset. Then the plots got bigger and bigger. Thirty-something houses they're building on Markmoor Farm.'

'Was Trevor involved in it when he worked there?'

'No.' Elaine was getting indignant now. 'Anything with development potential they dealt with, and he was left with the rest.'

'But he knew about it?'

'Yes, he knew. Like I said, he was going to blow the whistle, and that's why they got rid of him. There was a bloke threatening to sue, I seem to remember. They'd undervalued his late mother's house in Berrow, bought it, and then within six months had got permission to put eight houses on the plot. They paid him off, according to Trevor. They'll deny it, of course.'

'There was a restrictive covenant in Trevor's contract with Eastman and Webb. He wasn't allowed to work within five miles of Burnham for two years after he left. So, why didn't they enforce that when he set up practically next door to them? Ask yourself that.' Ken wagged his finger. 'They didn't want to risk it all coming out in court, that's why.'

'I need to ask you about Markmoor Farm Holidays,' said Dixon, turning to Elaine. 'I gather you ran the business with your ex-husband?'

'At least you know about that,' mumbled Ken. 'Before my time, I'm afraid. Richard Webb up to his old tricks again, ripping people off. Elaine got a fraction of what she was due.'

Elaine looked up, her face hardening. 'We always suspected the pylons were a scam and Trevor said he had proof. Don't ask me what it was or where he got it, because I don't know, but he said it proved the pylons were deliberately sited near the farm to get us to sell. Then they were moved later. There was no way we'd get permission to develop the land west of the lane with the pylons right on the boundary, and even if we did, no developer would want it. That left us with eight hundred thousand instead of one point six million.' She gave a vicious cackle. 'The only saving grace was that Lionel came off worse. We'd not long divorced – he refused to get solicitors involved and we agreed I'd get everything east of the lane and he'd get everything on the west. That was thanks to Trevor.'

Ken stifled a laugh. 'It meant Lionel got two hundred grand for his bit, and Elaine got six hundred for hers. Still a fraction of the true value.'

Dixon was staring at a colour photograph on the wall above the sideboard next to Ken's armchair. It looked like a school photo, rows of figures standing behind others who were sitting down. Only in this photo, they were all dressed in green and wearing berets. He walked around behind Ken's chair and read the names underneath.

'And no action has ever been taken against anyone over this?'

'Not as far as I'm aware.'

'Right, well, thank you for your help.' Dixon looked at Louise and nodded, then started edging towards the door as she shut her notebook and followed. 'We'll be in touch the moment we find anything.'

'Just make sure that you are,' said Elaine, through her tissues. 'We want to know what's happening.'

'I'll keep them informed, Sir,' said Karen, once they were out in the hall.

'If you get the chance,' Dixon was standing on the doorstep, gesturing to the Dachshund sign in the front window, 'tell them to get rid of that. It puts them at risk of dog theft. That's all they bloody well need on top of everything else.'

'Friendly bunch, estate agents,' said Louise, when they were sitting back in Dixon's Land Rover. 'I bet the annual dinner was a real blast. What's their surname again?'

'She was Elaine Bishop, then Harper and now she's Elaine Haynes.'

'Busy bunny.'

'Let's see if a complaint was ever made by Webb after that fight.' Dixon was putting on his seatbelt. 'And we need to have a word with this Brian Townsend fellow as well. Look something up on the internet for me, will you?'

'Hang on, I've got a voicemail from Jane.' Louise flicked on speakerphone.

I expect you're in with Trevor Bishop's mother. Just a quick one to let you know we've found his car. It's in the trees at the far end of Durleigh Reservoir – the western end. Roger's on his way over there now. I said I'd meet him there.'

'Shall we go back in and tell them?' asked Louise.

'We need more answers first.'

Dixon waited while Louise opened the web browser on her phone.

'Yeah, what is it?'

'621 EOD Squadron. Ken Haynes was sitting on the end of the front row in that photo. Officers and NCOs, August 2002.'

Louise was tapping her phone screen with her index finger, then she looked up. 'Explosive Ordnance Disposal and Search Regiment, Royal Logistic Corps. That's bomb disposal, isn't it?'

'It is.' Dixon was turning out on to the main road. 'And if you know how to dispose of a bomb, you know how to make one.'

Chapter Twenty-One

Dixon parked on the grass verge opposite the trees at the far end of the reservoir.

The five bar gate was open, several vans parked on the rough track in the trees beyond, but the entrance was blocked by multiple strands of blue tape, a uniformed officer leaning on the gate post.

'Here already,' said Poland. He was standing by the open boot of his Volvo, putting on a pair of wellington boots.

'We'd just seen his mother and stepfather over at North Petherton when we got the call,' replied Dixon. He was crossing the road, expecting the uniformed officer to remove the tape, but instead he took out his mobile phone.

'I'm sorry, Sir. I'm not to let anyone through without permission from the crime scene manager.'

Dixon gritted his teeth. 'I'm sure that doesn't extend to the SIO.'

'He said *especially* the SIO.'

'What about the pathologist?' asked Poland, slamming the boot of his car and picking up his cases.

'I'm to ring him and he'll come and get you.'

'Do it,' said Dixon, scuffing the ground with his foot. 'And tell him if he doesn't let me in there, I'll arrest him for obstruction.'

'Don't tell him that last bit,' whispered Poland.

The officer turned away, taking a few steps along the edge of Enmore Road to get out of Dixon's earshot.

Jane was first to appear, running along the edge of the track from the direction of the camera flashes going off in the trees behind her.

'He's a right jobsworth,' she said, pulling her mask below her chin with one hand and taking off her goggles with the other. Then she slid back the elasticated hood of her hazmat suit. 'You got the email about the new crime scene managers?'

'If I did, I didn't read it.'

'What he says, goes. And it's no use protesting, he just quotes chapter and verse at you from the regs.'

'This is going to be good,' said Poland, gesturing along the track.

Dixon noticed the clipboard first, then horn-rimmed glasses behind the goggles as the man approached. A moustache was just visible behind the face mask.

'Harish Patel, crime scene manager. Call me Hari,' he said, glancing down at Roger's two metal cases. 'You'll be DI Poland. Let him through. You can suit up by my van, Sir.'

'What about me?'

'And you are?'

'I'm just the SIO in the case, Detective Chief Inspector Dixon.'

'Forensics haven't finished yet, Sir, and I've already granted access to one investigating officer. Regulation—'

'I haven't got time to stand around here waiting for forensics to finish.'

'I'll need to ring my senior officer.'

'You do that.'

Dixon watched Poland wriggling into his hazmat suit at the back of the Scientific Services van parked nearest the gate while he listened to Patel's end of the telephone conversation with Donald Watson.

'I've got an SIO here, Don, the one you warned me about. He's kicking up that I won't let him through and I've already let one in.' He glanced at his clipboard. 'DS Winter. DCI Dixon, yes. Oh, right. Yes, I'll do that. If you say so.' Patel dropped his phone through the window of his van on to the driver's seat. 'Sorry, Sir. I can sign you in when I've signed DS Winter out. It's not technically correct but Mr Watson says we can do it on this occasion.'

'How very generous of him.'

'We're just trying to limit the potential for contam—'

'I get it. Really.' No doubt their paths would be crossing from time to time, so best not to fall out with him if at all possible. A bit like a traffic warden – always best to keep them on side too.

Once in his hazmat suit, Dixon followed Poland and Patel along the line of stepping plates towards the burnt out car. The plates had been laid in otherwise undisturbed grass in the middle of the track, lines of flags either side, one white and one red. The set of red flags turned right before they reached the car, and stopped between two trees.

The boot of the car was open, the whole of the back end destroyed by the fire. Both tyres had blown out, the rubber melting; the paint had gone and the rear window had shattered. Dixon looked along the side, balancing on the edge of the stepping plate. The white paint was largely untouched down the side of the vehicle, except for a few scorch marks extending from the boot.

'The passenger compartment is fairly intact,' said Patel.

'At least there was no fuel tank to blow,' said Poland. 'Looks like the batteries didn't catch either. If that had happened it'd have burnt for days.'

'Accelerant was poured in the boot. It burnt out fairly quickly, but left bugger all for us to find, I'm afraid.' Patel could have been ex-military; shoulders back and all that. 'Whatever it was, it was odourless. Lighter fuel, possibly, but we can check that.'

'Same stuff he used in Webb's squib,' said Dixon.

'Ah, the exploding firework.' Patel breathed in sharply behind his mask. 'We'll check the passenger compartment when we get it back to the lab, obviously, but there are two sets of tyre marks, so I'm guessing the killer had his own car.'

That explained the red flags.

The body was lying in the boot, curled into the foetal position, the flesh charred and blackened.

Poland leaned in and looked at the neck, the scene lit by two arc lamps, one on either side. 'The flesh has burnt away, unfortunately, so I can't see the wound on the AirDropped video. There may be traces of it under the microscope, but I can't tell until I get him back to the lab. ID will be teeth and DNA, which will take a while.'

'If he had a wallet in his back pocket, it was destroyed in the fire,' said Patel. 'His jacket too.'

'In the video, you can see the accelerant being poured from a red plastic fuel can—'

'The killer must've taken it with him,' interrupted Patel. 'We've searched the area and it's not here. Can't see the remains of anything like that in the boot either.'

'Maybe he's planning to use it again?'

'The thought had crossed my mind, Roger.'

Dixon walked back along the stepping plates and looked at the tyre marks in the long grass off to the side. 'Any footprints?' he asked.

'They were careful to walk in the long grass, so there's nothing, I'm afraid,' replied Patel.

Parked in it too. He'd do that in his Land Rover, no problem, but would someone do that in a car that wasn't a four wheel drive? It narrowed it down a bit, but not much or enough. 'What's along there?' he asked, gesturing to a line of flags leading off into the trees, following the telltale flattening of the long grass.

'There was a pile of vomit. I've bagged it up for analysis.'

'What was it?'

'Looked like scampi and chips to me, but I can't say I got any closer than I had to.'

Dixon followed the path through the grass – no stepping plates to bother with – and stopped short of three flags marking where the vomit had been, a circle of closely cut grass in the middle, right at the base of a large oak tree and beneath a rectangular hole where the bark had been cut away. Fresh too.

'I got photographs of that,' said Patel, watching Dixon's every move.

'Is there any sign of the bark in the car?'

'Not in the passenger compartment.' Patel shrugged. 'If it was in the boot then it's long gone.'

Dixon got his first look at the number plate around the front of the car: T B15H0P.

Nice.

'He should have been pulled over for that,' said Patel, who had followed Dixon around to the front. 'You're not allowed to muck about with the spacing of the letters.'

'How much is one of these?'

'You can get a second hand one for about forty grand, depending on the mileage. New ones are seventy plus.'

Bishop Property was doing well then.

'Have you had a look in the passenger compartment?'

'There are some long blonde hairs on the passenger seat and headrest, so someone's been sitting in it at some point, but that's it.'

'He was getting a divorce, but his girlfriend works for him. She's got blonde hair.'

'That explains that,' said Patel.

'Anything else, Roger?' asked Dixon.

'I've looked inside his mouth. There are some signs of scorching, so he was probably alive when the fire started, but not for long, I'm relieved to say, and he wouldn't have felt anything. He was past that. I'll be doing the post mortem as soon as I get him back to the lab in case you want to come over.'

'Thanks.' Dixon headed for his Land Rover, but was still within earshot for Patel's aside to Poland.

'So, that's him, then. The boy wonder.'

'It is.'

'Under investigation for killing a man, by all accounts.'

Chapter Twenty-Two

'Will this do?' asked Potter, looking pleased with herself.

'It will.'

'Two teams of eight, each led by a sergeant, plus what you had yesterday. You'll have to get a bit better at delegating,' she said, smiling at her own parting shot as she turned for the stairs.

Dixon recognised some, but not all. They were sitting in silence, watching his every move.

Whiteboards first, and more images taken from social media.

Trevor Bishop, age thirty-six – a bit old for nineteen year old Liv, perhaps, but then that was hardly any of Dixon's business. Jane had written 'ex-wife, son and daughter' underneath an image of Faye and two young children.

The images of the staff members at Bishop Property might have come from the firm's Facebook page, some of them doing a sponsored walk. There were four, including Liv and an older woman, wearing pink tabards with numbers on them. Trevor must have been there too, offering moral support and holding up an umbrella emblazoned with the Bishop Property logo.

'Their website's hopeless,' said Jane. 'No staff photos at all. That was the breast cancer walk on the beach last August.'

A third whiteboard had appeared, a photograph sellotaped top middle, the name 'Adam Waller' written underneath. Taken from his firm's website, possibly, or LinkedIn; formal, wearing a suit and tie, big smile for the camera.

'Waller rang us this morning from a landline that's been traced to Harrison Samuels estate agents in Burnham, asking to speak to the officer in charge.' Maggie appeared at Dixon's shoulder. 'He does their residential sales and lettings. Jumping the gun, probably, but we've tried to get back to him and he's nowhere to be found. His mobile's off, no one's seen him at his office since he went out at ten to do a viewing. I even sent uniform to check on him at home and he's not there either. He was supposed to be at the show home near the Crossways from eleven – that new development at West Huntspill – but that's all closed up and no one's seen him there since yesterday.'

Dixon stifled the expletive that had almost got away from him. 'Parents?' he asked, his mouth suddenly dry. Maggie would have checked, of course she would, but it bought him a few seconds to recover his composure.

'Not seen him either. We're checking through his friends on Facebook. No luck so far.'

'Do Harrison Samuels have any other offices?'

'They've got a North Petherton office, but he's not there either.'

'A change of priorities has been forced on us,' he said, turning to face the incident room. 'Adam Waller, estate agent aged twenty-nine, is missing.' He pointed to the photograph. 'He was last seen at the show home on the West Huntspill development yesterday, and is still alive until we know otherwise. I think we have to assume there is a threat to life.'

'He's already dead.' A voice at the back. 'Someone's got it in for estate agents.'

'Do you know something we don't?' asked Dixon, matter of fact.

'No, Sir.'

'Maggie,' he said. 'Get one of the new teams on the hunt for Waller.'

'Yes, Sir.' She was now sitting at the front with Jane.

'Dave and Mark, stay on the CCTV with the same team you had yesterday. You'll have the footage from Burnham carnival to go through now as well, so it's a huge job. Sorry.'

He ignored the eye rolling and muttering coming from their direction.

'The other team from Portishead can start working on the witnesses – Bridgwater and Burnham carnivals. We made a start yesterday talking to them on the phones, so you'll know who to speak to first. There are a lot, I'm afraid, and it'll be good old fashioned donkey work, but it's got to be done. You know what to look for: footage on their phones, photographs. It's my belief the killer was there, so find him. And remember, if we can find the killer, we might very well find Adam Waller too, one way or the other.'

'Yes, Sir.' In unison.

'DS Hobson, where are you?' asked Dixon.

'Here, Sir,' Jenny's arm appearing from behind a computer.

'There was a pile of vomit in the trees not far from Trevor Bishop's car. Scampi and chips, according to our frighteningly efficient new crime scene manager, Hari Patel. That sounds like a pub lunch to me, possibly with his killer. His throat was cut and he was bundled into the boot of his car.'

'Leave it to us, Sir.'

'Let's see if we can find his Tesla popping up on any number plate recognition cameras. Might give you a head start.'

'What about us, Sir?' asked Louise.

'We'll start with Trevor Bishop's ex-wife. She works at Harrison Samuels, doesn't she?'

'And she was at Burnham last night.'

Chapter Twenty-Three

Dixon was standing on the pavement outside the Railway Tavern in Burnham, the music blasting out through the open doors.

'Is it a B&B?' he asked.

'They do rooms, yeah.' Louise was standing in the window, reading the signs.

'You got AirDrop on, Lou?' Dixon took out his iPhone, selected 'General', then 'AirDrop'.

'Let me check.' She sighed. 'Yeah, it's on Contacts Only.'

'Let's check it works first.' He selected a photo at random – Monty on the beach – then 'AirDrop: Louise Willmott'.

'Got it.'

'Just decline it,' said Dixon. 'Now go and stand over by Bargain Booze and I'll send it again.'

'No, nothing.'

'What about the middle of the road?'

Louise stood on the white line while Dixon sent the photograph again.

'Yeah, got it this time.'

'That's about thirty feet, which means anyone on *Those Magnificent Men in Their Flying Machines* could have sent the video.' Dixon turned back to face the pub, looked up. 'And anyone in those upstairs windows too.'

'I'll go,' said Louise, disappearing inside the pub as Dixon put his phone to his ear.

'Where are you?' asked Jane.

'Outside the Railway Tavern. I've just been checking the AirDrop range with Lou. Anyone on the cart going past at the time could have sent it. It was the Ham Hill club with their Flying Machines.'

'I'll tell Maggie and she can look on the CCTV.'

'Get on to the club and get a list of everyone on that cart. And tell her to check the stewards too, and the charity collectors with their buckets.'

'Will do.'

'Lou's getting a list of guests in the pub, but get Maggie to see if there's anyone in the upstairs windows. One of the cameras may have picked them up. Is there any news from Birmingham?'

'No.'

'We're over to Harrison Samuels next.'

'All the upstairs front rooms were booked,' said Louise, emerging from the pub just as Dixon was dropping his phone in his jacket pocket. 'I've got a list, but they all had guests, so there were God knows how many people up there.'

'What other agents are there in the town?' asked Dixon.

'You've got Eastman and Webb, Bishop Property and Harrison Samuels,' replied Louise, glancing up at the 'Loading bay' sign on the pole behind Dixon's Land Rover. 'Plus you've got the web-based ones.'

It was odd how you never really notice an estate agent's, unless and until you're house hunting that is, thought Dixon, as he crossed the road towards the large double fronted shop, opposite the Baptist Church. He must have walked past it umpteen times. He stopped in the window and looked at the properties on offer, recognising some from his travels. 'Walking distance of the beach' was mentioned on some of them, always near the top of the selling points, and it would certainly be top of his list. Jane had already mentioned selling her flat and buying a place together. Kids, a mortgage; it would be a Labrador next, although Monty might have something to say about that.

'There she is,' said Louise. 'Sitting at the back on the phone.'

Three of the six desks were occupied, two of the staff on the phone, the third reading a newspaper.

There was a nice house in Gore Road, the sandy track at the top coming out on the beach opposite the lighthouse. He shuddered. Four times a detective superintendent's salary didn't even get him halfway there. Four times his and Jane's salary combined got them closer, but nothing like close enough.

'What the hell has happened to house prices?' he muttered.

'Tell me about it,' replied Louise. 'We bought a flat a couple of years ago and it's almost doubled in price already. You need to get yourself on the ladder, Sir.'

A bell rang above the door as Dixon pushed it open, wondering how long it would take the young lad sitting at the front to pounce. Dark trousers and white socks were visible under the desk; no tie either.

The answer was not very long at all. 'Can I help?'

Still, most people just look in the window at an estate agent's; if you actually go in, you must really be interested in buying a house. Or not, thought Dixon, as he took out his warrant card. 'We wanted a word with Mrs Bishop,' he said.

'Oh.'

That's right; not a couple looking for a house.

Faye Bishop looked up from her desk, a phone still clamped to her ear, Dixon assuming from her hand gesture she would only be two minutes.

Louise picked up a copy of the free Somerset property newspaper that was sitting in a rack just inside the door, Dixon watching her fold it up and stuff it in the top of her handbag. Going up the ladder, no doubt.

'That one's only a few doors up from you, Sir,' she said, pointing to an end-of-terrace cottage in Brent Knoll. 'Still within walking distance of the Red Cow and it's only two-eighty. Bit of a garden at the back for Monty too.'

The large sign at the top of the display offered one point five per cent selling commission, Dixon doing the maths in his head: four thousand two hundred pounds plus VAT.

No wonder property prices are going up.

'Are you looking for somewhere?' asked the young lad, clearly unable to stop himself.

'Not at the moment, thanks.'

'Would you like to go on our mailing list?'

His question coincided with Bishop's ex-wife hanging up. 'There's a room at the back we can use,' she said, standing up. 'You wanted a word about Trevor, I suppose?' She spoke as she walked, her back to Dixon and Louise as they weaved their way between the desks. Then she stopped in the doorway of a small office.

'We did, Mrs Bishop. And Adam Waller.'

'I'm using my maiden name again now. Smith, but please call me Faye.'

'I met a Ray Smith at the Avalon Carnival Club.'

'That's my dad; he's the club secretary over there. It's how I met Trevor, through the carnival, although he was Markmoor.'

'Are you an estate agent too?' asked Dixon, watching her sit down behind the desk.

'Admin assistant, technically, but I do the work of an estate agent. I even do viewings sometimes.'

'When did you and Trevor divorce?'

'I was traded in for a younger model, if you must know. You've met Liv.' She sneered. 'Last year, so it's still pretty raw, although we haven't actually got the decree absolute yet, so we're still married – *were* still married – legally at least. I should have known, I suppose, Trevor working in an office full of young girls.'

'Tell me about him.'

'He was good at his job, I'll give him that. And we agreed a financial split quickly, a generous one, to be fair to him; he never missed a payment either. Yet, anyway.' Tears were forming in the corners of her eyes. 'He even took out a life insurance policy, written in trust for me and the kids, so we'd be all right if something happened to him.'

'Can you think of anyone who might have wanted to—?'

'Not really. Your lot asked me that last night and there's no one. He's fallen out with all sorts of people over the years – it goes with the territory.' She shook her head. 'Richard Webb would be the obvious one, but someone's tried to kill him as well, haven't they?'

'There was a fight between Trevor and Richard at the County Ground last month, in the car park after the estate agents' annual dinner. Do you know what that was about?'

'First I've heard of it. Sorry. Come to think of it, though, Trevor did say something a bit odd a few weeks ago when he was picking up the kids. He had them every other weekend.'

Dixon waited.

'It was a Friday evening and he seemed a bit agitated,' continued Faye. 'When I asked him what was wrong, he said it was just Richard, up to his old tricks again.'

'Richard Webb?'

'I suppose so. I didn't really think any more of it, to be honest. And now he's dead.' Her eyes glazed over. 'Telling the kids was the hardest thing I've ever had to do. I've taken them out of school for a few days – my mum's got them. You try explaining Daddy's not coming back to a four year old.'

'I hope I never have to,' said Louise, with her best reassuring smile.

'Did Trevor ever mention any transactions he had on with Richard Webb?'

'They had deals on all the time,' Faye replied. 'It's the nature of the business and it's a small town. He'd have a client selling their property to one of Richard's clients, who was selling their property to one of our clients. It's all part of the dreaded chain.'

'There are rumours flying about, that Eastman and Webb were undervaluing property.'

'That old gem. It's been doing the rounds for ages, which probably means they've been at it for ages. I know Trevor was unhappy about it. It's why he left, although they'll tell you he was giving backhanders for probate instructions.'

'And was he?'

'He called it commission, but it was true, yes.'

'And was he still doing it when he set up on his own?'

'Until the bloke at the solicitors got caught helping himself to the client account. Why the hell not? Solicitors pay referral fees for conveyancing work.'

The window behind Faye looked out into an alley, bins lined up ready for collection at the back of the properties on the seafront.

'What did the other agents in the town think of that?'

'They were just annoyed he was doing it and they weren't, I think.'

'Did anyone ever make their feelings known?'

'Not that I can remember. And if they did, Trevor would have told them to mind their own business.'

'Can you think of any specific examples of Richard Webb undervaluing property?'

'There were a couple of biggies that raised a few eyebrows.' Faye leaned back in her chair. 'A smallholding at East Huntspill was the last straw for Trevor. Richard told the owner there was no chance of planning permission being granted, and the next thing you know Eastman Homes are building twenty-eight houses on it. They did the same over at Burtle – forty that time.'

'And Trevor was never tempted?'

'Once, he did it. A client wanted a quick sale and was happy with the valuation, so he bought the bungalow himself. A loft conversion and a lick of paint and he sold it for seventy thousand more than he paid for it.' Faye sniffed. 'That was the only time, and he did feel bad about it.'

'Bishop Property was doing well enough without—?'

'Estate agents don't make as much money as you might think,' said Faye, turning defensive. 'The advertising costs are huge, and a Rightmove listing isn't free. Travel, staffing, insurance, rent on the shop, business rates. Trevor was doing all right, but he was hardly raking it in. The only reason Hilary and Richard appear to be doing so well is because of their *other activities*.'

Dixon was looking at the various certificates mounted in frames on the wall. Estate Agent of the Year, South West Region 2018 and 2019 among them.

'Are Harrison Samuels a big firm?'

'Not really. We've only got the two offices; this one and the one at North Petherton.'

'And where is Mr Townsend?'

'Out on a viewing. He should be back in a minute.'

'I'm sorry,' said Dixon, sitting down at the desk, 'but there are some difficult questions I have to ask.'

'Fire away.' Faye put her hand over her mouth, the realisation of what she had just said washing over her, the tears welling up. 'Oh shit, sorry.'

'Don't be. You were there last night when a video of Trevor's body was AirDropped to the staff at Bishop Property. D'you have any idea who might have done that?'

'No, sorry. It was horrible. I wish I hadn't watched it; hardly slept a wink. Poor Trevor. Was he dead before the fire started?' She flinched, hardly daring to ask the question.

'No.' Matter of fact. Dixon had already decided he would give a different answer to Trevor's parents, but he needed to see other people's reactions to the news.

The blood drained from Faye's face. Then the tears started to flow.

'I'd no idea,' she sobbed. 'Who would do such a thing?'

'Whoever did it was sending a message,' continued Dixon. 'How well d'you know Adam Waller?' he asked, deciding that a change of subject might help.

'Reasonably well. He's a nice enough lad.' She was drying her eyes with a paper handkerchief. 'We flirted a bit, y'know, when he knew I was getting a divorce. Nothing ever happened, of course.'

No hint of a blush, so she was probably telling the truth. 'How long have you worked together?'

'He was here when I joined the firm last year. I had to get out of Bishop Property when I found out what was going on. Trevor and Liv – you can imagine it, can't you. The looks and the giggling behind my back.'

'Do you know where Adam might have gone?'

'No idea, sorry. I don't know him that well. He's got his own place in Highbridge, but I expect you've been there.'

'We have.'

'He had a viewing at ten-thirty, but never turned up. The buyers rang in a bit of a strop, so I've had to make them another appointment for later this week. Adam's still got the keys.'

'The property address?'

'Channel View, Coast Road.'

'Maggie sent a car over there earlier, Sir,' said Louise. 'No sign of him.'

'What can you tell me about Markmoor Farm?' Dixon asked, turning back to Faye.

'Nothing you haven't heard already, probably. Richard and his husband cooked up a nice little scam there, with the pylons. Trevor was pissed off because he regarded it as our kids' inheritance.'

'He told his mother that he could prove it was fraudulent.'

'I don't know anything about that, I'm afraid. We only really talked about the children, and that just about kept the peace.' Faye was looking past Dixon, to the front of the shop, the jangle of the bell on the door attracting her attention. 'Here's Brian now if you wanted a word with him?'

Dixon watched Townsend being told the police were in the office; hushed voices and pointing to the back room. Faye stood up and waved.

Jacket over the back of a chair at a vacant desk, then Townsend appeared in the doorway. 'You'll be here about Richard and Trevor, I imagine. How can I help?'

'Did you know them?' asked Dixon, standing up.

'I've worked in the town for twenty years, and I'm the president of the Somerset branch of the NAEA. I know everyone and pretty much everything they get up to as well.'

'There was a fight between Richard and Trevor at the annual dinner.'

'Actually, it was more of a scuffle. A few punches were thrown, none connecting, mercifully. It was more the sort of pushing and shoving you'd see on a rugby pitch. Richard ended up on his backside. I wrote to them both letting them know it was not the sort of behaviour that reflects well on the profession.'

Townsend was tall, with short greying hair, neatly pressed shirt, and cufflinks. Dixon recognised the NAEA logo on his tie as well.

'Did you find out what it was about?'

'Look, they've got history between them. Trevor used to work at Eastman and Webb and the parting of ways was less than amicable, shall we say? I do know it was something to do with the pylons, so probably about that development over at Markmoor – Trevor seemed to think Richard had ripped off his mother. I was standing by my car, so maybe ten yards away, when it started, and I heard Trevor mention "pylons" and "usual tricks". That's it, I'm afraid. Oh, and "you're going to pay for it this time".'

'And this wasn't reported to the police at the time?'

'Lord, no. A fight at the association annual dinner? The local rags would've loved that. Our advertising spends with them wouldn't have stopped them running that story, with glee.'

'When you say pylons, you'll be referring to the new ones, from Hinkley Point C up to Avonmouth?'

'I assume that's what Trevor was referring to, yes,' replied Townsend. 'But that's just me putting two and two together. They went near Trevor's parents' campsite over at Mark. Our chartered surveyor, Gerard Pollock, valued it with and without the pylons, from memory. Made a bit of a difference to the hope value.'

'Are you involved in the carnival as well? Everyone else seems to be.'

'We're patrons of the North Petherton carnival,' replied Townsend. 'We have an office over there, so it's a corporate sponsorship. We do the fireworks in Burnham, with the Chamber of Trade.'

'What about you personally?'

'Oh, I used to, back in the day. It was the social side of it, mainly.'

'Which carnival club?'

'Gremlins. "Ghost Ship" was my last, in 2006.'

'Did you ever squib?'

'Good God, no. They were homemade when I started and it was far too dangerous.'

'You'll have to forgive me, Sir, but we need to ask you where you were yesterday afternoon.'

Townsend flushed, his eyes darting around the office. 'Would you mind if we stepped outside?' he whispered.

'Not at all, Sir.'

'Office gossip, you know how it is,' said Townsend, closing the front door behind them. 'I was with Faye. We . . . er . . . were at my place, if you must know.' He was staring at his feet, his face a shade of crimson. 'All afternoon, till four or so anyway. Her mother picks the kids up from school and then Faye collects them from her place after work. We're both single, so . . .'

Dixon turned to look at Faye through the front window. She nodded, then shrugged.

Chapter Twenty-Four

Dixon hesitated on the pavement outside Harrison Samuels, the movement in the window catching his eye as the young lad who had pounced on them took down a poster adjacent to the front door with an embarrassed smile. Townsend had barked the order when he had gone back in, the bell above the door jangling once again.

Burnham-on-Sea Fireworks, Sunday 5th November, sponsored by Burnham and Highbridge Chamber of Trade and Harrison Samuels Estate Agents.

'Check their work diaries, will you, Lou, and I think it's time we had another word with Richard Webb's husband, Ian. Put a bit of pressure on him about this pylon business.'

Louise took out her phone and dialled a number, Dixon still watching what was going on inside Harrison Samuels. Not a lot, was the answer, although the newspaper had gone since Brian Townsend had got back.

Dixon hadn't been listening to Louise's conversation, although the words 'down by the lighthouse' did catch his attention.

'A black Labrador,' said Louise. 'You walk back towards the town; we'll drive round to Allandale Road and walk out to meet you.' She looked at Dixon, her eyebrows raised. 'We're on our way now,' she said, before hanging up.

Dixon would have to brush the sand off his shoes before he got home; Monty would be livid, missing a walk on the beach. It was a favourite spot, the end of Allandale Road. You could even park with a grandstand view up and down the beach; ideal for a bag of chips, the lights of Hinkley Point visible even on the gloomiest of nights.

Lines of seaweed marked that morning's high tide, water still draining out of muddy channels in the sand.

'He's the other side of the bloody mud.' Louise was looking down at her smart shoes, the toes already coated in sand.

'He's got wellies on, so he can come to us,' said Dixon, watching a large black Labrador with a red collar, chasing a rubber ball. Monty would probably recognise it, even if he didn't.

'Fancy coming out for a walk when your husband's on life support.'

'Dog's got to have a walk, Lou, come rain, shine or bereavement.'

'Yeah.'

'How is Mr Webb?' asked Dixon, watching Szopinski picking his way across the muddy channel.

'The same. The doctors say they will keep him in a coma.' He swallowed hard, blinking away a film of moisture. 'They will let me know when they're bringing him round, so I can be there.'

'And who's this?' asked Dixon, stroking the dog.

'Henry.' Szopinski squinted at Dixon. 'You have a white Staffie, I think?'

'I do.'

'We dog walkers are an odd bunch. We recognise the dogs always, but not the people.'

'Funny you should say that.'

'I should tell you my real name is Jan, but I change it to Ian when I come to England.'

'Does the name Trevor Bishop mean anything to you?'

'He is an estate agent, like Richard. They used to work together.'

'Mr Bishop is dead.'

'Trevor is dead?' A mixture of surprise and relief, possibly. 'How?'

Dixon ignored the question. 'Were you at the estate agents' annual dinner, Ian?'

'No.'

'Why not?'

'Richard likes to keep our relationship quiet. I did not mind, and that was the way he wanted it.'

'I'm told Richard and Trevor had a fight.'

'Trevor Bishop was drunk,' Szopinski replied, leaning over and clipping a lead on Henry's collar. 'He go after Richard in the car park, shouting and swearing. Richard tried to push him away. That's all it was.'

'Shouting about what?'

'He was accusing Richard of ripping someone off.'

'And had he?'

'No.' Indignant.

'We will find out, Ian, one way or the other.'

'Mogę stracić pracę,' he whispered, puffing out his cheeks.

Dixon glanced at Louise, who was scribbling in her notebook.

'The campsite at Mark,' continued Szopinski.

'Markmoor Farm Holidays?'

'Yes.' Szopinski was brushing away worm casts with his foot, his eyes fixed on the sand beneath him.

'When we spoke last night, you said you couldn't remember anything about it.'

Szopinski responded with an apologetic sigh. 'I tell Richard about the line of the pylons before it was made public. They were going to be in the next field and he uses that information to buy the land cheap. Then he wants me to get the pylons moved, so they can develop the land for houses. It was a client of Bishop, or his mother, I think – that is why he was so angry.'

'Did you get the pylons moved?'

'Two hundred metres. I make the recommendation, that is all. There was a campaign to take the pylons further away from the village and the planning people decided it. Richard said if I can get them moved even a little, the land becomes more valuable for the homes. They can build more and bigger, make more money, but it was not my decision.' Szopinski sighed again. 'Who wants to buy a house under a giant pylon?'

'Seems like a motive for murder,' said Louise, watching Szopinski letting his dog off the lead again before trudging back towards the lighthouse a few minutes later.

'Especially if you're the owner of the campsite and you think Bishop was in on it. Remember, it was Bishop who suggested the land was split when they divorced, giving his mother the bit to the east of the lane. Harper might think he was ripped off by Webb *and* Bishop in that scenario.' Dixon was typing into Google Translate on his phone. 'The land to the west of the lane would've had a fraction of the value with giant "T" pylons in the next field.'

'I wouldn't want to camp under one, let alone live under it.'

'Quite. And you'd be pretty pissed off if someone conned you into selling your campsite for a song on that basis, only to find the pylons are moved a couple of hundred metres away. That's more than enough to make a huge difference.'

'Try it without the "y" on the end,' said Louise, tipping her head to look at his screen upside down.

'"I might miss work",' said Dixon.

'Yeah, change the "k" for a "c".'

'"I may lose my job".' Dixon slid his phone back into his jacket pocket. 'You certainly may, Ian. Check with Jane and see who she spoke to at Energen, then we'll go and rattle their cage, I think.' He was kicking the sand off his shoes at the top of the steps from the beach. 'Where are Energen?'

'In the Energy Innovation Centre off junction 23.'

'Then we'll go and see how Roger's getting on with the post mortem.'

Louise frowned at her phone. 'No reply from Jane. I'll try Mark.' She dialled another number, then put her phone to her ear. 'Yeah, hi, Mark. I was looking for Jane . . . oh, right. Yeah, I'll tell him.'

'Where is she?' asked Dixon, when Louise rang off.

'You don't want to know.'

Chapter Twenty-Five

Jane had seen them coming in the reflection in her screen. Two suits; the same ones who had collared Dixon the day before.

Mark had done his best, a whispered 'incoming' from behind his computer.

She had resisted the temptation to turn around as the footsteps closed in on her along the landing. She had been expecting it; Dixon had warned her. She was a material witness – there on the night – and it was inevitable they would interview her. 'Just tell the truth' had been his advice.

It was her first visit to the Professional Standards Department. Soundproofed, just like the Safeguarding Unit, the silence inside ominous when the door slammed behind her.

Detective Superintendent Carlisle had already made the introductions standing over Jane at her workstation; the walk along the landing, deliberately slow, undertaken in silence. It had given her the feeling of walking to the gallows.

'As you may be aware, we are investigating a complaint against Detective Chief Inspector Dixon,' said Carlisle, when Larkin had closed the door of the interview room. 'He has been served with a Regulation 15 notice arising from events that took place at his cottage on the night of the sixteenth of November last year. We understand that you were present on the night in question?'

'I was.'

'Were you in a relationship with DCI Dixon?'

'Yes.'

Just answer the question, don't volunteer any extra information they haven't specifically asked for.

'A relationship between serving officers.' Carlisle was sucking his teeth. 'Had it been disclosed?'

'Detective Chief Inspector Lewis, our line manager, was aware of it.' Jane was resisting the temptation to fold her arms. She had conducted enough interviews of her own to be aware of body language.

'DCI Lewis is dead.'

The image flashed across Jane's mind; the squeal of the brakes on the train. Maybe they didn't know she had been there when it happened? Volunteering information, though. A statement of fact, not a question too. She stayed silent.

'Are you still in a relationship with DCI Dixon?'

'Yes.'

'Were you living together at the time?'

'Not then, no.'

'You had an address in Bridgwater?' Carlisle was looking down at the papers open on the table in front of him. 'A flat, I think.'

'That's right.'

'Do you still own it?'

What the fuck's that got to do with anything? Tempting, but Jane thought better of it. 'Yes.'

'How often had you stayed at Dixon's cottage in Brent Knoll in the weeks leading up to the sixteenth of November last year?'

'Three or four nights a week, maybe.'

'Had you seen a shotgun in the cottage at any time before the sixteenth of November?'

Time to take her own advice: *deep breath and count to ten.* She glanced down to find her arms folded tightly across her chest. 'No.'

'Were you aware that DCI Dixon kept a number of weapons in the cottage?'

'DCI Dixon did not keep any "weapons" in the cottage.'

'What about the ice axe?'

'That is a piece of climbing equipment, not a weapon.'

'He's a climber, is he?'

'He was.'

'Why does he keep the ice axe, if he no longer climbs?'

'Sentimental reasons. He had it with him when he climbed Mont Blanc. You can see it in the summit photo.'

'And the trench cosh?'

'It belonged to his great-grandfather.'

'Where were they kept?'

'Both were in his sock drawer under the divan bed from memory, although he didn't switch the light on for obvious reasons. I gave a detailed statement at the time, so I'd suggest you refer to that.'

'All right, let's move on to the events of the night. What's the first thing you remember?'

'Nick woke me up. He said we'd got company, told me to call it in. He said one had a gun, so to get Armed Response. And he told me to keep hold of his dog. I was only to let Monty go if they got past him. Then he got the ice axe and cosh from the divan drawer and went downstairs, closing the door behind him. This is all in the witness statement I gave at the time.'

'Who were these men?'

'We didn't know at the time. It was only afterwards we found out they were Albanians.'

'What happened next?'

'The shotgun blast first. I was still on the phone and the call handler heard it.'

Carlisle reached across and tapped the notebook in front of Larkin. 'We'll get the recording of the call.'

'Yes, Sir.'

'Go on,' said Carlisle, turning back to Jane.

'Then a shout, then it was all over. I came out on to the landing at the top of the stairs and two men were on the floor. The door curtain had come down and was lying on top of one of them, and Nick was standing there with blood pouring down his chest. He still had the ice axe in his left hand and was holding the shotgun in his right, by the barrels.'

'Where was the trench cosh?'

'Hanging down from the loop around his right wrist.'

'Where was the blood coming from?'

'He'd been stabbed a week or so before and he'd opened up the wound again.'

'Not the machete then?'

'No.'

'How did you find out these men were Albanian?'

'DCS Collyer from Zephyr came to see Nick in Weston hospital. The organised crime unit were engaged in some drugs op and said our murder investigation was treading on the wrong toes. Our victim worked at a stables being used for betting scams and drug importation, as it turned out. Collyer said they'd probably paid us a visit to warn us off.'

'After Dixon closed the bedroom door behind him, could you hear where he went?'

'No.'

'Was he carrying the shotgun at that point?'

'The ice axe and the trench cosh. He was holding the axe in his left hand, by the head of it, with the handle down the outside of his forearm.' Jane was rubbing the outside of her left arm with her right hand. 'There's a big gouge in the handle now, where he used it to deflect the blow from the machete.'

'Did you see that happen?'

Bristling now. 'If that is what he says happened, then that is what happened.' Jane knew there was more to come. Carlisle had been softening her up with the easy questions; she knew the drill well enough.

'How would you describe your relationship at the time?'

'It was early days. We'd only been seeing each other a few weeks.'

'Had you moved any of your belongings into the cottage?'

'Just overnight things. A toothbrush, stuff like that.'

'So, you wouldn't necessarily have known if Dixon had a shotgun in the cottage?' All became clear in one question; the direction of travel – *they're trying to say it's Nick's gun*. 'Hidden under the stairs, perhaps. In the spare bedroom. In the sideboard?'

'The shotgun belonged to the Albanian, and he brought it into the cottage. One had the gun and the other had a machete.'

'Did you see them in the street?'

'No.'

'So, the first time you saw them was when you came out on to the landing after the fight?'

'Yes.' Try as she might, Jane couldn't argue with that.

'You can't possibly know what weapons they were carrying, in that case.' Carlisle was looking increasingly pleased with himself. 'Your information comes entirely from DCI Dixon, doesn't it?'

'Nick did not have a shotgun in the house.'

'We have a statement from Ardita Besmir. Mr Besmir admits breaking into the cottage with Mr Raslan, but says that until recently he had no recollection of events. He too received a blow to the head. He now says he was advised to plead guilty to aggravated burglary based on the facts as presented at the time. He admits that he and Mr Raslan entered the property carrying the machete, so does not plan to appeal his conviction, but he denies that either of them was carrying a shotgun. What d'you say to that?'

'It's bullshit.'

'Mr Besmir says that he was carrying the crowbar he had used to break open the back door, and Mr Raslan was carrying the machete, but they both had them down by their sides and were retreating from the property when they were attacked by DCI Dixon.'

'More lies.' Jane was shaking her head. 'What about the shotgun blast?'

'Ah, I'm glad you asked me that.' Carlisle gave a sarcastic smile. 'Mr Besmir says that DCI Dixon switched on the lights and confronted them with the shotgun. There was a struggle, the gun was discharged, then he and Mr Raslan began retreating from the property, their arms down by their sides, when DCI Dixon attacked them with the gun, swinging it like a baseball bat. At that point, of course, they were both attempting to leave the property and presented no threat, which makes DCI Dixon's actions wholly unreasonable.'

'If true.'

'You held the gun. Is that correct?'

'By the barrels. Nick handed it to me when he went upstairs to throw some clothes on.'

'Which explains the presence of your fingerprints. But, let me ask you this . . .'

Jane would have given anything to be able to reach across the table and wipe that bloody smirk off Larkin's face.

'If DCI Dixon's version of events was correct, his fingerprints would only appear on the barrels of the shotgun overlaid with yours, and yet a further check of the gun has found his prints on the stock and a partial print on both triggers. What does that tell you?'

'That someone in forensics has fucked up or is on the take.'

'That's quite an allegation to make, Sergeant.'

'You rattle off this crap and then tell me *I'm* making quite an allegation?'

Chapter Twenty-Six

'Are you sure you want to do this now?' asked Louise, frowning as Dixon turned in to the Energy Innovation Centre.

'We'll be no use at Express Park now, especially if Jane's already in there with them.' He parked in the visitors' space next to the front door. 'Besides, she can handle it.'

'She'll probably lose her rag.'

'Can't blame her for that,' said Dixon, switching off the engine. 'I did.'

The bright orange reception desk matched the stair carpet, the grey tiled floor leading through to a canteen with yellow chairs. Dixon dreaded to think what the interior designer's bill might have been. Maybe he'd give it a try if Professional Standards were able to make something stick; throw enough shit about and some of it is bound to stick to something. 'Mr Burnett is expecting us.'

'That's a bit of a stretch,' whispered Louise, her eyes wide. 'I only spoke to him on the phone and we didn't fix a—'

Dixon waved her protest away with the back of his hand, watching the receptionist reaching for the telephone.

'And who may I say is here?'

'Police.'

'Oh, right.'

'We'll be in there,' said Dixon, gesturing to the cafeteria.

'You're not serious?' Louise followed, albeit reluctantly, judging by the huffing and puffing going on behind Dixon.

Tea and a KitKat; Dixon could do with the sugar. That was his excuse and he was sticking to it. He wondered how Jane was getting on, hoping that, whatever it was that was coming his way, he would be able to keep her out of it; perverting the course of justice, possibly, if they were able to prove she lied in her original witness statement, but she hadn't. Assault was more likely, if she really did lose her rag. He'd find out soon enough, he thought, dropping a sugar cube into his tea.

The receptionist started gesticulating wildly, and pointing in their direction, Dixon pretending not to notice out of the corner of his eye. 'I haven't given them visitor's passes,' she said. 'They walked off before I—'

'It's fine, Denise.'

Then a man appeared in the doorway.

'You're looking for me, I think,' he said hesitantly. Dark suit and a white shirt open at the collar, the tie hanging over the back of the chair in his office, probably. 'How can I help?'

'Is there somewhere we can talk privately?'

'Of course. Bring that with you.'

Up the orange stairs and into a meeting room, the projector screen still down, blocking the view out of the window. A water cooler in the corner, blank white walls, and multicoloured chairs this time, Dixon opting for the red one.

Introductions made. 'I want to understand how the line of the pylons was arrived at,' said Dixon.

'Oh, that.' Burnett shifted uneasily in his seat. 'I thought all that was done and dusted now. Cost me five years of my life, that did. All the unpleasantness that went with it.' He gritted his teeth. 'That has got to be the most stressful thing I've ever done.'

Dixon waited, sipping his tea.

'Everybody wanted it moved. And wherever we moved it, there were people there who wanted it moved as well. We couldn't win.'

'Why didn't it just follow the line of the existing pylons?'

'It does in places, near enough, but it can't follow it exactly. We need both lines for a time, until the switch over, and then we can start to dismantle the old one. So, we were left surveying the land to find a new route pretty much adjacent to the old, but it wasn't always possible. Ditches, woodland, housing, soft ground. Just over thirty-five miles, and we were the surveyors responsible for finding the line. Then, when it went public, we were the poor sods in the firing line.'

'Why not put it under the sea?'

'Money. It would've added a pound a month to everyone's electricity bill. It's all of us who end up paying for it, don't forget.' Burnett had stood up and was filling a plastic cup with water. 'All those sodding public meetings. I learnt a few new words at some, I can tell you.'

'Some campaigns were successful, and the pylons were moved.'

'They were. Where we could, we tried to accommodate people's concerns, and the planners decided that it went too close to settlements in a couple of places. The tinfoil hat brigade were out in force.'

Dixon noticed Louise glaring at Burnett.

'We had it all: giant "T" pylons, they said, when actually they're only thirty-five metres tall, compared to forty-six point five metres for the existing steel lattice pylons, but oh no, they're fine, it's the new ones we don't want. And we don't want them in *my* backyard. The sad fact is though that someone has to have them in their backyard.'

'How many compulsory purchases were made?'

'Only two in the end. Both north of the Mendips.'

'Who was responsible for the line around Mark?'

'Ian. That would be Ian Szopinski. He came up with a good line, solid footings, accessible, but it took it slightly further east than the existing line and a bit too close to the village. Some of them went nuts. If you look at the line now, there's a slight kink in it where it curves around to the west of Mark.'

'Why wasn't that done in the first place?'

'We were looking for the most direct route to keep the cost down, and don't forget that it's moorland out there, soft underfoot. And it floods. All these things have to be taken into account.'

'So, Ian was solely responsible for that part of the line?'

'Originally, yes.' Burnett took a sip of water. 'He'd have done the surveys, spoken to the various landowners and stakeholders.'

'What about those whose land the pylons went *near*? Holiday parks, for example.'

'Not them, no, only the direct landowners. It's not really anybody else's business, is it?'

'Unless the pylon is right next to your campsite, surely?'

'Not even then, really. Ian's job would've been to find sites for the foundations over a particular stretch between point A and point B, the more direct the better. That's it. As accessible as possible, one every three hundred metres. You try it. It's not that easy. All sorts of stuff gets in the way.'

'Like villages,' mumbled Louise, under her breath.

'We went round it in the end, as I say. They put up a very good case, to be fair to them. There was a local councillor, and he got the local MP involved. It was easier to go round it in the end, particularly when they started raising funds for a judicial review.'

'And whose decision was it in the end?'

'The Planning Inspectorate, and the energy minister would've given the final say-so.'

'Did anyone privately express any surprise that the line went so close to the village at the time?'

'The original line?' Burnett was standing with his back to the projector screen. 'I suppose some of us were a bit surprised, yes. I remember the campsite owner – I assume it's him you're referring to – got hold of some early leaked plans and was very unhappy about it, but then he sold out and it all went quiet for a time. It was only a couple of months later, when we went public with it, that the villagers kicked off.'

'And how long has Ian worked for you?'

'We were set up specifically for this project and he joined us right at the start. He'll be out of work when it's all finished, sadly. We all will be. There's always work for land surveyors, mind you. We'll probably all end up at Sizewell C. Then the next one after that.'

Two stone pillars marked the entrance, the shiny new signs announcing 'Badgworth Court', the drive beyond lined with conifers; shafts of light from lamps on the manicured lawns lit up the front of the old manor house.

'Please tell me he doesn't own the whole thing,' muttered Dixon, looking across at the illuminated fountain as his Land Rover rumbled up the drive.

'Number 3,' replied Louise. 'It's round the back.'

'I'm in the wrong business.'

Dixon followed the drive around to the back of Badgworth Court and parked in the small visitors' car park. He counted eight garages in the block.

'Yeah, there are eight flats and houses,' said Louise, looking at her phone. 'One of them's on the market for seven-fifty. Very nice.'

'Every day another episode of *Escape to the Country*.' Dixon followed the gravel path that led to a large front door; the staff entrance at one time, possibly. 'It's all very well living in one of these places, but the service charges will kill you,' he said, the gravel crunching under his feet. 'Communal grounds, lighting, insurance.'

'Eleven acres. There's a tennis court, pond and a croquet lawn too,' added Louise. 'There's even a bloody cricket pitch!'

'Nice.'

More lights on the path gave way to a large lantern over the front door of number 3. Dixon glanced in the large sash window at the side, a cat sitting on the table in the kitchen drinking from a saucer.

'If you have to ask, you can't afford it,' he said, ringing the doorbell.

The scrape of wooden chair legs on a tiled floor carried through the closed window of the kitchen. Sandstone tiles, marble work-tops, a central island; you could have fitted the whole of the ground floor of Dixon's cottage in it.

'I was wondering when it would be my turn,' said Gerard Pollock, folding his arms. He left Dixon to close the door behind them and returned to his seat in the far corner of the dining area, an empty chair pulled out from under the table, in front of a book and a glass of something with ice floating in it.

A leather flying jacket with a fur collar, a hat and goggles were visible through the open door of the utility room, hanging on a coat hanger.

Dixon sat down at the dining table, Louise taking out her notebook and leaning on the worktop.

'Richard Webb and Trevor Bishop.'

'I've no idea why someone might—'

'Does Markmoor Farm Holidays mean anything to you?'

'It was a holiday complex on the edge of Mark. I was asked to value it a couple of years ago. I'm a chartered surveyor, and a partner in Harrison Samuels, as you probably know.'

'Both Bishop and Webb had been involved with it.'

'The bloody pylons, that was it,' said Pollock, wagging his finger. 'I'd valued it a year or so before when the owner was getting a divorce. Then he got me back a bit later to revalue it on the basis that there was a line of four hundred thousand volt pylons in the adjacent field. The land had what we call "hope value" – it gives it an enhanced valuation because there's a prospect that planning permission might be granted for development. I'm afraid the pylons rather crushed the owner's hope value and his hopes.'

'Did you check whether the pylons really were going to be in the adjacent field?'

'Wasn't asked to, and it wouldn't exactly be my remit. He just presented me with this plan showing the line of them and asked me what effect the pylons would have on the valuation. Nothing's proven, of course, but some people don't like living near overhead electricity cables and it can even have an effect on whether planning's granted at all. And if you were a developer, would you want to buy it? Why take the risk?'

'Have you still got the plan?' asked Dixon.

'I may have a copy on my file, although it'll be in store by now. I can certainly have a look tomorrow. You need to understand, these weren't – aren't, I should say, because they're going up soon – your ordinary pylons, the Eiffel Tower type you see everywhere else. These are whoppers, bloody great "T" pylons, huge things. A real blot on the landscape, and they'd have passed right along the edge of his holiday complex, according to the plan he had. They've been moved a bit since, further west, after the villagers kicked up, but at the time the plan had them within fifty feet of his lodges. It would've been game over for his business and any hope of selling the land, and I told him so.'

'Can you remember the figures?'

'Not off the top of my head.'

'Then what happened?'

'He sold it, as far as I know. At a knock down price, I suspect, then the pylons were moved further west and I know they're building on the plot now, so he got right royally shafted at both ends, poor chap.'

'You had no further involvement in it?'

'No.'

'And Richard Webb?'

'Well, it's Eastman Homes developing it, so that's Hilary's husband. Thirty-seven houses.'

'What about Trevor Bishop?'

'Was he involved in it as well?' Pollock looked puzzled. 'I didn't know.'

'What can you tell me about the owner, then?'

A large television was sitting on the display cabinet behind Pollock, an odd looking standard lamp in the corner, a print propped against the wall on top of an ornate radiator cover, but no pictures or prints were hanging. The furniture looked like a job lot, from Laura Ashley probably, the place more like a show home than anything else. No family photographs anywhere, either.

'Lionel Harper, early sixties maybe, but that was then. Beard. Always wearing shorts, even in winter; the long ones with the side pockets, you know. Seemed angry, but then he had reason to be, both times I saw him. First he was getting a divorce, and then the second time it was the pylons and I had to break the news to him that his life's work had just crashed in value.'

'Did he fight it?'

'Couldn't, really. It wasn't on his land, for a start, and National Grid can compulsorily purchase anyway. They don't buy the land, just what's called an easement, which in this case is a right to pass the pylons *over* the land.'

'He's a solicitor as well,' said Louise, gesturing to Dixon.

'Oh, right,' replied Pollock, rolling his eyes. 'Sorry.'

'Were you involved in any other cases with Trevor Bishop and Richard Webb?'

'Not recently; myself, that is. The agency will have transactions on with them all the time, but I don't really deal with the residential stuff. That's Brian Townsend's department.'

'How d'you get on with Adam Waller?'

'Fine. He's worked for us for a couple of years now, and we give him pretty much free rein on the residential property side. He supervises the lettings as well as the sales. Very good, he is.'

'And you've not seen him today, I suppose?'

'No, sorry.'

'Do you pay him well?'

'Have to, otherwise he'll set up on his own next door.'

'Just like Trevor Bishop did to Eastman and Webb?'

'There's a lot of it about,' said Pollock. 'Look, Adam does all right. We pay him a good salary and he gets a decent bonus.'

Dixon stood up. 'Are you involved in the carnival, by any chance?'

'Ham Hill Carnival Club. We're doing *Those Magnificent Men in Their Flying Machines* this year. I'm the one sitting in the biplane.'

'Do you squib?'

'I have done in the past.'

'You'll let us know if you see or hear from Adam Waller,' Dixon said, making for the door.

'Er, yes, I suppose I can. I'll be working from home for the next few days, though. I've got a couple of viewings here.' Pollock looked sheepish. 'Buy it, move in, do it up, sell it, and on to the next one. Can't help myself, I'm afraid. And it's tax free.'

Chapter Twenty-Seven

Dixon dropped Louise back to her car at Express Park with orders to go home and get some rest, and half an hour later parked outside a dark and deserted Pathology Department at Musgrove Park Hospital. He tried the front doors, which were locked, and then walked around the side of the building, towards the dull glow of light fighting its way through frosted glass at the far end.

Dixon tapped on the thick glass, reinforced with a wire mesh insert. They were taking no chances with the lab windows.

A large shadow loomed up on the inside. 'Who is it?'

'It's me, Roger.'

'Give me a minute. Meet me round the front.'

'Just open the fire door.'

'An alarm goes off if I do that.'

Dixon was standing in the porch at the front entrance, replying to a text message from Jane, when the lights came on in the reception area.

Where are you? Jx

Musgrove. Bishop's PM. Any sign of Waller?

Jane was typing a message, the speech bubble flickering on the screen, as Poland unlocked the doors.

Not yet. Been in with PSD! Jx

'You'd better come in,' Poland said, reading the message on the screen of Dixon's phone as he locked the doors again behind them. 'Dragged her in, have they?'

'Professional Standards. They'll have been interviewing her about the Albanian thing.'

'She enjoying being back on CID?' asked Poland. He was dressed from head to foot in green, his plastic apron smeared with blood. Thankfully, he'd remembered to rip off his latex gloves before he pulled his mask down below his chin.

'Loving it, although she's not got long before she'll be off on maternity leave.'

'April, isn't it?'

'End of April.' Dixon hesitated in the open door of the lab, the charred body of Trevor Bishop stretched out on the slab in front of him.

'Here,' said Poland, handing him a mask and the jar of Vicks VapoRub. 'This'll help.'

'Thanks.' A large blob on his top lip, then Dixon flicked the elastic loops of the mask behind his ears and pinched the wire on the bridge of his nose.

'His hands were tied behind his back,' said Poland. 'Blue nylon rope. It melted and largely burnt away in the fire, but there are still traces of it left. See here,' pointing with a scalpel. 'There might be more of it in the boot of the car. I've told Scientific to keep an eye out for it.'

What was left of the soft tissue had been removed from Bishop's neck and was sitting in a stainless steel bowl on the side. Dixon grimaced and turned away.

'I had to do that so I could look at it under the microscope,' continued Poland. 'Sorry, should have said.'

'Cause of death?'

'A deep incision to the throat and consequent blood loss. Left to right, so your killer is right handed.' Poland drew his thumb across his neck to illustrate. 'Very little smoke inhaled into the lungs, as we hoped, so he was probably at the point of death when the fire was started.'

'What about a time of death?' asked Dixon.

'That's going to be difficult, given the extent of the fire damage. There are still traces of rigor mortis, there's some muscle on his right calf, so that's maybe eighteen hours. Stomach contents look like scampi and chips, so he probably had lunch yesterday as normal and was killed not long after that, say between two and four.'

'Sounds like a pub lunch,' said Dixon.

'There was beer.'

'And it's definitely Bishop?'

'Dental records are a match. I'm just waiting for DNA.'

'So, he meets his killer for lunch in a pub, then is killed between two and the video timed at 15.09, then it was AirDropped just before eight that night.'

'I spoke to Donald,' said Poland. 'He said there was a large quantity of blood under what's left of the carpet in the boot. He thinks Bishop might have been standing at the back of the car, maybe even leaning in, had his throat cut and was then bundled straight in. The right carotid artery was severed, so the fire must have been started within a minute or two of the incision being made.'

'So, if he was driven to the woods in the boot, they must have been close by.'

'*Very* close by.'

'Which makes it more likely he met his killer in the woods. There were two cars there, don't forget.' Dixon was leaning back against the vacant slab, his back to Bishop's body, adjusting his face mask. 'The killer ties Bishop's hands behind his back, marches him to the boot of his shiny new Tesla, and slits his throat before pushing him in.'

'Wouldn't have taken a second,' said Poland.

Dixon was waiting for the electric gates to open at the bottom of the ramp to the staff car park. If he was going to be arrested for something, far better to have his car under cover.

Three missed calls from Jane. Still, telling him what had been said would be a disciplinary matter for her and he wasn't having that, wasn't putting her in that position. If nothing else, they might need her salary coming in.

The incident room was quiet, phones ringing out. Only four workstations were occupied, the tops of heads visible as the occupants whispered to each other behind the partitioning. Jane's handbag was on the floor, next to an empty chair.

Dixon sat down and spun round to look at the whiteboards, a new photograph stuck top middle. 'Who's that?' he asked.

Mark's head shot up from behind the computer opposite.

'You're here.'

'Well spotted.'

'Er, right, yeah, it's that programme seller at the Bridgwater carnival we can't account for. Everyone else has been identified. We've asked the carnival committee and no one knows who he is. That's the only other shot we've got of him, unfortunately. Always got his back to the bloody camera.' Mark clearly couldn't help himself. 'Shouldn't you be . . . ? I mean, we thought you'd be steering well clear of this place.'

Dixon had stood up and was staring at the grainy photograph. 'Where's it from?'

'It's the security camera in the phone shop.'

A bobble hat and a hi-vis tabard. Sideways on; no facial hair was about the best anyone could say. 'And no one knows who he is?'

'Nope.'

'It could be Harper, couldn't it?' asked Louise, standing up from behind a computer.

'I thought I told you to go home?'

'Here we go,' said Mark, nodding towards the Professional Standards Department at the far end of the atrium.

'What the bloody hell is going on?' Louise almost snarled. 'These bloody people. Why can't they just leave you to get on with the job?'

It was a nice thought, and it had crossed his mind. Several times. 'They'll tell you they're just doing theirs,' he said, trying to see both sides.

Fuck that.

Dixon glanced out of the corner of his eye, watching the door swing shut behind Carlisle and Larkin as they set off along the landing towards him.

'Where's Jane?' he asked.

'Probably trying to get hold of you,' replied Mark. 'She took her phone with her, wherever she went.'

'Just tell her to go home and get Monty out of the cottage. All right?'

'Yes, Sir.'

'Tell her to do it now. They'll be executing a search warrant and I don't want some twat going after my dog with one of those snare things.'

Dixon turned to face Carlisle and Larkin, who were now walking across the incident room towards him. The lift was coming up on the far side of the atrium, Jane watching events unfold from behind the glass.

'Always turn into the wind,' he whispered, smiling at Louise.

'Good luck, Sir,' she said.

Carlisle and Larkin stopped in front of Dixon, Larkin standing to one side, between Dixon and the door, glaring at Louise and Mark. The classic arrest position.

'Detective Chief Inspector Nicholas Dixon, I am arresting you on suspicion of the murder of Besim Raslan.' Carlisle was clearly enjoying the moment too much. 'You do not have to say anything, but it may harm your defence if you do not mention when questioned something you later rely on in court.'

'This is fucking ridiculous,' hissed Mark.

'Wind your neck in, Constable,' snapped Larkin.

'Anything you do say may be given in evidence.'

Chapter Twenty-Eight

Carlisle and Larkin had walked slowly to the glass lift on the far side of the atrium. Deliberately so, almost certainly, to extract maximum embarrassment.

Dixon had known everyone was watching the procession. Just as every head had turned on the way down in the glass lift; even on the ground floor, where too many uniformed officers to count had their faces glued to the glass partition to sneak a look.

The custody sergeant's face had been a picture; more used to seeing Dixon checking in a suspect, rather than being checked in. She had been forewarned and managed to mask her double take when murder was mentioned. Almost.

'I'm sure you understand, Sir,' she said hesitantly. 'We have—'

'Questions you have to ask, boxes you have to tick.'

'Yes, Sir.' Avoiding eye contact now, staring at the custody sheet on the desk in front of her.

'Surname?'

'Dixon.'

'First name?'

'Nicholas.'

'Time?'

'Time of arrest was eighteen thirty-seven,' replied Carlisle.

'Offence?'

'Suspicion of murder.' Carlisle again, even the custody officer at the adjacent counter leaning around the partition to sneak a look.

'Place of arrest?'

'Police Centre, Express Park.'

'We've got your photograph and biometric data on the system and we can dispense with the blood test, I think. Do you want a solicitor?'

'Yes.'

'I thought you were one,' Larkin said sarcastically.

'A solicitor who acts for himself has a fool for a client,' was Dixon's reply.

'Duty solicitor's in with someone at the moment, Sir, so we'll have to put you in a cell while you wait,' said the custody sergeant, with an apologetic wince.

'That's fine.'

'Any medical conditions we need to be aware of?'

'I'm type 1 diabetic,' replied Dixon, placing his insulin pen in the tray with his phone, belt, shoelaces and wallet. 'I'll need my insulin and something to eat about seven o'clock.' He took a half-eaten packet of fruit pastilles out of his jacket pocket. 'I'll keep these, if I may. Just in case my blood sugar drops.'

The long walk to the cell, the jangle of keys. He had thought his composure might crack when the door slammed behind him, but it hadn't.

White walls all around, apart from the inside of the grey steel door; sitting on the concrete plinth that doubled for a bed, a miserable bit of rolled up foam against the wall at the end, the smell of bleach stinging the insides of his nostrils. A sure sign a drunk and disorderly had been in there before him.

It was a far cry from a wild and open beach in winter, the rain coming in horizontally, his dog sniffing along the lines of fetid seaweed.

The murder of Besim Raslan. Dixon knew there must be new evidence coming from somewhere, but what? There was no way on God's clean earth it would be based on anything Jane may or may not have said, so it must be something else.

Take a deep breath and count to ten. *And remember, old son, there's no way a jury will convict you of anything – repeat it often enough and you might actually start to believe it.*

It was self defence; the dead of night, intruders breaking into his cottage. Perhaps his legal training had given him an irrational faith in the judicial system? Either way, it looked as if he'd soon be finding out.

Voices outside. The viewing hatch slid open, before slamming shut just as quickly.

'Just open the door, will you.'

Dixon recognised Charlesworth's voice, followed by the jangling of keys again.

'Wait outside.'

'I'll need to lock you in, Sir,' said a suitably chastened custody officer.

'Well, Nick.' Charlesworth waited until the door was being locked behind him. 'What *have* you done?'

'Nothing, Sir.'

'Of course you haven't. I'm not sure where this rubbish is coming from, but we'll get to the bottom of it, have no fear.'

'I gave a detailed statement at the time and it was looked at by the IOPC.'

'I've read it, but the problem you've got is the other Albanian is now saying the shotgun was yours and you assaulted them with it as they were retreating from your cottage. If that's right—'

'It's not.'

'You said you only held the shotgun by the barrels, but your fingerprints have been found on the stock and both triggers.'

'Then they must've been planted there.'

Charlesworth was pacing up and down in front of Dixon, not that there was room for more than three. He was avoiding eye contact too – there was a lot of that going on. 'Who would do that?' he demanded, stopping and turning to face Dixon.

'It was a complaint from the Albanian family of the dead man that triggered the Reg 15 Notice. And now an Albanian has miraculously recovered his memory.' Dixon shrugged. 'I'd have to say the Albanians would do that. Zavan's lot out of the old bookies in Whiteladies Road.'

'What about the fingerprints?'

'Bought and paid for. I look forward to reading the technician's witness statement and it'll be interesting to see if he or she holds up under cross-examination too, although they'll probably disappear before any trial, not that they know it yet.'

'This Raslan fellow was in a permanent vegetative state by all accounts, not expected to regain consciousness. There'd even been talk of switching off his life support machine before he died.'

'I wouldn't be surprised if they helped him on his way in that case,' said Dixon. 'To give them leverage.'

'It was a cardiac arrest, according to the post mortem.'

'I'll be getting Roger Poland to have a look at it in the first instance.'

'They probably want you on their payroll,' offered Charlesworth, pacing up and down again. 'Now you've been promoted, and especially if you'd got the super's job.'

'That may be it.'

Charlesworth might be on side, but he'd cover his own arse first and foremost. Two years in a law firm had taught Dixon a great many things, one of them being that there are certain people you only take into your confidence if you want everybody to know your business. Office politics; it was worse than police station politics.

'My understanding is you'll be released under investigation after the interview,' continued Charlesworth. 'So, that means suspension from duty, of course. Full pay unless and until you're charged. Deborah Potter's taking on the carnival thing. Just don't do anything stupid.'

'I won't, Sir.'

'If there's anything you need, and I mean *anything*, use my name and I'll authorise it.'

Time to see if Charlesworth would put his money where his mouth was – figuratively speaking, of course. 'My guess is I'll be getting a visit from Zavan, so it would be good if I could be wearing a wire. They'll probably check for that, though, so a backup would be useful. One of the micro recorders in the collar of my coat, something like that.'

'They're expensive.' Charlesworth was examining Dixon over his horn-rimmed glasses. 'But I'll see to it. The requisition can go through in my name.'

'Thank you, Sir.'

'I must say, you're being very calm about all of this. I'd be climbing the walls.'

'I have an irrational faith in the jury system, Sir. It comes from being a solicitor, I think.'

'Let's hope it doesn't get that far.'

'What the fuck is going on here?' Jane shouted, running across the road with her warrant card in one hand, phone in the other – video recorder on.

She had heard Monty barking before she switched her engine off in the car park of the Red Cow, three police vans and several unmarked cars lined up along the pavement outside the cottage on the other side of the road.

Uniformed officers were milling about outside, others in plain clothes peering in the front window, tapping on the glass and laughing.

'We're waiting for Armed Response,' replied a dog handler holding a snare.

'In case we have to shoot it,' said another, with a battering ram in one hand.

'Don't be so bloody stupid.' Jane pushed past them. 'Let me through.'

Her arrival had at last attracted the attention of the plain clothes detectives at the window. 'Who are you?' demanded the one who had been tapping on the glass.

'Detective Sergeant Winter. I live here.'

'The cottage belongs to DCI Dixon and we're here to execute a search warrant.'

'I live here as well, and that's my dog as much as it is his.'

'We can't let you in. The bloody thing's going berserk.'

'Hardly surprising with you idiots tapping on the window.'

'May I remind you that is no way to speak to a senior officer, Sergeant.'

'And that is no way for a senior officer to behave.' Jane paused, long enough to make the point. 'Sir,' she said emphatically. 'You should be aware I have footage of you banging on the window deliberately to antagonise my dog, so if any harm comes to him, we'll be holding you personally responsible. Is that clear?'

'That dog is a danger to—'

'*You* maybe,' interrupted Jane. 'He doesn't suffer fools. And you can expect a formal complaint to be made about your conduct when DCI Dixon sees this film.'

Not that she would show it to him; *he's got enough on his plate at the moment.*

Several thumps at the inside of the front door, accompanied by more snarling and growling; Monty was showing no sign of calming down in the immediate future.

'You don't need that,' Jane said, turning to the dog handler with the snare. 'And I've got a key, so you don't need that, either,' glaring at the battering ram. 'Now, I'm going in to get my dog, and then you can execute your search warrant till you're blue in the bloody faces. All right?'

Jane walked around to the back of the cottage and put her key in the lock. Another thud, against the inside of the back door this time. 'It's me, you idiot,' she said, pressing her face to the frosted glass. Then she pushed open the door a crack, Monty's muzzle appearing, sniffing the air, then her hand.

She pushed open the door far enough to squeeze through sideways, all the time careful not to allow Monty to get out, blocking his exit route with her knees. Then she flicked the light on and knelt down, the dog burying his head in her arms, whimpering softly.

'It's all right, old son,' she said, scratching him behind his ears. 'I'm here now.' She was watching the plain clothes officers looking in the front window of the cottage, keeping tabs on her, no doubt, so she didn't tamper with evidence; not that there was any to tamper with.

A dog treat or two from the jar on the worktop, more scratching behind the ears, then she clipped on Monty's lead and opened the back door.

'And you should know better.' Jane scowled at the dog handler. 'You could see they were deliberately winding him up.'

No reply.

'He was going nuts,' said the officer with the battering ram.

'He was doing his job.'

'Yeah.'

'Thank you, Sergeant,' said the detective. He was holding a piece of paper in his outstretched hand. 'The search warrant.'

'You can stick it—' Jane thought better of it, just in time. 'On the side in the kitchen,' she said, stalking off towards her car, Monty trotting along beside her. 'And drop the latch on your way out.'

The duty solicitor turned out to be Michael Salter, of Michael Salter & Co. Dixon hadn't been unimpressed the last time they had crossed swords, and it had only taken Salter twenty minutes to get the measure of this case, once he'd got over his surprise.

'I need to see a copy of your original witness statement,' he had said, his hand on the doorknob. 'I should have been given it. Pure bloody incompetence, you know what they're li—' Salter stopped himself when he remembered he was talking to a police officer. Too late, but no harm done. Dixon knew the score.

Now he was sitting in the corner of interview room one, waiting while Salter read his statement.

'Seems perfectly clear to me. And entirely reasonable. What did you say at your disciplinary interview?'

'I just kept referring them to it. At that stage they had nothing new to put to me and were just fishing.'

'Good.'

Carlisle and Larkin walked in and sat down on the other side of the table; another interview where Dixon would be grateful for the room with the table, only this time he was the suspect.

Introductions over, Dixon left Salter to it, listening impassively to the sparring going on.

'My client will not be answering questions arising from matters already covered in his comprehensive witness statement dated sixteenth November last.'

Salter must have repeated that phrase at least six times before Carlisle finally got the message.

'All right then, let's move on to pastures new. We have a statement from Ardita Besmir, who is now able to recall the events of that night. He says that Mr Raslan was carrying the machete and he a crowbar. He maintains that the shotgun was yours. What d'you say to that?'

'He's lying,' replied Dixon.

'Really. Tell me then, why would he lie?'

'You'd need to ask him that.'

'He says there was a struggle between you and Mr Raslan, during which the gun was discharged, and then both of them were retreating from your cottage when you attacked them with the shotgun, swinging it like a baseball bat.'

Dixon remained silent.

'What d'you say to that?' asked Carlisle.

'My client has already made it clear that Ardita Besmir is lying.'

'About which bit?'

'All of it,' said Dixon.

'Do you deny that it was your shotgun?'

'Yes.'

'In your statement, you said that you held the gun by the barrels and dropped it straight into an evidence bag after the incident without touching any other part of it.'

'That is correct.'

'How then is it that we've found your fingerprints on the stock and both triggers?'

'It is my client's position,' said Salter, diving in, 'that the fingerprints on the stock and triggers are not his, but that, if they are, they have been placed there by a person or persons unknown. You will not be surprised to learn that we will be insisting on an independent examination of the shotgun by a fingerprint expert of our choice.'

'You're saying the prints were planted, you mean?'

'Precisely.'

Dixon was content to leave Salter to it; a phrase involving a dog and barking yourself sprang to mind.

'We will also be insisting upon a second post mortem,' continued Salter.

'Why?' Larkin had been unable to contain himself, but soon regretted it when Carlisle glared at him.

'Why would you want to do that?' Carlisle frowned. 'It was a cardiac arrest, pure and simple.'

Dixon decided to step in. 'If you need me to spell it out, then you won't understand, Sir. It would also tell me that you have absolutely no understanding whatsoever of the people we are dealing with.'

'Who?'

Dixon glanced at Salter. 'Res ipsa loquitur. I refer to the direct translation, of course.' Salter would know, one lawyer to another.

'What is that – Latin?' demanded Carlisle.

'The thing speaks for itself.' There was a lyrical tone to Salter's voice.

'What people?'

'For all I know, you're on their payroll, Sir,' replied Dixon, matter of fact. 'The fingerprint technician certainly is.'

'You're sure of that, are you?'

'Well, I never touched the triggers or the stock, so you tell me how my fingerprints got there.' Dixon folded his arms. 'If you want to pursue this elaborate charade, that is entirely a matter for you, Sir. But you're having your strings pulled.'

'You're not doing yourself any favours here, y'know,' Carlisle huffed, closing the file on the table in front of him.

'I'm quite happy to take my chances in front of a jury.' Dixon knew Charlesworth would be watching. Potter too, probably. 'You'll be telling me next you're on my side, Sir.'

'Which pathologist will you be getting for the second post mortem?' asked Carlisle, turning to Salter.

'We'll be asking Dr Poland to look at it in the first instance,' replied Salter. 'He will advise us of a suitable pathologist for a second post mortem, if appropriate.'

'Does he do private work?'

'He does.'

'All right. You'll be returned to custody pending the search of your cottage, Dixon. This interview is terminated at twenty-one fifty-two.'

Chapter Twenty-Nine

'Released under investigation,' Charlesworth had said.

How long does it bloody well take?

Dixon was stretched out on the miserable foam mattress, his hands behind his head, wondering if Jane had got to the cottage in time to stop someone going after Monty with a snare. He was also beginning to wonder if they had found something during the search. It was the only possible explanation for why he was still lying there, twiddling his thumbs.

Even Professional Standards couldn't take this long to release someone under investigation, surely? There were only three forms to fill in, after all.

A knock on the door, then the vision panel slid open.

'What time is it?' asked Dixon.

'Gone midnight,' came the reply. 'Detective Sergeant Winter dropped in your blood testing kit and night insulin. There's a cup of tea and a couple of biscuits if you need them as well.'

'Thank you.' Dixon stood up and walked over to the door.

'I'll need to wait for the insulin and the testing kit, I'm afraid, Sir.' The custody officer's voice had reduced to a whisper, clearly unsure whether he should call Dixon 'Sir' or not. He was avoiding eye contact too. 'She asked me to tell you she's got your dog and he's fine. She's left him with Dr Poland for the night.'

Dixon sat down on the edge of the concrete plinth and used the lance to draw blood from his fingertip, then lined up the end of the testing strip with the droplet and waited for the bleep. 'I'll need the biscuits.'

'If you need anything else, let us know.'

'I will.' Dixon handed back the testing kit and insulin – jab done through his shirt – and thought he might as well ask. 'I was told I was going to be released under investigation?'

'I'm not really sure . . . I think they're going to interview you again. They're just waiting for your solicitor to get here.'

Then the panel slammed shut with that disturbing metallic 'clank'.

They had found something then. The Albanians were being thorough. Still, they'd had plenty of opportunity with Monty safely out of the way on Bonfire Night.

Sent to prison for a crime he didn't commit. Now, there was an ignominious end to his career if ever there was one, and certainly not what his parents had expected. He sighed. Murder would never stick, though; they'd never be able to prove he intended to kill Raslan, so that made it manslaughter at worst.

Seven years.

The vision panel snapped back, dragging him back to his senses before too much doom and gloom set in.

'Interview. Your solicitor's here.'

The walk was a challenge with no shoelaces, but he got there without falling flat on his face. Michael Salter was waiting for him, sitting with his legs crossed, reading what looked like a witness statement. Corduroys and a pullover; dressed in a hurry when he was dragged out of bed.

'They're saying they found shotgun cartridges under your bed,' said Salter, when the door was closed behind Dixon. 'And I'm guessing you'll say they were planted?'

'I will, because they were.'

'What if they've got your DNA on them?'

'That's hardly surprising if they're under my bed.'

'Four shells, in a box.' Salter slid the statement across the table. 'It explains why they haven't released you, and it probably means they've got enough to ask for a charging decision from the CPS, I'm afraid.'

A knock at the door. 'Are you ready?'

Carlisle and Larkin looked sombre rather than smug this time. Maybe it was the time of night?

Dixon wasn't listening to the formalities, instead wondering what Jane was up to. Staying out of trouble, hopefully.

'You're still under caution,' said Carlisle. 'Now, as you may be aware, we executed a search warrant at your home this evening. During that search we found your ice axe and trench cosh, and . . .' – he paused for dramatic effect – 'a box with four shotgun cartridges in it. What have you got to say about that?'

'It was planted,' said Dixon, folding his arms.

'Who by?'

'The same people who arranged for my fingerprints to appear on the shotgun butt.'

'The cartridges are from the same batch as the empty shell casings found in the gun at your property last year. What do you say to that?'

'They're nothing if not thorough.'

'All right, you say they've been planted.' Carlisle leaned forward, his elbows on the table in front of him. 'How on earth would anyone be able to do that with your dog in the house? The search team certainly couldn't get in until Sergeant Winter turned up.'

'We never leave Monty in the cottage on his own on Guy Fawkes Night and, as you know, both Sergeant Winter and I were on duty that night, so he went to her parents'. Anyone watching the cottage would have known that and had ample opportunity to plant the shotgun cartridges.'

'Are you telling me that dog's frightened of fireworks?'

'Yes.'

'He doesn't sound the type to be frightened of much at all.'

'I take it you don't own a dog,' said Dixon.

'Would you like to know where the cartridges were found?'

'My solicitor said they were found under my bed.'

'Under the divan drawer, to be precise. The officer had to pull the drawer right out, off its runners, and there they were.'

'A good place to plant them. I'd be unlikely to find them first.'

'Where did you buy them?' asked Carlisle. 'It must've been illegally, because you don't have a shotgun licence.'

'I don't have a shotgun licence because I don't have a shotgun. And I did not buy these cartridges, or any others for that matter.' Spelling it out. Again.

'If we're just going to go over old ground, Inspector, I will advise my client to answer no further questions,' said Salter. 'He's made his position clear in relation to the gun, the fingerprints and the cartridges. Now, is there anything else you have to put to him tonight?'

'We're having the cartridges tested for DNA, Dixon,' said Carlisle, his eyes narrowing.

'They were found under my client's bed,' said Salter. 'So, it's somewhat inevitable they will have his DNA on them, don't you think?'

'This interview is terminated at one fifty-three. You will be returned to custody, Dixon, and you should know that we will be referring the matter to the Crown Prosecution Service in the morning for a charging decision.'

◆ ◆ ◆

It had been a long night, and Dixon would have spent much of it tossing and turning if the bed hadn't been so bloody uncomfortable.

Morning had brought with it the usual shift change too, the new custody officer adamant he knew nothing about Dixon's insulin, a situation soon resolved when the custody sergeant stepped in.

Breakfast had come and gone, Dixon still sitting there twiddling his thumbs mid-morning when the vision panel slid across abruptly.

'You're going to be charged, Dixon,' Carlisle said. 'I take no pleasure in it, but we are where we are.'

Deep breath, count to ten.

It was an unusually large crowd, oddly enough. No other 'customers' in the custody suite hadn't helped, but everyone had made an effort to be there. After all, it's not every day you get to see a detective chief inspector charged with murder.

Three officers helping the custody sergeant, Dixon flanked by Carlisle and Larkin. His mind was racing as he leaned forward and signed the custody sheet.

'And initial here, and here.'

He was only grateful his hand wasn't trembling.

'Nicholas John Dixon, you are charged that on first November in the county of Somerset you did murder Besim Raslan contrary to common law. Do you have anything to say?'

'No.'

The custody sergeant nodded, almost imperceptibly. 'You'll be appearing at Taunton Magistrates at two o'clock. Your solicitor has been advised and will see you there. All right?'

◆ ◆ ◆

A loud thump on the door echoed around the tiny cell. 'You're up next. Twenty minutes.'

'What time is it?' shouted Dixon, sitting up.

'Four o'clock.'

They know how to keep you waiting, these bloody magistrates, thought Dixon. Still, he'd managed to grab another couple of hours' sleep. He took the fruit pastilles out of his jacket pocket and popped a couple into his mouth, letting the sugar sit under his tongue. Odd, the effect of stress on blood sugar levels. Or maybe the slight tremble in his hand was fear?

He'd never taken that much notice of bail applications, but then he'd never been on the receiving end of one before. Murderers rarely bother to apply for it, let alone get it.

Keys jangling.

'Right, up we go,' said the custody officer.

Dixon rubbed his wrists as he climbed the stairs to the dock, shoelaces back in now so falling flat on his face was unlikely. The handcuffs had been a pain in the arse, though.

'Are these really necessary?' he had asked.

'Rules is rules,' had been the gruff response, softened with an apologetic shrug. 'And it's only while you're in transit.'

He looked up as he reached the top of the stairs, much as he had done when he was led out to the van in the caged area at the back of Express Park. That had been a mistake; a multitude of faces pressed to the glass in the upstairs windows, trying to catch a glimpse of him in handcuffs. Dave Harding, Mark Pearce and Louise among the crowd, a nervous wave from Lou; no sign of Jane though.

The light was going outside, the gloom creeping in through the skylight windows in the courtroom.

Lost a complete day, he thought. Might have to get used to the idea of losing a few more too.

The dock offered an unusual perspective on the courtroom scene; unusual for him, anyway. The backs of heads below, all looking up towards the bench, where three magistrates were sitting, looking down their noses at him.

Still, a late hearing wasn't all bad; the press box was empty, the court reporter's pub lunch dragging on a bit, probably.

He pretended not to notice Jane and Roger sitting in the public gallery. Jane looked white as a sheet; stress and diabetes was one thing, but stress and pregnancy another altogether.

The Crown Prosecutor stood up, keeping his back to Dixon; hoping he wouldn't recognise him, perhaps. 'Your Worships, this is a murder charge, which will obviously be committed to the Crown Court for trial. I should add that the defendant is a serving police officer with the Avon and Somerset force.'

'We know,' said the Margaret Rutherford lookalike sitting in the middle of the three. 'We ought to declare that the defendant is known to us, having appeared before this court on numerous occasions.'

'He is known to me as well, Your Worship,' said the Crown Prosecutor, turning around to face Dixon at last, his face flushed.

'I'm assuming you'll be making a bail application, Mr Salter,' said the magistrate.

'I am, Your Worship, yes,' he replied, jumping to his feet. 'The charge is to be vigorously defended. You're familiar with the facts of the case?'

'We are.'

'The defendant will say that he was acting in self defence, the only substantive issue then being ownership and use of the shotgun in the struggle that ensued and whether or not the force applied was reasonable, both matters for a jury, of course. In the meantime, the defendant is a responsible member of the community, a highly decorated serving police officer, who presents no flight risk whatsoever. He is getting married on Christmas Eve and his fiancée is pregnant. She is here in this court.' Salter spun round, a theatrical wave of his arm in Jane's direction.

'What is the Crown's position?'

'The Crown does not object to bail, Your Worship,' replied the Crown Prosecutor, ignoring the wild gesticulations from Carlisle, who was sitting behind him. 'It then becomes purely a matter of whether, and if so what, conditions are applied to it.'

Dixon glanced across at Jane, but her head was bowed, her eyes fixed on the floor in front of her.

'I would be seeking unconditional bail, Your Worships,' said Salter.

'What about contacting witnesses?' asked the magistrate, her question addressed to the prosecutor.

'The main prosecution witness is in prison. There's also a Detective Sergeant Winter, but my understanding is that it is to Sergeant Winter that the defendant is to be married and they are likely to be husband and wife before any trial takes place.'

'That is correct, Your Worships,' confirmed Salter. 'If I may say so, there seems no real purpose to be served by the imposition of

233

any conditions in this case. My client has no intention of fleeing – indeed, he wishes these matters to be placed before a jury as soon as possible – so even a condition that he report to a police station daily would seem entirely unnecessary.'

'What about surrendering his passport?'

'I'm instructed that he doesn't have one, Your Worships. It expired earlier this year and he has not yet renewed it.'

The prosecutor stood up. 'Your Worships, the Crown is content for bail to be granted with only one condition, if that assists, namely that the defendant resides elsewhere. His own home is the scene of the incident on sixteenth November last and there may yet be further forensic tests to be carried out.'

'Seems reasonable, and there'll be no need for us to give reasons in that case. We just need an address then,' said the magistrate. 'Mr Salter, someone is trying to attract your attention from the public gallery.'

Good old Roger.

Salter walked over to the public gallery, spoke to Poland, their conversation whispered, and then returned to the bench. 'Your Worships, that is Home Office pathologist Dr Roger Poland, who has very kindly said that the defendant can reside with him until his trial.'

Carlisle slid out from behind the desk and stormed out.

'Good,' said the magistrate, ignoring the commotion. 'The defendant will stand.'

Dixon did as he was told.

'Your case is to be committed to the Crown Court for trial, and I hardly need ask if you understand what that means. In the meantime, you will be granted bail conditional upon you residing with Dr Poland; the court clerk will take a note of the address. And may I add one last thing?' She smiled. 'Good luck to you.'

'Give me ten minutes to complete the paperwork,' said the custody officer when they reached the bottom of the stairs. 'Crikey, you look like you're going to . . . it's over there. There's no lock on it.'

Dixon closed the door behind him, lifted the seat and vomited.

Chapter Thirty

Jane ran across the car park and threw her arms around Dixon when he emerged from the side entrance at Taunton Magistrates Court.

'I never thought you'd get bail,' she said, lunging forward to kiss him on the lips.

He turned his head at the last second, the kiss landing on his cheek.

'Are you all right?' she demanded. 'What's that you're eating?'

'An Extra Strong Mint.' He licked his lips, an unfamiliar tremble in his voice. 'The security guard gave it to me.'

'Why?'

'You don't want to know.'

'You threw up your lunch.' Poland had followed Jane across the car park. 'You can't fool a medic,' he said, grimacing.

Jane still had her arms around Dixon's waist. 'Have you been sick?'

'When I got back down to the cells.'

'You'll need something to eat. Have you checked your blood?'

'I'm fine. I just need my Land Rover out of the staff car park, and my dog.'

'He's at my place,' said Poland. 'We left the telly on for him and there was a squirrel in the back garden to keep him entertained.'

'Thanks, Roger. Look, I—'

'Think nothing of it, and you're both welcome to stay as long as you like. It's a big place and there's only me rattling around in it.' Poland turned for his car. 'So, what happens now?'

'A plea and directions hearing in the new year, then the trial in the summer, maybe. You know how long these things take.'

'You'll be around for the birth then, whatever happens.' Poland put his arm around Jane's shoulders.

'It'll be sorted one way or the other long before that.'

'You've got a plan?' she asked.

'Nothing for you to worry about. You just concentrate on staying out of trouble.'

'Yeah, right.' She fished a phone out of her handbag. 'Here, I've got you that old iPhone out of the drawer in the sideboard and put a pay-as-you-go SIM in it. You've only got twenty quid credit, though.'

'Where's your car?' asked Dixon.

'Roger's house.'

Dixon knew it wouldn't be long before he picked up a tail, keeping half an eye on the main road outside the Magistrates Court for a black Range Rover.

A black Range Rover. The last time he had crossed paths with the Albanians they had a whole fleet of the things, and they would be paying him a visit sooner rather than later, no doubt.

To collect.

'I think I'd better leave my Land Rover where it is – safely out of the way in the staff car park.'

'You're welcome to use mine.' Poland lobbed him the keys. 'I should be walking to work anyway and it's not that far. There's not a lot of fuel in it, though. Sorry. And I'll need my cases out of the back.'

'Thanks, Roger.'

Jane's text arrived as Dixon was filling up Poland's car with diesel twenty minutes later.

I love you and we'll get through this Jx

He sighed, knowing his reply would not be what she was expecting, but it would have to do this time.

Need to find the Rural Crimes team. Where is he?

He ignored the fuel station attendant waving at him from the kiosk, and the voice that came over the tannoy. 'No mobile phones. Pump 4, please.'

It hadn't been the first time that day everyone had stared at him.

Nige is here, in the canteen.

Dixon tapped out a reply – *Gold Corner pumping station. 30 mins* – then went into the kiosk to face the music.

Dixon had caught a nice pike the last time he'd been at Gold Corner, out on the South Drain, although the owner of the fishing rod had been shot in the eye and pushed in the river. Still, the fish had gone back alive and well, at least.

238

He parked at the far end of the car park, just in case there were any CCTV cameras on the pumping station.

Cole arrived in an unmarked car, closely followed by Jane in her VW Golf. She parked behind him and took off her seatbelt, slumping back into the driver's seat when Dixon waved at her to stay where she was.

The less she knew, the better. For her own sake.

'I heard what's going on, Sir,' said Cole, climbing out of his car. 'Whatever I can do to help.'

'I was hoping you'd say that, Nige.'

'I remember it. I got there not long after, bagged up the evidence. An ice axe and a leather stick.'

'It means Professional Standards may well want to have a word with you.'

'What do I tell them?'

'The truth, Nige. Nothing more, nothing less.'

'Oh, right. Well, is there anything else I can do?'

Dixon leaned back against the bonnet of Poland's Volvo. 'I'm suspended, strictly speaking, so I can't give you an order, as such.'

'Bollocks to that.'

'We've been getting lots of reports of dog fighting in Berrow Dunes, near the nature reserve. That would be your remit, as rural crimes officer?'

'Yes, Sir.'

'Several concerned members of the public mentioned it to me when I was stuck doing Neighbourhood Watch liaison meetings. They said the perpetrators have been arriving by car along the flats and the fighting takes place in the dunes, in amongst the buckthorn.'

'What do you want me to do about it, Sir?'

'I'd suggest placing the area under surveillance. You'll need to requisition full surveillance equipment: a video camera with a zoom lens and a high-powered microphone. Get a night vision camera too, just in case. Watch the beach and you'll see them arrive that way.'

'Dog fighting?'

'Ideal for a surveillance operation, wouldn't you say?'

'How long?'

'As long as it takes.'

Chapter Thirty-One

'We must stop meeting like this,' said Dixon, when Jane finally got out of her car, Cole's rear lights disappearing along the lane.

'What was that all about?'

'Best you don't know.'

Jane was standing with her hands on her hips. 'I just don't get it,' she said. 'Where the fuck is this new evidence coming from? And what the hell is it all about?'

Dixon kicked a loose stone across the road into the hedge. 'The Albanians want me on their payroll.'

'That's the price of this all going away?'

'Probably. The fingerprints will disappear as if by magic, and Ardita Besmir will have a sudden lapse of memory again.'

'Fuck them.'

'I couldn't have put it better myself.'

Jane put her arms around him and kissed him on the lips. 'What are you going to do?'

'Roger's going to have a look at the post mortem, and he can recommend someone to do another if there's anything there. Then there's an independent report on the fingerprints. In the meantime, I'm going to take Monty for a walk or two and watch the carnival investigations unfold from a distance.'

'Potter's taken it over. Waller's still not turned up and she's rearrested Lionel Harper.'

'What for?'

'Don't ask me,' replied Jane, releasing her grip on Dixon. 'I'm out of the loop now.'

'Anything else?'

'The same accelerant was definitely used on Bishop and on Webb, but apart from that Scientific haven't come up with anything at all. The batteries on the Tesla didn't go up, but there's still bugger all to find there.' Jane shook her head. 'She's going to interview Harper again later with Maggie, which leaves me out on my ear. I think I'm being sidelined since you've been . . .'

'Sorry.'

'It's hardly your fault, is it.' She turned for her car. 'I'd better get back, anyway. I'll swing by the cottage, pick up some stuff and see you at Roger's later.'

'I'm used to him now.' Roger Poland was standing on his doorstep with his hands on his hips, watching Monty cocking his leg against the rear wheel of his Volvo.

'Thanks, Roger.'

'Jane rang me when they pulled you in and she stayed here last night, so I know what's been going on,' said Poland, shutting the front door behind Dixon. 'I've taken the rest of the week off work. Thought I might keep you out of troub . . . keep you company. Are you all right?'

'Fine,' he replied, watching the dog set off along the passageway towards the kitchen, the smell of cooking irresistible.

'You eaten?'

'Not yet.'

'I've got some pasta thing on the go, if you fancy it. There's plenty for two and you'd be doing me a favour.' Poland shuddered. 'It looks disgusting.'

'Thank you.'

'I'm not long back from the lab. I thought I'd better pop in and see what's been going on. Tea, coffee, there's a beer in the fridge?'

'Beer.'

'I had a quick look at the post mortem report for your Mr Raslan. He died in Bristol, so Leo did it. You know Leo Petersen?'

'I do.'

Poland opened a bottle of beer and handed it to Dixon, with a glass. 'Sit yourself down,' he said, gesturing to the kitchen table. 'Is Monty all right with pasta?'

'If there's no sauce on it,' replied Dixon, taking a swig from the bottle. 'You'll get a letter from my solicitor, but I'm going to be asking you to look at the post mortem officially. Then, if you think it worthwhile, we can get another one done.'

'You think Raslan was murdered?'

'The Albanians have got me right where they want me, and it all starts with the death of someone who was in a permanent vegetative state anyway. They probably think they did him a favour and it was his family who lodged the formal complaint, so they'll be being looked after, no doubt.'

Poland was stirring the pasta sauce that was noisily bubbling away in a frying pan on the hob.

'Then my fingerprints mysteriously appear all over the place and his accomplice suddenly remembers the events of that night.'

Another swig. 'In great detail. Not to mention shotgun cartridges under my bed.'

'I'll check they did a full tox screen then,' said Poland. 'I don't doubt Leo's conclusion that it was a cardiac arrest, but it's what caused the cardiac arrest you'll be interested in.'

'Precisely.'

'I did sneak a look at Raslan's notes.' Poland emptied a bag of pasta into a pan of boiling water. 'He had raised potassium levels, so potassium chloride is the most likely culprit, if you're right. A paralytic like succinylcholine would be no good because he was already on a ventilator, and besides, that wouldn't cause a cardiac arrest. He would've just stopped breathing.'

'Can you test for potassium chloride?'

'Not really, I'm afraid to say. The body breaks it down into potassium and chloride, both naturally occurring chemicals you'd expect to find. Raslan was suffering from renal failure too, so the fatal dose would've been much lower. And his records document hyperkalaemia, or raised potassium levels, over several weeks anyway. I'm not sure I'm going to be much help, I'm afraid, old chap.'

'Brilliant.'

'Someone must've got access to him in the ICU, so maybe check his visitors at the hospital?'

'I wouldn't put it past them to embed someone at the hospital,' muttered Dixon. 'They're nothing if not professional. I'm guessing they'll let me sweat for a couple of days before making their approach, promising to make it all go away if I play ball.'

'I'll have a look, by all means, but don't hold your breath, that's all I'm saying. I'm just not sure a tox screen is going to be the silver bullet you're looking for.'

'Charlesworth's being very good about it – offered me every assistance. It's just the Professional Standards Department, really. It's all their Christmases at once, a DCI in their sights.'

'Jane said you were pretty cut up by Raslan's death,' said Poland, a wooden spoon in one hand and a colander in the other.

'I was, I suppose, for an hour or two, but this business soon cured me of that.'

'It was him or you.'

Dixon braced himself for the clichés to come trotting out. Poland was doing his best, all the same.

'What else were you supposed to do? Let them kill you in your bed?'

'It's fine, Roger, really.'

'What's going on with the carnival investigation?' asked Poland, clearly deciding that a change of subject was in order.

'Deborah Potter's taken that over. There's a suspect in custody; he had plenty of motive, means and some opportunity. We're just waiting on the forensics, really.'

'You don't seem terribly enthusiastic about him.' Poland slid a plate of pasta across the table to Dixon, but he was watching Monty sniffing a small dollop on a plate on the tiled floor. It wasn't a good sign when the dog turned away, instead preferring to sit in the French windows, staring into the darkness.

'Have you got any cheese to grate on it?' asked Dixon.

Poland turned around to find Dixon doing his insulin injection through his shirt.

'How many times have I told you about that?' he grumbled.

'Yes, Mother.'

The pasta tasted better than it looked, mercifully.

'How is it?' asked Poland hesitantly.

'Better than prison food,' said Dixon, forcing a smile.

'You won't go to prison. No jury will ever convict you.'

He appreciated Poland's optimism, and the effort he was making. But the prospect of prison for a police officer was too horrible to contemplate. The alternative was spending the rest of his career

245

in an Albanian pocket, or until he was found out. And he would be found out. Corrupt police officers always are. Even if it is *eventually*.

No, once again, Jane had summed it up best.

'Fuck them.'

◆ ◆ ◆

Jane arrived back at Express Park just before ten o'clock to find the incident room deserted apart from Louise, who was sitting at a workstation.

'Looks like it's you and me,' she said, when Jane appeared at the top of the stairs. 'Maggie's working with Potter now.'

'Yeah.'

'He got bail then?'

'He did.'

'Potter sent everyone home, apart from Dave and Mark and the CCTV lot. They're still going back through the footage, looking for that unidentified programme seller in the hi-vis tabard. No sign of him yet.'

'Anything else come up?'

'Two payments of ten grand each going into Trevor Bishop's bank account. And you'll never guess who the payee was.'

'Surprise me.'

'Ian Szopinski. Potter's sent a team to pick him up.'

'Where is she?'

'Interviewing Harper again, although I'm not sure how far she's getting. Mark watched it for a minute on the monitor and he was "no commenting" everything. How's Nick doing? I mean *really*.'

'He'll be all right. He's getting Roger to look at the post mortem on the Albanian.' Jane dropped her handbag on the floor next to Louise's desk. 'Look after that for me, will you? I'm just nipping downstairs.'

She used the back stairs, bursting through the door just as keys were jangling on the inside.

'We shut at ten.'

'This is urgent,' said Jane. 'Please.'

The man stepped back – knew what was going on, probably – and besides, he should have had a call from Charlesworth's office by now. A retired uniformed sergeant, now employed as civilian admin staff and running the stores. 'This is for DCI Dixon?' he asked.

'Yes.'

'I've got it here,' he said, reaching for a small box off to the side, behind the Perspex screen. 'A full wire kit – which I'll probably not see again – and a micro recorder.'

'Do I need to sign for them?'

'Not this time.' The man shook his head, smiling at the same time. 'It's not often a civilian staffer gets to speak to the ACC. He did remember me, mind you. We were at Bristol together, back in the day.'

'Thank you.'

'My pleasure, Sergeant,' said the man. 'And wish DCI Dixon luck.'

'I will.'

DCS Potter was standing in front of the whiteboards when Jane reappeared in the incident room, the surveillance equipment safely stashed in the glovebox of her car.

'Ah, there you are,' said Potter. 'How is he?'

'Bearing up,' replied Jane.

'None of us believes this crap, I hope he knows that.'

'He does.'

'And we'd all have done exactly the same in his position. At least, I hope I'd have had the guts and presence of mind to do it, anyway.'

'I'll tell him you said that.'

'You do that.' Potter turned back to the whiteboards. 'We need him on this case, really, instead of sitting at home feeling sorry for himself.'

'Did Harper say anything useful?' asked Jane.

'He didn't say anything at all and we've got no real reason to continue holding him,' Potter replied impatiently. 'I want you and Louise to focus on the estate agents' computers. Chase up High Tech for their report in the morning. All right?'

'Yes, Ma'am.'

'Is that it?' whispered Louise.

'Looks like we really are surplus to requirements.' Jane curled her lip. 'Which is odd, when she's grumbling about being understaffed.'

'Katie will be fast asleep by now,' said Louise, looking at her watch. 'You've got that to look forward to.'

'What?'

'Getting home long after your kid's gone to bed.'

Chapter Thirty-Two

It had been a little white lie, but a lie all the same: taking Monty for a late night walk on the beach. Jane needed sleep, so Dixon had even promised to be quiet when they got back.

Instead, he was sitting outside a house in Clyce Road, Highbridge, watching for any sign of life.

The less Jane knew, the better.

The streetlights were still on, casting an eerie glow across the front of the small end-of-terrace house, only just visible through the overgrown vegetation in the front garden. The curtains were drawn in the bay window, a crack in the frosted glass of the front door.

The car seemed out of place. Last year's number plate on a shiny silver Mercedes of some description that was parked on four paving slabs resting on a sparsely gravelled drive, the stones spilling out into the road. Anyone getting out of the passenger side would get soaking wet from an overhanging shrub that was dropping its leaves on the roof; enough to confirm the car hadn't moved for a couple of days.

There was a light on inside the house, glinting through gaps along the top of the curtains – where some of the hooks had snapped off – a faint glow visible behind the front door.

Dixon waited. Much longer and the streetlights will go off, he thought, pulling on a pair of latex gloves. Yes, technically speaking it was none of his business any more, and the shit he was in would only get deeper if he was found to be interfering in the investigation, but Potter had scaled back the search for Adam Waller and even vetoed a search of his property, apparently on the grounds that he hadn't been involved in the Markmoor Farm thing.

He slid out of Poland's car and pushed the door shut, holding the handle open at the same time to soften the click. Then he crept down the side of the Mercedes, stepping on the patches of bare earth to avoid crunching the gravel.

A tiny red light in the rear view mirror started flashing; a motion activated dash cam, probably.

Sod it.

Closer now, Dixon noticed condensation running down in between the panes of the double glazed bay window. *In need of refurbishment.*

He followed the path around the side, stepping over the gaps where the slabs had been taken to park the car on, and looked in the back window.

The light from the hall illuminated the chessboard lino on the floor, but not much else, so Dixon shone his torch in the kitchen window. Poland always kept a torch in the glovebox in case the Volvo broke down.

Definitely in need of a new kitchen. The blood on the light switches wouldn't be a great selling point either.

The back door was standing ajar, the wood splintered, a deep gouge in the frame where it had been levered open. The handle had broken off the old mortice lock and was lying on the step.

There was no going back now anyway, footage of him creeping past the Mercedes safely stored on the hard drive of the dash cam, almost certainly, so he pushed open the door with his elbow and stepped into the kitchen.

Blood was smeared along the wall from the door frame to the light switch, someone fumbling for it in the dark, possibly. More blood on the old chrome taps of the sink; a pint glass half full of water also smeared with blood. Whoever had switched the light on hadn't switched it off, judging by the blood trail.

Dixon followed a line of drips on the hall carpet, the red dots standing out even against the pattern; old, like his grandmother used to have.

More blood on the light switch in the hall, and the door frame. He pushed open the living room door with his toe, flicking off his torch as the light streamed into the hall.

A whispered 'Hello?' followed by 'Police, anyone home?'

He noticed the blood first; everything else was just detail.

Two sofas, one behind the door on his left, the other against the wall in front of him, both facing a curved television screen in the corner. The gizmo was sitting on the arm of the sofa to his right, the television on standby. No pictures on the walls; a couple of DVDs and games lying on the floor in front of the TV stand; a small plastic steering wheel too.

A portable gas fire, one of those with the gas bottle in the back, was standing on the hearth, a box of matches on the mantelpiece above. If this place is rented, Dixon thought, the landlord needs his arse kicking into the middle of next week.

Then came the blood. Two large puddles of it had soaked into a blanket that had been draped over the sofa. Dixon was no blood pattern analyst, but someone – Waller, probably – had been sitting in the middle of the two-seater sofa, his hands resting on the blanket either side of him, wrists slashed. He glanced on the floor in front of the sofa, a Stanley knife lying on the bloodstained rug, the blade red with yet more blood.

Back out into the hall.

'Hello? Adam?'

Dixon pushed open the bedroom door with his left hand, the torch in his right, held as a weapon this time – *Carlisle would be pleased.*

Empty.

The sink in the bathroom was smeared with blood, some of it diluted, the dregs of more washed down the plug, so the tap had been turned on at some point.

He followed the drip-trail back to the front door, two small pools of blood on the mat just inside the hall, the Yale lock on the inner door on the latch. A pile of post was sitting on the floor in the porch behind one of those front doors that was never locked. There wasn't even a keyhole.

The hall table was hardly visible under the pile of junk mail and free newspapers that hid an old landline, the cable still plugged into the wall socket next to what looked like writing just above the skirting board.

Dixon squatted down and shone the light on his phone at the letters – 'I.S' – the blood dried and soaked into the wallpaper. He took a photograph of it, and of the Yale lock on the inner door.

Then, careful not to step in any of the blood, he retraced his footsteps to the kitchen, stepping out into the back garden as he put his phone to his ear.

'Where've you been?' asked Jane, yawning. 'You've been gone ages.'

Monty had jumped up on the end of the bed and was lying with his head resting on her feet.

'I went round to check Waller's place,' replied Dixon. 'I need to keep busy.'

'You shouldn't be—' She stopped mid-sentence, leaning up on her elbow. 'What's happened?'

'Looks to me like he sat on the sofa and tried to slit his wrists. There's not enough blood for him to have succeeded, though.'

'Where is he?'

'Gone.' Dixon was sitting on the edge of the bed, a toothbrush sticking out of the corner of his mouth. 'His bungalow had been broken into. Someone had jemmied open the back door.'

'Please tell me you called it in.'

'Couldn't very well not. There's a dash cam on Waller's car so I'll be on that. Whoever broke in will be as well, hopefully. I did tell Scientific to get the footage off the hard drive.'

'Where's Roger?'

'Watching the rugby. It's a tour match, down under.'

'At least you didn't take him with you. That's something, I suppose. How did you get in?'

'The back door was open.'

'That's bloody marvellous, that is. You're on bail for murder, in case you'd forgotten.' Jane was sitting up now. 'Charlesworth'll go ballistic!'

'So will Deborah Potter, but that's just tough. She was the one who called off the search for Waller.'

'That was me, actually. She told me to, though.'

'There you are then.'

Dixon slid his T-shirt off over his head, revealing the wire and microphone taped to his chest. He began peeling the tape off slowly.

'Any Albanians following you?' asked Jane.

'They'll let me sweat for a couple of days, I expect. I would.'

'What about the micro recorder?'

'I've got that rolled up in the hood of my old coat, then it's tucked inside the collar with the microphone poking through the seam. They'll never spot that.'

'If they do, you're buggered.'

'You know just what to say, don't you?'

'I'll come and visit you in prison,' said Jane, with a wry smile.

'Piss off.'

'You'll have Professional Standards trying to pin Waller's disappearance on you as well. Your DNA will be everywhere in there.'

'Bollocks. Any concerned member of the public would've done the same. There was blood all over the light switch in the kitchen.'

'That's your story and you're sticking to it.'

'I am.'

'Where d'you think Waller's gone?'

'I don't think he's *gone* anywhere. I think he's been taken; and we've got until North Petherton Carnival on Friday night to find him.'

'You're joking!'

'Something happened at Bridgwater on Saturday and Burnham on Monday; North Petherton's next,' Dixon said, handing Jane his phone. 'This was scrawled in blood on the wall just inside the front door. My guess is whoever took Waller left him lying on the floor there while he or she went to get their car.'

'Ian Szopinski,' said Jane. 'Must be, he's the only one with those initials.' She frowned. 'Potter's got him in custody though. She picked him up when we found the payments going into Bishop's bank account. Blackmail is a good motive for murder.'

'What time was he brought in?'

'Mid-afternoon.'

'It could've been him who's taken Waller in that case, but he was in Birmingham when Bishop was murdered.'

'She's interviewing him in the morning.'

'Can you be there?'

'She's got me and Lou chasing up the report from High Tech,' Jane replied. 'Keeping us out of the way, more like. She's letting Harper go in the morning as well, unless forensics have come up with anything by then.'

'They won't.'

'This is bloody ridiculous. I'll never get back to sleep now.' Jane threw back the duvet. 'D'you want a cup of tea? I'll see if Roger wants one as well.'

Jane had gone by the time Dixon woke the following morning; just after nine, despite the fact it was well past Monty's breakfast. Still, he'd had a late night. They both had.

He was standing in the kitchen, eating a bowl of cornflakes and wondering what Monty was growling at, when he noticed Deborah Potter at the small window in the front door. Jeans and a polo shirt, unshaven; it was no way to welcome his line manager, although it was unlikely to be a social call.

He opened the front door before Potter knocked.

'What the bloody hell are you playing at?'

'Do come in, Ma'am. Roger's got some coffee somewhere, if you'd like one?'

'I suppose we should be grateful you didn't break in.' Potter sat down at the kitchen table, looking around the room at the same time.

'The back door was open and there was blood on the light switch. I just did what any concerned member of the public would've—'

A wave was enough to stop Dixon mid-sentence. 'If you want to rub Charlesworth up the wrong way, you're going the right way about it.'

'Thank you, Ma'am.'

'It wasn't a bloody compliment!' Potter was keeping a close eye on Monty, who was sniffing her shoes. 'He'll throw the bloody book at you, and don't think he won't just because it's you. The sun shining out of your arse only takes you so far with the ACC. Coffee. One sugar.'

Dixon flicked on the kettle.

'Where's Dr Poland?'

'Still in bed, I think, Ma'am. He's taken a few days off work, says he's going to keep me out of trouble.'

'Fat chance of that.' Potter's usual invitation to call her Deborah when they were alone was conspicuous by its absence. 'There's still no sign of Waller,' she continued. 'He's not pitched up at any of the local hospitals and there was definitely someone else in the house, according to Scientific, so it looks like he's been taken rather than gone of his own free will. There are drag marks outside as well. Shoes, they think.' She was leaning back, still watching Monty, who was now sitting on the floor next to her. 'How did you know?'

'I didn't. I thought it might be a possibility, so I went to check.'

'A bunch of bloody estate agents fighting like rats in a sack.' Potter sighed as Dixon handed her a mug of coffee. 'Have you got *any* idea what's going on?'

'Not really, Ma'am,' replied Dixon. 'I had thought Harper had motive. He has for Bishop and Webb, but I'm not sure how Waller fits in.'

'Szopinski is a strong suspect. He was being blackmailed by Bishop, and now we've got the writing on the wall at Waller's bungalow.'

'He was by his husband's hospital bed in Birmingham when Bishop was killed, don't forget.' Dixon hesitated, unsure what else to say. The truth was that the investigation had been going nowhere fast, except around in circles, perhaps. Hundreds of witnesses and hours of CCTV footage had led to precisely nothing.

'I know you've got other things on your mind,' continued Potter. 'We made enquiries at the hospital and it turns out there was an Estonian agency worker there, portering. Since disappeared into thin air, apparently. It might be pure coincidence, of course.'

'I doubt that.'

'What's the surveillance equipment for?'

'You know about that?'

'I do.'

'I'm expecting a visit from the Albanians, with an offer to make it all go away if I do their bidding.' Dixon opened the patio door, allowing Monty into the garden, much to Potter's relief.

She took a swig of coffee. 'At the briefing this morning, Jane said Waller might be killed at the North Petherton Carnival on Friday night. I'm guessing that came from you?'

'It's a possibility.'

'Well, he's still alive, if the blood loss alone is anything to go by. Look, we can just about turn a blind eye to what happened last night, Nick, but you're going to have to stay out of it now. We simply cannot have a murder investigation compromised by an officer himself on bail for murder. Is that clear?'

'Yes, Ma'am.'

'We're way beyond bunking off a bit of management training this time. You are not the SIO any more. I am. And you're in enough trouble with Professional Standards as it is.'

Chapter Thirty-Three

The briefing at eight hadn't lasted long, most of the time spent on the hunt for Waller. Two sets of footprints in the blood, one of which had been confirmed as Waller's overnight, had convinced Potter he hadn't done a runner after a failed suicide bid. That had been her initial reaction, dismissing the broken lock on the back door as part and parcel of the rundown state of the house. 'It could have happened at any time,' she had said.

The second set of footprints in the blood – Dixon's ruled out – had changed all that. 'We're going to work on the assumption something is planned for the carnival on Friday night at North Petherton. It's Thursday today, so that gives us a day and a half.'

'How are you getting on with the computers?' Potter's question had been addressed to Louise, almost pointedly.

'We're seeing the tech guy at ten.'

Jane was convinced she was being sidelined. Pushed out. She glanced at Maggie, now working with a detective chief superintendent and loving every minute of it. *Yes, Ma'am, no Ma'am, three bags full, Ma'am.* Either that or it was because Jane was pregnant. They'd kept it quiet for as long as they could, but there came a point when not even a baggy pullover would hide 'the bump'.

She ducked down behind her computer when the briefing broke up, listening intently as the team drifted off in different directions. Some had been staring at her when the news of Waller's disappearance overnight was broken, as if it was her fault the search had been scaled back. Some, anyway; most knew better.

'A word, please, Jane.' Potter was standing over her, her hands on her hips; the same sharp two piece suit; highlights – or were they lowlights? Jane never had understood the difference – in her shoulder length bob.

She followed Potter along the corridor and out on to the top floor of the staff car park, Potter leaning back against the wall behind the door, sheltering from the light drizzle that was drifting down.

'How's he holding up?' she asked.

'He'll be all right.' Jane folded her arms, although it was as much about the weather as it was body language.

'Look, I don't want you to think you're being pushed out.'

'That's exactly what I was thinking, actually.'

'I know it must feel like it.' Potter was nodding and shrugging at the same time. 'I'm guessing Nick will be out on the beach with Monty?'

'Probably.'

'It's a shame. I know the way he works and no one's going to have a better handle on this investigation than him. He'll have watched everything, read everything, and he's got a memory like an elephant. We can't really afford to be without him if we're to find Waller before tomorrow night, but we have to be, I'm afraid, and it places you in a very difficult position.'

'Piggy in the middle.'

'Not only that, but you're a witness in the Professional Standards investigation.' Potter looked skyward when the drizzle turned to rain. 'This is just a friendly word of advice, Jane, but you need to make sure you don't talk to Nick about what's going on. It might be different if it was a simple disciplinary matter, and God alone knows we could do with him, but he's been charged with murder, which I hardly need tell you is an entirely different kettle of fish.'

'You don't need to tell me.'

'And it would be gross misconduct on your part.' Potter slid her staff pass over her head and held it in front of the sensor, the lanyard dangling down. 'We really don't want to find ourselves with disciplinary proceedings being taken against you as well.'

'No, Ma'am.'

'Work with Louise and keep your nose clean.' Potter sighed loudly as she moved her pass up and down in front of the sensor. 'Why won't this bloody thing—' her sentence punctuated by the bleep. 'At last,' she said, snatching open the door. 'We can allow Nick what happened last night, but that's got to be the last. You must've told him we'd given up on Waller?'

Jane hesitated.

'Don't answer that.' Potter allowed the door to slam behind them. 'Just remember what I said, for your own sake.'

Jane had turned the volume down nice and low, but kept looking over her shoulder at the door. After her friendly chat with Potter, she really couldn't risk being caught snooping.

She was watching the monitor as Potter and Maggie Baldwin interviewed Ian Szopinski in the adjacent room. There was a chase to be cut to and Jane had twenty minutes or so before Louise would start to wonder where she was.

Just ask him about the bloody money!

Polish, openly gay; it was all very interesting.

'There you are,' said Louise, pushing open the door. 'We need to be go—' She broke off when she saw what Jane was watching. 'What's he said?' she asked, sitting on the edge of the table next to her.

'Not a lot,' replied Jane, turning back to the screen. 'Yet.'

'Yes, Richard was married when we met,' said Szopinski.

'Happily?' asked Potter.

'Obviously not.'

'And how would you describe your relationship?'

'Good.'

'Was Richard aware you were being blackmailed by Trevor Bishop?'

Boom!

The question took Szopinski by surprise too, albeit fleetingly. 'It wasn't just me, we both were. Bishop found out about the pylons and wanted "a piece of the action", as he put it.' Szopinski leaned back in his chair and looked up at the camera. 'It was either that or he go to the papers and blow the whole thing wide open. His mother and stepfather would've sued us as well.'

'What *thing* would he have blown wide open?'

Szopinski's solicitor whispered in his ear, much to the obvious annoyance of Potter.

'It is fine. It will all come out now anyway.' Szopinski turned back to Potter. 'Richard ask me to put the pylons right next to Markmoor Farm Holidays. Millions were at stake, he said; the plan was to use the pylons to buy the plot at a knock down price and then move them. He say there'd be a campaign by the villagers and that would explain the move. He would make sure of it, give them some money to pay for leaflets and posters. There was even a website.'

'Just to be clear then, Ian, you're admitting that you conspired to put the pylons so close to Markmoor Farm Holidays that your husband, Richard, could buy the land at a price significantly less than the true market value?'

'Yes.'

'And Trevor Bishop was using that information to blackmail you?'

'He was.'

'How did he find out about it?'

'He have an email I send to Richard from my Gmail account.'

'What was this email about?'

'The timing of the official announcement that the pylons were going to be moved. Richard ask me to get it delayed until after the purchase had completed. It was just about the dates.'

'Where did he get this email?'

'God knows.'

'Is this what the argument between Richard and Trevor Bishop was about at the annual dinner?'

'I wasn't there. Richard is embarrassed about us. He say people wouldn't understand. But, yes. Bishop had already had two lots of ten thousand and wanted more.'

Potter fixed Szopinski in a cold stare, pausing for effect. 'Is this why you killed Bishop?'

'I didn't kill him.'

'You cut his throat, bundled him into the boot of his car and then set it on fire.'

'No.'

'You said your relationship with Richard was good.'

'It was. Is.'

'But we've spoken to a neighbour who said that Richard moved out of your flat a couple of months ago.'

'News to me,' mumbled Louise.

'And me,' replied Jane.

'They talked about shouting and banging about,' continued Potter. 'Fighting, breaking glass.'

'It is not true.'

'Granted, he hadn't changed his address officially, but we've found the B&B he'd been staying at.'

No response.

'Shall I tell you what I think happened?' It may have been a question, but Potter didn't wait for a reply. 'You found out that Richard had been using you.'

'No.'

'He wasn't *really* interested in you. He just used you to put the pylons nice and close to Markmoor Farm Holidays so he could buy it for a song. And when he'd bought it, he—'

'No. We are married. We love each other.'

'That's what he told you, is it?' Potter let out a small laugh of disbelief. 'And you fell for it hook, line and sinker.'

'It is not true.'

'And when you found out, you tried to kill Richard as publicly as you could. What was that, revenge for keeping your relationship in the closet?'

Szopinski was fighting to keep his composure, wiping away the tears as fast as they were cascading down his cheeks.

'When did you first meet Adam Waller?'

'I never meet him.'

'Yes, you have.' Potter slid a piece of paper across the table. 'You're both on the same dating website. Look.'

'That's an old profile, from before I met Richard and settled down.'

'What the neighbours describe doesn't sound much like *settling down*, Ian.'

'They're lying.'

'Why would they lie?'

'I don't know.' Szopinski clenched his fists. 'They never like us living there anyway. A pair of queers. I see the looks on their faces.'

'Where is Adam Waller?'

'I don't know.'

'We know he's still alive, Ian. So, where is he?'

'You're not listening to me.'

'My client has already answered your question, Superintendent,' said the solicitor.

'We went to Mr Waller's property in the early hours of this morning and there's blood everywhere; your initials written on the wall just above the skirting board. In blood.' Potter let that one hang, using the opportunity to slide a photograph across the table.

'He'll start going "no comment" in a minute,' said Louise, nudging Jane's elbow. 'Then they'll be coming out. We'd better get a wriggle on.'

Jane stopped in the doorway and looked back at the monitor, just as Szopinski lifted his head.

'No comment.'

Chapter Thirty-Four

'I saw Potter taking you off to one side after the briefing,' said Louise, as they drove out of Express Park in Jane's car ten minutes later.

'A friendly reminder not to speak out of turn to Nick.' Jane raised her eyebrows. 'It's a misconduct matter, as if I didn't know.'

'She doesn't want his help then.'

'Probably doesn't think she needs it now.'

'She's let Harper go. No reason to hold him. No evidence either.'

'I bet Dave and Mark will be chuffed,' said Jane, accelerating along the dual carriageway. 'They'll have to go through all the CCTV and photos again, looking for Szopinski this time. At Bridgwater Carnival and Burnham.'

'There's hours of it.' Louise smiled. 'I tell you what's bugging me though. Let's assume Szopinski really did try to kill Webb and then killed Bishop – what's the AirDropped video all about? Why would he send that to the staff of Bishop Property?'

'No idea,' replied Jane. 'Have you read the High Tech report?'

'Yes.'

'You'd better ask the questions, then.'

TG Media occupied office space above a plumbing supplies unit on the Walrow Industrial Estate.

'They sponsor the Somerset Association of Estate Agents.' Louise was scrolling on her phone. 'And run the computer networks for quite a few of the local agencies, looking at the testimonials.'

'Which ones in Burnham?' Jane asked, as she pulled on the handbrake.

'All of them.'

Dixon was standing on the road bridge, looking along the River Huntspill, his elbows resting on the parapet, huge windows revealing the steel turbines inside Gold Corner pumping station behind him, the prevailing wind whipping the surface of the water into white horses. No swirl under the bridge and no roar from behind him either; the pumps were off. Time enough for that when the winter rains get going good and proper, he thought, remembering his visit to Northmoor Green in a boat, the water up to the first floor windows.

Monty was on his long lead, sniffing along the grass verge, the occasional tug on Dixon's wrist telling him the dog was interested in something just out of reach.

Confident he was not being followed, Dixon had parked under the trees and walked along to the river. Now he was watching the traffic racing past on the M5 in the distance: lorries, cars, vans, a carnival cart by the looks of things, although that must have been on the A38 beyond.

Gold Corner was a good place to meet. Single track country lanes would make a tailing car easy to spot, particularly if it was a black Range Rover. The Albanians would know he was expecting a visit; only the where and when was in doubt. *When* would be up to them, but it was down to Dixon to fix the *where* and Gold Corner pumping station would not do at all. That was reserved for meeting someone else.

'God, that was irritating,' huffed Jane, appearing beside him. 'What a pain in the arse that bloke is.'

'Far too busy worrying about what he was going to say next, instead of listening to the damn question.' Louise frowned. 'Don't you just hate people like that?'

'You get back in the car, Lou,' said Dixon. 'There's no need for you to risk a disciplinary.'

'Don't you worry about me, Sir. I'll be fine.'

'Any sign of them?' asked Jane.

'Not yet,' replied Dixon. 'What did he have to say for himself?'

'Not a lot; nothing useful anyway. It's a small agency and they do computer networks for small businesses, online search marketing, pay-per-click campaigns, a bit of graphic design, that sort of stuff. The owner is a bloke called Taylor Gooch. Rabbit pie, he is. You can't get a word in edgeways.'

Louise was flicking through her notebook. 'They sponsor the annual dinner and do a lot of marketing to local estate agents. They always place an ad in the newsletter and there's a banner on the association website. Cornered the market, according to Gooch. He's got them set up all pretty much the same: Microsoft Exchange Server, Outlook for email. They're all using a cloud based management tool called QBrix Agent as well. It's a customer resource management thing that covers sales and lettings. It generates reminders and letters.'

'Accessible remotely?'

'And on a phone.'

'Anything else?'

'There's workplace analytics software installed on the servers. He seemed a bit embarrassed about that, to be honest,' replied Louise. 'Sort of admitted it had been installed without the staff knowing. Sounds like a breach of privacy to me. Eastman and Webb, Bishop Property and Harrison Samuels have all got it.'

A similar thing had been installed at the firm of solicitors Dixon had trained at. 'To facilitate remote working' had been the reason given, but everyone knew what it was really about. 'Who had access to it?' he asked.

'Administrator access only,' replied Louise. 'So, that's Richard Webb and Hilary Eastman at their firm, Trevor Bishop obviously, Gerard Pollock and Brian Townsend at Harrison Samuels.'

'It's just so they can keep tabs on people,' said Jane. 'That's the way Gooch described it anyway. Make sure they're at their computers working when they're supposed to be, at appointments when they say they are. It gives access to email as well, so they can check if any complaints are coming in.'

At least the law firm had been up front about it, so they all knew they were being spied on.

'The administrator dials in to the server using a numerical IP address; then they've got username and password login access.' Louise was reading from her notebook.

'I'm not sure how this all fits in with Szopinski,' said Jane, leaning back against the wall. 'Potter seems to think she's got him for the whole lot. We watched a bit of the interview.'

'Trevor Bishop was blackmailing him over the pylons thing – two lots of ten thousand pounds – and Richard Webb had used him to get the land cheap and then left him,' said Louise.

'What about Adam Waller?'

'Szopinski and Waller are both on a gay dating app, so High Tech are looking into that. Forensics too. She'll charge him if they find anything.'

'His initials written in blood on the wall was the clincher,' said Jane. 'He went "no comment" after that. But it still doesn't explain the AirDropping.'

'Waller is still missing?' asked Dixon.

'As far as we know. We'll find out when we get back to Express Park.'

'He's probably dead by now,' said Louise, resignation in her voice. 'He'd lost a lot of blood.'

'And is the tech guy involved in the carnival?'

'Nope,' replied Louise. 'Been once or twice, but it's the same every year and he's bored with it, he says. He's certainly not a carnival club member or anything like that. I checked the lists.'

'What about Szopinski?'

'No.'

'It all makes sense if you ignore the AirDropped video,' said Jane. 'Szopinski finds out Webb used him just to buy the land, so he rigs his squib to kill him as publicly as possible. Then you've got two lots of ten grand and Bishop wanted more, so he slits Bishop's throat and sets fire to the car with him in it.'

'The squib was his revenge for being kept in the closet. That was the way Potter put it to him,' said Louise.

'And Waller will be down to the dating app. If we can prove they met on there, then maybe something went wrong between them?'

'Potter's releasing Harper then?'

'Already has by now.' Louise looked at her watch. 'We'd better get back or she'll be checking our mobile phone signals.'

'She hasn't got the number of my burner, don't worry. How did Bishop find out about the pylon thing?' Dixon asked. 'He must have had some evidence to have got twenty grand out of Szopinski.'

'A copy of an email sent from Szopinski's private Gmail account to Webb,' replied Jane. 'That's what he said in interview.'

'Where did Bishop get it from?'

'Szopinski didn't know.'

'What about the tech guy, Gooch?'

'He didn't know either, but Potter wants us to find out.'

'It could be one of the deleted emails on the Eastman and Webb server,' said Louise. 'The High Tech report lists several days where all the emails were deleted. They're trying to restore them, but it's likely to take several days.'

Dixon kicked a stone along the lane, holding Monty back when the dog tried to chase after it. 'Several days we don't have if we're to find Waller alive before North Petherton tomorrow night.'

Jane hesitated in the window of Eastman and Webb and glanced at the properties for sale, conscious that Dixon was parked in the Baptist Church car park and watching her every move; listening too. She leaned forward and adjusted her hair, making sure the earpiece in her right ear was suitably covered.

The wire had been requisitioned for Dixon's visit from the Albanians, but it made sense to let him listen in. Louise had agreed, although if it came out, there was no way they would let on that she knew what had been going on; no use in everybody having to look for a new job.

It was their best chance of finding Waller too.

'That's a nice one,' said Louise, pointing at a lavender cottage with an arched window; a nice garden backing on to open fields too. 'D'you think you'll ever get the old stick-in-the-mud to move?'

'I heard that.' Dixon's voice in Jane's earpiece.

'He's got other things on his mind at the moment,' replied Jane.

'Yeah.'

A glazed front door; every estate agency seemed to have a bell above the door. Two red leather armchairs, a coffee table strewn with property magazines and the free newspaper. Then three desks either side of an aisle leading to more offices and a small kitchen at the back.

Four of the desks were occupied, Jane recognising them from Saturday night at Bridgwater, not that she could put names to the faces; it had all been a bit of a blur. 'Name, address, phone number', and on to the next. Some of them had certainly been there filming Hilary and Richard squibbing though.

She recognised Hilary Eastman, her office door standing open. A second door was closed, the lettering on the nameplate bearing an uncanny resemblance to that of a gravestone. It's just the font, Jane thought, blinking the image away.

'Any news on Richard?' asked Hilary, appearing in the doorway of her office.

'I'm afraid not,' replied Jane. 'It's likely to be weeks rather than days.'

Hilary nodded slowly. 'What can we do for you?' she asked, returning to the leather chair behind her desk.

'We needed to ask you a few questions, if you wouldn't mind,' replied Jane. She stepped into the office and closed the door behind them. 'Trevor Bishop was blackmailing Richard. Did you know?'

'No.' Hilary folded her arms. 'What about?'

'There's an email that appears to suggest the siting of the pylons adjacent to Markmoor Farm was done deliberately to enable Eastman Homes to purchase the land at an undervalue. Then the pylons were moved and—'

'That's ridiculous.'

'It's just an allegation,' Jane said airily. 'But it does point to a possible motive for Trevor's murder.'

'First I've heard of it and I'm sure it'll be news to my husband as well.' Hilary stood up. 'Do you need to see anyone else?'

'It was an email from Ian Szopinski to Richard, sent to his Eastman and Webb email address, and we were wondering if you knew how Trevor Bishop might have got hold of a copy of it?'

'I've really got no idea, I'm afraid. Our systems are secure and we've got the usual antivirus stuff in place. You're welcome to speak to TG Media.'

'We have, thank you.'

'Oh, right.' Hilary frowned. 'Are you suggesting someone here forwarded it to Trevor or printed it off?'

'I'm not suggesting anything,' replied Jane, matter of fact. 'I'm just asking the question. Is there someone here who might have done that? Someone he got on well with?'

'Certainly not!'

'Well, we've taken up enough of your time,' said Jane, turning round.

Louise closed her notebook and dropped it into her handbag, following Jane into the corridor. Hilary was standing at the back of the office, about to show them out, when she was handed a piece of paper by the receptionist.

'Another one?' Hilary flicked the piece of paper with the back of her fingers. 'We haven't even been out to value this one yet! Pass me the phone,' she said, with a heavy sigh.

Jane was making her way towards the front door. 'We'll show ourselves—'

'Stay,' said Dixon, his voice in her earpiece, although it felt more like he was looking over her shoulder.

'Mr Jeffries, Hilary Eastman at—' Another sigh. 'Yes, but when did they contact you?' Hilary turned around and leaned back against the edge of the reception desk, her left hand across her forehead. 'We haven't even valued your house yet; it's in the diary for tomorrow. I'm sure he was very convincing. Two-nine-five for a bungalow in—' She looked at Jane, her eyes wide. 'You've already signed up with them?' Hilary screwed the piece of paper into a ball and threw it on the floor. 'Well, good luck. I'm afraid you're going to need it at that price. Yes, I'm sorry too, but you know where we are when you're still stuck on the market in six months' time.'

The phone went down with a bang.

'Problems?' asked Jane.

'Just another agent contacting our clients. We all do it, so I can't grumble too much. When a property goes on the market with another agent, the client gets a flyer from us through their letterbox. Trouble is, they've been told their property is worth way over the odds. They'll end up having to drop the price; they always do. And by then anybody who might have been interested in it at the right price will have found something else. The first six weeks is critical.'

Chapter Thirty-Five

Dixon had known they were being watched for several minutes; a head occasionally popping up from behind a computer visible despite the 'For Sale' notices in the window of Harrison Samuels. Second desk on the left, a small child slumped in the chair at the first, kicking her feet against the drawers. Dixon was no body language or lip reading expert, but the irritated glances from the other side of the office and the embarrassed shouts of 'Stop that!' were obvious even from across the road.

It must be the hoodie, Dixon thought, watching Poland flicking through his emails on his phone. He'd noticed the occasional stare, few bothering to hide their assumption that he was up to no good. He'd never worn a hoodie before; never felt the need to keep out of sight before. Investigating a murder when he was on bail for one was a good enough reason, even without the Albanians on his tail. No, there'd be time enough for them when the carnival business was sorted. Until then they'd have to bloody well wait.

Poland drew breath as if he was about to say something, then remembered that Dixon was listening to the conversation taking place in Eastman and Webb on his earpiece. He sighed, then turned back to his phone.

Not being able to see what was going on was a pain; the reactions, glances, blushes, nervous tics – more often than not, they told him more than the answers to the questions. Still, Jane and Louise knew what they were doing.

Dixon could hear the interview drawing to a conclusion. 'Ask her about her relationship with Trevor's ex-wife,' he said.

'One last thing – tell me about your relationship with Faye Bishop, or Smith, she's using her maiden name now,' said Jane, after a slight pause.

Dixon heard Hilary's sigh over the wire. 'We bump into each other in the High Street sometimes and have the odd deal on together from time to time. She used to come to some of the staff parties when Trevor worked here, but that was a while ago now, as you know.'

'I'm getting something to eat,' said Poland, opening the driver's door. 'D'you want anything?'

'A sandwich.'

'What?'

'Not tuna, thanks.' Dixon put his hand up to his earpiece, more as a signal to Poland than anything else. 'Ask to have another look in Webb's office and tell me what you see,' he said, when the car door slammed.

'Would you mind if we had another look in Richard's office, while we're here?' asked Jane.

'If you must.' Hilary's reply was accompanied by another loud sigh, which carried over the wire.

'Walk me round the room,' said Dixon. 'Pictures on the wall; you know the sort of stuff.'

The sound of a door closing, then Jane's voice. 'There's a fireplace with an arty-farty picture of the lighthouse above it; angry sky

276

and some filter on it making everything look dark and ominous. It's quite nice, actually.'

'I wouldn't want it on my wall,' mumbled Louise. 'Makes me feel cold just looking at it.'

'There are two framed photos on the mantelpiece – one of a boy playing rugby, running with the ball, and the other a girl on a horse. Then there are three filing cabinets.' Jane was opening the drawers, judging by the noise. 'All empty, but we've got the files at Express Park. On top there's a few books, a tape measure, some stationery; crap like that.'

'Sit at his desk and tell me what you see.'

'A space where his computer was. We've got that as well. There's a keyboard, with the cable loose on the desk, and a mouse. There's one of those leather desk blotter things.'

Dixon sighed. 'Anything written on the blotting paper?'

'A few doodles, nothing to get—'

'Bring the top sheet. Roll it, don't fold it.'

'Yes, Sir.' There was a barb to that one, Dixon letting it hang while Jane rolled up the blotting paper.

'There's a slide out tray, with a few paperclips and treasury tags,' she continued, pushing it back with a clunk. 'The drawers are all empty; cleaned out. There was a desk diary, but we've got that as well.'

'What else?'

'A freebie calendar pen pot on the windowsill with a few pens in it. It's from an accountant in Bridgwater.' Dixon heard the pens rattling as Jane picked it up. 'Last year's. Then there's a couple of chairs in front of the desk and a glass topped table in the far corner. That's got some plans open on it.'

'The old Shapwick School site,' said Louise. 'Lots of houses, so they look like development plans. Done by an architect in Taunton.'

'Bring them.'

The tap on the passenger window took Dixon by surprise. He had been leaning forward, concentrating, the hoodie obscuring his face and his view of Harrison Samuels.

'I thought it was,' said Faye, smiling. 'It's Inspector Dixon, isn't it?'

Poland had taken the keys with him, so the window wouldn't open when Dixon jabbed the button. 'Yes,' he said, opening the car door, careful not to knock over the girl standing a little too close.

'All hush-hush, is it?'

'I'm not on duty, actually, Ms Smith,' replied Dixon.

'Oh.' She swept the hair back off her face. 'And do call me Faye. This is Amelia. Mel for short. Say hello to the nice man,' she said, tugging the girl by the hand.

'Hello.'

'And who's this?' asked Dixon, leaning over and pointing to the teddy bear in Mel's hand. She was holding the bear upside down by the foot, his ears dragging on the ground.

'Bear.'

'I wanted to call him Baloo, but she wasn't having any of it,' said Faye, her face brightening at the thought. 'I had to pick her up from school early today – she was a bit sick – now I'm off to pick up Jack from school. Granny's having a day off today. Then we're going to Secret World, aren't we?' Tugging Mel by the hand. 'For an ice cream.' She turned to Dixon and whispered, 'Somewhere nice to try and cheer them up.'

'Good luck.'

'Thanks,' with a heavy shrug. 'You got kids?'

'Not yet,' replied Dixon, conscious that Jane was listening on the wire.

'You can have mine, if you like,' Faye said, leaning over and picking up Mel. 'I'm just kidding. It never ends when you're a parent.' She glanced over her shoulder at her office on the other side of the road. 'Looks like I might be out of work soon as well.'

'Really, why's that?'

'The firm's not doing so well. It's all the online competition; bung it on Rightmove, a call centre to arrange the viewings. We can't compete with that, according to Brian. The North Petherton office will be the first to go, so I should be all right for a while. You've got my phone number?'

'Er, yes, at Express Park.'

'Call me,' said Faye, turning away. 'When you're off duty.'

'She's chatting you up,' said Jane, over the wire.

'It happens all the time,' whispered Dixon, climbing back into the passenger seat. 'I've got used to it now.'

'Yeah, right.'

The black Range Rover with privacy glass looked out of place on the seafront, Dixon watching it from the safety of Roger Poland's Volvo, parked in the Baptist Church car park. Even so, he slid down in the passenger seat as far as he could and pulled the hoodie down over his face.

The Range Rover had stopped opposite the end of College Street, the front passenger door opening and a man dressed in black from head to toe jumping out and running across to check the beach below.

You're wasting your time there, matey, thought Dixon. Dogs aren't allowed on that side of the Pavilion.

'Is that them?' asked Poland, climbing into the driver's seat.

'Yes.'

'They *are* looking for you then.'

'To offer me my "get out of jail free" card.'

'Here.' Poland dropped a sandwich into Dixon's lap. 'No chocolate.'

'Et tu, Roger.'

The sound of the bell in Dixon's earpiece confirmed that Jane and Louise were coming out of Eastman and Webb, further down College Street; and there they were, emerging on to the pavement just beyond the Zalshah. Jane was looking across to the Baptist Church.

Then she spotted the Range Rover up on the seafront.

'The Albanians are here. Go in the curry house,' said Dixon, watching them duck into the Zalshah. 'Get Ravi to let you out the back door. Where's your car?'

'Oxford Street car park.'

'They'll be looking for a blonde ponytail, so don't tie your hair up. Where's Liv? We need to see her again.'

'At her parents' in Chilton Trinity. One of the bungalows backing on to the fishing lakes there.'

'I'll see you there in twenty minutes.'

Poland parked in the turning circle at the end of the cul-de-sac, Dixon looking down the side of the bungalow at the fishing lake beyond, an angler on the far bank hunched over a rod, another sitting in a small tent.

The curtains twitched as Jane and Louise squeezed past the two cars parked on the drive they had blocked in with Jane's car.

'Liv's through in the kitchen,' said the middle-aged woman who opened the door before Jane had rung the bell; at least, if she did, Dixon hadn't heard it over the wire. 'D'you mind if I stay with her?' she asked in a hushed voice. 'I'm her mother. Only, she's a bit nervous. We've never had any dealings with the police before.'

'That's fine,' replied Jane. Dixon could imagine the reassuring smile.

Chair legs on a kitchen floor, the rattle of a cup and saucer. 'You've left another one. It's stone cold,' said Liv's mother. 'I'll make another. Would you like one, Sergeant?'

'Thank you.'

'Sugar?'

'One, please.'

'And what about you?'

'Yes, please. No sugar for me.' Louise's voice.

'Liv's got a flat in Burnham she rents, but she's staying with us for a few days.'

'You look like you've done a fair bit of crying,' said Jane. A tissue being ripped out of a cardboard box. 'Here, you've still got bits of mascara on your cheek.'

'Thanks.' Dixon recognised Liv's voice. 'You will find whoever did it, won't you?'

'We're doing everything we can,' replied Jane. 'How long had you known Trevor?'

'I first met him when he interviewed me for a job. A couple of years ago that was. I didn't have any experience, but he said he could train me up. I went for an interview at Eastman and Webb and they offered me a job as well, but Trevor was paying more and I was trying to get my own place.'

A kettle was boiling in the background, cups and saucers being placed on the side.

'And when did your relationship start?'

'You don't pull any punches, do you?' said Liv's mother, a tray of tea rattling before being placed on a table. Then the sound of chair legs on a tiled floor.

'We haven't got time for the niceties, I'm afraid.'

'Not long after,' said Liv. 'We were at a viewing and the house was empty, then we went for a drink afterwards at the Crossways. After that it was hotels. I know what people are saying, but it wasn't just a fling. He'd left his wife and we were going to get a place together and get married when his divorce came through. We talked about it. We were going to start a family too, of our own. He just needed to take it a bit slow to begin with because of his kids. And, yes, I knew he was married, with two young children. I knew that, but . . .'

'I'm not here to judge, Liv,' said Jane.

Someone was stirring tea with an exaggerated rattle of the spoon. 'It takes two to . . . y'know.' Liv's mother again.

Dixon could hear the awkward silence. 'Ask her about her relationship with Trevor's ex-wife,' he said.

'Tell me about your relationship with Faye,' said Jane, after a slight pause.

Dixon heard Liv's sigh over the wire. 'We bump into each other in the High Street sometimes and she always ignores me, crosses the road. Trevor says – said – she always refers to me as "the child".'

'What about your relationship with the children?'

'I don't have one, as such. That was why Trevor was still living with his parents. Faye said he couldn't see them if he was living with me; that she'd fight him every step of the way.'

'Ask her what Faye was doing there on Monday night,' whispered Dixon.

'What was Faye doing at the carnival on Monday night?' asked Jane.

'She'd come over to see a couple of the girls she used to work with. I know she's still in touch with Ella and Claire. They're like this.'

Like what? Dixon plumped for crossed fingers, probably.

282

'What sort of work did you do at Bishop Property, Liv?' asked Jane.

'I started off doing the typing, then I'd go with Trevor on viewings, do the measurements, that sort of stuff. He always did the valuations, agreed rents and fees with clients, but I've been doing pretty much everything else. Chasing up solicitors on the phone, that sort of thing.'

'Did you have your own caseload?'

'Some of the straightforward residential sales to look after.'

'What d'you know about a campsite at Mark?'

'That was Mr Harper and Trevor's mum's; the family business,' continued Liv. 'They had a campsite, with some lodges on it. I'd gone over there with Trevor when he'd done an initial valuation. Then they got Gerard Pollock from Harrison Samuels to do a formal valuation for the divorce. Mr Harper didn't trust Trevor, he said. He was worried he'd take his mother's side and value it in her favour, so they agreed on someone neutral to do it. I can't remember the figures, but then the pylons happened.'

'And what happened after that?'

'I didn't hear any more about it, really. Trevor dealt with it. The next thing was Mr Harper has sold it for eight hundred thousand and Trevor went nuts. You've heard about the punch-up at the annual dinner?'

'You were there?'

'Yes. Everybody knew about us by then so Trevor said it would be fine; he wanted to show me off, he said.'

A loud sigh from Liv's mother.

'Richard was shouting about suing Trevor for libel and slander, or whatever it is, saying he'd been spreading lies about him. He tried to hit him, so Trevor knocked him down. That's all, really. It was all over in a second.'

'Did Trevor have a file open for the sale?'

'I never saw one, but he had a filing cabinet in his office. Always locked. We have to keep copies of everything. He'd done a long letter and put a lot of time into it, he said, because of the size of the place. He'd suggested selling it as a going concern, but it was all wasted effort thanks to Richard.'

'D'you know if any other agents were involved?'

'No, sorry.'

'Do you have a lot of probate sales on?'

'We valued quite a few and there was a local firm of solicitors that used to give us a lot of instructions. Trevor said it was because he took the bloke out to lunch once a month. And to the races at Taunton.'

'Did you see anything at the carnival on Monday night, before the video was AirDropped to your phone?'

'Not really. I had a friend there and she'd brought a bottle of voddy.'

'Really, Liv,' said her mother, an air of resignation in her voice, half-heartedly slamming her cup down on to a saucer by the sound of things. 'I thought you'd stopped all that.'

'It was just a one off.'

'Binge drinking always is.'

'We were going to get a place together,' said Liv. 'When Trevor had got his divorce sorted out.'

'Did you know that Trevor was blackmailing Richard Webb and his husband, Ian Szopinski?' asked Jane.

'He wasn't.' Liv sat up sharply; or someone did – chair legs moving.

'There were two payments of ten thousand pounds each into Trevor's bank account. They came from Ian.'

'I didn't know anything about that. Trevor never said anything.'

'He had a copy of an email Ian sent to Richard.' Jane paused, watching for a reaction, probably.

'I never saw any email,' protested Liv. 'And he never mentioned it to me.'

'Did he say where he got it from?'

'No. Like I said, he never mentioned it to me.'

'And there's nothing you can tell us about twenty thousand pounds landing in Trevor's bank account?'

'Nothing, sorry.'

'You said you were training.'

'To be an estate agent, yeah. I started off doing bits and pieces, following Trevor around, learning the ropes. Now I deal with the smaller properties and the rentals, although we haven't got many of them. So, I take the initial call from the client, meet them, take the measurements and photos. Then Trevor would help me value their house or flat; anything too big and he would take it. I'd started doing the two-up two-downs, smaller flats and stuff. It's not difficult, you just look at Rightmove, see what else is about, add a bit to flatter the client and get the business. You can always drop the price later if it doesn't sell.'

'What about agreeing the commission?'

'That's easy. There are extras on top: glossy printed brochure, featured listing on Rightmove, that sort of thing. Apart from that, it's one point five per cent plus VAT. Always. I'd just say "It's not my decision, I'm afraid", and leave it at that.'

Chapter Thirty-Six

'This is all rather fun, isn't it?' Poland had parked under the trees at the far end of the car park, well away from the Environment Agency van outside the pumping station. 'All this cloak and dagger stuff.'

'I'm glad you're enjoying it,' said Dixon.

'It's much more interesting than rummaging through someone's stomach contents.'

'I'll try to remember that.'

Poland was watching a car approaching along the lane. 'They're here.'

'We haven't seen the Range Rover again,' said Louise, climbing out of the passenger seat of Jane's car. 'Probably buggered off home.'

'They'll try Berrow and then Brean,' said Jane. 'I bet they're watching the cottage too.'

'I'll let them find me when I'm good and ready. Gits.'

'There's a briefing at six, so we haven't got long,' said Jane. 'What do we do now? Potter's still going after Szopinski.'

'It stopped being Szopinski when Waller disappeared. Yes, he had a motive for killing Trevor Bishop, but that's it. His motive for attacking Richard Webb is tenuous at best, and why Waller and why the AirDropped video?'

'Where does Waller fit in?' asked Louise.

'He doesn't.' Dixon leaned back against the post and rail fence, his hands thrust deep into the pockets of his hoodie. 'He calls the Bridgwater switchboard, asks to speak to me, and the next thing we know is he's missing.'

'They were both members of one of these dating websites, don't forget,' said Jane. 'Szopinski and Waller.'

'It doesn't add up. I've met Szopinski and he's no killer, even in the face of blackmail. He'd do a runner rather than kill his blackmailer.'

'He's got a dog, so he can't be a killer,' said Louise, grinning.

'Adolf Hitler had a dog,' replied Poland.

'Did he?'

'Look, this has got nothing to do with Szopinski. I'm not even sure it has anything to do with Markmoor Farm Holidays. What it does have everything to do with is the estate agents. I need to see the High Tech report on their computers and phones.'

'Whose?' asked Jane.

'Everybody's. Has it got Waller's QBrix login details in it?'

'His computer's still being examined, but we've got Webb's. How the hell do we get it out of Express Park, though?'

'I need to see their files too.'

'Which ones?'

'All of them.'

'All of the estate agency files. How the f—?'

'We were only supposed to be keeping them for a couple of days,' said Dixon. 'They'll have been copied by now, so tell Potter you're taking them back and bring them here on the way. We'll wait for you.'

Jane looked at Louise and raised her eyebrows. 'You don't have to get involved in this, Lou. It's a disciplinary, you do know that.'

'Stop saying that, will you. I'm fine with it,' replied Louise, with a wave of her hand. 'Really.'

'I met Trevor Bishop's ex-wife,' said Dixon, a sideways glance at Jane.

'I heard.'

'She said Harrison Samuels were in financial trouble, so do a bit of digging there. Check the others too. They're probably trading as limited companies, so do a company search and get the latest sets of accounts, if we haven't done so already.'

'That's not all she said.'

Dixon grinned. 'I've got my chaperone, stop worrying.'

'Three's a crowd, and all that,' said Poland.

'You're not helping, Roger.'

'Sorry.'

'And how do we explain all this to Deborah Potter?' asked Jane.

'You'll find a way.'

'Ah, there you are,' said Potter, when Jane and Louise appeared along the corridor from the staff car park. 'Have you found out who gave the email to Trevor Bishop?'

'No, Ma'am,' replied Jane, dropping her handbag on to a vacant workstation. 'Hilary Eastman knew nothing about the blackmail, and neither did Liv.'

'Hilary would say that, wouldn't she? She was probably in on the pylon thing – it was her husband's bloody company that bought the land, wasn't it? Anyway, let's move on.' Potter turned away, clearly not expecting an answer to her question. 'Who was looking at Szopinski's social media?'

'There's not a lot, Ma'am,' replied Maggie, her back to Jane at another workstation. 'A couple of cryptic posts on his Facebook timeline about having to keep his relationship quiet, but nothing more than that. We've printed them off.'

'Had he met Waller, then?'

'Not according to the dating site.'

Potter gritted her teeth. 'Where have we got to with the search?'

'Nowhere,' said Maggie coldly. 'Waller's phone's offline. We've got people watching his house, and his parents haven't seen him and neither have any of his friends; the ones we know about, anyway. The dating site was quite forthcoming with his recent contacts and none of them have seen him either. No new posts on social media.' Maggie turned to the uniformed officer sitting next to her. 'What else?'

'No bank transactions,' he said. 'Nothing on the CCTV and his car's not moved.'

'Stay on the CCTV then, that's our best bet. We'll get his photo out to the local news as well and see if that comes up with anything. When are we interviewing Szopinski again?'

'His solicitor's due back at eight this evening, Ma'am,' replied Maggie.

Jane selected the printer furthest away from the front of the incident room and sent three High Tech reports to print, appendices too – she'd fallen for that one before: Trevor Bishop's phone, Richard Webb's phone and then the recipients of the AirDropped video. It would be a bundle about an inch thick by the time it finished, and would never fit in her handbag.

'Right, that's it.' Potter clapped her hands. 'Back to it, everybody.' Then she pointed at Jane. 'You, with me.'

'Good luck,' mouthed Louise, her eyes wide and following Jane as she got up and walked after Potter towards the back door.

Potter held open the door on to the top floor of the staff car park, letting it slam behind Jane.

'What does *he* think?'

'I haven't—'

'Of course you have.' Potter sighed.

'You said I wasn't to—'

'I know what I said, but I never thought for a minute you'd stick to it. And, besides, we need his help.'

Jane took a deep breath. 'He doesn't think Szopinski's got anything to do with it.'

'Why?'

'Motive, opportunity, personality. And Waller changes everything.'

'If he's got anything to do with it.'

'Nick thinks he has.'

'Where is Nick?'

'Dodging the Albanians. A black Range Rover's been doing the rounds.'

'What do they want?'

'To offer him a way out of his current predicament.'

'So he *has* been framed?'

Jane had to stop herself looking on the floor for the penny that had just dropped.

'Is there anything I can do?' continued Potter.

'Not really.'

'And what's all that stuff you're printing off?'

'He wants to see the High Tech reports.'

'Give them to him, but I didn't authorise it if you get caught. Anything else?'

'The estate agents' files. I was going to drop them back to their offices.'

'And let him have a look at them on the way, I suppose?'

Jane did her best to remain impassive; maybe a flicker in her eyes giving her away.

'Do it.' Potter was waving her pass in front of the door sensor. 'Just don't get caught.'

◆ ◆ ◆

'I saw the black Range Rover again.' Jane dropped a box of files on the kitchen table. 'They did a drive-by at Express Park, into the visitors' car park and out again, bold as brass.'

'They'll have to wait. I'll make myself available when I'm good and ready,' replied Dixon. 'Were you followed?'

'No.'

'Good job your Land Rover is out of sight,' said Poland. 'Are there any more?' he asked, gesturing to the box.

'Three.'

'I'll give you a hand.'

'Was he all right?' asked Jane, watching Monty sitting in the French windows, staring at a white cat in the tree at the far end of Poland's garden.

'He didn't eat my sofa, which was a relief.'

'He was fine,' said Dixon, smiling. 'And Roger didn't notice the puddle, so . . .'

'What puddle?'

'I'm joking.'

'I've only got the High Tech reports on the phones,' said Jane, raising her voice as she disappeared along the corridor. 'They haven't finished with the computers yet. Tomorrow morning at the latest, they said.'

One arm tied behind his back Dixon could live with, but this was starting to feel like both.

'Potter collared me and asked what you thought of Szopinski,' said Jane, dropping another box on the table. 'She knows you're looking at these too. I'm on my own if I get caught, apparently, but then that's par for the course.'

'Nice.' Dixon was pouring the dregs of a can of lager into his glass. 'Where's Lou?'

'Gone home.'

'You'd better lock your car,' said Poland, appearing in the doorway. 'I've left the other boxes in the hall.'

'Thanks.'

'I do a very good spag bol, if you fancy it? There's a jar of sauce in the cupboard and some mince in the freezer; soon defrost in the microwave.'

'That'd be lovely, Roger, thank you,' replied Jane, shouting from the front door where she was standing, jabbing her key fob in the direction of her car at the bottom of Poland's drive.

'There's a bottle of red wine too.' Poland grinned. 'This is all very exciting. It's like that bit from *The Godfather* when they go to the mattresses. That bloke was cooking—'

'Clemenza,' muttered Dixon.

'Right.' Poland frowned. 'I thought you only watched old black and white films?'

'I can make an exception for *The Godfather*.' Dixon had dragged the nearest box across the kitchen table and was standing up, fishing files out one by one.

'That's the Markmoor Farm box,' said Jane. 'You've got the agents' files and the solicitors' dealing with the conveyancing, buyer and seller. Plus the Energen Land file as well.'

Dixon dropped the files back in and closed the lid. 'Needs to go to the Serious Fraud Office.'

'I'll tell Deborah Potter.'

'She knows.'

The next box was marked 'Bishop Property' and was full of thin red files. Dixon upended it on the table, the files sliding across the tabletop like a wave rolling up the beach, taking the salt and pepper with them.

'That's all the current stuff and the last twelve months, but his file on Markmoor is in the other box, remember.' Jane had sat down at the table and was watching Poland opening the wine.

'None for Jane.'

'Of course not, sorry,' said Poland, with an apologetic smile. 'I've got some tonic water somewhere, but it might be a bit flat now, I'm afraid.'

'Tea's fine,' said Jane, stifling a huff.

Dixon picked a file at random and opened it. Wafer thin; not much to show for the sale of a six hundred thousand pound property. A copy of Bishop Property's signed terms and conditions of business; the sales particulars, where the photos looked nothing like the real thing.

Jane leaned across and snatched it from Dixon's hand. 'Nice garden,' she said, looking at the photographs. 'Must've used a drone for that one.'

The memorandum of sale. Dixon had seen them umpteen times before, during his stint in the property department. Six months, done under protest; buying and selling other people's houses, getting shouted at by clients for holding things up and chased by the estate agents to speed things up. It had been the trainee solicitor's job to take those calls; the shortest of short straws.

More like the shit end of the stick.

'What exactly are you looking for?' asked Poland. He was watching a frozen block of minced beef in the microwave.

'A motive. I'll know it when I see it.'

Bishop Property's invoice. Six hundred thousand pounds at one point five per cent is nice work if you can get it, thought Dixon. Nine grand plus VAT. A copy of a letter sending it to the seller's solicitor when contracts had been exchanged, and another sending a receipted invoice after it had been paid on completion.

The correspondence pin, such as it was, consisted of copy emails and the viewing details, a separate form for each. Name and address; own property on the market/sale agreed; cash/mortgage.

And the telephone notes, records of almost daily calls made to the seller's and the buyer's solicitors asking for an update, chasing up this and that and generally making a nuisance of themselves. Dixon had been on the receiving end of it and it had certainly been motive enough for murder.

Still, he might be a bit biased, and if he was selling a house he'd like to think the estate agent was on the ball.

Bollocks.

It was standard stuff: '15th May, 3pm – chased seller's solicitor; waiting to hear from buyer's solicitor'. Then next on the clip: '15th May, 3.05pm – chased buyer's sol; waiting to hear from seller's solicitor'.

You couldn't make this stuff up.

Someone with the initials 'T.B.' had got involved after that, trying to get to the bottom of exactly who was waiting for what. Maybe Trevor Bishop had earned his money? Turned out it was the surveyor holding things up: Gerard Pollock of Harrison Samuels.

Dixon was not usually a believer in coincidence, but this time he'd make an exception. He snatched the sales particulars from Jane, slotted them back in the file and dropped it on the floor next to his chair.

Small world.

On to the next.

A current file this time. A modern box on the new estate behind Tesco. Two hundred and thirty thousand; one point five per cent.

Jane had taken the sales particulars again. 'Walking distance of the beach, my arse.'

'Depends on how long you've got,' said Poland, blinking furiously as he chopped the onions. 'You two should move. Too many people know where you live.'

'Like the Albanians,' grumbled Jane.

'Precisely.'

A QBrix record sheet had been stapled to the inside of the file. Simple stuff; Dixon had seen similar management records on legal files. Names, addresses and contact details for the client; identified – tick; signed T&C – tick; Rightmove – tick; PrimeLocation – not ticked; solicitor – not ticked; sale agreed – not ticked. Asking price was an interesting one, several empty boxes below it ready for reductions and the date reduced.

Commission was preprinted – the standard one point five per cent.

Then came the viewings, a box for each to coincide with the form, and below them the reminder dates for follow up and review, the first three ticked off.

'Is it still on the market, this one?' asked Jane.

'We've agreed it's not within walking distance of the beach,' replied Dixon, snatching the sales particulars out of her hand. 'And besides, I'm facing a murder charge at the moment.'

'Yeah.'

'You got a computer, Roger?' asked Dixon, looking up to find Poland standing over him with a glass of wine in his hand.

'A laptop.'

'Can we borrow it?'

Poland looked nervous as he placed the glass on the table in front of Dixon. 'What for?'

'I need to have a look at this QBrix thing. We've got Richard Webb's login details so we can get into Eastman and Webb's system.'

'On my laptop?' Poland grimaced. 'Are you mad? They'll be able to see you've logged in, surely? My IP address and everything.'

'Don't panic,' said Jane. 'We'll install the Onion Router and log in via the dark web. No one can trace that. Not even us.'

◆ ◆ ◆

'Are you sure about this?'

Poland's 'spag bol' had gone, the dirty plates stacked in the dishwasher, and he was now standing behind Jane, who was sitting at the kitchen table installing the Onion Router on his laptop.

Dixon had gone back to the boxes of files, having only stopped reading when Jane kicked him under the table. 'The supper's ready and you've forgotten your jab,' she had said, with a steely glare.

'Make yourself a hat out of tinfoil, Roger,' he said. 'Either that or you can put a saucepan on your head. Always helps.'

'Very funny.'

'I'll uninstall it afterwards, don't panic,' said Jane.

'What does it do?'

'It relays the traffic through multiple computers and encrypts it before we get to the Eastman and Webb server, like the layers of an onion. If they look at the logs, they'll see someone's been in, but they'll have no idea who and your internet service provider can't see what you've been looking at either.'

'Good grief.' Poland shook his head. 'Why isn't everyone using it all the time?'

'Don't know, really. Nothing to hide, I suppose.'

Dixon had started on the Eastman and Webb files, the current ones having the same QBrix record sheet stapled to the inside of the front cover. The first file had the initials 'R.W.' in the agent box, 'Woodlands, an imposing gentleman's residence' with an asking price of eight hundred and fifty thousand; definitely one that would have been dealt with by Richard Webb personally. Sale agreed had been ticked, the figure of eight-two-five handwritten in the adjacent box. Solicitor – ticked. After that, reminder dates came thick and fast, the initials 'J.C.' responsible for the follow-up calls, whoever that was.

The preprinted one point five per cent had been crossed out in the commission box and one point two per cent written in and initialled by R.W. Still a lot of money; the invoice had already been prepared in anticipation of exchange of contracts: nine thousand nine hundred pounds, plus VAT.

'Right, I'm into this QBrix thing,' said Jane. 'Looks like you can sort by client name or the address.'

Dixon was leaning over Jane's shoulder. 'Click on that one,' he said, pointing to an address in Rectory Road.

'Sale agreed at eight-two-five. I guess we won't be moving there then.'

The tabs along the top of the screen looked very similar to the probate case management software Dixon had used as a trainee solicitor. 'Mail Merge' to generate the letters; 'Documents' for the sales particulars, memorandum of sale and the all-important invoice. 'Contacts' would be the solicitors and surveyor, probably, and 'Photographs' was presumably where they could be uploaded.

'Shall we have a look at them?' asked Jane.

'No.'

'Reminders' would flash up the diary alerts for individual transactions, no doubt, and the 'Client Record' was almost identical to the sheet that had been stapled to the inside of each file.

'Try another one.'

'Gore Road,' said Jane, sitting up. 'Now that's definitely within walking distance of the beach.' She clicked on the entry and sighed. 'Five-seven-five.' Then gave an exaggerated shrug. 'Oh, well.'

'Let me find the file.' Dixon started rummaging through the files scattered across the table, several falling on the floor.

'Here it is,' said Poland, leaning over.

Dixon looked at the Client Record sheet on the inside of the file, then compared it to the entries on the screen.

'I need to make a couple of telephone calls,' he said, snapping the file shut.

Jane frowned. 'It's gone ten at night.'

'In that case, I need to take Monty for a walk. Vivary Park's not far from here, is it, Roger?'

'It'll be shut.'

'Fences are made for climbing over.'

'I know that face.' Jane looked at the screen quizzically, then back to Dixon. 'You know what's been going on, don't you?'

Chapter Thirty-Seven

'Are you looking to buy?'

The nearest streetlight was fifty yards away, so Dixon could just about make out the outline. A hoodie, naturally, the trousers a lighter shade, possibly. It was hard to tell in the light.

The man – boy – was sitting on a bench, sheltering from the drizzle, his hands deep in the pockets of his coat; one clutching drugs, the other a knife, probably.

Dixon had seen it all before.

Monty started growling softly.

'I'm a detective chief inspector in the Avon and Somerset Police out for a walk with my dog. You need to be somewhere else. Now.'

'You gonna nick me?'

'I have staff for that.'

He watched the boy sprint off across the grass, hurdle the waist-high railings, and disappear around the corner.

Vivary Park at night should have been deserted. The gates at the top of High Street were locked at dusk, but it had been easy to lift Monty over the railings round the back, opposite the cricket pavilion.

The old station must be a good place to deal drugs, thought Dixon, sitting down behind the high hedge; screened from prying eyes. Most customers could probably hop the railings, too, even in the rain.

Monty sat down in the gap in the hedge, staring out across the park – keeping guard – his wet coat glistening in the light from Dixon's phone. Shame; he'd left the dog's waterproof coat in the back of the Land Rover.

'Relax, old son. They'll never find us here.'

The more he thought about it, the more their plan made sense. Raslan dies, the other intruder changes his statement, plant a few shotgun cartridges in the cottage, a few fingerprints appear on the gun butt and, bingo, the Albanians have a senior police officer in their pocket. Whether Raslan had died of a cardiac arrest or been helped on his way hardly mattered, either. The plan worked both ways.

Dixon felt for the hidden micro recorder buried in the collar of his coat. The approach would come sooner or later, and he would make himself available when this carnival business had been sorted out. It was bad enough being on bail for murder; in hiding too was becoming a pain in the arse.

The Albanians had done him a favour of sorts, all the same. Now when he thought about Raslan, and the scene unfolded in his head all over again – swinging the shotgun, the crack of the skull – all he felt was anger.

Two figures were standing in the bandstand in the middle of the park, silhouetted against the dull glow of the streetlights from the far end. Kissing and holding hands. Two kids who'd sneaked out of one of the local boarding schools, possibly.

Now, that brought back some memories.

And now here he was, all these years later, sneaking about in the same park. Maybe now was the time to think the unthinkable? What if he was convicted of murder and sentenced to life imprisonment? Manslaughter was more likely because the Crown could never prove he intended to kill Raslan. Seven years, maybe?

If he was lucky.

Either way, Jane would be giving birth before the trial, so he could be there for that, assuming he was granted bail. A child was still an abstract idea, though. A bump. And how old would he or she be when he got out?

'What about you, old son?' whispered Dixon, looking down at Monty, still on sentry duty. 'Will you still be here when I get out?'

Footsteps; soft and closing in from the cricket pavilion. Monty had heard them too, ears up, head tipped.

'Are you selling?'

'Walking my dog.'

'Oh, right.'

It was a welcome interruption, oddly enough. Dixon had been starting to feel sorry for himself; not something he had done for a while – seventeen years, to be precise.

Best not to go there.

One step at a time. The carnival thing first. Then the Albanians.

Then maybe there was a serious conversation to be had with Jane. In fifteen months with Avon and Somerset Police he'd been stabbed, left to die in a cave, burnt and shot with a crossbow. Now Dixon was facing a murder charge, his own police force coming after him.

Hardly good father material.

He'd already thought the unthinkable once tonight, so why not do it again – a comfy desk in a solicitor's office?

Things aren't that bad, matey.

So, Richard Webb in an induced coma in Birmingham; Bishop dead, footage of it AirDropped to all and sundry at the Burnham carnival; Waller missing. And several days spent barking up the wrong tree.

Potter had hit the nail on the head: 'A bunch of bloody estate agents fighting like rats in a sack.' Someone had even suggested leaving them to it – Mark Pearce probably, skulking behind his computer.

Four hours Dixon had spent going through the files. Jane and Poland had left him to it just before 1 a.m. Then he'd tiptoed out of Poland's house with Monty. Taking his dog for a walk was thinking time, but there was so much else going on in his head . . .

The seed of a motive was drifting on the wind, never settling anywhere long enough to take hold.

Richard Webb's login had given Dixon access to the whole firm's QBrix system. And every single client – *every single one* – had agreed one point five per cent commission.

Or had they?

Chapter Thirty-Eight

'Did you use my towel when you got in last night?' Jane was standing over him, a wet towel in her hand, the muddy end dragging on the carpet.

'He was soaked,' replied Dixon, yawning and gesturing to Monty, who was curled up asleep on the end of the bed.

'You—' She thought better of it, instead picking up one of the neatly folded towels Poland had left on the chest of drawers. 'I'll have to use one of Roger's now.'

'I could hardly use one of his on the dog, could I?'

'You shouldn't have left his coat in your car, should you.' She dropped the High Tech reports on the phones on the bed next to him. 'You left these on the floor.'

'Thanks.' Dixon rolled over and closed his eyes. 'Any news on Waller?'

'Nothing.'

'Pick up your phone a minute, will you?' He reached across to the bedside table and picked up the old iPhone. 'I'm going to AirDrop you a video of Monty on the beach from six months ago and I want you to tell me where it goes.' A few taps of the screen. 'There.'

'Got it,' said Jane. 'It's gone into my photo album.'

'Whereabouts?'

'It's the top one. The newest.'

'Date received then, not the date the video was filmed,' said Dixon, rolling over and closing his eyes.

'Are you going to tell me what this is all about?'

'What time is it?'

'Six.'

'I've got some calls to make at nine and I need to see the High Tech reports on the computers.'

Jane sighed. 'You go back to sleep then, dear, and I'll text you when I get in.'

The smell of bacon cooking was better than an alarm, although Dixon was already awake, reading the High Tech reports on the phones.

Then the smell woke Monty, the dog sitting up on the end of the bed.

'Jane already gone?' asked Poland, when they appeared in the kitchen.

'She was gone by half six, Roger.'

'She didn't have anything to eat. I did tell her to help herself.'

Dixon was inspecting the contents of the frying pan. 'She'll have got something in the canteen, don't worry.'

'You're on to something then, I gather,' said Poland, cracking eggs into a Pyrex jug. 'Scrambled in the microwave all right?'

'Lovely,' replied Dixon, turning away to hide his wince. 'There's something not quite right in the files, but I need to make a few calls at nine o'clock to be sure.'

'Ten minutes,' said Poland, glancing at the clock on the wall. 'Toast?'

'Thanks.'

Dixon was letting Monty lick his plate ten minutes later when Poland reappeared in the kitchen and handed him the telephone. 'Here,' he said. 'Use the landline. And *that* needs to go in the dishwasher, if you don't mind.'

'Sorry.' Dixon dialled a number, flicked on the speakerphone and placed the phone on the kitchen table.

'Eastman and Webb, good morning. How can I help you?'

He could picture the scene. A bustling office first thing in the morning, kettle on, post being opened. Someone walking in late.

'Yes, hello. My aunt's recently died and we need to sell her house now that probate's been granted. It's in Burnham and I was wondering what your commission might be?'

'What's the address?'

'The Dunes, Allandale Road.' Dixon had parked opposite it often enough when taking Monty to the beach. 'It's detached, four bedrooms.'

'Would you like to speak to one of the estate agents?'

'Not at this stage, thank you. I'm just ringing around to find out the commission.'

'Oh, well, there's not really any point doing that. We all charge the same. One point five per cent plus VAT. It's the standard fee.'

'And you can't do any better than that? I got one point two when I was selling my own house and shopped around.'

'Can't, I'm afraid.'

'Can't or won't?'

'Can I take a name and get one of the agents to call you?'

'No, it's fine, thank you.' Dixon snatched the phone off the table and rang off.

'What's the problem with that?' asked Poland, frowning.

'*We all charge the same.*' Dixon dialled another number.

'Bishop Property Services.'

'Yes, hello. We need to sell my late aunt's house now that probate's been granted. It's in Burnham and I was wondering what your commission was?' Dixon was on a roll now.

'We charge one point five per cent for a standard residential sale. That's plus VAT, of course, but I'm afraid I can't make an appointment for an agent to come out to see you until next week now. We've had a bereavement. There's no charge for the initial market appraisal, though. Is next week any good?'

'I'm just ringing around to see if I can do any better than one point five per cent.'

'You won't, I'm afraid. That's the standard fee in this area.'

Dixon made his excuses and rang off. 'One last one.'

'Harrison Samuels. How can I help?'

He recognised Faye Smith's voice immediately, mouthing 'you do it' at Poland and jabbing his finger at the phone on the table.

'Hello,' said Poland, scowling at Dixon. 'My aunt's died and we need to sell her house.'

'Oh, I'm very sorry to hear that. What's the address?'

'The Dunes, Allandale Road.'

'Well, the first thing we'd need to do is come out and have a look at the property, value it for you, and perhaps give you some advice as to any works that might be needed before it goes on the market. All of that's entirely free, of course, but if you do decide to go with us then the selling commission would be one point five per cent.'

'Plus VAT?'

'Yes. Always plus VAT, I'm afraid. Can I book you in for an inspection? There's no charge.'

'Not at this stage, thank you. I'm just ringing around to see what people are charging.'

'We all charge the standard one point five per cent. Sometimes more, depending on the service – if you want a colour brochure, perhaps, or a featured listing on Rightmove. Never less, though.'

'Thank you. I'll be in touch,' said Poland, as Dixon leaned forward to disconnect the call. 'Is there a property called The Dunes in Allandale Road?' he asked.

'I park outside it when I'm taking Monty on the beach.'

'What if they know it's not for sale?'

'They won't.'

'So, what's it all about then?'

'Price fixing.'

'I should've been a police officer,' said Poland, parking under the trees at Gold Corner pumping station. 'I'd have been good at it.'

'Like Morse.'

'Or, what's that other one called?'

'Clouseau.'

'You cheeky—'

307

Jane tapped on the passenger window before Dixon had a chance to open the door. 'That's the High Tech reports,' she said, when he wound down the window, thrusting a large brown envelope into his hand. 'Did you make your calls?'

'He did,' replied Poland, grinning. 'They're price fixing.'

'Just give me a minute to flick through this stuff, will you?' asked Dixon. 'Does Potter know where you are?'

'She does.'

'What did she say?'

'That she hoped to God you know what you're doing. She wanted to know what to do with Szopinski as well.'

'Tell her to let him go,' said Dixon, turning his attention to the bundle of paper in his lap.

'She won't do that. She's convinced it's him because of the blackmail and the writing on the wall at Waller's place.'

Dixon flicked through pages and pages of technical reports on the software installed on Richard Webb's computer, most of it Microsoft and most of it totally irrelevant. Webb's email and calendar was in Outlook, which he had expected. And one of the appendices consisted of 'Deleted Emails', which would be worth a proper look at some point, although there was no way of knowing who had deleted them.

The digital telephone call log listed all of the numbers dialled from the telephone in Webb's office; that made up another appendix, as did his internet search history extracted from Internet Explorer.

The section on the QBrix transaction management software was all very interesting, but Dixon had seen that for himself, so he flicked straight to the workplace analytics: screenshots, printouts. Webb had administrator access to it and could see what everyone in his office had been up to. How long they had spent browsing the internet, typing emails and letters, on the phone, updating QBrix. Even usernames and passwords for private accounts accessed on the work computer.

It was a snooper's paradise.

Documents generated by QBrix were stored centrally on the office exchange server, and included letters, memoranda of sale and invoices. Samples had been included in the appendices; the Woodlands memorandum was there, the commission given as one point two per cent – the same on their invoice.

It had said one point five per cent on QBrix.

Dixon snapped the bundle of papers shut and dropped it into the passenger footwell of Poland's Volvo. Then he turned to the report on Trevor Bishop's computer.

'I brought a Thermos of coffee, if anyone fancies a cup,' said Poland.

'Thanks, Roger,' replied Jane.

'I'm all right, Dr Poland, thank you,' said Louise. She was leaning on the wall, looking along the Huntspill River.

'Call me Roger, for heaven's sake.'

'We'd better leave him to it,' suggested Jane, watching Dixon frantically turning the pages of the report.

The software installed on Bishop's was identical to Webb's, but then it had been installed by the same IT company, so they probably had their standard configuration for estate agents. Minutes ticked away as Dixon skim-read the appendices.

Nothing.

Last but not least was Trevor Bishop's internet search history. Webb's had not been terribly enlightening: BBC News, Landlord Today; Webb had been looking for a new car as well. Bishop's, on the other hand, was all but empty. Maybe he did all his web browsing on his phone?

Dixon knew that Bishop had gone into his office on the Sunday morning after the Bridgwater carnival. A few emails had made it into a separate appendix to the report, but the real gem was in his search history. The one and only entry:

CMA leniency.

Chapter Thirty-Nine

'What do we tell her?'

It had been a fair question, Jane thought, and Dixon's answer had been a simple one: 'Nothing for now, unless you have to.'

She's going to love that.

Deborah Potter would have to know soon enough, Dixon had said, but until he had the answers he needed from High Tech he only knew *why* and not *how*; not even half the story.

Who would have to come later as well, but not too late for Waller, God willing.

Louise had done her best, but hadn't been able to get any sense out of High Tech on the phone. 'You know what they're like. He said they won't be able to look at it until Monday now, at the earliest. They've got another rush job on.'

'You told them there's a threat to life?'

'Yes.'

'And that it's the North Petherton carnival tonight?'

'Yes.'

And so Jane and Louise had left for Express Park to get Deborah Potter to ring the High Tech Unit. They knew the question she had to ask, but couldn't really tell her why she had to ask it.

Nice.

An order from a detective chief superintendent should do the trick, all the same.

They arrived back at Express Park just before eleven to find Potter in meeting room two with Charlesworth.

'What the hell do we do?' whispered Louise.

'Only one thing to do,' replied Jane, knocking on the door.

'Yes, what is it?' shouted Charlesworth.

Jane pushed open the door. 'We need a word with the chief super . . .' Her voice ran out of steam, hoping Potter would take the hint.

'Now?'

'Yes, Sir.'

Potter turned in her seat. 'Give me ten minutes, will you, Sir,' she said, standing up. 'This might be important.'

The adjacent meeting room was vacant, Louise already holding the door open.

Potter perched on the edge of the table, her eyes darting to the partition, keeping a careful watch on Charlesworth through the glass. She clearly didn't want the ACC to know she had enlisted Dixon's help. 'Well?'

'The High Tech report is incomplete, Ma'am,' said Louise, closing the door. 'I've tried ringing them but they say they can't look at it again until Monday at the earliest.'

'We just need to know if the workplace analytics software installed on the victims' computers can be accessed remotely,' said Jane. 'The report doesn't say one way or the other.'

'You need to know, or Nick needs to know?' Arms folded now.

'No comment.' Jane tried a wry smile.

'Does he know what's been going on?'

'Yes, Ma'am. He just needs this last piece of—'

A wave of Potter's left hand cut Jane off mid-sentence, as she picked up the phone with her right. She was watching Charlesworth in the reflection as she dialled the number, flicked it to speaker-phone and replaced the handset.

'High Tech.'

'This is Deborah Potter. Put me on to whoever is dealing with the Webb and Bishop computers, will you?'

'That's me, Ma'am. How can I help?'

'We need to know if the workplace analytics software is accessible remotely.'

'I've just had a DC bending my ear about that. I couldn't see anything obvious when I looked at it—'

'Can you look at it again, please? Now.'

The hesitation was long enough to be noticeable.

'We are in a threat to life situation,' continued Potter. 'I think that was explained to you.'

'Sorry, yes, Ma'am. Give me half an hour. I'll need to get the hard drives out again.'

'Ring Louise Willmott when you've got an answer.' Potter replaced the handset and turned to Jane, her eyebrows raised. 'Can you at least give me something to calm him down?' she asked, with an almost imperceptible nod in Charlesworth's direction.

'Nick said he knows the motive and this is the last piece of the jigsaw.'

'And it's nothing to do with Markmoor Farm or Szopinski?'

'No, Ma'am.'

'Cela commence, as Hercule Poirot would say.'

'That's him.' Poland was watching the rain running down the windscreen of his Volvo. 'I'd have been like him.'

'You've certainly got the walk for it.'

'Thanks.'

They were parked in the 'customers only' spaces in front of Somerset Plumbing Supplies, a shiny two-storey commercial unit at the newer end of the Walrow Industrial Estate, a set of metal steps up the outside of the building leading to office space above. 'To Let' signs blocked the windows at the far end, TG Media stickers filling the three windows nearest the steps.

'That must be his car,' said Dixon, pointing to an Audi estate parked in front of another TG Media sign bolted to the low wall.

'Good cheap office space, I imagine,' said Poland, pouring himself another coffee from his flask. 'Ideal if you're mainly online.'

A good point, not that Dixon would tell him.

'Someone's spotted us in the plumbing supplies office. We must look a bit suspicious sitting here.'

'Let's hope they haven't called the police. Here we go,' Dixon said, putting his phone to his ear. 'How did you get on?'

'She was in a meeting with Charlesworth, but we got her out and she made the call. High Tech have just got back to us and, yes, the workplace analytics is accessible remotely. There's nothing obvious, no reference to it, so unless you were looking for it you wouldn't see it, but it's there. He's pulled off the logs and emailed them over, but it's just a list of IP addresses; no two the same. Whoever's using it is masking their IP.'

'It'll take days to go through them all,' said Louise, in the background.

'There's no time—'

'Get over to Walrow. We're waiting for you in the car park.'

'Taylor Gooch?'

'He installed it, so he should know who's logging into it, shouldn't he?'

◆ ◆ ◆

Curiosity had got the better of Dixon, and he was already leaning across from the top step and trying to get a look in the side window of TG Media when Jane and Louise turned into the car park.

Poland had gone around the back and was standing on a stack of pallets. 'Frosted glass round here,' he shouted, reappearing from around the corner, brushing his hands together. 'The loo, probably. There's an extractor fan.'

'Have you rung the bell?' asked Jane, stopping on the top step.

'There's no one in there.' Louise was squatting down on the landing, looking through the letterbox.

'Can I help?' The man had come out of the plumbing supplies office and was standing below them in the car park, his hands on his hips.

'Police,' replied Jane, warrant card at the ready. 'We're looking for Taylor Gooch.'

'Not seen him, I'm afraid.' The man shook his head. 'That's his car, but as I say, I've not seen him today.'

'Is there anyone with a key?' asked Louise.

'Our manager's got one, but he's not in the office today. Do you want me to ring him?'

'No time for that,' muttered Dixon.

'There's a pile of bricks round the back,' offered Poland. 'I'll get one.'

'I'll do it,' said Jane, intercepting Poland before he reached the top of the steps. She took hold of the brick and swung it at the glass adjacent to the Yale lock. 'At least I'm on duty, so have a lawful excuse.' Then she began smashing away the shards of glass stuck in the frame, before reaching in and opening the door.

Dixon squeezed past her, snapping on a pair of latex gloves. 'Here,' he said, handing a pair to Poland. 'I've got a feeling we'll be needing you, Roger.'

Four desks, filing cabinets, certificates on the wall; Microsoft Exchange Server certified, Google Adwords accredited, Oracle Developer Advanced, the list went on. Several photos of someone in black tie receiving an award for something or other too.

'That's him at the Somerset Business Awards. Best Use of Technology Award,' said Louise. 'Unfortunate.'

There were two doors at the back of the office, the one on the left ajar. Poland had been spot on: the loo. The door on the right was locked.

'This must be the server cupboard.' Dixon put his ear to the door. 'You can hear the fans whirring.'

'Can't see a key,' said Jane. She was searching the desk in front of the door, a jacket slung over the back of the chair. Then she tapped the mouse, bringing the computer back to life. 'It's just gone to sleep. It hadn't been switched off, so he must be here somewhere.'

'In there,' said Poland. He was pointing at the bottom of the server cupboard door, where a trickle of blood was soaking into the edge of the carpet.

'Call it in, Lou.' Dixon picked up a fire extinguisher and began hitting the door frame, the wood around the lock splintering a little with each blow. 'A battering ram would be useful.'

'Do you want to wait for uniform to get here?' asked Jane, her eyebrows raised.

Three more hits, then the frame around the lock disintegrated, the bracket dropped to the floor and the door swung open.

Metal racks mounted on the walls either side were filled with computers, thick bundles of cables running along the back of each shelf. Green and red lights flickered on each of the boxes, which were standing vertically side by side, lines of them.

Poland reached in and flicked on the light, careful not to tread in the pool of blood. 'Dragged in feet first by the looks of things. Throat's been cut and there's a blow to the back of the head. Here.' He was leaning over, pointing. 'I'd say he was hit from behind when he was sitting at his desk, dragged in here and finished off. Either that or he was already in here, working perhaps, when the killer struck. Blood spatter will soon tell us.' Poland shone his torch at the computer units, looking for blood. 'These ones are all black so we'll need luminol. You won't see it with the naked eye, not in this light.'

'How long?'

'The blood's not fresh. So some time last night maybe. I'll need to get him back to the lab though.'

'See if anyone saw anything, Lou,' said Dixon. 'CCTV too. There may be some covering the car park.'

'Yes, Sir.'

'He's not going to be telling us who's been using the work-place analytics now, is he?' Dixon was sucking his teeth. 'And that's exactly why he's been killed.'

'He probably rang his killer after we visited yesterday,' said Jane. 'Poor sod.'

Dixon was looking at the screen of Gooch's computer, which had now come on, revealing a news story on the Somerset Live website: 'Local Estate Agent found murdered'. He had read the same article on his phone, mainly to check that no mention had been made of the AirDropping. 'We'd better clear out and leave the scene for Scientific,' he said, turning for the door. 'And I could really do with being somewhere else before the cavalry arrive. Specially our new crime scene manager.'

'Take my car,' said Poland. 'I'll hang on here. May as well do something useful even though I'm supposed to be on holiday.'

'We'd better get somebody round to Gooch's flat,' said Jane.

'Potter's ten minutes away,' said Lou, leaning in the front door. *Time to go.*

'Where are you off to now?' Jane was shouting after Dixon as he jogged across the car park towards Poland's Volvo. He jumped in, turned out of the parking space just as Poland slammed the boot, and wound down the window.

'One last throw of the dice before we have to start going through the estate agents one by one. And if we have to do that, Waller's dead.'

'Assuming he isn't already.'

'We always assume that unless and until we know otherwise.'

'Yeah.'

'Meet me at Gold Corner in an hour. And bring Potter.'

Chapter Forty

Somewhere suitably posh. Detached with a large garden.

Expensive.

Dixon was creeping along Rectory Road, looking up at the houses. He stopped across the entrance to the vicarage, remembering games of cricket in the drive; the stumps leaning up against the garage door, his friend Tim's run up so long he started on the pavement on the other side of the road.

Happy days.

Next door would do. They'd climbed over the wall often enough to get the ball back.

He checked the sold prices on Rightmove, the property not listed at all; it hadn't changed hands for years. Perfect.

Two quid on the Land Registry website would tell him who owned it.

High hedges hid the large detached house, the black and white painted timbers of dormer windows on the second floor visible over the top; six bedrooms at least.

No estate agent would be able to resist.

'Eastman and Webb. How can I help?'

'Yes, hello,' said Dixon, his voice gruff. 'My mother's gone into a care home and we need to sell her house. I've got a lasting power of attorney. Could someone come and have a look at it with a view to putting it on the market?'

'Yes, of course. It won't be until next week now, I'm afraid. What's the address?'

'Rectory Road, number 52.'

'Oh, right. Mrs Eastman could come and see you tomorrow morning, if that's any good?'

'Yes, fine.'

'And what's the name?'

'David Cook. My mother is Beryl.'

'Can I just take a number for you, Mr Cook, or is it the mobile you're ringing from?'

'That's it.'

'How about ten-thirty tomorrow then?'

'Fine.'

'That's lovely. I'll put it in the diary now.'

Dixon rang off and dropped his phone on the passenger seat. Bait set.

Dixon was sitting on the wall at Gold Corner, his back to the pumping station, his feet dangling over the water swirling as it flowed out from under the bridge. He was watching the traffic speeding past on the motorway in the distance, a couple of miles away at least, although it was impossible to judge in the light. Thick cloud, darkness maybe an hour away if he was lucky.

Impossible to see the traffic too, although he could have sworn he'd spotted a black Range Rover heading south.

His phone was lying on the top of the wall next to him.

Silent.

Occasionally, he'd tap the screen to see if there were any notifications. He'd already checked the volume umpteen times, cranking it up to the max.

It was a call not to be missed.

A line of cars appeared around the bend in the lane, maybe half a mile away. Dixon recognised Jane's at the front of the convoy, followed by Dave's, then Potter's.

Another tap of the phone screen. It was just a theory at this point, until the bloody thing rang.

Where's your evidence?

The question was hanging over him already, and Potter hadn't even asked it yet. She would, though, that much was inevitable.

And he didn't really have an answer unless and until his phone rang.

He was about to find out how much faith the detective chief superintendent had in him; whether the simple fact that he had never been wrong before was enough. That everything had dropped into place would help, of course. Every single thing.

His phone ringing would be the icing on the cake, like picking up the blank tile in Scrabble when you're on the brink of an eight-letter word. Not your run-of-the-mill seven letter word either – definitely an eight. He tapped the screen again, before turning around and dropping off the top of the wall, the convoy parking under the trees.

Potter didn't bother to pull in, leaving her car on the roadside, engine running.

The look on the face of the Environment Agency bloke working in the pumping station was a picture – he'd probably be ringing the police to report a drug deal, thought Dixon.

'How did you know Gooch was dead?' demanded Potter, striding along the lane towards him, Maggie Baldwin caught in her slipstream. Then came Jane, Louise, Dave and Mark, with Roger Poland at the back, keeping a safe distance.

'It was a reasonable assumption, based on the evidence.'

'What evidence?'

There we go.

Dixon leaned back against the wall, the others forming a semicircle around him, Potter in the middle.

'It's a cartel,' he said.

'What, like the Colombians?' Mark Pearce grinned.

'No, not like the Colombians.' Dixon scowled at him. 'You've been watching too much Netflix.'

'Sorry, Sir.'

'A price fixing cartel. All three estate agents have put their heads together and agreed to fix the price they charge for selling a house. It's a clear breach of competition law and they can be fined tens of thousands of pounds by the Competition and Markets Authority, which is more than enough motive for murder.'

'Yes, but what about the writing on the wall at Waller's place, the "I.S"? It must be Ian Szopinski, surely?'

'It could be any one of three things,' said Dixon. 'It could really have been Waller pointing us in the direction of Szopinski. Or it could have been the killer taking the opportunity to point us in Szopinski's direction. Or it could mean something else altogether.'

'What?' demanded Potter.

'One point five.'

Potter's stance softened, her hands moving from her hips to her pockets. 'Go on.'

'I rang round all the agents this morning and it's impossible to get any of them to agree to less than one point five per cent commission. Every single property entered on Eastman and Webb's QBrix software shows the same fee. Even the Record Sheets stapled to the insides of the files have the commission preprinted at one point five per cent. But on some of Richard Webb's files, he's altered that by hand to one point two.'

'He was undercutting?'

'He was, Ma'am,' replied Dixon.

'Which is why someone tried to kill him?'

'Undercut everyone else in the cartel and he could snaffle all the sales going, put the others out of business. After all, everyone rings around for the cheapest quote, don't they? And I don't think they did try to kill him.'

'Eh?'

'He was being punished. The fact that his QBrix software still records one point five per cent tells me that someone else had access to it. Someone whose job it was to make sure they were all sticking to the agreement. What Webb didn't know was that this person also had access to everything on his computer via the workplace analytics tool, so he or she could see not only the QBrix entries, but also his emails and documents.'

'The invoices and memoranda of sale would show the actual figure agreed with the client.' Potter nodded her understanding. 'One point two per cent.'

'Exactly.'

'So, all that Markmoor Farm Holidays and pylon stuff was a load of bollocks. We went in completely the wrong direction?'

'We were *sent* in completely the wrong direction, Ma'am, but that's another matter.' Dixon tapped the screen of his phone again. Nothing.

'What about Trevor Bishop then? Was he undercutting the cartel?'

'Not as far as I can see. He was killed because of his internet search history.'

'The killer can see that as well?'

'The workplace analytics tool gives him full access to Bishop's computer, so yes.'

'Which explains why Gooch was killed as well,' said Potter. 'He must've given the killer the login details for the workplace analytics and had to be silenced.'

'Maybe he was demanding money to stay silent?' asked Louise.

'Maybe he was. Hardly matters now though,' replied Potter. 'Does it?'

'I suppose not.'

'So what was it in Bishop's internet search history?' asked Potter, turning back to Dixon.

'He went into the office on Sunday morning, probably after he heard about what happened to Richard Webb the night before, and searched for "CMA leniency". The Competition and Markets Authority operates a leniency policy and that gives a whistle blower total immunity from any prosecution and fines – and these are huge fines, ten per cent of turnover – provided they cooperate fully. Most importantly of all, though, is that they must be blowing the whistle on a cartel that is not already under investigation, which explains why he said nothing when we brought him in for questioning on Sunday night. To get his immunity, he needed to contact the CMA first.'

'Have we checked with the CMA?'

'Not yet.' Dixon shrugged. 'I didn't want them checking my credentials at the moment, oddly enough.'

'Quite.' Potter turned to Maggie Baldwin and raised her eyebrows.

'I'll do it now, Ma'am,' said Maggie.

'And Waller?'

'He rang us from his office landline,' replied Dixon, tapping the screen on his phone. 'The workplace analytics is installed at Harrison Samuels as well, so the killer would've seen that in Waller's digital call log.'

'We'll need to be careful how we handle this,' said Potter. 'Ideally, we need to find Waller before we go wading in. If the killer gets wind that we're on to him, Waller's as good as dead.'

'If he isn't already.' Mark Pearce again.

'What's so fascinating on your bloody phone?' asked Potter, watching Dixon glance at the screen.

'When Jane and Lou were in Eastman and Webb's office yesterday, Hilary Eastman took a call from a client saying they'd been approached by another agent and were placing their property with them instead. She sounded livid.'

'You were listening in?' Potter frowned.

'Long story.'

'I remember,' said Jane. 'She couldn't work out how the other agent had got the details. She hadn't even been out to see the property yet, let alone placed it on the market.'

'Did she say who this other agent was?' demanded Potter.

'No.'

'The other agent must've got the details from Hilary Eastman's Outlook diary on her computer via the workplace analytics tool,' said Dixon. 'It was a big house – too good an opportunity to miss – so I've baited a trap. I've made an appointment for Hilary to visit a property

I'm selling in Rectory Road, tomorrow at ten-thirty. A nice big one; eight hundred grand's worth at least. When my phone rings, it'll be the killer trying to get in first.'

'What the bloody hell is that?' asked Mark.

Jane rolled her eyes. 'Now you know why his phone is always on silent.'

The theme from *The Vikings* on full blast.

'Quiet, everyone,' said Potter.

Dixon turned away, placing his phone to his ear. 'David Cook,' he said.

'Mr Cook, I gather you're selling a relative's property under a lasting power of attorney and I was ringing to offer my assistance. I'm an estate agent in Burnham, probably better suited to a property of this type than Eastman and Webb, if I may say so. They tend to deal with the lower end of the market, if that makes sense.'

'It does.'

'Could I perhaps come and visit? I'd be happy to offer you my market appraisal, entirely free of charge, of course. No obligation. Eastman and Webb do charge a valuation fee. Did they tell you that when you spoke to them?'

'No, they didn't.'

'Ah, I'm afraid they often do that. I'm guessing someone's going into a care home, if you're using a lasting power of attorney?'

'My mother.'

'I'm sorry to hear that. What's her name, if I may ask?'

You may.

'Beryl Ada Cook.'

'The property is also registered in the name of . . . I'm guessing . . . your father?'

You've done your homework.

'My father, Anthony, yes. He died in 2011 and we never got round to sending his death certificate to the Land Registry, I'm afraid,' replied Dixon. 'I'm told the solicitors can sort that out when they're doing the conveyancing.'

'Of course they can. Would tomorrow at ten-thirty suit?'

'Er, yes.' Dixon hesitated, deliberately. 'I think I'll cancel Eastman and Webb if they charge a fee.'

'Good idea.'

'One last thing.' Dixon turned back to Potter, his fingers crossed in his pocket. 'Can I take your name?'

Chapter Forty-One

'Oh, shit.'

'What is it, Lou?' asked Dixon.

'Brian Townsend was the one presenting the award to Taylor Gooch. Remember? The picture on the wall in Gooch's office.'

Dixon remembered. 'The Somerset Business Awards.'

'Best Use of Technology,' continued Louise. 'Sponsored by Harrison Samuels Estate Agents.'

'He's also the president of the Somerset branch of the National Association of Estate Agents.' Dixon gritted his teeth. '"I know everyone and pretty much everything they get up to as well", he said. Now I know how.'

'Talk about hiding in plain sight,' said Potter. 'I take it you've got a plan.'

'We need to find him and get him under surveillance; hope he leads us to Waller. In the meantime, we look at all the properties being sold with vacant possession. If he's alive, Waller will be in one of them. Start with those that have got outbuildings.'

'Just Harrison Samuels?' asked Jane.

'No. Townsend's got access to the properties on the books of the other agents as well, so it could be any one of them. Look for one that's been on the market for a while, perhaps. Rural, out of the way.'

'Well done, Nick,' said Potter, turning for her car. 'I'll see you get the credit for this.'

Dixon watched the cars speed off one by one, a cheery wave from Jane as her wheels spun on the gravel.

'Pub?' asked Poland.

'I thought you were going to deal with Gooch?'

'My assistant turned up, so I thought I'd leave him to it and keep you company. It was pretty straightforward and he doesn't need me breathing down his neck.'

'Thanks.'

'And you got all of that just from looking at the files?'

'The files and QBrix. Once I knew the workplace analytics was accessible remotely, it all dropped into place. Gooch's murder just confirmed it. There can't really be any other reason he was killed.'

'Maybe I'll stick to post mortems.'

'Here, you drive,' said Dixon, lobbing Poland the car keys.

'Where are we going?'

'I've just done a search of Harrison Samuels properties listed on Rightmove, highest price first. There's a vacant smallholding over at Woolavington that'll be as good a place as any to start. It's got outbuildings with lapsed planning permission to convert into office units, and an old stable block; being sold with development potential at an asking price of one point three million.'

'When did it go on the market?' asked Poland, opening the driver's door of his car.

'Last year.'

Ten minutes later they screeched to a halt in front of Chilpitts Farm. It had seen better days; even the Harrison Samuels 'For Sale' board was leaning over, partially hidden by brambles.

Dixon looked up the track leading to the derelict farmhouse. 'This isn't it,' he said. 'No one's been up that track for weeks.'

'Shouldn't we at least go and have a look?' asked Poland, frowning. 'Is there another way in?'

'Nope. I looked on Google Earth.'

Dixon was scrolling through more listings on Rightmove. 'Let me see if the search parameters are any different on PrimeLocation.' He stretched his shoulders while he waited for the page to load. 'Yes, they are. Look, you can search for "Rural/secluded" and "Chain free".'

'What's if it's not on PrimeLocation?'

'Then we're stuffed. Here we go. Now, that's perfect for a man who likes to hide in plain sight. Brean Down Farm. The opposite end to the fort. Everybody who goes to Brean Down goes up the steps and turns left. No one goes to the quarry at the Uphill end. And even if they do, it's hidden by trees from above.'

'There's a quarry at the Uphill end?'

'With an old farmhouse. Empty and "in need of modernisation", for sale by auction on . . . if not sold before. Looks like it might flood, which explains why it's been on the market for a while.'

'How long's a while?' asked Poland, doing a three-point turn.

'Two years.'

Coast Road was inches deep in sand, Poland's tyres sliding on the bend at the Brean beach access slip. Dixon was amusing himself spotting rust on the static caravans slowly decomposing in salt spray driven on the prevailing wind. It was either that, or watching the speedometer as Poland cheerfully ignored the thirty miles an hour speed limit.

'He should've waited,' Poland said, his wheels on the grass verge to avoid a car that had come out of the National Trust car park.

'Maybe he wasn't expecting you to be hurtling along at sixty?'

'You'd be doing the same.'

'I can stick a blue light on my Land Rover.'

'Either you want to get there or you don't.' Poland accelerated past the Tropical Bird Garden, switching his lights to full beam as his Volvo bounced along the farm track at the base of the Down. 'There's a torch in the glovebox.'

'You have that,' said Dixon. 'I've got my phone.'

Poland slowed as he reached the end of the track. 'What d'you want me to do?'

'Go round to the right, park somewhere and we'll walk back.'

The grass verge was wide enough for Poland's car. 'Should we check those barns as well?' he asked, switching off the headlights.

'Looks like a working farm to me. If Waller's here, he'll be in the old farmhouse, back there.'

'And what if he's not?'

'We've wasted an hour.'

Fresh tyre tracks in the mud, the parking area deserted. A good sign.

The house was dark; trees on the steep slope behind it over-hanging and resting on the roof tiles. The only light was com-ing from across the River Axe, which snaked inland between the end of Brean Down and Uphill. Streetlights, houses, a couple of fireworks going up from the Weston Bay Yacht Club on Uphill beach now the light was fading; half a mile away, and yet half an hour in the car.

'Four garages? Who the bloody hell needs four garages?'

'Someone with four cars?' The doors were locked, Dixon rattling the handle of each in turn. Then he shone the light on his phone in the side window. 'They're separate garages and I can't see into the next one. There are windows in the back wall so I'll squeeze along here to get a look in.'

'I'll wait for you,' said Poland, glancing up at the brambles towering over the block.

'Thanks.'

Branches clawing at his coat; the brambles may have lost their leaves, but they haven't bloody well lost their thorns, thought Dixon, as he pushed his way through the undergrowth, shielding his eyes with one hand, his phone in the other.

An old Mini was rusting away in the second garage, rubble on the floor in the third. The fourth was empty. Dixon kept going, emerging at the far end of the block.

Poland had gone by the time he was back where he started, a light flickering inside the old farmhouse. Grey stone, the windows boarded up.

Modernisation, my arse.

The kitchen units had gone, leaving their outline in laminate flooring that had been laid around them; the wall tiles had gone too, their outline left in grout yet to be chipped off the wall; lead pipes where the sink had once been, under the boarded-up window. Only an old Aga and a rusty radiator remained untouched.

Poland had already moved on, the beam of his torch in a room at the far end of the corridor. Dixon followed.

'That must've been the living room,' said Poland, emerging from the end room. 'There's a TV aerial on the floor. If Waller's here, he won't be upstairs either.'

'Why not?'

'No stairs.' Poland shone his torch at the back of the hall, opposite the front door, where a handrail bolted to the wall rose diagonally to a landing.

'There was a ladder in the garage,' said Dixon.

'I'll go,' offered Poland.

Dixon was admiring a new electricity meter in the walk-in cupboard next to the kitchen door when he heard the sound of breaking glass, Poland reappearing seconds later with a cheesy grin and the ladder tucked under his arm.

'I tripped and fell and my elbow went through the glass,' he said.

'Just make sure you pay for the damage.'

The ladder swiftly replaced the stairs, Poland's foot on the bottom rung. 'Up you go,' he said. 'And you'd better take this,' handing Dixon the torch. 'That phone's no bloody good to man nor beast.'

'Thanks.'

'If he's not up there, we can look for a cellar next.'

'There won't be one,' replied Dixon, shining the torch in Poland's eyes. 'I looked on Google Earth and the high tide comes in right round the front of the house. A cellar would flood in the blink of an eye.'

'Talking of which!' Poland had turned away, blinking furiously.

'Sorry.'

Dixon stepped across from the top of the ladder on to the landing and listened.

Nothing.

Each room in turn; torch and phone, he tiptoed through the first open door; top of the landing on the right. Nothing, except a chill wind whistling through the gaps in the planks nailed across the inside of the window.

Back out on to the landing, the next door was shut; another bedroom at the back of the house.

Must be.

He pushed the door with the torch, then tried turning the handle.

Jammed: best case. Locked: worst case.

He took a step back, lifted his left foot and kicked the door just above the handle. It swung open.

Dixon turned away, his hand across his mouth, desperately trying to suppress the urge to vomit.

'What is it?'

'Give me a minute, Roger.' Phone in his back pocket now; torch in his right hand, his left clamping a wad of scented dog poo bags across his nose and mouth, Dixon edged into the room.

Two windows either side of the fireplace, both boarded up. Wallpaper peeling, cobwebs.

One of those old butane gas fires in front of a mattress, a man lying on the floorboards next to it, naked from the waist up and chained to an old column radiator, his wrists wrapped in bloody bandages. Dixon stepped over a washing-up bowl – the source of the smell – and pressed his fingers into the side of Waller's neck.

A faint pulse.

'Need you up here, Roger,' Dixon shouted, taking off his coat and laying it over Waller.

He checked the fire. Switched on, the last of the butane long since burnt out.

Hypothermia then.

'Is it him?' Poland asked, raising his voice over the clunking of the aluminium ladder as he climbed towards the light.

'Yes, it's Waller. Freezing cold to the touch, but there's a faint pulse.' Dixon shone the torch on the washing-up bowl. 'Watch out for that. He's been using it for—'

'I get it.'

'I'll ring Jane.'

'Let's get him off these floorboards first,' said Poland. 'The bloody draught is whistling up through them.'

Together they lifted Waller on to the mattress, then Dixon dialled Jane's number.

'Where are you?' she asked, before he had even drawn breath.

'Brean Down Farm. We've found Waller.'

'How the bloody hell did you do that?'

'Can we worry about that later?'

'Yeah.'

'He's alive, but only just, so you'd better get an ambulance on the way.'

'Scientific?'

'He's chained to a radiator, so yes, the full works.'

'Leave it to me.'

Dixon rang off and turned to find Poland down to his shirt-sleeves, his coat draped over Waller's upper body and his pullover wrapped around his head. 'He's only young,' Poland said. 'Poor sod.'

'Any injuries?'

'Can't see any, apart from his wrists. There's the odd bruise, but it's hypothermia that's the danger.' Poland was rubbing Waller's shoulders. 'C'mon, boy, stay with us.'

'He was probably all right until the gas ran out.' Dixon shone the torch on a pile of clothes in the corner, at the foot of the mattress. 'Looks like he took his own clothes off.'

'Paradoxical undressing. I've seen it before. The mind playing tricks; telling you you're hot when actually you're freezing to death.'

'Is there anything else we can do for him?'

'Not really.'

'What about a fire?'

Poland turned his head to listen to the sirens in the distance. 'By the time you've got that going, they'll be here.'

'I haven't got any matches anyway.' Dixon stepped over Waller and lay down next to him on the mattress. 'Body warmth it is then, Roger. You lie the other side.'

Chapter Forty-Two

'We got lucky.' Dixon was leaning against the passenger door of Poland's car, holding the hood of his top down over his face while the air ambulance touched down in the field next to the track. The downdraft of the rotor blades was sending loose hay high into the air, the landing zone lit by the headlights of several patrol cars.

'Luck doesn't come into it,' said Potter.

An ambulance had got to them first, Dixon beating a hasty retreat, leaving Poland to brief the paramedics on Waller's condition. Then had come the first of the patrol cars, followed by Jane and Louise in convoy with Deborah Potter.

Jane had sent Dixon a text, which should have given him ample time to get clear, but it arrived late and he'd only got as far as Poland's Volvo before Potter caught up with him.

'You make your own luck,' he said. He allowed himself the ghost of a smile, but even that soon faded.

'You certainly seem to.' Potter was standing with her back to the helicopter, oblivious to the bits of hay landing in her hair. 'Did he say anything?'

'Way beyond that, I'm afraid.' Dixon curled his lip. 'Touch and go, according to Roger.'

'Was he part of the cartel?'

'I doubt it, not directly anyway. Waller's just an employee; Gerard Pollock and Brian Townsend own Harrison Samuels, so it would have been their decision. They'd have told Waller not to go below one point five per cent. Pollock'll be the one paying the fines. Either way, that's the Competition and Markets Authority's problem.'

'Don't they switch those bloody things off?' Potter glanced over her shoulder at the helicopter, the rotor blades still turning.

'Here he comes,' said Dixon, nodding in the direction of the farm, where four paramedics were carrying a stretcher towards an open five bar gate, Poland following along behind them. Two Scientific Services vans had stopped on the corner to allow them through.

'They've got him on a warm drip and wrapped him in space blankets,' said Poland, jogging over. 'They need to get his core temperature up, but he should be fine, they said. Saved by a search of PrimeLocation. Who'd have thought it?'

Potter looked at Dixon and raised her eyebrows.

'Chain free and rural,' he said.

The stretcher was slid into the back of the helicopter, the roar of the engine as the helicopter took off putting a stop to further conversation.

'Have you been in?' asked Poland, lowering his voice as the noise of the helicopter receded into the distance.

'Not yet,' replied Potter.

'See if Scientific have got some Vicks for under your nose, would be my advice.'

'Like that, is it?'

'He's been in there for days, chained to a radiator.'

'Maybe I'll give it a miss.' Potter turned to Dixon. 'Where do we find Brian bloody Townsend then?'

'Harrison Samuels is a patron of the North Petherton carnival. They've got a small office there, next to the chemist.' He slid a crumpled booklet out of his coat pocket – open at the back page, folded back on itself and then in half again – and handed it to Potter. 'That's the carnival programme. They also sponsor the Harrison Samuels Cup for the Best Feature Cart. The prize giving is at seven at the Walnut Tree. He's hardly going to miss that, is he?'

'It starts at the rugby club and goes all the way up the A38 to the Huntworth roundabout,' said the traffic officer behind the wheel of the speeding patrol car, the blue light reflecting off the roofs as they raced out of Bridgwater. 'Our best bet's the back road in from North Newton. I'll get as far up Mill Street as I can, then you'll have to walk the rest of the way.'

'We'll run,' said Potter, sitting in the passenger seat.

Jane was crammed in the back, with Louise and Maggie, her warrant card at the ready. The car slowed on the bridge over the M5, lights in the distance streaming along the A38 towards North Petherton.

'The first carts have left the rugby club,' said Louise. The lights were moving north, the lead carts disappearing behind the houses along the A38, only the glare of the thousands of bulbs giving away how far they'd got.

A patrol car was parked across the road at the junction with Baymead Lane, blocking access to the main road, a cart creeping past at the far end.

'You won't get much further,' said a uniformed officer, leaning in the driver's window. Then he noticed Potter. 'Sorry, Ma'am. Give me a sec. You should be all right as far as the school.'

'Thank you.'

'The school'll do,' said Jane.

The driver was revving the engine impatiently while the officer reversed the patrol car out of the way. Then he accelerated through the gap, the officer blocking the road again behind them.

'At least we know Townsend's going to be stuck on foot,' said Potter. 'Better switch the blue light off as well. No one's going to see it on a night like this anyway.'

Mill Street was blocked by a gang of youths, some kicking a football backwards and forwards across the road, others swigging from a bottle. They started banging on the bonnet of the car when the driver sounded the horn, but a flash of the blue light soon had them running off down side streets, the bottle left rolling into the gutter.

The sounds of the carnival made their way into the passenger compartment as they crept along Mill Lane, as did the smells, all of them familiar to Jane.

Fish and chips and cannabis.

A steward wearing a hi-vis tabard standing in the entrance to the school car park flagged them down. 'You won't get much further, I'm afraid,' he said.

'Get as far as you can,' said Potter, leaning across and waving her warrant card at him.

'You can leave it here, if you want,' the steward replied. 'Anywhere you can get in.'

A narrow entrance with a turning circle at the far end and three parking spaces, all of them occupied; a large sign saying 'Staff only'.

'Katie starts here next year,' said Louise. 'I'll have to get used to the school run.'

Jane was looking down at her screen, which had just lit up. 'Dave and Mark are here. They're outside the Walnut Tree. There's a gala dinner going on inside.'

'Tell them to see if he's in there, but be discreet. We'll be there in a minute,' said Potter. 'Just leave the car here. Block them in.'

Potter jumped out of the car and sprinted along Mill Street towards the Walnut Tree, Jane, Louise and Maggie right behind her. The hotel sign was visible on the far side of the road, over the heads of the crowd waiting patiently for the procession to reach them.

Jane weaved her way through the queues of people, clouds of smoke billowing from e-cigarettes as they waited for their fish and chips, burgers, candyfloss, toffee apples; the stands blocking the end of Mill Street.

Then she was pushing her way through the crowd to the edge of the road, ducking under the rope and sprinting across the A38, the first carts now a couple of hundred yards away, the sights and sounds familiar from Bridgwater and Burnham.

She ducked under the rope on the far side, right behind Potter, the crowd parting to let them through.

A flatbed trailer had been parked against the wall in the entrance to the Walnut Tree car park. It was lit up by several lamps, a microphone on a stand positioned opposite several bales of straw. A man was standing by the microphone, tapping it with his index finger, a large crowd gathered in front of him beneath a North Petherton Carnival sign that had been painted on a wooden board and nailed to the side of the trailer.

'You made it then?'

'We did,' replied Potter, turning to find Dave and Mark emerging from the Walnut Tree, much to the obvious relief of the doorman.

'He's not in there, Ma'am. We had a good look around.'

'Testing, testing, one, two, three. Ah, it's working,' said the man standing at the microphone. 'The procession will soon be here, so let's make a start with the prize giving, if I could have the dignitaries and special guests on stage, please?'

'He'll be down at the front and getting up on that trailer any second now. Block his exits.'

'Yes, Ma'am.'

'We'll start with the award for Best Tableaux Cart, sponsored by Newton Country Stores, and it goes to Ham Hill Carnival Club for *Those Magnificent Men in Their Flying Machines*.'

Cheers and applause drowned out the approaching carts just for a moment as the trophy was held aloft by a Biggles lookalike, several people still clambering up on to the trailer behind the presentation party.

Jane was working her way towards the front of the crowd, Louise right behind her. She glanced across at Potter and Maggie, pushing their way through the crowd towards the far end of the trailer. That left over the wall behind it as the obvious escape route. 'Where did Dave and Mark go?' she shouted, turning to Louise.

'Out into the road, I think.'

The awards ceremony was winding up now, as the carnival procession approached along the main road.

'Lastly we have the Harrison Samuels Cup for Best Feature Cart, which goes to Middlezoy, for *Curse of the Kraken*.'

And there he was. Brian Townsend stepped forward, trophy in hand, ready to congratulate the winner. Wearing a Rotary Club tabard over a blue coat, and a red bobble hat.

A shake of the hand, the trophy handed over to a pirate, and Townsend stepped back into the shadows behind the straw bales at the back of the trailer.

Time for thanks to go to the organising committee, obviously; polite cheers and applause.

Jane glanced across at Potter, who was only feet away from the trailer, the noise from the carts approaching along the A38 growing louder by the second.

Then four uniformed officers appeared, pushing their way through the crowd that was now filing out on to the pavement to see the first of the carnival carts drawing level with the car park. The officers reached the bottom of the steps up on to the trailer, their path blocked by people clambering down.

'Where the hell did they come from?' shouted Jane.

Townsend stepped back into the shadows.

'He's seen them,' said Louise.

'Get ready. If Nick's right, he'll run.'

Chapter Forty-Three

'This is as close as I can get,' said Poland, the end of Watery Lane blocked in front of him, cars parked on both sides of the road. 'I'll never turn around either, so I'm going to have to back out.'

'I can run the rest of the way,' said Dixon, jumping out of the passenger seat.

Roger's reply: 'I'll catch you—' cut off by the slamming of the car door.

Dixon sprinted along the pavement, past North Petherton Library, weaving his way through the stragglers at the back of the crowd, most of them standing on tiptoe, trying to get a glimpse of the procession that was creeping towards them.

Then Dixon was working his way along the back of the car park outside the Walnut Tree. He pulled his hoodie down over his face as he weaved between the parked cars, in the shadows now as he crossed to the far wall and began making his way forward again, towards the front of the trailer, just as Brian Townsend was presenting the trophy to someone dressed as a pirate. An eye patch and a false moustache, but no hat – not Blackbeard then.

Townsend was wearing a hi-vis Rotary Club tabard over a blue coat, a red bobble hat – and it all dropped into place. Dixon had seen him before, at the Bridgwater carnival.

'Want a programme, mate? Two quid.'

Townsend turned and jumped up on to the wall behind the trailer, then stepped across on to the flat roof of a garage.

What the hell?

Suddenly there was movement in the crowd: four uniformed officers were pushing past dignitaries on the steps, Jane pushing her way out into the road.

Dixon stepped up on to the wheel, then hopped up on to the flatbed trailer, before following Townsend on to the roof of the garage behind, just in time to see him drop down into the lane on the other side.

The first cart was level with them now, the glare of the lights and the noise making it possible to see Townsend, but impossible to shout to anyone. Mercifully, Louise had spotted Townsend's escape route and was hastily backtracking, pushing her way out into the road, behind the crowd watching the procession.

Dixon dropped down off the garage and followed Townsend out on to the pavement, weaving in and out of the stragglers at the back of the crowd lining the kerb.

Then Townsend was gone; ducked down and under the rope.

Dixon followed, just in time to see him cross the road in front of the Mendip Vale Carnival Club cart. A rather unconvincing Santa Claus and scantily clad elves. He tried to ignore the Christmas music and the snow machine as he ran in front of the cart into a crowd of stewards on the far side – all wearing hi-vis tabards.

Uniformed officers were running towards him, stopping the carts, the procession being stopped behind him.

No sign of the bobble hat.

Jane ran past on the other side of the road, pointing ahead of her. Townsend must have doubled back to the other side.

The carts were getting familiar now: *Sprit in the Sky, Highway to Hell, Those Magnificent Men in Their Flying Machines.* Then Dixon saw Jane climbing up on to *Curse of the Kraken* behind the towing vehicle.

The Spanish galleon was still rocking from side to side, but the eerie green lighting went off as Jane reached the platform, following Townsend along the side of the galleon towards the back of the cart. The hi-vis tabard had gone, as had the bobble hat. Changing his appearance on the hoof.

Nice try, but no cigar.

Dave, Mark and two uniformed officers began climbing up the front of the cart and weaving their way in between the rowing boats and the pirates looking on in astonishment.

Townsend reached the back of the cart, his way up blocked by the generator, his way down by two more uniformed officers on the ground. He turned and lunged at Jane, spinning her round and clamping his left arm around her throat, his right hand behind her head, pushing it forwards – millimetres from snapping her neck.

The music went off on the carts in front and behind, shouts from the crowd carrying for the first time.

'Stay back!' Townsend was backing away from Dave and Mark, towards the base of the power unit, dragging Jane with him.

Dixon ducked down and ran along the side of the cart, out of sight of those above him, before climbing up on to the cart, hidden by the ship, which had stopped rocking from side to side and was now frozen in a sharp list to starboard.

He looked up and saw Blackbeard leaning over the side of his cradle.

'Give me your gun,' whispered Dixon.

'It's plastic!'

'Just give it to me.'

A plastic flintlock pistol. It would have to do.

Dixon crouched low and edged around the stern of the galleon. Two steps across the platform, then he pressed the barrel of the gun to the back of Townsend's head.

'Armed Police. Release your hostage; face down on the floor, hands behind your head.'

No response.

Jane was wriggling, Townsend tightening his grip if anything.

'Armed Police. This is your final warning.' Dixon jabbed the barrel into the back of Townsend's skull. 'Get down on the floor with your hands behind your head.'

'Fuck you.'

'Command, this is SA74, permission to engage. Suspect is not releasing hostage. I have a clear shot. Range point blank.'

'All right, all right,' shouted Townsend, slowly releasing his grip on Jane. 'Don't shoot.' Hands in the air now. 'Don't shoot me!'

Townsend turned his head as Jane lurched forwards, bent dou ble by a rasping cough.

'Do not look at me,' shouted Dixon. 'Down on the floor. Now.'

On his knees first, then lying prone, his hands behind his head. Mark handcuffed him. 'Brian Townsend, I am arresting you on suspicion of the murders of Trevor Bishop and Taylor Gooch and the attempted murder of Richard Webb. You do not have to say anything, but it may harm your defence if you do not mention when questioned something you later rely on in court.'

Jane straightened up, rubbing her throat at the same time.

'You all right?' Dixon asked, his hand on her shoulder.

'I'll be fine.'

He handed her the plastic pistol, mouthing the word 'fingerprints'.

'Anything you do say may be given in evidence,' continued Mark, watching Jane busily smudging Dixon's prints on the gun with the palm of her hand.

Then Dave stepped forward to help Townsend to his feet.

Dixon dropped off the side of the cart and disappeared into the crowd, pulling the hoodie down over his face as he fell into step with *Right Here, Right Now*, the music and lights coming back on all along the procession.

Chapter Forty-Four

Dixon stopped on the motorway bridge and looked back towards North Petherton, the carnival procession underway again, the last of the carts now well clear of the rugby club, lights moving slowly north on the A38, the cacophony drifting towards him on the westerly breeze.

Three sets of headlights were coming along Newton Road – no flashing blue, mercifully. No sirens either.

The last of the line screeched to a halt next to him, Poland leaning across the empty passenger seat. 'There you are,' he said, smiling through the open window. 'It's taken me ages to get round. They've got him.'

'Really?'

'Jane got herself caught up in it, but a member of the public came to her rescue. Potter's sent her to Musgrove Park to be checked over. She's in an ambulance going out the other way, via Farringdon.'

'She's all right?' demanded Dixon, snatching open the passenger door.

'I spoke to her and she's fine. It's just a precaution.' Poland accelerated away, the door slamming shut. 'Where did you get to?'

'Round and about.'

'Yes, this bloke jumped on the cart and came up behind Townsend. He had her by the neck, but this fellow pretended to be Armed Response and Townsend let her go. Then he just disappeared into the crowd. Left behind a plastic flintlock pistol, he did.'

'What was he wearing?'

'Blue jeans and a hood . . .' Poland's voice tailed off, the realisation finally dawning. 'That's why you scarpered, isn't it?' He sighed. 'I am a complete arse.'

'I wouldn't say that, Roger. Not a complete one, anyway.'

Dixon eventually found Jane in Willow Ward, otherwise known as the maternity unit. Poland had pulled a few strings to find her, the receptionist in the A&E Department refusing to give out any details because Dixon wasn't Jane's next of kin.

Not yet, anyway.

Jane was sitting on a bed in the triage area, flicking through a copy of *Somerset Life*. 'They gave me the once-over in A&E and sent me over here. I've got to have an ultrasound scan, apparently.' She dropped the magazine on the bedside table. 'I told them we've got one booked for next week at Weston, but they wouldn't listen.'

'Are you all right?' Dixon asked, kissing her on the forehead.

'Fine. They're worried about oxygen levels or something, but it was only a few seconds before you got there and I was able to breathe through my nose the whole time.'

Poland was hovering in the doorway.

'Come in, Roger,' shouted Jane. 'You're going to be a godfather, so you're practically family anyway.'

'Am I?'

'I hadn't said anything,' muttered Dixon.

'Yes, you are.'

'Oh, right. Lovely.' Poland smiled. 'Aren't I a bit old?'

'No, you're not.'

'Did Townsend say anything when you nicked him?' asked Dixon, sitting on the edge of the bed next to Jane.

'Kept going on about how he had an alibi for Bishop's murder.'

'Let's worry about that tomorrow, shall we?'

'Turns out he was the squib maker for the Gremlins Carnival Club, though, back when the squibs were homemade,' continued Jane. 'Potter will be interviewing him later tonight and I'm going to miss it. What's the time?'

'Just after ten.'

'She's in for a late night then. She probably won't finish shouting at uniform until the early hours, blundering in with their size elevens. She told them to stay out of sight, but they just couldn't help themselves.' Jane grinned. 'Armed Response, indeed. With a plastic gun. What the hell was that all about?'

'He wasn't to know the barrel pressed to the back of his head was plastic, was he?' Dixon shrugged. 'And it did the trick. He let you go.'

'And all that crap about "SA74, permission to engage" . . . ?'

'Convinced him, though, and that's all that matters.'

'Now everyone's looking for the hero from the crowd who came to my rescue. The mysterious man in the hoodie!'

'Did anyone see me?'

'Only Lou, Mark and Dave, and they won't say anything. I'm sure Potter *thinks* it was you, but she's got no way of proving it.'

'Right then, you've been in the wars and we need to check you over,' said the nurse appearing in the doorway, clipboard in hand. 'Tell me what happened.'

'I'm a police officer and I was assaulted while making an arrest.'

'Not the one at the carnival? It was on the radio.'

'She was held around the throat,' offered Dixon. 'In an arm lock.'

'Well done you. Any abdominal injury?'

'No, thank God,' replied Jane.

'Right, well, it's time for your ultrasound,' said the nurse. 'Who's staying and who's going to wait outside?'

'This is my fiancé.' Jane took Dixon's hand. 'And that is the godfather of whoever's in here,' she said, rubbing her abdomen. 'They're both staying, please.'

It was just after midnight when they finally got out of Musgrove Park, the nurse having refused to allow them to leave until Jane had been seen by the duty obstetrician.

'All perfectly normal' had been a relief.

Now they were sitting in Poland's living room, Dixon with a large glass of Scotch in one hand, the black and white ultrasound image in the other.

'Why didn't you want to know the gender?' asked Poland.

'Ruins the surprise,' replied Jane, taking a sip of hot, sweet tea. 'I'm just grateful everything's all right. And it's not twins.'

'One at a time will do nicely,' mumbled Dixon.

'Lucy will go ballistic when she finds out she missed the first scan. She was coming down specially for it next week.'

'She can still go,' replied Dixon. 'They told us at Musgrove to keep that appointment. Just don't tell her you've already had one.'

'Where will you be?'

'In custody, probably.'

'Don't be so bloody stupid. I thought you said you had a plan. Those recorders and microphones.'

'We'll have to get my Land Rover out of the car park tomorrow afternoon, then I can make myself available for my visitation.'

'Why the afternoon?'

'We'll be busy in the morning.'

'Oh, what fun,' said Poland, rubbing his hands together. 'And there was me thinking it was all over.'

Dixon was staring at the ultrasound scan, ignoring the huffing and puffing coming from Jane.

'Are you going to tell us or what?' she demanded, her impatience eventually getting the better of her.

'It's all in the High Tech reports.'

'I read them and I didn't see anything.'

'Time for bed.' Dixon stood up, placing his empty glass on the arm of the sofa. 'Dave, Mark and Lou, Burnham Baptist Church, nine o'clock in the morning. Potter can come if she wants.'

'What about me?' asked Poland, grinning. 'Can I come?'

Chapter Forty-Five

'What are we doing here then?' asked Deborah Potter, climbing into the back seat of Poland's Volvo.

'Tying up loose ends,' replied Dixon.

'I didn't know there were any.' She sighed. Loudly. 'We even got a statement from Adam Waller this morning.'

'What did Townsend say in interview?'

'No comment, but we've got more than enough.'

They were sitting in the Baptist Church car park opposite the double fronted offices of Harrison Samuels estate agents in College Street, Burnham. Dave Harding and Mark Pearce were already in position at the back of the premises, with orders to let themselves be seen and arrest anyone who came out that way. Jane and Louise were standing on the pavement, pretending to look at the properties in the window, despite the drizzle that was coming in horizontally on the wind. Either that or the high tide was breaking over the sea wall some fifty yards away.

'What about the search of his house?' asked Dixon.

'Still going on, but we've found his workshop in an outbuilding. Squib-making stuff and the accelerant. Even a red petrol can just like the one you can see in the video.' Potter leaned forward in between the front seats of Poland's car. 'Look, what's going on?'

'Two people working together, each with different motives.'

'For killing the same people?'

'Just one of them.'

'You'd better come in with us,' said Potter.

Poland sat up in the driver's seat. 'What about me? Can I—?'

'No.' Potter and Dixon in unison.

They left Poland listening to the clunk of his windscreen wipers and walked across the road.

'It was you last night, wasn't it?' whispered Potter, leaning into the wind. 'On the cart.'

'No comment.'

'I thought as much. You'd better hope video of it doesn't pop up on Facebook.'

Jane had gone into Harrison Samuels and was holding the door open. Two of the desks were occupied; a skeleton staff in the office on a Saturday morning, the rest out doing viewings or sitting in a cell at Express Park.

'Can I help?' asked Gerard Pollock. 'There'll be some more in at nine-thirty and others in and out all day. Saturday's the busiest for viewings as a rule.'

'We've been in contact with the Competition and Markets Authority, Mr Pollock,' said Potter. 'They'll be investigating the price fixing cartel and no doubt will wish to speak to you in due course.'

Pollock's face flushed. 'That was nothing to do with me. I'm a chartered surveyor. Brian runs that side of the business.'

'You're a director of the company?'

'Yes, but—'

'Then you're jointly liable. Probably get disqualified too.'

'Look, you need to speak to Brian – I warned him, I bloody warned him – he'll be in in a minute.'

'He won't, as it happens.' Potter spun round, looking for Dixon. 'Mr Townsend was arrested last night on suspicion of the murders of Trevor Bishop and Taylor Gooch and the attempted murder of Richard Webb.'

'You're joking?'

'No, Sir.'

'Brian, you bloody idiot.' Pollock slumped back into his chair, shaking his head. 'You think you know these people. We've worked together for twenty years and he goes and does this.'

Dixon had sat down at the coffee table at the front of the office, hidden from the road by the window displays, and flicked his hoodie back off his face. Then he picked up a property paper and pretended to look through it, all the while listening to Pollock's excuses.

'Has he admitted it?'

'Not yet, Mr Pollock,' replied Potter. 'But we don't need him to. We have more than enough evidence.'

Dixon glanced around the office – all eyes were watching Pollock, even Dave and Mark's peering through the window at the back; watching his every move, every reaction.

Except Jane, of course, but then she knew what was about to happen.

Potter turned to her. 'It's over to you, Jane, to make the arrest, if you will, please.'

Pollock sat up, bracing himself for the inevitable.

'Thank you, Ma'am,' replied Jane. 'Faye Bishop, I am arresting you on suspicion of the murder of Trevor Bishop.'

'Me?' Faye sprang to her feet, sending her swivel chair crashing into the filing cabinet behind her.

Potter spun round and looked at Dixon, her eyes wide.

He just nodded. Slowly.

Pollock's sigh of relief was glaringly obvious to all, despite his best efforts to stifle it.

'You do not have to say anything,' continued Jane, 'but it may harm your defence if you do not mention when questioned something you later rely on in court. Anything you do say may be given in evidence.'

'You think I murdered Trevor?'

'A nice pub lunch to chat about the kids, was it?' Dixon stood up. 'Scampi and chips. Then you lured him to the woods – I'm guessing on the promise of sex – and watched while Townsend cut his throat,' he said, matter of fact. 'Then you set fire to Trevor in the boot of his car, a box of matches in one hand and your phone in the other. The camera never lies.'

'What d'you mean, "the camera never lies"?' Faye's eyes darted from front door to back door, only to find all exits blocked.

'Brian Townsend is a foot taller than you. It's the camera angle.'

'I wasn't there!'

'How else did the footage get on your phone?'

'I told you. I received it when it was AirDropped at Burnham carnival. Everybody else got it as well.'

'You sent it from Trevor's phone, to everyone listed in his contacts, but you never got it.'

Potter was still staring at Dixon. Louise was too.

'I did receive it, I tell you.' Tears now, falling softly down Faye's cheeks. 'I deleted it at first and then recovered it. You saw me.'

'When did you delete Trevor from the contacts list on your phone?'

'Ages ago, when he first left me.'

'Felt good, I bet.'

'Yes, it did, actually.'

'The problem is, your phone is set to receive AirDropped files from contacts only, so you couldn't have received the video from Trevor's phone, could you?'

No reply.

'You gave a statement in which you said you received the AirDrop, but that was a lie. Pure and simple. Because if you had received it, there'd have been two copies of the footage on your phone, wouldn't there?'

'Rubbish!'

'The original footage when you filmed Trevor's death, and then the AirDropped copy.'

'That is the AirDropped copy on my phone.'

'What did you do that afternoon?'

'After I finished with Brian, I picked up the kids from my mum about four o'clock and took them to Secret World. I told you. We often go there.'

'And there are photos of them on your phone taken at Secret World that day. Trouble is, those photographs appear in your photo album *after* the footage of Trevor's death, which means the footage was on your phone *before* you went to Secret World.'

'It was AirDropped at the carnival, I tell you!'

'If it had been AirDropped at the carnival, it would appear in your photo album *after* the Secret World photos, not before. AirDropped images go into the photo album in the sequence they are received. Not only that, but there's nothing in the "Imports" folder, which means the video on your phone was not imported by AirDrop.'

Faye hesitated, the tears drying up. 'I've got an alibi for Trevor's murder,' she said, trying a change of tack.

'You gave Brian Townsend an alibi, but more importantly, that gave you one as well, didn't it? Both false, as it turns out. Were you really sleeping with him or was it all a lie?'

'It's true, I tell you. I was with Brian.'

'What about Andrew Platt? Did you sleep with him as well, to get him to tell us about Markmoor Farm?'

'He's just a boy, playing his silly computer games; follows me round like a puppy.' Faye folded her arms tightly across her chest and sat down on the edge of the swivel chair. 'All right then, why? I'm not involved in the price fixing, I'm just an employee, so why did I do it?'

'Let's ignore the life insurance, shall we? Because it was never about the money, was it?'

No response.

'And start with the AirDropping,' continued Dixon. 'You sent that to the whole staff of Bishop Property, but that was just smoke and mirrors; the real target was Liv. You waited until she had her phone out, filming the carnival, and sent her the footage. You wanted her to know what had happened to Trevor – to see it for herself – and you loved every minute of it, crying your crocodile tears.'

'Yes, I bloody well did. The little tart. Thinking she could waltz off with my husband.' Faye sneered, all pretence gone.

Dixon had pressed the right buttons.

'I told him I'd kill him if he ever left me for her,' continued Faye, her face hardening, nostrils flaring. 'I warned him. She's just a bloody child. So, yes, I decided to help Brian. He said Trevor was going to blow the whistle on the cartel and that he'd have to kill him. I thought he was joking at first, but he wasn't. Poor sod's got nothing to lose anyway; the bloody business is going down the pan.'

'Is it?' Pollock sat up.

'You want to check the accounts more often, Gerry,' said Faye, with a vicious laugh. 'So, I sent Trevor a text asking him to meet me – lunch, then a trip to the woods. It was *our* secret place, where we used to go before we got married. We'd carved our names into the bark on a tree there, but Brian cut it out and threw it in the car.' The anger was draining away, Faye's voice slowing as the realisation dawned on her; not so much that she'd been caught, more what she'd done.

'Tell me about the email Trevor was using to blackmail Richard Webb and Ian Szopinski,' said Dixon.

'I gave it to him. Brian pulled it off Richard's computer with the workplace analytics thing he was using and I gave it to Trevor. I wanted him back and thought it might . . .' Her voice was thin, hollowed out somehow, the anger gone. 'I swear to God I thought he was dead when I set the car on fire. I really did. He didn't deserve to die like that.' She looked up at Dixon, wiping the sweat from her lips with the back of her hand. 'How the hell do I explain that to my children?'

Chapter Forty-Six

'He's making his feelings known, I see.'

Dixon was sitting on the low wall outside the police centre at Express Park while he waited for Jane to drive his Land Rover out of the staff car park, Monty cocking his leg on the Avon and Somerset Police sign. He had pretended not to notice Charlesworth watching them from the upstairs window, or the black Range Rover filling up with fuel at the Esso garage a couple of hundred yards away.

Charlesworth had made his move first and was striding across the visitors' car park towards him. 'Seems the press are keen to track down the hero of the North Petherton carnival,' he continued. 'Won't give us moment's peace. There's even a social media campaign to give him a medal.'

'Shame you don't know who he is, Sir,' said Dixon, watching the Range Rover out of the corner of his eye, a feeling of apprehension rising from the pit of his stomach.

'No one got a good look at him, not even Sergeant Winter, oddly enough. I'll give it a mention at the press conference this afternoon and, you never know, someone may know who he is.

Otherwise, it will have to remain a mystery.' Charlesworth offered a sarcastic smile. 'It's not as if I can tell them it was an off duty police officer currently on bail for murder, is it?'

'Well, you'd need some evidence it was.'

'It would've been the media coup of the year.' Charlesworth sat down on the wall next to Dixon. 'Still, it's not bad as it is, thanks to you. Deborah Potter told me you were instrumental in bringing this carnival thing to a satisfactory conclusion; two murderers behind bars in less than a week. It'll do our reputation the power of good. Any sign of your Albanians?'

'I wouldn't necessarily describe them as *mine*, Sir. And I've been keeping out of their way until this carnival business was over,' replied Dixon. 'Don't look, but they're in that black Range Rover at the garage.'

'That's them?' asked Charlesworth, resisting the temptation to turn his head.

'It is.'

'And you're wearing the wire?'

'I am.'

'Now's your chance to get some evidence. Professional Standards *want* to believe you've been framed, but at the moment it doesn't look good, what with the shotgun cartridges in your cottage and the fingerprints.' Charlesworth was watching the black Range Rover out of the corner of his eye. 'They're pretending to check the tyres now.'

'Jane's just getting my Land Rover out, so I'll be on my way in a minute.'

'You're not going on your own, surely?'

'What else can I do?' Dixon stood up. 'She's here,' he said, watching the electric gates of the car park opening. 'Time to face the music.'

'Give me an hour,' said Charlesworth. 'Have lunch in the canteen, or something. We really can't afford to lose officers of your calibre.'

Jane pulled up opposite Dixon and slid out of the driver's seat, just as Charlesworth reached the front doors of the police centre. 'What did he want?' she asked.

'Just passing the time of day.'

'Yeah, right.' Jane frowned. 'Where's your hoodie?'

'I dropped it in the clothing bank.'

'It didn't suit you anyway.'

'There's not a lot of point trying to hide my face when I've got him by my side,' replied Dixon, leaning over and scratching his dog behind the ears. 'Monty stands out a mile.'

'I suppose he does. So, what happens now?'

'We've got an hour to kill. Then I take him for a walk.' A sideways glance at the petrol station; the Range Rover gone.

Dixon turned out of the police centre an hour later, watching Jane waving at him. Then, when she thought he wasn't looking, she turned and ran up the ramp to the staff car park.

The Range Rover picked him up before he was halfway along the dual carriageway; three cars back, matching his speed. Best to pretend he hadn't noticed, for the time being, at least.

He had already decided on the motorway; less chance of being intercepted, forced down a country lane, away from people and traffic cameras. That this was happening now was his choice, and it would happen at a place of his choosing. On home ground.

One junction north on the M5, the Range Rover a steady three cars back.

Perhaps a half-hearted attempt to give them the slip; they'd expect that, surely? And Dixon needed them to know he was expecting them.

He accelerated up the short off slip at Burnham-on-Sea, round the roundabout in the wrong lane, then he cut across the traffic to take the second exit.

Trying to outrun a Range Rover Sport in an old Land Rover Defender.

Hardly.

Maybe he could lose them in the town traffic?

Left by the church, right by the Post Office; Dixon was on the seafront now, a second black Range Rover further down, parked on the double yellows outside the Pavilion – it must be a second one, they could never have got there, surely?

Gits.

He accelerated along Berrow Road, all the time keeping an eye out for Jane's blue Golf.

Both Range Rovers were behind him now. It hadn't helped that his Land Rover was quite so visible. Or maybe it had? After all, he wanted to get it over and done with, one way or the other.

Drizzle started to fall as Dixon took the bend at Berrow Church. He switched his sidelights on, hoping the gates to the beach would be open; they usually were at this time of year. Being charged six quid parking for the privilege of being framed by the Albanians would have been taking the piss.

He made the turn on to the beach road without indicating. Down the ramp on to the firm, wet sand; the drizzle had seen off any other dog walkers and day trippers – not that there were many on a dank and grey November day.

He followed the line of stinking black seaweed until he was opposite an old tree stump and then reversed up to the wooden bollards pile-driven into the sand to protect the dunes, switching off his engine and jumping out of the Land Rover just as the Range Rovers accelerated off the beach ramp.

Dixon clipped on Monty's lead and let the dog jump out of the back of the Land Rover, dragging him back behind the bollards just as the Range Rovers slid to a halt in front of him.

The passenger door of the nearest opened and a man climbed out, at the same time drawing a gun from a shoulder holster under his black jacket. He pointed the gun at Monty.

'We've had this conversation before,' said Dixon, matter of fact.

Then the rear passenger door of the Range Rover opened.

Zavan could have been wearing the same black trousers, black polo neck sweater and black jacket as last time, even though their paths hadn't crossed for nearly a year. There was no way of knowing. He barked an order in Albanian, the man quickly replacing his gun in the holster.

'I tell him you will arrest him or die trying if he shoots your dog.' Zavan nodded slowly. 'But then I forget, you are suspended, are you not?'

'You wanted a chat?'

'I have got myself a dog. A German shepherd. You are right, it is good to own a dog. You are not an easy man to find.'

'Whatever.' Dixon hated that word, but now it seemed to sum up his situation. He was studying Zavan, watching his every move, every twitch. And he was under no illusion.

Another order in Albanian and the smaller man stepped forward. 'Arms up!'

Dixon watched his phone spinning into the sand dunes. 'It's all right, boy,' he said, giving a gentle tug on the lead when Monty started growling.

Then the man lifted Dixon's shirt, revealing a wire cable taped to his chest.

'You were expecting us, I see,' said Zavan with a wave of his hand, Dixon stifling a grimace when the man ripped the tape off his ribcage. Then, pulling on the cable, he reached around Dixon's back and unclipped the recorder off his belt. The microphone was next, behind Dixon's shirt collar.

'You must think we are idiots, Nicholas. Search him,' ordered Zavan.

He'd have made a good poker player, staring ahead impassively as the other man rummaged through his pockets, allowing himself a shallow intake of breath when the man ran his fingers along the collar of his coat, before it was ripped down his back and off his arms; the hood unfurled from the collar, the micro recorder dropping on to the sand.

'You do not disappoint,' said Zavan, watching his lieutenant pick up the recorder and rip the microphone cable from the small black box, before stamping both into the sand. 'Come, now we can talk, can we not?'

Dixon waited.

'We have much to talk about,' continued Zavan. Trimmed his beard since last time too. 'There is my cocaine, for a start.'

So that's what this is all about.

'We sent the *Sunset Boulevard* out to collect it from a cruiser off the Azores. A little yacht from a place like Burnham, who would check that for drugs? It was perfect. All the way from Colombia the cruiser had come; they say they make the transfer, but when the yacht sinks there is no sign of the merchandise. *My* merchandise. Twenty million pounds is out there somewhere,' with an exaggerated wave of his arm out to sea. 'Someone has it and I want you to find it for me.'

'Why would I do that?'

'Because if you do not, you go to prison for murder.'

'Find it yourself.' Dixon forced a smile. 'I'll take my chances in front of a jury, thanks all the same.'

'What chances?' Zavan threw his head back and laughed. 'Your fingerprints are on the gun. I know. We put them there. Bought and paid for. Everyone has their price.'

'I don't.'

Zavan tried an arm around Dixon's shoulders, his fingers digging into his arm. 'Come now, you found who killed the owner of the yacht. And with a crossbow of all things! But it still leaves my cocaine. You find that too, I think.'

'You think wrong.'

'Be sensible. If you agree to find it for me, then we make all this shotgun business go away. And we can make it worth your while too.'

'Money?'

'Maybe you can get your promotion and a transfer to Zephyr?' Zavan grinned. 'And we will be friends forever.'

'You made me think I killed a man, that I was responsible for the death of Besim Raslan.'

'Besim was dead anyway, in – how you say – a vegetable state? A potassium chloride overdose; we do him a favour. And we look after his family now, back in the homeland.'

'What about the shotgun cartridges?'

'Locks can be picked and we have always known where you live. When you know the game, it is easily played. Your Professional Standards Department is so efficient, is it not?' Zavan's eyes narrowed. 'You are getting married? You must let me pay for the honeymoon. Not Albania, it is too cold at that time of year. What about the Seychelles?'

'A kind offer, but you'll forgive me if I decline.'

'I get it. You need time to think. Take your time, take as much time as you want, as long as it is not *too* long.'

'I don't need time. I've made my decision and the answer is no. You'll have to find your own bloody cocaine.'

'Then you will go to prison and rot in a cell. And remember, there is nowhere we cannot get to you.'

'I don't matter.' Dixon was unusually calm, but then he had known this was coming for days and had lain awake at night, rehearsing the conversation over and over in his head. 'What matters is that people like you don't win, because when we let that happen, we're all fucked.'

'We buy the jury too.' Zavan threw his head back, forcing an exaggerated belly laugh. 'You think you're untouchable.'

'You've been watching those American films again, haven't you?'

'Come, we are wasting our time here. We go,' snapped Zavan, turning towards his Range Rover. 'You make a big mistake, Nicholas.'

The second Range Rover was revving its engine, the sound suddenly drowned out by the rotor blades of the police helicopter as it roared low over the sand dunes. Then three police vehicles accelerated off the end of the beach slipway, their wheels spinning in the sand as they turned towards the Range Rovers.

A police van stopped on the slipway, blocking the only escape route, the beach to the north and south blocked by more wooden posts pile-driven deep into the sand; different sizes and heights, the gaps between them random, they looked like rotten teeth, the lines stretching out to sea, stopping a few yards short of the incoming tide.

Zavan drew his gun, pointing it at Dixon. 'Get in,' he said, gesturing to his Range Rover.

'No.'

'Then you die.'

'Go now and you can get round the end of the wooden posts. There are no more between here and Burnham. Get off the beach by the start of the sea wall.'

'You help us?'

'What choice do I have?'

'We go,' said Zavan.

The Range Rovers reversed at speed, the doors still open, showering Dixon's Land Rover with sand, before doing hand-brake turns, the doors slamming shut as they sped down the beach towards the end of the wooden posts, the incoming tide gradually closing the gap.

'Armed Police. Get down on the ground, hands above your head.'

'3275 Detective Chief Inspector Dixon,' he said, obeying the command. He turned his head to watch events unfold further down the beach, still holding on tight to Monty's lead.

He smiled to himself. The locals knew; the police knew too, the pursuit vehicles stopping on the firm sand, but the Albanians clearly didn't.

The Range Rovers started to slew from side to side on the mud, their tyres spinning before sinking up to the wheel arches.

Stuck fast, both of them, fifty yards or so short of the end of the wooden posts.

'That's Chief Inspector Dixon. The Albanians are in the Range Rovers.' He recognised Charlesworth's voice. 'Get up, Nick.'

'Thank you, Sir.'

The Armed Response officers had taken up position by their vehicles, their weapons pointed at the Range Rovers, the helicopter hovering further out to sea.

'We'd better get back behind your Land Rover,' said Charlesworth. 'Just in case.'

Two figures were crouching behind Charlesworth's car: Carlisle and Larkin. A nice touch bringing them along, thought Dixon, as he watched Jane push past an officer at the bottom of the slipway and start running along the base of the dunes towards them.

Then the loudhailer started, directed at the Range Rovers, still sitting silently in the mud. 'Armed Police. Get out of the cars with your hands up.'

'We'd better have BARB on standby with their hovercraft in case we need a mud rescue,' said Charlesworth to the uniformed officer crouching next to him.

'Yes, Sir.'

Still no movement from inside the Range Rovers.

'Will they surrender?' asked Carlisle, addressing his question to Dixon.

'How the hell should I know?'

'They're your friends, aren't they?'

'I'm guessing it's thanks to you they're stuck in the mud, Nick?' asked Charlesworth.

. Doors opening. Slowly. Two men climbed out of each Range Rover, their feet sinking in the grey slime.

'Armed Police. Drop your weapons.'

Zavan's hands were up, a gun in his right.

'They're all carrying,' said Carlisle, ducking down behind Charlesworth's car.

'Drop. Your. Weapons.'

Dixon heard Zavan shout and saw him move, then turned away as the shots rang out.

Eight. Two each.

Dixon watched the Armed Response officers edging out across the mud to where Zavan lay, face down.

Then the order came over the radio. 'All units. Stand down.'

Jane took her chance, sprinting across the sand towards where Dixon was crouching behind his Land Rover with Monty.

'How'd it go?' She threw her arms around him and kissed him. 'I thought for a minute they were going to kill you.'

'Zavan just wanted to talk. This time.'

'A friendly chat with your mates, Dixon?' Carlisle sneered. 'Doesn't look good, does it?'

'Did they kill Raslan?' asked Jane, ignoring him.

'He admitted it.'

'It wasn't you.' Jane puffed out her cheeks. 'Thank God for that.'

'Please tell me you've got the recording,' said Charlesworth.

'No, he hasn't,' muttered Larkin, with a smirk.

'They found the wire, unfortunately, Sir.'

'What about the micro recorder in your collar?' demanded Jane.

Dixon gestured to his coat, which was lying in the seaweed, the hood ripped out of the collar, the recorder trodden into the sand next to it.

'That's it then. We've had it.' She crossed her arms over her abdomen and glared at Carlisle and Larkin, who were still skulking behind Charlesworth's car. 'Those two vultures are going to have a field day. What the hell are we going to do?'

'All is not lost. You're forgetting our Rural Crimes Unit,' replied Dixon, turning towards the sand dunes. 'Did you get all of that, Nige?'

Nigel Cole was sliding down the sand, a long-range microphone in one hand and a camera with a zoom lens in the other. 'I got the lot,' he shouted, with a broad grin. 'Loud and clear, Sir.'

'Well done, Nick!' said Charlesworth, patting Dixon on the back.

'These bloody people,' hissed Jane, a smile creeping across her lips. 'Who the hell do they think they're dealing with?'

Author's Note

I very much hope you enjoyed reading *Carnival Blues* as much as I enjoyed writing it.

The Somerset Carnivals are said to be the largest illuminated processions in the world, and I hope I have been able to capture something of the atmosphere. It's a great fun night out that comes highly recommended by me!

Squibbing aficionados will no doubt spot that I have taken several liberties with current practice and procedure. Needless to say, I have done so in the hope of creating an entertaining mystery, but I am reliably informed that squibbing is now so tightly controlled and regulated that the attempted murder of Richard Webb would simply not be possible these days. Health and safety is paramount and rightly so.

The squibs are stored centrally, for example, rather than by the carnival clubs themselves, and the whole process is overseen by the Bridgwater Guy Fawkes Carnival Squibbing Officer, Dave Creedy. It is Dave who assures me that squibbing is safe, and so confident am I that I have accepted his kind invitation to have a go at the 2022 carnival. Thank you, Dave. I can't wait!

Another liberty I have taken is with the date when the squibs ceased to be homemade. This has been lost in the mists of time, so long ago was it, but to have used anything close to the correct date would have made all the leading characters in the book octogenarians.

You will not be surprised to learn that I prefer to call it 'poetic licence'.

I wrote the Author's Note for *Dying Inside* during the winter lockdown of January 2021 and expressed the hope that by the time you read that book, life might be starting to return to something close to normal. As I sit here writing this note in December 2021, a new coronavirus variant is dominating the news cycle. So, here's hoping that by the time you are reading *this*, the nightmare is well on the way to being behind us.

There are several people to thank, as always. First and foremost is my wife, Shelley, who reads the manuscript on a daily basis. I would also like to thank my unpaid editor-in-chief, Rod Glanville. And David Hall and Clare Paul who, once again, have been extraordinarily generous with their local knowledge.

And lastly, I would like to thank my editorial team at Thomas & Mercer, whose patience has still not run out – in particular Victoria Haslam and Ian Pindar.

Damien Boyd
Devon, UK
December 2021

About the Author

Photo © 2013 Damien Boyd

Damien Boyd is a solicitor by training and draws on his extensive experience of criminal law, along with a spell in the Crown Prosecution Service, to write fast-paced crime thrillers featuring Detective Inspector Nick Dixon.